A TEXTBOOK OF COLLEGE ENGLISH
IN
ECONOMICS AND MANAGEMENT

经济管理专业英语

（第三版）

戴贤远　主编

北京大学出版社

PEKING UNIVERSITY PRESS

图书在版编目(CIP)数据

经济管理专业英语(第三版)＝A TEXTBOOK OF COLLEGE ENGLISH IN ECONOMICS AND MANAGEMENT/戴贤远主编.—北京:北京大学出版社,2006.7

ISBN 978-7-301-02412-6

Ⅰ.经… Ⅱ.戴… Ⅲ.①英语-经济管理-高等学校-教材 ②经济管理-英语-高等学校-教材 Ⅳ.H319-43

书　　　名:经济管理专业英语(第三版)
著作责任者:戴贤远　主编
责 任 编 辑:徐万丽
标 准 书 号:ISBN 978-7-301-02412-6/H·0237
出 版 发 行:北京大学出版社
地　　　址:北京市海淀区成府路 205 号　100871
网　　　址:http://www.pup.cn
电　　　话:邮购部 62752015　发行部 62750672　编辑室 62765014　出版部 62754962
电 子 信 箱:xuwanli50@yahoo.com.cn
印　刷　者:世界知识印刷厂
经　销　者:新华书店
　　　　　　730 毫米×980 毫米　16 开本　17 印张　302 千字
　　　　　　1994 年 7 月第 1 版　2000 年 8 月第 2 版
　　　　　　2006 年 7 月第 3 版　2007 年 1 月第 3 版第 2 次印刷
定　　　价:24.00 元

第三版前言

《经济管理专业英语》1994 年 7 月出版发行,以后的 7 年里印刷了 4 次。2000 年 8 月,《经济管理专业英语(第二版)》发行,到 2006 年,一共印刷了 7 次。目前中国有上百所大学的教师,使用这部教材,教授经济管理领域各个专业的专业英语课程。

好的教科书有生命力,教师、学生都喜欢。一部教科书,授课教师连续使用十几年,能够使教学有连续性,提高教学效率和教学水平。年复一年,这样的教科书还能辅助教师评价各届学生之间的差别,以及教师教学结果上的差别。每一年的教学,教师都会有新的思想,这些新思想促成教与学的进步。

在《经济管理专业英语(第三版)》出版发行之际,需要再次强调专业英语课程的主旨。教授专业英语课程,对于教师来说,是教授英语;学习专业英语,对于学生来说,是学习英语。如此,专业知识的讲授和学习,只是这门课程的辅助部分。

《经济管理专业英语(第三版)》在内容安排上,依旧保留了过去选定的经济管理领域教科书中讨论基本概念的那些内容,强调教学内容的延续性,但是阅读材料中增加了 6 篇文章,使教科书的每一部分都配有一篇阅读材料,促进学生阅读能力的提高。长期来看,阅读能力,在实用的英语能力中,无论如何也是最重要的一项能力。

此外,近两年来,学生的就业竞争加强了,所以英语实际应用能力的重要性日趋突出。目前一个明显的现象就是,那些英语口语和英语写作能力强的学生,能够比较容易地获得较好的工作,特别是在银行、合资企业和外资企业里。为此,《经济管理专业英语(第三版)》增加了学习提示(Suggestions for Further Study)。本教科书总共 14 个部分中,每部分都增加了一个"学习提示"(Suggestions for Further Study)。全书 14 个部分的"学习提示"联结起来,展示了完整的专业英语学习的思路,并且与英语的实际应用紧密相连。依次,这些学习提示涉及学习方法概说、新单词的记忆、读、听、写、说、写作精要、语感、业务信函、注释格式、参考文献格式、个人简历格式、内部便笺以及翻译要则。

在《经济管理专业英语(第三版)》出版发行之际,感谢 Christopher Jeffries 教授和 Donald Elliott 教授花费时间校改本书的学习提示部分;再次感谢美国的 Irwin/McGraw-Hill Publishing Company 公司、Scott, Foreman and Company 公司、Prentice-Hall, Inc. 公司和 John Wiley and Sons, Inc. 公司为本教科书

提供了重印版权许可；同时也感谢 Paul E. Sultan，John E. Weinrich，K. M. Hussain，Ronald M. Copeland，Peter H. Rushton，Christopher Jeffries，Donald Elliott，Dal Didia，Alisa Mosley，Geungu Yu，James R. Smith，Jean-Claude Assad，Richard L. Russell，Dennis O. Anyamele 和高一虹教授，感谢他们不断地为国际学术与教学交流活动做出贡献。

戴贤远

2006 年 5 月于清华园

再 版 前 言

　　《经济管理专业英语》自 1994 年 7 月出版发行以来，7 年里已经印刷了 4 次，目前中国有几十所大学的教师，使用这部教材教授经济管理领域各个专业的专业英语课程。

　　在过去的 7 年里，全国各个大学的本科生和研究生的英语水平有了很大的提高，国际上流行的经济管理领域的许多美国原文教科书也在中国出版发行了，所以，教师和学生在课本和教与学的内容安排上，有了更多的选择，这是一件非常好的事情。

　　专业英语课程的主旨，对于教师来说，是教授英语；对于学生来说，是学习英语；专业知识的讲授和学习，只是这门课程的辅助部分。

　　《经济管理专业英语》这部教材在内容安排上，7 年前全部选用了经济管理领域教科书中讨论基本概念的内容，强调教学内容的延续性。这次再版所增加的阅读材料，内容涉及的也都是经济管理领域中的一些基本概念。

　　专业英语课程的教学与公共英语的教学应该有很大的差异。专业英语课程有相对独立的要求。首先，读懂课文是起码的要求。除了极个别难点，对文中的句子和词的理解，甚至不应该在课堂上提及。其次，要重视培养翻译能力。翻译的标准不应该仅仅停留在是否能够译出，而要强调译文格式的规范与文字的流畅。再次，应该加强写作。通过对课文中文字词的分析，完成对一般写作和商业信函写作能力的培养。教学要关注素质培养，要求学生根据语感行文和修改写作中的错误，同时遵守语法规则。第四，强调交流的过程。读与听、写与说均需完成双向交流的过程。说和写时，别人要懂；读和听时，自己要懂。

　　《经济管理专业英语》的第二版增加了 8 篇阅读材料，强调阅读和理解的过程。阅读是英语学习中占第一位的工作，也是学生提高英语水平的一个最基本的手段。对于学习第二语言的人来说，读不懂就听不懂；不读或读得少，就不可能有相对永久性的词汇量，也不可能从根本上学到写作需要的各种知识和技能。汉语学习和英语学习的要领有一点是相通的：中文读得多，汉语就好；英文读得多，英语就好。至于人们时常谈及的语言学习环境的好坏，不过是指视听方面接触某种语言的机会的多寡。

　　在《经济管理专业英语》第二版出版发行之际，再次感谢美国的 Irwin/McGraw-Hill Publishing Companies 公司、Scott, Foreman and Company 公司、Prentice-Hall, Inc. 公司和 John Wiley and Sons, Inc. 公司为本教科书提供了

重印版权许可；同时也感谢 Paul E. Sultan，John E. Weinrich，K. M. Hussain，Ronald M. Copeland，Peter II. Rushton，Christopher Jeffries，Donald Elliott，Dal Didia，Alisa Mosley，Geungu Yu，James R. Smith，Jean-Claude Assad，Richard L. Russell 和高一虹教授，感谢他们为国际学术与教学交流活动所做出的贡献。

戴贤远

2000 年 7 月于北京师范大学

前　言

如果有人问:在中国的学校里,哪一门课最难?虽然不同的学生在不同的学习阶段有各种各样的看法,但最后人们总会得出一个类似的、被大多数人认可的结论——最难的课是英文。首先,这门课年复一年延续的时间最长,起于中学甚至小学,结束在研究生的最后一堂专业英语课。其次,这门课花的时间最长。不知有多少人把多少年的早晨给了这门课,更不必说在这门课上花的时间了。再次,有些同学念完研究生后,听与说方面不及母语是英语的五岁的孩子,写则不及八岁孩子。这样看来,英语是难,可它难在哪儿呢?最重要的是,怎样才能解决这些困难呢?另外,读、听、写、说究竟哪个重要?最后,英语学到什么程度才算可以了呢?这些问题对于经济管理专业的学生似乎更难,因为这类专业涉及广泛,远非数学、物理或工程专业可比。

下面我们就来一一回答上面提出的问题。

经济管理专业英语的范围究竟有多广呢?严格地说,这范围没有清楚的界限。但是,MBA专业的八门基础课可以说是经济管理专业英语的基本范围,它们是:微观经济学、宏观经济学、决策统计分析、管理信息系统、生产管理、市场学、财务管理与组织行为学。本教科书正是以这个系统为基础编的。鉴于英语与国际货币和银行、国际营销、国际商业、国际经济、国际贸易的密切联系,本教科书延伸部分的课文均选自这几方面。为适应同学们毕业后实际工作的需要,本书的最后一部分是工作与商业信函写作的格式,这是将来从事运用英语的工作的同学必不可少的知识。

英语究竟难在哪?据笔者接触的一届又一届的中学生、大学生和研究生来看,无一不说是背单词难。其次就是"说",因为发音不好,所以也就不好意思说。英文写作因为用得少,所以这一真正的困难事儿不怎么被人提起。现在我们就来看看解决"背单词难"和"开口难"这两个问题的办法。

学英语最初的一两千个单词是要背的,并且是毫无疑问的,但是所有学专业英语课的同学统统已经过了这个阶段。另外的五六千常用词再靠背行吗?不行,特别是从五千到八千的那三千词靠背就更困难,绝大多数本科生和相当一部分研究生不能跃过这个阶段就是一个证明,这也是人们越学越说背单词难的原因。

已故北京大学西方语言文学系教授徐锡良先生说过,学英语不用背单词,因为背下来的词多数迟早会忘掉,而阅读留在记忆里的词是最牢固的。这道理很简单,只不过多数同学没认识到罢了。打个比方说,一个大学生刚入学,校园里的张张脸对他来说都是陌生的。以后,在教室里,在操场上,在文艺队、体育队和食堂里,不断地碰见同学,先是面孔,然后是名字,久了了解得就更深。谁也没有有意背,为什么都记住了呢?词也一样,读第一页见到的很生,第三页再见到就记住个词头词尾的,第八页遇见这词发音也记住了,到第十五页、二十页,用法都会了。这里重要的是:阅读时一定不能懒得查字典,如同校园里碰见的人,你不打听,就不会知道他叫什么。想掌握单词,阅读量就一定要大,读得多,见词的机会和次数才多。不去文艺队、体育队,也就很少认识那里的人;不读某类书,也就不会那类词。英语有大约六千个词是随处可见的,其余两千说是常用词,也许读三十页书才碰到一次。如果一个人见五六次或八九次才能记住一个词的话,学会最后那两千常用词的阅读量是可想而知的。根据人们的经验,不读相当的书,这些词是学不到的,而"背"对绝大多数人来讲是徒劳的。

多数同学到了学专业英语的时候仍被发音困扰,因为播音员和教学音带的声音确实是太好了。但是,世界各地实在是有很多的例子可以让人们重新从实用角度来看"说",这实际上也是一个"发音"与"口音"的对阵。为什么"托福"考600多分的同学刚到美国时听不懂中东教授的简单问候?为什么有些英语系的教授听不懂电影《根》里美国南方黑人的对白?为什么不同国家的英语广播员的声音全都不一样?为什么生意场上中东人、远东人、欧洲人操各种各样的英语?问题全都在口音。所以,当同学们开始学专业英语时,对于"说"要有一个全新的概念——话说出来,如果对方听懂了,这个交流也就完成了。至于说话的声音,它永远要受口音或乡音的制约,大可不必为此不好意思。

发音只有两点最重要:一是重音错不得,二是清辅音不能读重了,因为重音错了或是清辅音读重了,会使词听起来面目全非,听话的人也就听不懂说话人的意思。

上面讲的道理解决了同学们记单词的困难和不好意思开口的问题,但这都是一般性问题。除了上述学专业英语的一些一般层次的问题以外,专业英语还有高一层次的问题,那就是翻译。本书是经济管理方面的专业英语教程,同学在阅读、理解和翻译课文时,有些句子和概念很难译,除了语言习惯外,也有语言艺术在里面。说到难翻译的句子,不外乎是一些中英文表达方式大不相同的长句子。至于解决的办法,著名翻译家傅雷早有表述。他虽是翻译文艺作品的,但他的论述对经济管理专业英语的翻译方法也是有指导意义的。因为经济管理专业英语的翻译中,除了严格的概念表述外,语言的处理是很重要的一部分。

傅雷先生有两段话是很重要的:

> 以效果而论,翻译应当像临画一样,所求的不在形似而在神似。以实际工作而论,翻译比临画更难。

倘若认为译文标准不应当如是平易,则不妨假定理想的译文仿佛是原作者的中文写作。那么原文的意义与精神,译文的流畅与完整,都可以兼筹并顾,不至于再有以辞害意,或以意害辞的了。(傅雷,《高老头》重译本序,1951)

领会了傅雷先生的话,再把经济管理专业英语里的长句子中的从句、介词宾语及同位语部分分别断开,在中文中以逗号和分号断开长句来写短句,翻译中的困难就会大大减少了。

解决了经济管理专业英语中的主要困难,再来谈谈抓重点的问题,也就是读、听、写、说哪一个最重要。

人的母语是从环境中学来的,或是学别人讲话,或是从景物反应到词或话,最后才是从书本上的文字中学。但第二语言则不是,尤其是中国学生学英语,多数是对书上的文字发生反应后学到的。因此,说的过程中的"景物—中文—英文"的反应过程及听的过程中的"英文—中文—景物"反应过程是普遍存在的。由此而言,读和写对中国同学的英语学习来说是第一位的,因为读不懂也就听不懂;不会写也就不会说,况且听和说对反应速度的要求要比读与写高得多。

余下的最后一个问题是:英语学到什么程度就算行了呢?

就这个问题来讲,绝对的回答是学无止境,相对的回答是要看工作需要,而一般的衡量标准是:在一个人读、听、写、说的过程中,如果翻译的过程在他的反应过程中消失了,他的英语也就很好了。值得提一句的是,尽管翻译的过程在脑子里消失了,说和写的时候,词语选择的过程还是存在的,不过都是英文词罢了;读和听那时当然只是抓意思,不会再有语法方面的考虑。

以上是关于经济管理专业英语的内容及学习方法的讨论,希望能对使用本书学习这门课的同学有所帮助。书中如有谬误,待以后改进。另外,本教科书的编写工作得到了国际上一些教授和出版公司的大力协助,编者在此表示感谢。感谢我最崇敬的 Paul E. Sultan 教授为本教科书提供课文并校阅部分注释;感谢 John E. Weinrich, K. M. Hussain, Ronald M. Copeland, Peter H. Rushton 及高一虹博士为本教科书撰写、提供课文或是校阅注释;感谢美国 Richard D. Irwin, Inc. 公司, Prentice-Hall, Inc. 公司, Scott, Foresman, and Company 公司, John Wiley and Sons, Inc. 公司和 McGraw-Hill Book Company 公司为本教科书的出版提供必要的重印版权许可。北京师范大学经济系 90 级本科生和 91 级研究生为本教科书提出许多有益的建议,在此一并表示感谢。

戴贤远

1993 年 8 月于北京师范大学

PREFACE

If some people raise the question, what is the most difficult course for the Chinese students? There would be all kinds of answers given by different students at various stages of study, but eventually people would come to a similar conclusion: The most difficult course in China is English.

First, this course extends for a very long period, starting from either elementary school or middle school, ending with the last English class of graduate study.

Second, year after year, most students spend a lot of time on it. No one knows how many charming mornings are devoted to reading English, not to mention the total amount of time students spend studying through their school years.

Third, some students find, even after over ten years of study, that their listening and speaking are still behind those of a five-year-old American boy, while their writing, lags behind that of an eight-year-old.

For this reason, it is quite reasonable to think that English is really difficult. But, what are the key problems and how are they to be solved? In addition, of the four aspects of English study, namely, reading, listening, writing and speaking, which plays the most critical role? Lastly, when can we say a student has mastered English? It seems that the above problems are even tougher for students majoring in business administration which, compared with mathematics, physics and engineering, covers an even broader scope.

Now, let's start to explore the solutions to the above problems.

What is the scope of *College English in Economics and Management*? Strictly speaking, a fixed boundary is absolutely out of the question, yet we may say the eight foundation courses in an MBA program are the basic areas covered. They are: microeconomics, macroeconomics, statistics for decision making, management information system, operations management, marketing, managerial finance, and organizational behavior management. The first eight parts of this textbook are targeted for these fields. Since *College English in Economics and Management* closely relates to money and banking, managerial strategy, international marketing, international economics as well as international business, texts related to these areas make up the last six parts. There is also an appendix entitled business writings in the back of this textbook. It is necessary to supply such an appendix for those students who will frequently use English as a basic tool in their work after graduation.

What are the biggest problems for Chinese students to learn English? My previous experience with high school students, undergraduate students, and graduate students tells me that none of them would exclude the obstacle of "learning words by heart." The other barrier would be "speaking." Poor pronunciation(actually it is a matter of accent in most cases)by the students is a source of embarrassment making them reluctant to speak. Writing in English is a skill seldom used in school and in future. Thus, people have ignored this toughest area.

Now that the problems are presented, how are we to solve them?

It is well known and broadly agreed that the first one or two thousand English words are kept in a beginner's mind through forced memorization. Yet all the students taking the class of *College English in Economics and Management* have passed this phase. Can a person keep in mind an additional five or six thousand words with the same method? Definitely not, especially for the last two or three thousand words in eight thousand common English words. The common failure of most undergraduate students and some graduate students in this stage has proved it.

The late professor Xiliang Xu, one of the best professors in his time in the Department of Western Languages and Literature of Peking University, once said, "It is not necessary to force words into a learner's memory on purpose, for many of the words kept in memory by enforcement simply wouldn't last long. Some disappear in just a couple of weeks. Words held in mind through reading are most stable." The reason is quite simple, but few people really understand it.

Here I would like to present a straightforward example. The first day on campus for a freshman is always exciting, yet he knows nobody. It seems to him that all the faces are strange. Afterwards, in classrooms or cafeterias, on athletic fields or with groups involved in arts and sports, he continues to meet people and continues to make acquaintances. First there are faces, then there are names. Day after day, he comes to know these people very well. No one has asked him to learn these people by heart on purpose, so how can he keep them in mind? It is the same with words. A word on page one may be new for people at first glance. But on the third page, if the word is met again, people will remember either the first or the last part of it. Till page eight, its pronunciation seems already familiar. On the fifteenth or twentieth page, if the word continues to show up, people even know how to use it. One thing needs to be mentioned—a student should never stop using a dictionary. Just like a person meeting a student on campus, without asking who she is, he will never know her name unless he obtains information from other sources. To learn more words, people have to read more. The more one reads, the more opportunities one has to meet words. A person who never visits sports team or an art group probably will never know people there. A person who does not read books in a certain field, will never learn the specialized vocabulary.

There are approximately six thousand English words which can be seen anywhere, including books, newspapers, magazines, and periodicals. The remaining two thousand words, though also called common words based on the theory of eight thousand common English words, might be found only once in every thirty pages. If one takes eight to nine encounters with a word to master it, the amount of reading required is quite clear. According to the general experience of people, it is impossible for a person to learn these words without a great deal of reading, while rote memorization is definitely not on the road leading to success.

Many students are still troubled by pronunciation in the stage of learning *College English in Economics and Management* due to the deep impression on the students by the high quality tapes. However, there are so many examples in the world which remind people of reconsidering the standard of "Spoken English". Actually this is a game theory of "pronunciation vs. accent". Why are some Chinese students with TOEFL scores over 600 not able to understand a Middle Eastern professor's simple greetings when they just arrive in the United States? Why are some very good Chinese professors in the Department of English not able to understand completely the black people's dialogues in the movie *ROOTS*? Why do announcers of English radio stations in different countries speak with different voices? Why do businessmen from the Middle East, Far East, or Europe all speak different kinds of English? The answer lies in their different accents. When people start to learn *College English in Economics and Management*, they should have a brand new concept, that is— when the words come to an end, if the speaker has been understood, then the communication is complete. As to the voice of speaker, it will surely be blocked or affected to a certain extent by native accent. People just need not be bashful about it.

However, there are two points in pronunciation which are very important: One is to avoid making mistakes in stress; the other is not to emphasize consonants, because either of the two cases would make a word sound distorted and disrupt communication.

So far, what we have discussed are just some ordinary problems, such as how to keep words in mind or how to get rid of shyness. Besides these, there are also some problems at higher levels as people study *College English in Economics and Management*. One of them is translation. This textbook is concerned with economics, business and management. Some sentences in the texts are very tricky in terms of the combination of reading, understanding and translating. On the one hand, the problem is caused by different customs in language expressions; on the other hand, it is caused by the art of language. When we say a sentence is difficult, we mean the kind of long sentence employing a different style of expression. As to the way leading to the solution, Mr. Lei Fu, a famous late translator, explained long ago. Although he was well known as the greatest master in the translations of literary works, his ideas can still help students learning *College English in Economics and Management*. Besides the concepts presented in this textbook, coping with the art of language is equally important.

Two paragraphs of words by Mr. Lei Fu are very important:

"In terms of the effect, in translation, as well as in copying a painting, one should catch the spirit of the words rather than the words themselves. As to the practice, to translate is much more difficult than to copy." (Lei Fu, "Preface for Retranslation, "*Le Pere Goriot*, 1951.)

"If people think translation should not be plain, then it is necessary to assume that a good work of translation done in Chinese by the author, would contain the spirit and expression of the original work, and the integration and fluency of translation, then are all well taken care of. Phrases won't distort the original spirit of the words and the spirit won't bother phrases either." (Lei Fu, "Preface for Retranslation, "*Le Pere Goriot*, 1951.)

Guided by Mr. Lei Fu's words, if students cut off the long English sentences and separate the subordinate clauses, prepositional objects, and appositives, and at the same time, use commas and semicolons to make the sentences translated into several very short subsentences, it will make the work of translation much easier.

Having solved the key problem in learning *College English in Economics and Management*, let's shift to other discussions on reading, listening, speaking and writing.

People learn their native language through the environment around them, either through others' talking or through the reflection of objects. The function of words in books ranks the last in the process of the formation of concepts in the native language. However, a second language is a totally different story, especially for Chinese students learning English. By and large, Chinese students learn English through their reaction to the words in books. Hence, the process of reaction in speaking, such as "object—Chinese—English", and the process of reaction in listening noted as "English—Chinese—object" widely exist among students. From this point of view, reading and writing compose the most important two factors in learning English. For a given sentence, if a Chinese student cannot catch the meaning through reading, then he cannot understand it through listening either. As to the ability of expression, if a Chinese student cannot write it, then he cannot express it through speaking either. Speaking obviously requires an even faster speed of reaction than writing.

The final question is: when can a student's English be considered adequate?

An absolute answer to this question is that there never is an end to studying; an objective answer lies in the needs and requirements in one's work; and the general standard used to evaluate a Chinese student's English states that if the process of translation in reading, listening, writing and speaking disappears from one's mind, his(or her)English is fine. What is worth mentioning here is that although the process of translation no longer exists in one's brain, the process of word selection is still there, but all in English. By that time, the considerations of grammar are thoroughly excluded. Reading and listening are nothing but a process of catching meaning.

The above are the contents of the textbook and a discussion of the methods of learning *College English in Economics and Management*. I hope it will be helpful for the students who will use this book. Meanwhile, suggestions and criticisms concerning this textbook are surely welcome. In addition, the completion of this textbook greatly relied on the assistance of others. First, I would like to appreciate my most respected professor Dr. Paul E. Sultan for his contributions to the texts and for his patient work in editing part of the Key Terms and Concepts. Appreciation also goes to John E. Weinrich, K.M. Hussain, Ronald M. Copeland, Peter H. Rushton, and Yihong Gao. Furthermore, I would like to express my appreciation to Richard D. Irwin, Inc. , Scott, Foreman and Company, Prentice-Hall, Inc. , John Wiley and Sons, Inc. , and McGraw-Hill Book Company for their permission to reprint passages. Students and graduate students of Beijing Normal University made a lot of suggestions and comments in my classes, here I would also like to express my sincere appreciation to them.

Xianyuan Dai

Beijing Normal University

August, 1993

CONTENTS

PART ONE
MICROECONOMICS

The Concept of Utility

Economists first began to analyze consumer behavior over a century ago when it was fashionable in psychological circles, to assert that much of human behavior could be explained by people's desire to realize as much "pleasure" and to avoid as much "pain" as possible. The pleasure-pain doctrine was quickly borrowed by economists[1] and applied to the sphere of consumer expenditures in what became the first systematic theory of motivated consumer behavior;[2] the basic economic thesis was that rational consumers would, quite intentionally, manage their purchases of goods and services so as to realize the greatest possible amount of overall total "satisfaction." Economists labeled the want-satisfying power of goods and services as "utility."[3]

The concept of utility refers to the pleasure or satisfaction associated with having, using, consuming, or benefiting from goods or services. The utility inherent in a good or service derives from whatever qualities it has that gives it want-satisfying capabilities. The sources and causes of utility are legion: better health, esthetic beauty or design, ease of use, flavor and taste, durability, convenience, luxury, comfort, a sense of individuality, pleasure, prestige, status, pride, security, ego gratification, and power—to mention the most obvious. Hence, utility has both objective and subjective features and, most particularly, utility is a matter of individual taste, preference, perception, personality makeup, and state of mind.[4]

As a consequence, the utility that a good possesses or is perceived to possess is variable, not absolute. In the first place,[5] no two people necessarily will view a good as having the same degree of want-satisfying powers—one person may derive great utility from smoking cigarettes while someone else finds them distasteful; Cadillacs may be important status symbols to some people(and hence have great utility), yet have little or no appeal to other people. Different people buy the same product for quite different uses and motivations. Peanuts, for instance, are bought by some people to serve at cocktail parties, by others to make peanut brittle[6], and by some to feed to squirrels, with potentially different utilities to each buyer in each case.

1

Moreover, the utility of a good can vary from time to time, or place to place. Rising gasoline prices quickly modified the utility many people placed on small cars.[7] Wool clothing does not have the same utility or want-satisfying powers for people living in short-winter climates as for those living in long-winter climates. But irrespective of the wide variations[8] that different persons may place on the utility of a good or service, the utility concept offers a purposeful basis for establishing consumer preferences for what and how much they will purchase[9] because it leads to comparisons of the amounts of satisfaction received from different consumption rates of different goods and services.

It is, of course, doubtful that the intensity of satisfaction one gains from an item can be represented precisely in cardinal rankings whereby numerical values are assigned to represent utility.[10] One may say that "broiled lobster is my favorite food" or "I enjoy broiled lobster more than any other seafood or meat"; but if asked "how much do you enjoy broiled lobster?" one can scarcely reply "about 17" and expect to convey understanding.[11] The subjective nature of the utility concept is, however, susceptible to ordinal ranking measure.[12] In ordinal preference patterns, one only has to be able to rank alternatives—from highest to lowest, best to worst, or most satisfying to least satisfying; no attempt is made to quantify the amount by which one alternative is better (or worse) than others.

Despite the fact that utility is not subject to precise quantification, it is still analytically useful to assume that utility can be represented by cardinal numbers. Doing so makes it easier to illuminate several important aspects of consumer behavior.

From Arthur A. Thompson, Jr. and John P. Formby, *Economics of the Firm: Theory and Practice* 6th ed. © 1993, pp. 36-37. Reprinted by permission of Prentice-Hall, Englewood Cliffs, New Jersey.

Key Terms and Concepts
Cadillac a brand name of car.

status symbols symbols which represent people's position or state, namely, wealthy or poor.

intensity of satisfaction a phrase used to describe how much the satisfaction is.

cardinal rankings one of the two ways to measure utility. In this way, numerical values are assigned to represent utility.

ordinal rankings one of the two ways to measure utility. In this way, utility is measured without a specified unit. Ordinal rankings provide the order of preference without absolute scale of difference in preference.

ordinal preference patterns   all kinds of preferences ranked by certain kinds of preference standards.

NOTES

1. The pleasure-pain doctrine was quickly borrowed by economists...   这种乐与苦的信条很快便被经济学家借用了……

2. ... applied to the sphere of consumer expenditures in what became the first systematic theory of motivated consumer behavior;...   ……（指前面说的乐与苦的信条）运用于消费者的消费行为中,并使之成为解释消费者行为的第一个系统理论;……

3. Economists labeled the want-satisfying power of goods and services as "utility."   经济学家把人们对商品和服务的需要与满足称为"效用"。

4. ... utility is a matter of individual taste, preference, perception, personality makeup, and state of mind.   ……效用决定于人的口味、偏好、感觉、个性的构成及思维的状态。

5. in the first place   首先

6. to make peanut brittle   来做花生糖片

7. Rising gasoline prices quickly modified the utility many people placed on small cars.   汽油价格的上升,很快地改变了人们对小型汽车的效用的看法。

8. irrespective of the wide variations   不考虑各种不同的情况（指不同的人对商品和服务的看法不同。）

9. ... the utility concept offers a purposeful basis for establishing consumer preferences for what and how much they will purchase...   ……对于人们买什么或买多少,效用的概念提供了一个有意义的根据来解释人们的这种偏好……

10. ... whereby numerical values are assigned to represent utility.   ……因此数值就被用来代表效用。

11. ... expect to convey understanding.   ……（人们很难）指望理解这其中的原因。

12. The subjective nature of the utility concepts is, however, susceptible to ordinal ranking measure.   但是,效用概念的实质还是适合于用顺序排列法来表示。

How Markets Function

A critical part of examining the market for a product is the structure of competition—whether there are many or few sellers in the industry. The terms "many" and "few" are delineated not so much by the numbers of firms as by the competitive interaction among firms.[1] There are "many" sellers of a product when no one firm has a big enough volume of business or enjoys high enough standing as a market leader for the remaining firms to react to its actions. Each firm is small enough and insignificant enough in the context of the whole market[2] that it is virtually an anonymous entity[3], hidden by sheer numbers from the watchful eyes of other firms.[4] In contrast, we say there are "few" sellers of a product whenever the actions of any one firm will be noticed and reacted to by rival sellers. "Few" means few enough so that firms find it imperative to follow each other's moves closely. Fewness of sellers also means that each firm is large relative to the size of the market in which it operates; often, when firms are few in number each firm is large in absolute size as well. The single-firm industry, or monopoly, is the limiting case of fewness.

A second key element in market analysis relates to whether the products of sellers are identical or differentiated. The products of sellers may be considered to be identical whenever and wherever customers evidence no particular preference for one firm's product over that of another firm.[5] This may arise because the item is produced by a process that confers certain measurable qualities which can be graded and which are unrelated to the seller producing it. For instance, choice-grade beef is choice-grade beef, and one cannot tell(nor does it really matter)whether it came from ranch A or ranch B. In such cases, the products of firms in an industry tend to be perfect substitutes;examples include cotton, sulfuric acid, natural gas, coal, cement, and coffee beans.

On the other hand, where the products of firms are distinctive and somewhat unique, they are not perfect substitutes for one another, and buyers may have good reason to prefer the product of one firm over that of another. However, the ultimate test of differentiation is in the mind of the buyer, and the perceived differences in the products of various firms may be either real or contrived. "Real" differences involving performance, materials, design, workmanship, and service are obviously important aspects of product

4

differentiation. But "contrived" differences brought about by brand names, trademarks, packaging, and advertising can also be important to buyers; for example, even though all brands of aspirin are chemically alike, many buyers evidence preference for one brand over others.

In addition, it should be recognized that a firm's product extends beyond the physical and functional characteristics of the item itself. [6] Although a large number of retailers in an area may sell Crest toothpaste, they may not be viewed as equally attractive to buyers of Crest. The sales clerks in one store may be more courteous, or its location more convenient, or its checkout system faster, or its delivery service more dependable, or its credit terms more accommodating. Such factors can cause buyers to prefer one seller over another, even though the item purchased is the same. The various brands of shoes, wines, cereal, cosmetics, tires, and soft drinks are all examples of differentiated products.

As might be expected, competition proceeds along different lines, depending on whether there are "many" or "few" firms and whether their products are identical or differentiated. Viewed from this perspective, four main forms of market structure and organization stand out:

1. Perfect competition—many sellers of a standardized product.
2. Monopolistic competition—many sellers of a differentiated product.
3. Oligopoly—few sellers of either a standardized or a differentiated product.
4. Monopoly—a single seller of a product for which there is no close substitute.

Arthur A. Thompson Jr. and John P. Formby, *Economics of the Firm: Theory and Practice* 6th ed. © 1993, pp. 265-266. Reprinted by permission of Prentice-Hall, Englewood Cliffs, New Jersey.

Key Terms and Concepts

choice-grade beef quality measure of beef packaged and sold at different prices.

perfect substitution refers to the products in very much similar qualities that a consumer would just as soon have one as the other.

Crest a brand name of toothpaste.

checkout system a system in store or supermarket to generate bills of payments for customers and complete the transaction with customers, usually automated in U.S.

credit terms   period of late payment to be offered by a seller.

NOTES

1. The terms "many" and "few" are delineated not so much by the number of firms as by the competitive interaction among firms.
   这里的词"多"与"少"不仅是看企业的数目,更重要的是看企业间的竞争活动。
2. in the context of the whole market   在整个市场范围内
3. an anonymous entity   不知名的实体
4. ...hidden by sheer numbers from the watchful eyes of other firms.   ……
   企业的数目很多,因而单一的一个企业(指某个不知名的实体)就不怎么被其他企业注意。
5. ...customers evidence no particular preference for one firm's product over that of another firm.   ……消费者不会对某一个企业的产品有特殊的偏爱,而对另一个企业的产品不感兴趣。
6. ...it should be recognized that a firm's product extents beyond the physical and functional characteristics of the item itself.
   ……应该认识到(就产品的效用而言),一个企业的产品不仅仅限于产品本身和功能上的那些特性。

Suggestions for Further Study

When a student starts to learn specialized English, the way he learns becomes very important. Before a student makes great progress in learning English, he first has to recognize the problems associated with learning the language.

Recalling previous English classes in middle schools or universities, one can easily find systematic loopholes. Those loopholes are as follows: First, the whole system of teaching and learning English is scheduled to be examination-oriented. Students have to spend a lot of time dealing with endless examinations. Second, students often think that vocabulary is the only obstacle in their study, therefore, they spend most of their time memorizing new words. They habitually hesitate on every new word and stop at every new word when reading. Third, the "step by step" pedagogy discourages students from more extensive reading. Other than the required textbooks, most students do not read much each year. Moreover, the textbooks students read are very thin. As a result of this, students do not learn much English even after completing eight or ten years of English classes. Fourth, problems can also be found in the standards applied to assess a student's English. At universities, many students recognize over six thousand English words and have high qualification scores but cannot express themselves clearly. More specifically, they cannot speak fluently or write well.

The systematic loopholes listed here remind people to look for better ways to learn English. The loopholes also remind people to set more realistic standards to evaluate a student's English.

To improve a student's English, there are no methods better than reading novels or English textbooks used at universities abroad. To learn a language, reading is always most important. From certain points of view, one should learn English the same way that he learns Chinese.

To assess a student's English practically, people should adopt a more meaningful rule which says that when the process of translation disappears in a student's mind, his English is fine.

Key Words Loophole

PART TWO
MACROECONOMICS

Outlays and Components of Demand

In the previous sections, we started with GNP and asked how much of the value of goods and services produced actually gets into the hands of households. In this section we present a different perspective on GNP[1] by asking who buys the output, rather than who receives the income. More technically, we look at the demand for output and speak of the components of the aggregate demand for goods and services.

Total demand for domestic output is made up of four components: (1) consumption spending by households; (2) investment spending by businesses or households; (3) government (federal, state, and local) purchases of goods and services; and (4) foreign demand. We shall now look more closely at each of these components.

Consumption

Table 2-1 presents a breakdown of the demand[2] for goods and services in 1982 by components of demand. The table shows that the chief component of demand is consumption spending by the personal sector. This includes anything from food to golf lessons, but involves also, as we shall see in discussing investment, consumer spending on durable goods such as automobiles—spending which might be regarded as investment rather than consumption.

Table 2-1   GNP and Components of Demand, 1982 (In Billions of Dollars)

Personal consumption expenditures	$1,991.9	64.8%
Gross private domestic investment	414.5	13.5
Government purchases of goods and services	649.2	21.1
Net exports of goods and services	17.4	0.6
Gross national product	3,073.0	100.0

Source: Data Resource, Inc.

8

Government

Next in importance we have government purchases of goods and services. Here we have such items as national defense expenditures, road paving by state and local governments, and salaries of government employees.

We draw attention to the use of certain words in connection with government spending. We refer to government spending on goods and services as purchases of goods and services, and we speak of transfers plus purchases as government expenditure.[3] The federal government budget, of the order of $650 billion, refers to federal government expenditure. Less than half that sum is for federal government purchases of goods and services.

Investment

Gross private domestic investment requires some definitions. First, throughout this book, investment means additions to the physical stock of capital. As we use the term, investment does not include buying a bond or purchasing stock in General Motors. Practically, investment includes housing construction, building of machinery, business construction, and additions to a firm's inventories of goods.

The classification of spending as consumption or investment remains to a significant extent a matter of convention. From the economic point of view, there is little difference between a household building up an inventory of peanut butter and a grocery store doing the same. Nevertheless, in the national income accounts, the individual's purchase is treated as a personal consumption expenditure, whereas the store's purchase is treated as investment in the form of inventory investment. Although these borderline cases clearly exist, we can apply a simple rule of thumb[4]: that investment is associated with the business sector's adding to the physical stock of capital, including inventories.

Similar issues arise in the treatment of household sector expenditures. For instance, how should we treat purchases of automobiles by households? Since automobiles usually last for several years, it would seem sensible to classify household purchases of automobiles as investments. We would then treat the use of automobiles as providing consumption services. (We could think of imputing a rental income to owner-occupied automobiles.[5]) However, the

9

convention is to treat all household expenditures as consumption spending. This is not quite so bad as it might seem, since the accounts do separate households' purchases of durable goods like cars and refrigerators from their other purchases. When consumer spending decisions are studied in detail, expenditures on consumer durables are usually treated separately.

In passing, we note that in Table 2-1, investment is defined as "gross" and "domestic." It is gross in the sense that depreciation is not deducted. Net investment is gross investment minus depreciation. Thus NNP is equal to net investment plus the other categories of spending in Table 2-1.

The term domestic means that this is investment spending by domestic residents but is not necessarily spending on goods produced within this country. It may well be an expenditure that falls on foreign goods. Similarly, consumption and government spending may also be partly for imported goods. On the other hand, some of domestic output is sold to foreigners.

Net Exports

The item "Net exports" appears in Table 2-1 to show the effects of domestic spending on foreign goods and foreign spending on domestic goods on the aggregate demand for domestic output. The total demand for the goods we produce includes exports, the demand from foreigners for our goods.[6] It excludes imports, the part of our domestic spending that is not for our own goods. Accordingly, the difference between exports and imports, called net exports, is a component of the total demand for our goods.

The point can be illustrated with an example. Assume that instead of having spent $1,992 billion, the personal sector had spent $20 billion more. What would GNP have been? If we assume that government and investment spending had been the same as in Table 2-1, we might be tempted to say that GNP would have been $20 billion higher. That is correct if all the additional spending had fallen on our goods. The other extreme, however, is the case where all the additional spending falls on imports. In that event, consumption would be up $20 billion and net exports would be down $20 billion, with no net effect on GNP.

Rudiger Dornbusch and Stanley Fischer, *Macroeconomics* 3rd ed. © 1984, pp. 43-45. Reprinted by permission of McGraw-Hill Book Company, New York.

Key Terms and Concepts

aggregate demand   refers to total demand in four aspects: (1) the demand of households for consumption goods and services, or consumption; (2) the demand of businesses for capital goods, or investment; (3) the demand of governments for goods and services, government expenditure; and (4) the net foreign demand for goods and services (exports minus imports).

GNP   gross national product.

transfers   or transfer payments. Expenditures for which no goods and services are exchanged, including welfare payments, social security benefits, and unemployment compensation.

physical stock of capital   refers to durable or long-lasting inputs, such as machinery, tools, and buildings.

NNP   net national product. Gross national product (GNP) minus the depreciation of the existing capital stock over the course of the period.

NOTES

1. ... we present a different perspective on GNP...   ……我们从另一角度来看国民生产总值……

2. a breakdown of the demand   需求的分类表

3. ... we speak of transfers plus purchases as government expenditure.   ……我们把转移支付和购买称为政府的支出。

4. a simple rule of thumb   简单的衡量方法

5. ... imputing a rental income to owner-occupied automobiles...   ……看做汽车拥有者靠租赁业务获得的收入……

6. The total demand for the goods we produce includes exports, the demand from foreigners for our goods.   对我们生产的产品的总需求包括出口产品，也就是外国人对我们产品的需求。

Macroeconomic Policy

Policy makers have at their command two broad classes of policies with which to affect the economy.[1] Monetary policy is controlled by the Federal Reserve System (the Fed). The instruments of monetary policy are changes in the stock of money, changes in the interest rate—the discount rate—at which the Fed lends money to banks, and some controls over the banking system. Fiscal policy is under the control of the Congress, and usually is initiated by the executive branch of the government. The instruments of fiscal policy are tax rates and government spending.

One of the central facts of policy is that the effects of monetary and fiscal policy on the economy are not fully predictable, neither in their timing nor in the extent to which they affect demand or supply. [2] These two uncertainties are at the heart of the problem of stabilization policy. Stabilization policies are monetary and fiscal policies designed to moderate the fluctuations of the economy—in particular, fluctuations in the rates of growth, inflation, and unemployment.

The recent fluctuations of the rates of inflation and unemployment, suggest strongly that stabilization policy has not been fully successful in keeping them within narrow bounds. [3] The failures of stabilization policy are due mostly to uncertainty about the way it works.

However, questions of political economy are also involved in the way stabilization policy has been operated. The speed at which to proceed in trying to eliminate unemployment, at the risk of increasing inflation, is a matter of judgment about both the economy and the costs of mistakes. Those who regard the costs of unemployment as high, relative to the costs of inflation, will run greater risks of inflation to reduce unemployment than will those who regard the costs of inflation as primary and unemployment as a relatively minor misfortune.

Political economy affects stabilization policy in more ways than through the costs which policy makers of different political persuasions attach to inflation and unemployment, and the risks they are willing to undertake in trying to improve the economic situation. [4] There is also the so-called political business cycle, which is based on the observation that election results are affected by economic conditions. When the economic situation is improving and the unemployment rate is falling, incumbent presidents tend to be reelected. There is thus the incentive to policy makers running for reelection, or who wish to affect the election results, to use stabilization policy to produce booming economic conditions before elections.

Stabilization policy is also known as countercyclical policy, that is, policy to moderate the trade cycle or business cycle. The cycles in the past 20 years have been far from regular. The behavior, and even the existence, of the trade cycle is substantially affected by the conduct of stabilization policy. Successful stabilization policy smooths out the cycle, while unsuccessful stabilization policy may worsen the fluctuations of the economy. Indeed, one of the tenets of monetarism is that the major fluctuations of the economy are a result of government actions rather than the inherent instability of the economy's private sector.

Rudiger Dornbusch and Stanley Fischer, *Macroeconomics* 3rd ed. © 1984, pp. 17-18. Reprinted by permission of McGraw-Hill Book Company.

Key Terms and Concepts

Federal Reserve System a coordinated group of financial institutes acts as the central bank of the United States, issuing paper currency, supervising the commercial banks of the country, and implementing monetary policy.

monetary policy the policy that the federal government takes to adjust the money supply, the availability of loanable funds, or the level of interest rates so as to influence general economic activity.

stock of money quantity of money related to money supply.

fiscal policy The federal government influences general economic activity by changing the level of government spending or taxes.

trade cycle regularly recurring periods of recession and recovery.

business cycle see "trade cycle."

NOTES

1. Policy makers have at their command two broad classes of policies with which to affect the economy. 政策制定者可以自由地运用两大类政策去影响经济。

2. ... neither in their timing nor in the extent to which they affect demand or supply. ……并不是在一定的时间和范围内来影响需求和供给。

3. ... suggest strongly that stabilization policy has not been fully successful in keeping them within narrow bounds. ……强烈地表明平衡政策还没有完全成功地在一定范围控制住通货膨胀和失业。

4. Political economy affects stabilization policy in more ways than through the costs

which policy makers of different political persuasions attach to inflation and unemployment, and the risks they are willing to undertake in trying to improve the economic situation. 政治经济在很多方面影响平衡政策,而不仅仅是通过有不同政治见解的政策制定者花在通货膨胀和失业上的代价,以及他们在试图改变经济形势时,愿意承担的风险。

Suggestions for Further Study

Nearly every Chinese student says that mastering new words is the biggest problem in learning English. Most Chinese students expect that there will be a day when they no longer encounter new words when reading books, newspapers, or magazines. However, few Chinese students understand that there are many more English words than Chinese words and it is just natural to come across new words when reading English materials.

What is the best way for a student to remember new words? Before this question can be answered, one has to understand what the worst way is. It is a way that thousands and thousands of Chinese students have tried for decades — repeating a word nearly once every second again and again, then starting the repetition of another. Unfortunately, using this method, a new word will not stay long in a person's mind. Most of the new words will fade quickly, either in weeks or in months.

The impact of repeating a word ten times in ten seconds differs from the impact of seeing a word ten times on pages of readings. Some six thousand words can be seen frequently anywhere. If a person sees new words on different pages time and time again, these words will stay in his mind. More importantly, new words learned in this way, will likely be retained for some thirty years.

Key Words New words

PART THREE
STATISTICAL ANALYSIS FOR DECISION MAKING

Why Sample

In this brief scenario, we are introduced to one of the most important tools in the decision making process of the business community—the survey. [1] Although often treated with disdain, it can be highly informative and of enormous assistance to everyone from the multinational executive officer to the small retailer in Oshkosh, Wisconsin. Perhaps, the survey represents the outstanding example of using sampling techniques to make inferences about populations.

But why sample? Why not target a particular population in which we are interested and then conduct a census of this population[2]? Certainly it would remove the uncertainty that inevitably accompanies drawing inferences from samples. [3]

Example

Statistics on the U.S. population have been collected and published decennially (every 10 years) ever since 1790, generally with increasing amounts of detail. The decennial census attempts to count every person, household, and so forth, in the population. It is designed to be the most complete census of the entire population. Perhaps because it is the biggest, it best illustrates the problems with census taking and why sampling is probably, even here, the best way to collect data. [4]

Let's look at the 1980 census and some of the problems associated with an attempt to measure every member of a population and, thus, obtain the actual parameters, not just estimates from samples.

Because the population is so very large, and, in some cases, scattered, the cost of the 1980 census will well exceed $1 billion! The massive undertaking officially got under way in the spring. [5] On

March 28, 1980, census forms were sent through the mail. Let's look at some of the problems that arose from the system used to collect the data. First, many citizens reported that they never received the form in the March mailing. The U.S. Postal Service said that the mailing lists were filled with errors. For example, 13 percent of the census forms in Manhattan were undeliverable because of bureau errors. Approximately 85 percent of the mailed forms were filled out and returned. Since the census attempts a complete count of all citizens, over 300,000 workers were recruited and paid to follow up mailed forms and to contact residents of out-of-the-way places.[6] Think of the monetary expenses involved here!

Timeliness, as we know, is a key factor. Unfortunately, the 1980 census found itself embroiled in legal difficulties.[7] Thus, not only was there a significant time delay, but one can well imagine the impact these litigations will have on the final costs.

Then, of course, census officials encountered the usually types of problems associated with any census. Many members of the population were inaccessible, unavailable, or simply unresponsive. Although the law provides penalties for not giving the bureau required information, one census bureau supervisor reported, "It's very difficult to count people who don't want to be counted." He indicated that such people include illegal aliens, welfare cheats, tax evaders, and others who feel the census invades their privacy. This particular type of problem—dealing with the part of the population that is not included—has already led to various legal skirmishes. For example, a federal judge upheld Detroit's contention that its residents had been undercounted. New York city officials claim that the 1980 census missed at least 800,000 of its citizens. In recent years, big cities have asserted that the bureau has missed huge numbers of blacks and Hispanics because its approach to counting citizens is antiquated. As of September 1980, the bureau faced lawsuits filed by cities (other than Detroit) such as New York, Philadelphia, Chicago, and Newark. According to The Wall Street Journal, all the suits are aimed at a readjustment of the 1980 figures.

Thus, we see, even the biggest census of them all has its

problems. Later, we shall examine some of the errors associated with these government censuses. The director of the National Opinion Research Center at the University of Chicago said, "Maybe [the Census Bureau] can count noses, but the more people they have to count, the less chance there is that they'll do it right."

Let's look at a few additional examples that illustrate why we sample.

The cost per minute of television advertising is determined by such factors as the time of the day, the day of the week, and the size of the estimated audience viewing a particular program. With approximately 98 percent of all U.S. homes owning at least one TV set, it is unthinkable that the TV viewing practices of the residents of all 75,000,000 homes could be obtained. The population is simply too large. Even if it were not, the cost would be prohibitive and the time required to collect and analyze the data might make the results as timely as last week's newspapers.

In order to assess the risk of serious injury or death to drivers and passengers in a given model compact car, the car is driven into a concrete wall at 35 miles per hour. A dummy, wired with sensitive electronic equipment, provides data on the possible consequences of the impact. Since the test involves the destruction of the vehicle, few cars would be available at the dealership if the entire population were tested in this way.

A government agency authorizes a study to determine the principal causes of mine disasters. The total population is not available since the sites of some of the disasters may be buried under tons of dirt and water. Or, a college is interested in the income and occupations of its alumni. For a variety of reasons, it may be impossible to query some members of this population. They may be dead, institutionalized, or inaccessible because they hold high political offices or for various other reasons. Hence, a sample must suffice to represent the population.

We have attempted to illustrate that there are a number of factors that make it necessary for us to sample rather than to attempt to measure the entire population.

In brief, the reasons for sampling are:

1. Economy. The larger and less accessible the population of interest, the greater the cost of obtaining a census vis à vis collecting a sample. [8] There are times, however, where the population is sufficiently small and accessible that cost differences are negligible.

2. Timeliness. Generally, it requires less time to collect, analyze, and report the data from a sample than to perform similar operations with a census. If the survey is required in order to make a timely decision, the sample survey has a distinct advantage. Again, if the population is sufficiently small and accessible, this advantage will be diminished. I should be emphasized that inferential statistical procedures are not required following the collection of census data. A mean or proportion is a parameter and is not an estimate.

3. Destruction of item. When testing destroys or impairs the operation of an item, there is no real choice but to sample.

4. Infinite population. When the population is unlimited, such as that resulting from an ongoing production process, sampling must be undertaken since a census is impossible.

5. Accuracy. Paradoxically, a sample may be more accurate than a census. This is especially the case in surveys that require much information from the respondents. Because of cost and time factors, a sample may permit detailed probing whereas a census frequently involves yes-no types of responses. [9]

Richard P. Runyon and Audrey Haber, *Business Statistics* © 1982, pp. 158-161. Reprinted by permission of Richard D. Irwin, Inc., Homewood, Illinois.

Key Terms and Concepts

sample   to draw data as an example to represent the population in a given research work so as to make inferences about population.

survey   statistical investigation.

population   the total collection of elements or items that fall into the scope of a statistical investigation.

dummy   an artificial human form electronically wired to measure force impact,

18

used in automotive crash testing.

mean   A mean is the sum of the values of a set of observations divided by the number of observations.

estimate   the numerical value of the statistic used to estimate a parameter.

NOTES

1. ... one of the most important tools in the decision making process of the business community—the survey.   在企业界的决策过程中最重要的工具之一——调查。

2. a census of this population   总体调查

3. ... drawing inferences from samples.   ······从样本中来推论。

4. Perhaps because it is the biggest, it best illustrates the problems with census taking and why sampling is probably, even here, the best way to collect data.   可能因为人口调查是最大的统计调查,因而它能够非常好地说明收集统计数字时的问题和为什么抽样调查即使在这样的问题中仍可能是收集数据的最好方法。

5. The massive undertaking officially got under way in the spring.   大量的调查工作在春天正式开始进行。

6. ... to contact residents of out-of-the-way places.   ······来与那些不在正常的居住地点的居民联系。

7. ... the 1980 census found itself embroiled in legal difficulties. ······1980 年的人口调查遇到法律方面的困难。

8. The larger and less accessible the population of interest, the greater the cost of obtaining a census vis a vis collecting a sample.   统计数字越多、越不易收集,抽样得到统计数字的成本就越高。

9. ... a sample may permit detailed probing whereas a census frequently involves yes-no types of responses.   ······一个样本可能需要仔细调查,而统计数字却常常只需"是"与"否"的回答。

Basic Concepts of Hypothesis Testing

We have seen that, in making decisions, we always have to deal with uncertainty. We can never be absolutely sure that any decision we make is correct (except perhaps after the fact—when it may be too late).[1] Although intuitive feelings and hunches often play a role in managerial decisions,[2] we need to have a more objective manner to reduce the uncertainty. Unfortunately, as we shall see, we can never completely eliminate uncertainty. We can, however, remove some of the guesswork and make our decisions in a more objective manner.

In this chapter we shall examine the role of hypothesis testing in decision making. We shall develop rules that will help us control and minimize the probability of error in choosing among alternative. To illustrate some of the basic concepts in hypothesis testing, let us look at an example.

Ever since the Arab embargo on oil following the Yom Kippur War in 1973, numerous products have entered the market claiming to substantially increase the mile-per-gallon ratings of the family "dream-turning-nightmare" machine.[3] Some involve additives that are mixed with the gasoline of the car, whereas others are devices that must be installed along the fuel line or attached directly to the carburetor.[4] All claim significant improvements in gasoline mileage. You have undoubtedly seen the advertisements, "Enjoy 10 percent to 40 percent improvement in your car's mileage ratings." On what basis are these claims made? Unfortunately, they often represent nothing more than testimonials by "satisfied" users, usually in the form of letters written to the manufacturer. We know that convenience sampling of this sort is rarely representative of the population of interest (i.e., all purchasers of the additive or device).[5] Moreover, few consumers are capable of conducting or motivated to conduct the objective and systematic research necessary to test the claims. Additionally, there is a strong psychological tendency for consumers to look for and find improvements in order to justify their expenditure of funds.

Fortunately, there are a number of federal and private agencies that are set up specifically to evaluate claims of this sort. Let's follow through both the logic and the procedures for testing the mileage claims. To begin with, the claim is either true or it is false: an additive either increases mileage or it does not. It is our role as researchers to establish procedures for deciding between these two alternatives. Stated in formal terms, these alternative possibilities are:

1. The additive has no effect on gasoline mileage.
2. The additive has an effect on gasoline mileage.

Since the first is often an hypothesis of "no effect," it is referred to as the null hypothesis(H_0). As we shall see, the null hypothesis may also specify a particular value of the parameter of interest. But characteristically it denies the effect we are seeking to evaluate. The second hypothesis, called the alternative hypothesis (H_1), asserts that the null hypothesis is false. Note that these two hypotheses are mutually exclusive and exhaustive. They cannot both be true or false at the same time. One must be true and one must be false. It is the role of our data collection and statistical procedures to decide between these two alternatives. But, if you think for a moment, you'll realize how difficult it is to conceive of proving the null hypothesis. Except for taking a complete census, which is not feasible considering the millions of cars on the road, we must rely on drawing samples from a population. We have already seen that these sample statistics distribute themselves about a central value,[6] such as the population mean or the population proportion. The sample means virtually never equal the population mean, and the sample proportions virtually never equal the population proportion. In addition, they almost always differ from one another and by variable amounts. How then can sample statistics be used to prove no difference? In a word, they cannot.

However, since H_0 and H_1 are mutually exclusive and exhaustive, rejecting H_0 allows us to assert H_1. Note that the proof is indirect. We assert H_1 by rejecting H_0. Also, statistical proof is always one-way. We may reject H_0 and assert H_1, but we cannot reject H_1 and, thereby, assert H_0. In brief, just as we cannot prove H_1 directly neither can we disprove it. For example, if two sample means happen to be identical, this does not prove no difference in the population parameters. In other words, we have not proved that they come from the same population, or from two different populations in which the population means are the same. We know that sample statistics, even if drawn from different populations, can occasionally be the same. It should be noted that the null and alternative hypotheses are always stated in terms of population parameters rather than in terms of sample statistics, although we use sample statistics to test the hypotheses.

Let's briefly summarize the logic of hypothesis testing up to this point. First, we set up two mutually exclusive and exhaustive hypotheses.

1. The null hypothesis(H_0):
a. Cannot be proved. We cannot prove the mileage additive or device does not work.

b. Can be rejected. If rejected, we assert H_1. We can reject the hypothesis that the additive or device does not work and thereby assert that it does work.

2. The alternative hypothesis (H_1):

a. Cannot be proved directly. We cannot directly prove that the mileage additive or device works.

b. Cannot be rejected directly. We cannot directly reject the possibility that the additive or device works.

Only by rejecting H_0 (b) can we assert our "indirect proof" of the alternative hypothesis.

But how do we go about rejecting H_0? This is where probability theory enters the arena. First, it should be emphasized that in hypothesis testing we assume that the null hypothesis is the true distribution. If, in the sampling distribution of a statistic under the null hypothesis, a particular result would have a low probability of occurrence, then one of two possible conditions has occurred. Namely, either the null hypothesis is true, and we obtained a result which had a very small probability of occurring, or the null hypothesis is not true. We choose to accept the latter condition, i.e., we reject H_0 and assert H_1.

How do we define low probability? The definition is arbitrary but not capricious.[7] Some researchers are willing to reject H_0 when the obtained statistic would have occurred 5 percent of the time or less in the appropriate sampling distribution. This criterion for rejecting H_0 is variously referred to as the 5 percent significance level, the 0.05 level of significance, or simply the 5 percent or 0.05 level. The criterion of rejection is typically represented by the Greek letter α (alpha). Thus, when we use the 0.05 significance level, $\alpha = 0.05$.

Other researchers set up a more stringent criterion for rejecting H_0 and asserting H_1, namely the 0.01 or 1 percent significance level (i.e., $\alpha = 0.01$). Only when the obtained statistic would have occurred 1 percent or fewer times in the sampling distribution of interest would the researcher be willing to reject H_0 and assert indirect proof of H_1. These two levels of significance are commonly used, although we will occasionally encounter other values, such as 0.10 or 0.001.

The level of significance that is set is not merely a matter of preference among different researchers or different statisticians. The choice has to do with the consequences of making one of two types of error—mistakenly rejecting a true H_0 or failing to reject a false H_0. The same researchers or statistician may use different levels of significance in different experiments.

Note that statistical proof is not absolute proof in any sense of the word. If our test allow us to reject the null hypothesis that the additive or device does not work, we have not demonstrated beyond all reasonable doubt that it does work. As we have noted repeatedly, statistical analysis and probability theory help to reduce uncertainty. They do not eliminate it altogether. Indeed, analysis of the logic of statistical inference reveals that there are two types of errors we may commit:

1. We may reject the null hypothesis when it is true. Thus, we may falsely reject H_0, that the additive or device does not improve mileage, and assert H_1, that it does improve mileage. Such an error of falsely rejecting H_0 is known as a Type I or Type α error. The probability of this type of error is given by α. Thus, if $\alpha = 0.05$, we will mistakenly reject a true null hypothesis approximately five percent of the time.[8] Hence, our claim to have demonstrated an effect of changed conditions (such as better mileage when mixing an additive with the gasoline) will be wrong about 5 times in 100.[9] Some might consider this risk of error too high. That is why some investigators use $\alpha = 0.01$ or less. They are more conservative about their willingness to claim an effect where there may not be one.

2. In the second type of error, we fail to reject H_0 when it is actually false. This class of error is known as Type II or Type β error. If the device or additive actually improved mileage and we did not reject H_0, we would have failed to claim an effect when there was one. Note that we do not claim to have proved H_0 but merely that we failed to reject it. We should not minimize the importance of a Type II error. Many promising lines of research[10] have undoubtedly been abandoned prematurely because the results of preliminary investigations were not encouraging.

An ideal situation is one that results in a balance between the two types of errors. In this ideal situation, we should be able to state in advance the probability of making both a Type I and a Type II error.

As we have seen, we may state the probability of a Type I error in terms of the value of α we employ. The probability of a Type II error is represented by β. How can we evaluate this probability? We can determine β only when H_0 is false and we know the true value of the parameter under H_1. Since this is rarely the case, it is difficult to evaluate this probability. However, procedures are available that permit us to estimate β even when the parameter is not known. These procedures are beyond the scope of this text.

There are certain strategies, however, that may be employed to reduce the probability of a Type II error. For example, the lower we set our α, the greater the likelihood of a Type II error. Thus, in general, if $\alpha = 0.05$, β will be less than if $\alpha = 0.01$. [11] Another way to reduce β is to increase the sample size. The larger the sample, the smaller the probability of a Type II error.

Table 3-1 summarizes the type of error as a function of the true status of H_0 and the decision we have made. Note that a Type I error can be made only when H_0 is true, and a Type II error only when H_0 is false. We see that $(1-\alpha)$ is the probability of accepting H_0 when it is true, and α is the probability of rejecting a true H_0. Thus, if $\alpha = 0.05$ and H_0 is true, the probability of accepting H_0 equals $1 - 0.05 = 0.95$. Or, stated another way, if the null hypothesis is true, there is a 95 percent chance that it will be accepted.

Table 3-1   The Type of Error Made as a Function of the True Status of H_0 and the Decision We Have Made

	True status of H_0	
Decision	H_0 true	H_0 false
Accept H_0	Correct	Type II error
	$(1-\alpha)$	(β)
Reject H_0	Type I error	Correct
	(α)	$(1-\beta)$

Richard P. Runyon and Audrey Haber, *Business Statistics* © 1982, pp. 224-228. Reprinted by permission of Richard D. Irwin, Inc., Homewood, Illinois.

Key Terms and Concepts

hypothesis testing   one of the basic subdivisions of statistical inference, dealing with methods for testing hypotheses about population parameters.

Yom Kippur War   war in Middle East starting on Yom Kippur in 1973.

null hypothesis   The basic hypothesis H_0 is generally referred to null hypothesis. Actually it is a statement that specifies hypothesized values for

24

one or more of the population parameters.

alternative hypothesis The opposite hypothesis of null hypothesis is designated the alternative hypothesis, or a statement that specifies that the population parameter is a value other than that specified in the null hypothesis.

population mean mean of the population. Usually it is not available since it is the average of the complete set of measurements or observations that interest the person collecting a sample.

population proportion relative frequency of occurrence with qualitative variables in terms of the complete set of measures or observations.

significance level a probability value that A influences B to allow the assertion that nonchance factors are operating.

NOTES

1. ... (except perhaps after the fact—when it may be too late).　……（除了在事件发生以后——不过那时已太晚了）。

2. Although intuitive feelings and hunches often play a role in managerial decisions, ...　虽然直觉和预感常在管理决策中起作用,……

3. ... to substantially increase the mile-per-gallon ratings of the family "dream-turning-nightmare" machine.　……极大地增加那些家庭里突然变糟的汽车的每加仑英里数。(注:汽油的紧张使许多很好的但耗油多的大汽车忽然变得不受欢迎。)

4. ... whereas others are devices that must be installed along the fuel line or attached directly to the carburetor.　……而其他设计必须安装在油路中或直接连接汽化器。

5. We know that convenience sampling of this sort is rarely representative of the population of interest (i.e., all purchasers of the additive or device).　我们知道这种方便的抽样方法并不能代表统计数字的全体(即全体购买添加剂或装置的人)。

6. We have already seen that these sample statistics distribute themselves about a central value, ...　我们已经看见这些样本统计值分布在中心值附近,……

7. The definition is arbitrary but not capricious.　定义是据情况而定的,但不是多变的。

8. Thus, if $\alpha = 0.05$, we will mistakenly reject a true null hypothesis approximately five percent of the time.　因此,如果 $\alpha=0.05$,我们将有5%

25

9. ...wrong about 5 times in 100.　……100 次里错 5 次。

10. Many promising lines of research...　许多有希望的研究思路……

11. Thus, in general, if $\alpha=0.05$, β will be less than if $\alpha=0.01$.　因此,总的来说,如果 $\alpha=0.05$, β 将比 $\alpha=0.01$ 时出现的可能性小。

Suggestions for Further Study

Reading ranks first in importance when studying a foreign language. Reading is also the most productive strategy in learning a foreign language. If a student can read a word, most likely he can understand the word in chatting or broadcasting.

Three situations make reading ineffective. First, one reads slowly, hesitating or stopping at every new word. Second, one reads fast, but stops at the wrong places and misses important ideas. Third, one reads fast and stops at the right places, but misunderstands the message or theme.

When reading, not every word is important, and this idea can be applied to Chinese reading materials as well. English learners in China like to stop at every new word, just because English is a foreign language. If one day they can ignore new words as they ignore new Chinese characters in evening news, they are free.

Key Words　Reading

PART FOUR
MANAGEMENT INFORMATION SYSTEM

Hotel Computer Applications

It was stated in the chapter introduction that an airline reservation system had spin-off applications for hotel reservations. [1] Hotels also use computers for applications such as accounting, inventory, and payroll. These applications will now be discussed in the context of an actual case study. The hotel chosen for the study, Hotel West (a fictitious name) is a private business, though part of a chain[2], in a town of 50,000. It has 200 rooms, 175 employees, and a variety of facilities, including an indoor pool, conference rooms, banquet halls, shops, bars, and a restaurant servicing primarily upper-middle class families and traveling businesspeople.

Hotel Reservation

The input required from hotel reservations is name, address, phone, date and time of arrival, length of stay, number in party, room preference (size, price, locations; e. g. poolside, quiet wing,) and special services requested (crib, wheelchair). Because desk clerks and receptionists are generally unskilled and not permanent staff, reservation equipment is designed to be simple to operate. In Hotel West, a terminal with a standard typewriter keyboard is used for entering name, address, and phone number of the client, and a special-purpose terminal with 76 keys and 16 lights is used to input other reservation data. Though this latter terminal appears confusing at first glance, it is actually easier and faster to operate than airline reservation systems. For example, when an October booking is requested,[3] the clerk need not remember a month code (such as 10) but merely presses the key marked Oct. in a group of 12 keys for months set in a row. Additional keys represent other crucial data, such as code keys for hotel identification, date, number and type of rooms required, or action requested (cancel, reserve), and all related keys are grouped together. The lights identify the status of the equipment (ready, in use), availability of different types of rooms (single, double), and room availability in nearby hotels. Equipment so specialized is expensive and can only be justified if the number of reservations and hotel size are sufficiently large to permit it to be cost-effective.[4]

Reservations for a room at Hotel West can be made by another hotel in the chain or reservations can be made by the client calling a reservation center.[5] When Hotel West initiates a room request on behalf of a customer for a room at another hotel in the chain, a computer tie-in with central reservations checks availability. Confirmation of the reservation and a copy of notification to the hotel in question are messages that the operator in Hotel West receives as printout, and which the client can use as a reservation confirmation. Table 4-1 shows how such a request is coded.

Table 4-1 Sample Hotel Reservation Dialogue

Mr. John Doe, staying at Hotel West, asks the desk clerk to make reservations at another hotel in the chain, Hotel Polka, code 352 for June 5th for one person for two nights for a single room with guaranteed payment. Doe's address is 4943 Karen Drive, Las Cruces, NM 88001.

INPUT TYPED BY CLERK:

Doe, John	(Name of guest, last name first)
4943 Karen Dr.	(Street address)
Las Cruces, NM 88001	(City, state, zip code)
5055231427	(Area code plus phone number)

Clerk also keys in data on the special terminal, 352 for the hotel code, June 5 for the date of arrival, the 1 key for the number of rooms required, 1BD 1PR key for 1 bed for one person, and the 2 key for the two nights desired, the action key AVAIL to inquire about availability of the room, and finally, the ENTER key to enter the data for processing.

COMPUTER MESSAGE CONFIRMING RESERVATION AT HOTEL WEST:

CONF 1RM 1BD 1PR 2NT MON JUN 05

GUARANTEED PAYMENT DUE IF NOT CANCELLED BEFORE 6PM[6]

MESSAGE TO HOTEL POLKA:

28

SOLD 1RM 1BD 1PR 2NT MON JUN 05
   GUARANTEED PAYMENT
4943 Karen Dr.
Las Cruces, NM 88001
SK

If the requested hotel has no bookings available, central reservations will supply data on room options at the nearest hotel in the chain.

The tie-in to central reservations costs Hotel West $8,000 per year with $1 charged for each reservation made by the system. Line charges vary from one chain to another,[7] some underwriting the expense as part of their service to member hotels. One can measure the gain from a centralized reservation system since many of the figures are available for a cost-benefit analysis; cost of reservation service, number of rooms reserved through the system, income from reservations, income otherwise lost from unoccupied rooms. However, intangible benefits, such as convenience to customers, should also be recognized.

The central reservations network can also be programmed to provide other information services as well. In 1979, when gas shortages discouraged travelers, one hotel chain relayed information on filling-station hours, and dollar and volume limits per vehicle of stations within a five-mile radius of each hotel in the 1,500-member chain.[8] Travelers or hotels could phone to obtain the information. The purpose was to prevent cancellations or empty rooms by providing information on gas availability to clientele.

Other Business Applications

Hotel West also has a minicomputer for other business applications that is independent of the reservation system. This minicomputer has five CRTs, a main office terminal, three at points of sale (restaurant and bars), and one at the housekeeper's station.[9] These terminals are used for room assignments, registrations, and billing (front desk activities), and for processing payroll, accounts receivable, general ledger, cash posting, printing of statements, and management reporting, as well as energy and inventory control (backroom accounting). Large hotels often have two computer systems for these functions, separating front desk and backroom accounting, and also providing backup in the backroom computer should the frontroom system fail at the check-in counter.

Hotel West's minicomputer is located in an alcove of the front office. Maintenance and training are provided by the small out-of-state firm that installed the equipment and developed the software, Communications Diversified, Inc. This firm, with only 45 professionals, can compete with large conglomerates like IT&T because it specializes, providing software packages that apply to only few industries. The hotel management software, for example, required little modification to fit Hotel West's needs, whereas the purchase of a general business application package would have required Hotel West to hire a programmer or system analyst to adapt the package to local conditions. [10] This specialization of software entrepreneurs, coupled with the drop in the price of minis, [11] is what has made computer applications cost-effective for small businesses.

In the following sections, several of Hotel West's specialized business applications will be described.

Room Status　In order for desk clerk to assign rooms to clients, the status of hotel rooms (occupied or empty) must be known. At Hotel West, room status is one report provided by the minicomputer. To obtain room status information, the clerk first requests the display of a menu of reports or programs on the CRT of the front desk terminal by pressing a key code to this effect. From this list, the code for room status report is determined. This code is keyed and the RETURN key pressed to indicate end of choice of report. The terminal will then display the number of rooms available on any given date (up to 20 years in the future) and rooms currently ready for occupancy by room number and type (single, double). Occupancy status is updated in real-time mode from the housekeeper's terminal as maids complete cleaning. This information not only serves the front desk for registrations, but pinpoints the location and progress of each maid, and identifies rooms ready for inspections.

Registration and Check-out　Registration is done on the CRT by the front desk clerk. The input required is keyed line by line from top to bottom, the terminal validating each entry by character and range validity checks. [12] When a required field is not provided, the system locks (does not proceed) until all required information is entered. In processing registrations, the computer updates the room inventory, informs the housekeeper (on a terminal) of the room assignment, and generates a guest folio of all registration information keyed by room number. Included is such data as time and date of check-in which the computer automatically records. A guest account is also created (room rent and tax) to be updated in real time for charges, for example, telephone calls or restaurant bills. [13]

At check-out, the computer will print an itemized customer bill upon a simple keyed command by the desk clerk. When payment is received, the clerk enters the method of payment (cash, check, credit card) and amount into the system for auditing purposes. The computer automatically updates the room inventory and signals the housekeeper that the vacated room is ready for cleaning.

Check-out using the computer system is fast and accurate, saving the client time since the system instantly generates the bill. [14] But registration by computer takes longer than traditional manual registrations primarily because more information is requested, information that the desk clerk manually keys into the system.

Control Applications Stock inventory, especially food and beverages, is one important control function performed by computer at Hotel West. Another is auditing: shift audits (done three times a day) and the night audit (an audit summary of all three shifts). The audits list all transactions, amounts, mode of payment, transaction clerk, and shift supervisor. [15] These computer audits eliminate the need for daily bookkeeping by an accountant. In addition, the audits serve as financial reports to management.

In addition, the computer regulates energy consumption at Hotel West. Upon registration of a client, room heat (or air conditioning) is automatically turned on; at check-out, the system turns heat off. Air circulation in unoccupied rooms is also maintained by automatically switching on heat or cooling periodically. At Hotel West, the computer is programmed to control energy demand during peak periods. To reduce energy surcharges, heat is switched off for short time spans when energy demand reaches a predetermined level. The computer also regulates power-consuming devices, such as pumps, lights, and signs. This automation and control reduces energy consumption at Hotel West, saving an estimated 15-30 percent on the hotel's energy bill.

Wake-up Service Wake-up is automated, the computer telephoning clients at the time requested.

By K.M. Hussain

Key Terms and Concepts

poolside along the side of a pool.

quiet wing the section of a hotel building where it is quiet.

hotel identification the code representing a hotel and used to distinguish it from others in the chain of hotels.

CRT cathode ray tube terminal. A display device on which images are produced on a cathode ray tube.

line charges a per use fee.

cash posting to write daily transactions into general ledger.

room inventory status of hotel rooms, which tells if a room is occupied or empty.

mode of payment way of payment, such as cash, check, or credit card.

transaction clerk the clerk who is responsible for a specified transaction.

NOTES

1. ... an airline reservation system had spin-off applications for hotel reservations. ……航空公司定位系统有预定旅馆房间的附加业务。

2. though part of a chain 虽是连锁系统的一部分

3. ...when an October booking is requested,... ……当有人定十月的房间时,……

4. Equipment so specialized is expensive and can only be justified if the number of reservations and hotel size are sufficiently large to permit it to be cost-effective. 专用设备很贵,只有当旅馆规模较大或是旅馆业务很好时,花资金建立这种系统才合算。

5. ... by the client calling a reservation center. ……通过顾客打电话给连锁系统的控制中心。

6. GUARANTEED PAYMENT DUE IF NOT CANCELLED BEFORE 6PM
如果下午六时前不取消的话,必须支付租金。

7. Line charges vary from one chain to another,... 定位服务的收费标准各系统均不同,……

8. ... one hotel chain relayed information on filling-station hours, and dollar and volume limits per vehicle of stations within a five-mile radius of each hotel in the 1,500-member chain.　······有一个 1,500 家旅馆的连锁系统，提供各家旅馆半径在 5 英里内的加油站的营业时间及对每辆车加油量和金额的限制方面的信息。

9. ... a main office terminal, three at points of sale (restaurant and bars), and one at the housekeeper's station.　······一个终端在主要的办公室，三个在有销售业务的地方（餐厅及酒吧），另一个在清洁人员服务台。

10. ... whereas the purchase of a general business application package would have required Hotel West to hire a programmer or system analyst to adapt the package to local conditions.　······因此，买一个一般营业管理系统软件，西方旅馆需要雇一名程序员或系统分析人员改写软件以适应当地的情况。

11. ... coupled with the drop in the price of minis,...　······伴随着微机价格的下跌，······

12. The input required is keyed line by line from top to bottom, the terminal validating each entry by character and range validity checks.　需要输入的内容，自上至下，一行一行地键入，终端则逐字逐段地检查输入是否符合要求。

13. A guest account is also created (room rent and tax) to be updated in real time for charges, for example, telephone calls or restaurant bills.　顾客的账目（房租和税）也按时间算好了，比如说电话单或餐厅账单。

14. ... since the system instantly generates the bill.　······因为系统很快打出账单。

15. The audits list all transactions, amounts, mode of payment, transaction clerk, and shift supervisor.　审计人员列出所有的交易项目、金额、付账方式、经手人员及领班人。

Word Processing

Word processing is another major application of computers for office management. The data processed is not numbers but text. With office costs rising yearly, businesses have begun to recognize the value of WP, a computerized system of hardware and software for transforming ideas into printed text. Computers can compose and format correspondence, and can edit, revise, update, duplicate, and file data for memoranda, contracts, reports, manuals, and reference materials. Word processors can also automate conversion of documents into machine-readable form,[1] provide copy storage, and facilitate the flow of information in an office through reference and retrieval capabilities. In short, WP aids document creation and record keeping. When WP equipment is linked to communication equipment, a further benefit, electronic mail, is possible.

Nature of Word Processing

An overview of word processing is as follows. Input may be in the form of printed material, such as documents, or mail converted into machine readable text by means of OCR (optical character recognition) or facsimile equipment; it may be gathered by voice recognition equipment; or may be entered by keystroking on a hard copy terminal[2] or CRT system, a process similar to typing. Word processors may also draw upon data (text) stored in computer memory for input. For example, a computer memory can store an encyclopedia of statistics, quotations, standard responses to common queries, and text previously processed. Information from trade journals may also be extracted and placed in storage for reference, or articles may be entered in their entirety after being indexed for retrieval.[3] There are currently 100,000 magazines on the market. Computer retrieval of information in these magazines helps businesspersons keep abreast of the latest developments in their fields for future document generation.

The text chosen for output is formatted under software control. This includes centering, left and right justification, and horizontal and vertical spacing on a page.[4] In conventional text preparation, 38 percent of all copy goes into the wastebasket because of typewriting errors. The nervousness a typist feels, particularly near the end of a page when an error will require retyping the entire page, is eliminated in word processing since corrections can be made one letter, one word, one line, or one paragraph at a time after the page is typed, the word processor making all the necessary format adjustments for corrections automatically.[5] Insertions and deletions can also be performed easily by one command. A dictionary stored in the memory unit can be referenced quickly to check on spelling and syllable divisions.

Text stored in memory, once edited, can be reproduced without mistake, a tremendous saving over conventional typing where each retyped copy is subject to error.[6] However, text in memory may have to be updated or revised. A final check must, therefore, take place after the output text is composed to be sure all editing has, in fact, been done. The document can then be printed. When the text has been prepared on a CRT, a code releases the text from the screen into memory and starts the printing. A second page of text can be composed while the first is being printed, or can be stored in auxiliary memory for later printing in batch mode if desired.

When the output is correspondence, the computer can be programmed to personalize letter, with names, addresses, and salutations added to the text. This capability was available in the mid-1960s with the magnetic tape Selectric Typewriter. What makes WP different is that sentences or entire paragraphs can be extracted from the data base and collated with other information provided through dictation, or reading by an OCR device in preparing the text. A change in wording, such as substituting the words "recreation vehicle" for "trailer" whenever it appears in the text can be done by a simple command under program control. Names and address lists can be drawn from computer memory, and letters for a selected list printed, such as letters to vice-presidents in a particular industry in zip code 88001. The system may also be directed to print letters and envelopes with a font chosen from a large variety of styles and sizes.[7] In addition, the system can keep track of time spent on each job to facilitate charging customer accounts for service.[8] This feature is particularly valuable for law and consulting firms.

If the word processor has telecommunications equipment and addresses have terminals, electronic mail with instant delivery can be transmitted instead of preparing copies of text. Text storage can be in the computer memory, on microfilm, microfiche, floppy disk, or a computer peripheral instead of hard copy.

General Mills is an example of a company using WP for correspondence. Some 10,000 letters composed from a set of 550 paragraphs stores in memory are mailed each month in response to letters regarding Bettery Crocker products. The letters appear customized. So do documents, such as contracts and manuals, prepared by word processors. The wide variety of office applications for word processors, and their speed, accuracy, and convenience are reasons business people are turning to this office use of computers.

When Word Processing

Word processors will never replace secretaries entirely. Personal correspondence and documents directed to a particular situation or recipient require conventional methods of preparation. WP is of value primarily for documents with a large receivership, for messages that are repetitive, and for documents that must be regenerated periodically with only minor revisions and updating of text. For such documents, word processing reduces lead time up to 50 percent, and proofreading by 10-95 percent. In addition, reproductions are highly accurate and have cosmetic formatting and lettering. [9]

The need for word processing should be established by a cost-benefit analysis before firms invest in the equipment. Fortunately, WP can be acquired in modules so that receptive departments can initiate word processing and demonstrate its value to other departments in the firm.

By K.M. Hussain

Key Terms and Concepts

OCR optical character recognition. The machine identification of printed characters through the use of light-sensitive devices.

centering to make line of word(s) on screen with equal margins on the left and right.

justification adjust the typed lines to fill the space on screen neatly.

syllable divisions divisions within a word, made in accordance with syllables.

batch mode putting data in a file for later printing.

Selectric Typewriter a device with the benefit of magnetic tape on which data can be stored by selective polarization of portions of the surface.

recreation vehicle vehicle with kitchen and restroom used for travelling and camping.

trailer small movable house pulled by vehicle for travelling and camping.

microfilm film used to store data. Its size is the same as the film used in a 135 camera.

microfiche film used to store data. Its size is much smaller than microfilm but similar to the film used in a 110 camera.

computer peripheral refers to magnetic tapes or other appurtenances used for data storage.

General Mills   name of a company.

Bettery Crocker   a brand name.

hard copy   a piece of paper with data or information printed on it.

lead time   period from design to production.

proofreading   work done by a proofreader who reads and corrects printers' proof.

NOTES

1. Word processors can also automate conversion of documents into machine-readable form,... 文字处理机能自动将文件转换为机器可以读的形式，……

2. by keystroking on a hard copy terminal 在有打印系统的终端上键入

3. ...articles may be entered in their entirety after being indexed for retrieval. ……所有文章可以在编目后输入，以供查询和调出。

4. This includes centering, left and right justification, and horizontal and vertical spacing on a page. 这包括向中心对齐，左右边缘的调整及字间和行距的安排。

5. ...the word processor making all the necessary format adjustments for corrections automatically. ……文字处理机自动地对修改过的部分作必要的格式调整。

6. ...a tremendous saving over conventional typing where each retyped copy is subject to error. ……由于不像用传统方法重复打时那样容易出错，所以就特别省事。

7. ...with a font chosen from a large variety of styles and sizes. ……字的式样和规格大小有许多形式可以选择。

8. ...the system can keep track of time spent on each job to facilitate charging customer accounts for service. ……系统自动记录每项工作花费的时间，从而使收顾客服务费的工作变得容易了。

9. ...reproductions are highly accurate and have cosmetic formatting and lettering. ……重复打印的文件不仅精确，并且有漂亮的格式和字形。

Suggestions for Further Study

Most times, to learn a foreign language, people learn words from reading. A prerequisite to effective listening is that one must be able to read and understand words in print before they can be aware of them in daily conversation or in news broadcasting. From this point of view, most problems people encounter in listening are not the problems of listening but of reading.

In modern society, there are many opportunities for students to improve their listening. These include English TV programs, English radio programs, as well as movies on VCD or DVD. Chinese students who go abroad to study find that their listening improves very fast, not only because of attending classes and reading textbooks, but also because of watching TV. Actually, TV shows are more helpful to the improvement of Chinese students' listening. Why? Normally, each week, a Chinese student away from their home country spends only eight or ten hours each week in class, but dozens of hours watching TV! Think of the impact of TV.

Key Words Listening

PART FIVE
OPERATIONS MANAGEMENT

Order Processing

When things are going well, operations is able to produce and deliver what marketing sells[1]. To keep things going well, operations management must play an active role in the processing of customer orders. In most cases, it is poor policy for the operations function to simply put into backlog any orders that sales is able to "scare up."[2] Instead, there should be a well-devised order processing system. Central to the system is the order promise. In this section we discuss orders in general, examine the order processing sequence, and then look specifically at order promising.

Orders

Even when considered only as a noun and only within an operations context[3], the word order has multiple meanings. For example, there might be individual sales orders, consolidation of sales orders into a few batch orders[4] (for total requirements of each item), scheduled production orders for major modules, planned orders for component parts from inventory planning, shop or work orders, purchase orders for component parts and raw materials, final assembly order, and shipment orders. Each type of order may have its own number system and set of documentation. Clearly, in a manufacturing company, you will not necessarily get the response you are looking for when you inquire, "Where's my order?"

Even in the service sector the customer order may break down into several subtypes. Consider, for example, a medical clinic. You, the patient, are an order;[5] when you go to X ray, an X-ray order number is assigned;[6] when you go to the lab, several lab orders are created;[7] when you are finished, there will be a billing order with its own number for total services rendered.

With these meanings in mind, we now turn our attention to the order processing sequence[8].

Order Processing Sequence

The sequence of order processing is as follows.

The first step is order booking, in which an order is booked by sales. The second step is order entry. Order entry, which is really a subprocess in itself, includes the organizational acceptance of the order into the order processing system. Order-entry activities might include:

*   Credit checks, especially for new customers.
*   Documentation of pertinent customer data, such as specifications.
*   Translation of what the customer wants into terms used by production.
*   Determining whether the order can be filled from stock (if so, the process might skip directly to step 10).
*   Assignment of an internal order number.

The next seven steps are operations functions. Step 3 is determining total requirements. Orders by several customers for the same product or service must be totaled. Additional translation might be required at this point, specifically, translation of sales catalog terminology into manufacturing part numbers.[9] Some companies employ as many as three sets of part numbers, which are used with three different scheduling procedures: (1) the final assembly schedule—for assembly of finished end products, (2) the master production schedule—for production of major modules such as frames and engines, and (3) a schedule for the manufacture of service parts, interplant transfer parts, customer optional parts,[10] and so forth.

Step 4, order positioning, accomplishes several things. First, a check is made to see if present schedules can accommodate new requirements. If so, the order is positioned—placed—in the schedule. We might say that the order receives its third "acceptance, " this time by the master schedule.

If the schedule is full and the customer is willing to wait, the order is accepted and positioned at the tail end of a backlog of orders. The preferred procedure in competitive firms is to make the goods, wholly or partially, based on a forecast. Thus, parts, major modules, and final assemblies are scheduled in advance. It is these schedules that are checked to see whether they will result in the goods requested by a customer at a desired future date.

Step 5 is the culmination of step 4. If the schedule can meet the customer order, an order promise notice goes to the customer. We will discuss the order promise step more fully a bit later.

In steps 6 through 8, customer identification is lost, and these steps are generally out of the realm of demand management. In step 6, inventory planning, accepted orders are divided into requirements for component parts. If the parts are not on hand, manufacture and purchase orders for parts are generated.[11] The component parts orders do not easily tie to a given customer, because common parts go into various end items ordered by various customers. Scheduling, at a detailed level, and purchasing constitute step 7: Schedulers carefully release the parts manufacturing orders[12] so as not to overload the shop; buyers release the purchase orders. Dispatching is step 8: Dispatchers control the priorities of parts orders as they queue up in the work centers to have certain operations done.

In step 9, assembly orders, the customer order reemerges as the basis for orders for the final assembly of end items (and accessories) into finished goods or end products. Shipment orders, geographically consolidated, constitute step 10.

It is clear that order processing is complex. Much of this book is devoted to explaining all the steps and techniques used to achieve good results—on-time completion of quality goods and services at a reasonable cost and flexibility to respond to new orders or other customer needs.

Order Promising

Order promising means making a commitment to the customer to ship or deliver an order. Order promise by operations management also serves as its commitment to the partnership that marketing and operations should have.[13] Speedy notice of order promise can provide salespeople with sound information[14] for use in making any delivery arrangements. Timely notice also helps get more sales. In return, the sales force may be able to more closely gear selling activities toward operating capacity; that is, salespeople may push sales of items that require use of idle or slack operations capacity and ease off on items that would strain other capacity.[15]

The only situation in which operations does not have an order promise function is the pure make-to-stock company. Here goods are made to a forecast and placed in distribution centers, and customer order processing is left to the marketing arm of the business. But few companies are strictly make-to-stock. Special large orders, orders for service parts, and so forth may be accepted. In that case, there should be a formal order promise procedure so that sales can give the customer some assurance that production is committed to meet the agreed-upon delivery date.

In client-oriented services, the order promise is known as an appointment. The order is not a legal promise; it just means that schedules have been checked and that, barring problems, the customer's order should be done on time. All parties realize that problems do occur and some orders are going to be late. Just as obvious to all is that the firm with the fewest late orders enhances its competitive position.

Richard J. Schonberger and Edward M. Knod, Jr. ,*Operations Management* 3rd ed. © 1988, pp. 99-102. Reprinted by permission of Richard D. Irwin, Inc. , Homewood, Illinois.

Key Terms and Concepts

operations management   a term shifting from industrial management, manufacturing management, production management, and production/ operations management, because people have found that concepts and techniques for managing production in factories are useful in government and services as well.

order promising   to grant a customer to ship or deliver an order.

batch orders   orders which consist of several orders, often small.

final assembly order   notice which tells people to proceed final assembly.

shipment orders   notice which tells people to ship or transport goods.

number system   parts or goods with their own codes so as to make management easier.

set of documentation   documents to tell the details in order processing.

billing order   notice which tells people the sum of payments.

order booking   making record of order.

order entry   inputting the details of order.

operations functions   concerned scope or tasks which management should deal with.

42

order positioning arranging when and how to proceed an order.

order promise notice making a commitment to the customer to ship or deliver an order.

accessories parts attached to a machine or a good，making it with extra functions.

NOTES

1. marketing sells 销售部卖的(产品)

2. ...it is poor policy for the operations function to simply put into backlog any orders that sales is able to "scare up." ……如果管理职能部门在销售部门还能凑合的情况下就只管把订单积压起来，那是一种很糟糕的做法。

3. within an operations context 在经营管理的范围内

4. consolidation of sales orders into a few batch orders 把零散的订货集合起来变为一些批量订货

5. You，the patient，are an order；... 你，一个病人，就好比一张订单；……

6. X-ray order number is assigned；... (当你去作 X 光检查)会(给你)指定一个 X 光检查的序列号；……

7. ...several lab orders are created；... ……就会有几种化验单(或检查表格)……

8. order processing sequence 订货处理的顺序

9. ...translation of sales catalog terminology into manufacturing part numbers. ……将销售目录里的名称转为加工部件的代号。

10. ...interplant transfer parts, customer optional parts，... ……不同工序需转送的零件,供顾客选择的零件,……

11. If the parts are not on hand，manufacture and purchase orders for parts are generated. 如果需要的零件没有,则需要填写制造或外购订单。

12. parts manufacturing orders 零件制造的订单

13. ...partnership that marketing and operations should have. ……销售部门和管理部门应有的协作。

14. sound information 充分的信息

15. ...salespeople may push sales of items that require use of idle or slack operations capacity and ease off on items that would strain other capacity. ……销售人员可能促成多销一些产品,因而需要使用闲置的生产能力,从而减轻另一些设备的压力。

Bring Design into the Business

If there is to be awareness of how designs affect other functions, designers need to work with and come to understand those functions. Product design has its greatest effect on three key functions: (1) operations, (2) marketing and the customer, and (3) suppliers.

Operations: The Next Process

The designer's "customer" is operations or, more likely, where operations planning is done. In manufacturing, one aspect of operations planning is manufacturing engineering[1] (sometimes called process engineering). Manufacturing engineers are equipment and automation experts. Machines—those now in use as well as any being considered for purchase—have limited capabilities. A certain machine may be able to cut aluminum but not brass, machine 14-mm. but not 18-mm. steel, or hold tolerances of 0.005 inches but no better. If the design is to be manufacturable, the designer must somehow acquire some of the manufacturing engineer's knowledge of machine capabilities.

For a number of years, IBM has fed that kind of information to designers through a program called "early manufacturing involvement (EMI)."[2] Under EMI, IBM assigns a manufacturing engineer to work in a development lab with product designers during a design project. More recently a number of companies, such as Deere and Company and Stanadyne Diesel, have adopted a more permanent solution: putting design engineering and manufacturing engineering under one manager. The single manager has full responsibility for enduring close coordination. An even more profound and rapidly spreading approach is to form design-build teams[3] composed of designers, engineers, other support people, and even line production employees[4].

Linkage with Marketing

The designer must also close ranks with the final customer—via marketing. Chrysler rescued itself from the grave largely by cost cutting. Design and marketing jointly played a central role. They developed a product

44

line with a narrow range of options having broad appeal[5] instead of the former practice of a broad range with narrow appeal. In other words, the new concept featured just a few standard design "packages" available to the customer.

From the Dodge Omni and Plymouth Horizon, some 8 million permutations of options (excluding colors) had been possible. The new design concept reduced the number of permutations to 42. Chrysler could then focus on making a small number of parts in very high volumes, which offered economy of scale and a narrower target for improving quality. As a result, the price Chrysler had to charge plunged in 1986 to $5,779, which was below that of almost all other cars sold in the United States.

Eliminating options and reducing "part counts" can backfire if not done right.[6] Customers' needs and wants are the foremost concern, and Detroit had been allowing options to proliferate because that seemed to be what customers wanted. Good design, however, can sometimes allow high variety with small part counts; that is, a modest number of parts designed[7] to fit together in many ways can yield a large number of end product variations (Legos, the toy construction blocks, come to mind). Modular design concepts also allow variety of end products while holding part counts down. For example, personal computer manufacturers offer a variety of compatible products—keyboard, mouse, extramemory, different screens, modems, and so forth—so that the consumer can tailor a system to meet personal needs and budget.

Interface with Suppliers

Design's third accommodation is with suppliers. Designers have major authority in choosing materials, which often is tantamount to choosing the supplier. Company policies, however, sometimes make it difficult for anyone but buyers in the purchasing department[8] to interact directly with suppliers. (Under past purchasing practices, there was really little chance for either buyer or design engineer to interact with suppliers; there simply were too many suppliers. The movement to reduce number of suppliers per part number makes it reasonable to visit suppliers.) Now some companies are beginning to relax such policies. Designers need to visit supplier plants, perhaps along with buyers, in order to learn the suppliers' capabilities.

Top companies are not content with just visiting suppliers. They also seek early supplier involvement, which means inviting suggestions for making the supplied materials or components function better for the customer's intended uses. Often the supplier's designers end up working concurrently with the customer's. Furthermore, instead of the customer's specs being hurled "over the wall" to the supplier[9], the customer may just specify critical performance specifications. That practice, sometimes called minimal specifications or minimal dimensioning, makes sense only when coordination between supplier and customer are excellent; otherwise, thorough specifications are usually desirable.

Richard J. Schonberger and Edward M. Knod, Jr., *Operations Management* 3rd ed. © 1988, pp. 625-27. Reprinted by permission of Richard D. Irwin, Inc, Homewood, Illinois.

Key Terms and Concepts

Chrysler one of the three automobile companies in the United States.

Dodge Omni Dodge is a brand name of car. Omni is the name of a model under Dodge.

Plymouth Horizon Plymouth is a brand name of car. Horizon is the name of a model under Plymouth.

economy of scale refers to the positive effects on unit costs of a firm as it increases its scale or plant size over the long run.

Lego name of a company which invented toy construction blocks. Later, people call these blocks "Legos."

compatible products products with specifications matching the requirements.

NOTES

1. manufacturing engineering　制造工程
2. "early manufacturing involvement (EMI)"　"制造前期工作"(指制造前期工作计划,即设计时便将制造中的问题考虑进去。)
3. design-build teams　设计与制造相结合的小组
4. line production employees　生产线上的员工
5. ...a product line with a narrow range of options having broad appeal...
   ……(搞了)一条产品线,产品从性能(或特征)上来讲,选择性较少,但适应性则较宽……(注:比如汽车的颜色,种类较少,但却能适应大多数消费者,而那特殊的颜色,尽管有成百上千种,也有人喜欢,但由于每一种只适合很少的人，所以厂家不去生产。）

6. ... can backfire if not done right.　……搞不好会把事情弄糟。

7. a modest number of parts designed　所设计的零件数量较少

8. buyers in the purchasing department　销售部的采购人员（这里 buyers 不是指消费者，而是指集团购买者）

9. ... the customer's specs being hurled "over the wall" to the supplier,...
　……把消费者对产品性能的要求一股脑地推给供应商，……

Suggestions for Further Study

To learn a foreign language, writing ranks second in importance to reading. In most cases, if a second language learner knows how to write, he knows how to speak.

When a Chinese student recalls his or her years in primary school and those early days when he or she just started to learn how to write Chinese, definitely he or she will think of the red marks his or her teacher made, for a character, or for a sentence. Little by little, day after day, year after year, boys become men and girls become women, with writing greatly improved or even matured.

At a university, if a student, without an instructor or professor to edit his writings, wants to learn writing but does not know how to write, what should he do? In this case, a dictionary can be very helpful, especially the dictionary *A Dictionary of Current English Usage* (《现代英语用法词典》，张道真编著，上海译文出版社) edited by Professor Daozhen Zhang. This is a dictionary specially designed for English usage. It helps a student to express what he is unable to express in English yet.

For university students, effective writing is crucial. Students need to learn the format of a résumé so they can present themselves well to society when they graduate. Students need to learn the format of a business letter so they can make a better impression when securing employment or applying to a foreign university. Students need to learn the format of footnotes and bibliographies, because when an undergraduate student writes an essay, a graduate student in a master's program writes a thesis or a graduate student in a doctoral program works on a dissertation, they need these skills. Fortunately, in the appendixes of this textbook, students can find samples of the formats of résumé, business letters, footnotes, and bibliographies.

To evaluate writing, many criteria exist. However, among the various alternatives, one is most practical. It says that small words and short sentences are good English. Explaining further, "important" and "big" are small words, and "significant" and "gigantic" are big words. The two sentences presented by Walt Disney in the last paragraph of the text "Free Markets and Growth" of Part Twelve International Economics in this textbook, "Change is inevitable. Growth is not." are good examples of short English sentences and "床前明月光" is a good example of a short Chinese sentence. When the later becomes long, it could be "老夫那张冰冷的梨花木大床前的地上铺满了昊天明月洒下的银色冷光。" Then the sentence has become very awkward. Remember, when writing, always make sentences as short as possible.

Key Words Writing

PART SIX
MARKETING

Pulling and Pushing Marketing Strategies
in a Market-Oriented System

The main objective of any organization is survival. For a market-oriented business, the route to that survival, in the long run, is the successful marketing of its products and services at prices which absorb its full costs of operations including a financial reward to its owners and a sum permitting it to sustain its growth.[1] A business can exist in the short run through obtaining State subsidies, receiving preferential tax treatment, or through net borrowing, the sales of its assets, default on its payments liabilities, the neglect of challenging opportunities,[2] or resort to other non-growth options. In the final analysis, however, the continuing viability of a business is the satisfactory marketing of its goods and services to meet the economic desiderata of the market place. It can do so either through PUSHING its goods and services to consumers through distribution channels or through PULLING its goods and services to consumers by means of promotional efforts[3] designed to motivate consumers to choose its particular goods and services. Its pulling strategies rely on sales promotions, personal selling and salesmanship, public relations, and advertising in all of its forms including sky writing, air borne streamers, "sandwich boards", hoardings or billboards, poster displays in buses, trams and trains, in taxis, leaflets, T-shirts, packaging materials, match boxes, and word-of-mouth, to name the most widely used.

The pull strategy can also include cooperative advertising by which the costs of advertising are shared by manufacturers and retailers on an agreed percentage basis. It is most prominently practiced in North American markets. Cooperative advertising sometimes makes use of fold-in inserts in newspapers and magazines, particularly when readers' profiles match a retailer's clientele. An unusual form of pull strategy, also prevalent in the United States, is an arrangement between manufacturers and film studios or sports organizers to display products (e. g. , Pepsi Cola, Marlboro cigarettes, Budweiser beer) either in film scenes or outdoor displays of the products themselves or their identifiable logos. [4] As such the promotions are blended into the background of the film or sports contest and viewed by viewers or spectators as part of everyday life.

Whether push or pull strategies are employed is a matter of the category of goods and services to be promoted, the willingness of channel occupants to participate, the size of the budget, market traditions and national or local culture, brand recognition, trade practices, consumer sophistication and buying behavior, stage of the product life cycle among other factors. Ordinarily both sets of strategies are necessary for optimum results.

Push Strategies

Push strategies rely on a wide variety of in-channel methods to induce, motivate, coerce, or otherwise bring about alliances and cooperative pushing efforts involving retailers, wholesalers, brokers, agents, and other middlemen to help ensure that the seller has his goods and services pushed to consumers. The thrust of the push strategy is toward middlemen, those who are in the distribution chain linking producers to final users. Push strategies include giving rebates cash payments, payments in kind, [5] or other awards to wholesalers and retailers who push the suppliers' ware and services on to consumers. Such rewards are given to cooperating distributors who stock or prominently display the supplier's goods or services. [6] The cash payments can be in the form of prizes or goods to be sold by distributors who design award-winning store or window displays of supplier's products. They are also awarded to distributors who give preferred shelf space, store space, or store location to the supplier's products. Sometimes, the award takes the form of a "spiv" or extra commission to distributors who "push" the supplier's particular brand on to buyers. Beer companies notably often arrange extra payments to bartenders who push their brands to the drinking patrons.

Pull Strategies

The pull strategies are directed at final users and are aimed at motivating them to ask for specific products or services by brand name or service identification.

The pull strategies comprise four thrusts: [7]

    * To discover new users or find new market segments of existing products or services;

    * To exploit existing products or services by finding new uses;

    * To increase product or service usage by motivating customers to use products or services more often or to use more of each during usage occasion;

    * To modify existing products or services so as to extend the product or service life cycle.

The most prevalent among the pull strategies are quizzes, questionnaires, contests, or sweepstakes. These pull strategies account for over 50% of all sales campaigns. The most notable among them in the United States is the decades-old Pillsbury Bake Contest in which entrants' cooking recipes are judged, in a nationwide television show, by a panel of "experts" to determine winners of large cash prizes and other awards. Contests can also be won through supposed impartial judgment of best entries containing an answer to a quiz question such as "I like Chinese Dynasty Wine because ... (in 25 words or less)."

Sales Promotions

Sales promotions, accounting for about 30% of marketing campaign expenditures aimed directly at consumers, can take place as part of in-store demonstrations. Free samples are given to potential customers to encourage them to try the product before adopting it. The samples are usually foodstuffs, beverages, laundry powders, and other non-durables. Domestic electrical appliances are also offered, but on a use-it-at-home short term trial basis. Promotions can also be in-the-home trials, with sales personnel demonstrating the proper use of such products as vacuum cleaners, cookware, ovenware, glassware, electrical juicers, and cosmetics. The promotions are launched through direct request from potential users who respond to direct mail,[8] fill in newspaper or magazine coupons, respond to door-to-door canvassers, or telephone prospectors. Avon products relies almost exclusively on door-to-door selling of its beauty products by trained cosmeticians.

A variation of this kind of promotion is the offer of a membership in a "trying and buying" club. Prospects are invited to apply for membership in order to be granted club privileges to buy products at special introductory low prices. The promotions include book subscriptions or credit cares. Usually members receive a numbered membership card, a free subscription to a periodical which describes the club's special promotions, and contains offers of products specially discounted for club members. In the case of cosmetics clubs, members are invited to arrange "make-up" lessons and to buy low-priced facial, body, and hair products. Airlines award members certificates based on paid air miles flown which entitle members to free travel upon the completion of a specified number of air miles flown. A British credit card company offers its members a two-day free hotel stay in selected hotels in the United Kingdom. Publishers and cassette companies offer members free or low-priced books or discs as an inducement to join. The variety of membership awards is almost endless.

The clubs are promoted through media campaigns, television, radio, magazines, newspapers, direct mail, outdoor advertising, mail box stuffers, on-the-street handouts, word-of-mouth, in-flight literature, or brochures at check-in counters or hotels. Another technique in the sales promotion mix is to stage a premium campaign in which prospective customers are asked to return labels or tops of food boxes or to supply other evidence of purchase in order to qualify for cash prizes, merchandise awards, discounts on purchases, free air travel, or holiday resort free accommodation[9].

Two other kinds of sales promotion which are not widely administered outside North America are:

* The giving of redemption stamps at points of purchase;
* Offering discount coupons to shoppers or potential shoppers.

The number of stamps given is based on a certain percentage of the monetary value of in-store purchases. The stamps are able to be redeemed at special shops which stock a wide variety of popular merchandise items which are available at no extra charge. The discount coupons can be redeemed either for free items or items at lower prices than prevailing one. The coupons are distributed as part of in-store promotions, through the mail, or as newspaper "flyers" or inserts, or located inside or outside the package. Coupons are also offered as a combination or package deal.[10] These so-called "cross promotions" offer a brand item together with a non-competitive brand or product. A biscuit company, for example, may offer its brand product in combination with cheese at a special price, or a cake mix company may offer its product with a companion box of icing.

The coupons are judged to be legal contracts[11] so that whether they are sponsored by manufacturers or retailers, their redemptions must be guaranteed in accordance with the specifications stated in the coupon offer.

In summary, the creation, design, implementation of pull and push strategies are the hallmarks of a successful enterprise destined to survive. The appropriate selection and execution of specific marketing strategies represent the challenges inherent in marketing management. However, no matter which of the above strategies are pursued, for optimum results, they must be integrated into a company's total marketing policy and its organizational objectives so as to ensure a company's success.

By John E. Weinrich

Key Terms and Concepts

market-oriented system a system in which price, output, and volume decisions are made through the interaction of supply and demand market forces rather than by a central government authority.

economic desiderata desired economic benefits resulting from the interaction of market supply and demand forces.

sky writing legible smoke trails from an airplane in which vapors spell out words or promotional phrases.

sandwich boards an advertising message on an attachment of two knee length flat pieces of wood which are suspended over the shoulders of a person.

packaging materials paper, cardboard, and other wrapping or containers for goods on which messages are written.

word-of-mouth messages given vocally by one person to another.

cooperative advertising an arrangement by which the costs of advertising are shared by the retailer and the manufacturer.

payments in kind payments in goods or services not in money.

spiv U.S.A. advertising jargon to describe secret payments to salesmen for manipulating customers to buy a specific brand.

Pillsbury Bake Contest a contest staged by a leading U.S.A. flour manufacturer in which contestants' baked cookies, cakes, bread, are judged for their taste, nutrition, look, and economy.

mail box stuffers printed advertising messages inserted in letter boxes in apartment complexes or residential homes.

on-the-street handouts leaflets containing messages given to pedestrians asking them to buy a particular product or service.

flyers a general terms for mail box stuffers, on-the-street handouts, or other one page printed messages directed to consumers.

cross promotion coupons on packages which offer a combination of products involving the advertiser's brand and a non-competing brand or product, usually at a reduced price.

consumer sophistication a degree of consumer awareness, whereby advertising messages are judged by their rationality, factual reality, and truthfulness rather than fancy or falsity.

NOTES

1. ... the successful marketing of its products and services at prices which absorb its full costs of operations including a financial reward to its owners and a sum permitting it to sustain its growth. ……（企业能够经营下去的途径是）成功地营销它的产品和服务,价格则要能做到回收全部成本,并使企业拥有者有一定的收益,与此同时还要有一笔资金保证企业的成长。

2. ... default on its payments liabilities, the neglect of challenging opportunities, ……拖欠债务款项,放弃挑战性的机会,(注:意思是以"求稳"来保企业。)

3. by means of promotional efforts 以促销方面的努力为手段(注:促销包括广告、人员推销、营业推广与公共关系四个方面。)

4. ... either in film scenes or outdoor displays of the products themselves or their identifiable logos. ……用影像放映或在户外展示产品及它们的标识语。

5. ... giving rebate cash payments, payments in kind,... ……给现金回扣,或类似的偿付,……

6. ... cooperating distributors who stock or prominently display the supplier's goods or services. ……储存或展示供应商产品或服务的合作分销商。

7. The pull strategies comprise four thrusts:... 引导策略包括四个有力措施:……

8. The promotions are launched through direct request from potential users who respond to direct mail,... 潜在顾客对邮寄广告反应后产生需求,进

一步引发促销活动。

9. holiday resort free accommodation　假日出游的免费食宿
10. Coupons are also offered as a combination or package deal. 　代金券也以搭配或组合产品为内容。
11. The coupons are judged to be legal contracts... 　代金券如同是一种法律契约……

The Many Faces of Personal Selling

Personal selling assumes many forms based on the amount of selling done and the amount of creativity required to perform the sales task.[1] Broadly speaking, three types of personal selling exist: order taking, order getting, and sales support activities. While some firms use only one of these types of personal selling, others use a combination of all three.

Order taking

Typically an order taker processes routine orders or reorders for products that were already sold by the company. The primary responsibility of order takers is to preserve an ongoing relationship with existing customers and maintain sales. Two types of order takers exist. Outside order takers visit customers and replenish inventory stocks of resellers,[2] such as retailers or wholesalers. For example, Frito-Lay salespeople call on supermarkets, neighborhood grocery stores, and other establishments to ensure that the company's line of salty snack products[3] (such as Doritos and Tostitos) is in adequate supply. In addition, outside order takers typically provide assistance in arranging displays. Inside order takers, also called sales or order clerks, typically answer simple questions, take orders, and complete transactions with customers.[4] Many retail clerks are inside order takers, as are people who take orders from buyers by telephone.[5] In industrial settings, order taking arises in straight rebuy situations[6]. For instance, stationery supply firms have inside order takers. Order takers, for the most part, do little selling in a conventional sense[7] and engage in little problem solving with customers. They often represent simple products that have few options, such as confectionery items, magazine subscriptions, and highly standardized industrial products.

Order Getting

An order getter sells in a conventional sense and identifies prospective customers, provides customers with information, persuades customers to buy, closes sales, and follows up on customers' use of a product or service.[8] Like order takers, order getters can be inside (an automobile salesperson) or outside (like Xerox salespersons who travel a lot and are only interested in peddling their products or services). Order getting involves a high degree of creativity and customer empathy[9] and typically is required for selling complex or technical products with many options. Therefore considerable product knowledge and sales training are necessary. In modified rebuy or new buy purchase situations in industrial selling,[10] an order getter acts as a problem solver who identifies how a particular product may satisfy a customer's need. Similarly, in the purchase of a service, such as insurance, an insurance agent can provide a mix of plans to satisfy a buyer's needs depending on income, stage of the family's life cycle, and investment objective. Table 6-1 compares order takers and order getters to illustrate some differences between them.

Table 6-1 Comparing Order Takers and Order Getters

BASIS OF COMPARISON	ORDER TAKERS	ORDER GETTERS
Objective	Handle routine product orders or reorders	Identify new customers and sales opportunities
Purchase situation	Focus on straight rebuy purchase situations	Focus on new buy and modified rebuy purchase situations
Activity	Perform order processing functions	Act as creative problem solvers
Training	Require significant clerical training	Require significant sales training
Source of sales	Maintain sales volume	Create new sales volume
Kind of products	Represent simple products with few options	Represent complex products with many options

Order getting is an expensive process. It is estimated that it takes about five visits with a customer to complete a sale, and the average cost of a single sales call is about $205. The average weekly (5-day) expenditure for a sales-

56

person's meals, transportation, and lodging is over $730. These costs illustrate why telephone selling, with a significantly lower average cost per call and little or no travel expenses, has become popular in recent years.

Sales Support Personnel

Sales support personnel augment the selling effort of order getters by performing a variety of services. For example, missionary salespeople do not directly solicit orders but rather concentrate on performing promotional activities and introducing new products. They are used extensively in the pharmaceutical industry, where detailers, as they called, persuade physicians to prescribe a firm's product. Actual sales are made through wholesalers or directly to pharmacists who fill prescriptions. A sales engineer is a salesperson who specializes in identifying, analyzing, and solving customer problems and brings know-how and technical expertise to the selling situation, but often does not actually sell products and services. Sales engineers are popular in selling industrial products such as chemicals and heavy equipment. In short, all salespeople do not sell to the actual user.

In many situations firms engage in team selling, the practice of using an entire team of professionals in selling to and servicing major customers. Team selling is used when specialized knowledge is needed to satisfy the different interests of individuals in a customer's buying center. For example, a selling team might consist of a salesperson, a sales engineer, a service representative, and a financial executive, each of whom would deal with a counterpart in the customer's firm.[11] Xerox Corporation emphasizes this approach in working with prospective buyers.

> Eric N. Berkowitz, Roger A. Kerin, and William Rudelius, *Marketing* ©
> 1986, pp. 493-95. Reprinted by permission of Richard D. Irwin, Inc.,
> Homewood, Illinois.

Key Terms and Concepts

order taking processing routine orders or reorders for products which have been sold by the company.

order getting selling in a conventional sense but engaging in identifying prospective customers, providing customers with information, persuading customers to buy, and closing sales.

sales support   necessary tasks to help customers, such as providing specific information concerning goods or doing a particular service on goods.

Frito-Lay   name of a food company.

Doritos   brand of a kind of snack usually in small package and sold by machine.

Tostitos   brand of a kind of snack usually in small package and sold by machine.

family's life cycle   a general process of a family through several distinct phases of their ages.

detailors   people who help a firm sell goods and know every detail of capacity of their commodities to meet unique customer requirements.

NOTES

1. Personal selling assumes many forms based on the amount of selling done and the amount of creativity required to perform the sales task.　人员推销有很多种形式,这主要要看销售量的多少和销售工作所具有的特殊要求。

2. ... replenish inventory stocks of resellers,...　……补充分销商的存货,……

3. the company's line of salty snack products　公司的咸味小吃产品的生产线(注:这里小吃产品指小包装的零食,有时也用作聚会时吃的食品。)

4. ... complete transactions with customers.　……完成与顾客的交易。

5. ... take orders from buyers by telephone.　……听电话接受顾客订货。

6. straight rebuy situations　直接的重购(注:工厂的常规订货定期重复进行,这种活动在市场营销学里称为"重购"。)

7. in a conventional sense　就习惯概念来讲

8. ... closes sales, and follows up on customers' use of a product or service.　……完成销售,跟踪顾客产品使用情况并提供服务。

9. customer empathy　顾客的同感

10. In modified rebuy or new buy purchase situations in industrial selling,...　在集团性销售中,对变动了的重购或新购……(注:集团性购买中,第一次购买在市场营销学中称为"新购"。)

11. ... a financial executive, each of whom would deal with a counterpart in the customer's firm.　……一个财务主管,他们每一个人主管客户的一个方面。

Suggestions for Further Study

In recent years, the importance of spoken English keeps growing, not only in various international contests on campuses, but also for all kinds of communication between companies or countries. Most importantly, in the job market, applicants for foreign conglomerates or international joint ventures have noticed that those students who speak English fluently definitely have better chances to be hired by banks, companies or other units.

Another phenomenon that should attract students' attention is that more and more undergraduate students or graduate students now speak English very well. These students, though participating in the same system of teaching and studying as other students, learn spoken English from other places. They may learn from a close English speaker, say a parent or foreign friend, or through some special training program. Alternatively, the current system of examination-oriented English teaching and studying is not very successful in teaching students to speak.

To learn spoken English, students should find an English corner or watch English TV programs and movies. This is definitely a good way from any point of view. Another way that is always neglected by Chinese students is reading English novels. Opening any novel, people will find that many pages are covered by people's dialogues and these dialogues present perfect oral English to readers. So, novels bring students to a special English corner too.

After having learned English for many years, people no longer talk about pronunciation. Why? The concerns of accent replace the concerns of pronunciation. Accent is native. Probably no one can entirely change his accent, even over all his life. Although no one can completely change his accent, when students speak English, there are still two key points to address. They are stress and consonant. If people change the position of the stress of a word or read a consonant heavily, the whole word is distorted in people's ears. Remember to keep these two points in mind.

Key Words Speaking

PART SEVEN
MANAGERIAL FINANCE

Motives for Using Debt

The "tax subsidy" due to deductibility of interest is often cited as a major advantage to the use of debt. [1] However, because of the effects of personal income taxes discussed above, a part of this advantage may be illusory.

The size of the net tax subsidy on debt is very much an unsettled question at present. Until this question is resolved, financial managers might be best advised to stay on the side of conservatism and assume that the tax advantage to shareholders from the use of debt is probably modest. [2]

Betting on the Future

Firms used debt long before interest was made deductible for tax purposes, so there must be other advantages. Earlier in this chapter, we learned that the effect of financial leverage on returns depends on the relationship between the firm's operating return on assets and the interest cost of debt. If operating return is greater than interest cost, then increasing financial leverage by replacing equity with debt will have a favorable effect on earnings. [3] Earnings and return to equity will be higher with debt than without. Conversely, if operating return is less than interest cost, the firm will be worse off with debt[4].

So, one motive for using debt is simply to gain the advantage of financial leverage that accrues if things turn out well. [5] A management convinced that the future is bright may want to "lever up" and thereby increase the return to owners. If management's predictions are correct, owners indeed will be better off because of the debt[6]. If the predictions are wrong, the piper must be paid.

Do the financial markets place a higher value on firms that bet on the future by using debt? If there existed managers that could predict the future with certainty, the answer would be yes. But even managers with access to the best information cannot do so, and suppliers of capital in the financial markets know they cannot. Debt can make the owners worse off, perhaps very much worse off, if things do not go well.

Earlier in this chapter, we discussed the effect of debt on the magnitude and variability of returns. We found that, in most cases, debt increases both the expected or most likely return and simultaneously increases the variability or riskiness of that return. The increase in risk offsets the increase in expected return in the eyes of suppliers of capital, and the current value of the firm is affected only to the extent of tax benefits.[7] We found this to be so in our discussion of the "EBIT pie" and division of EBIT among its various claimants.

The use of debt makes sense only if management is reasonably convinced that operating return on assets in the future will exceed the interest rate on debt. However, even where this is the anticipated outcome, it does not necessarily follow that debt ought to be used. Management must make a judgment that the prospect of higher returns justifies running the risk that returns may turn out to be lower. If the future looks sufficiently bright, management may decide to "bet on the future" via increased use of debt. However, the financial markets are unlikely to place a higher current value on the firm's securities simply because the gamble is being taken.[8] Any immediate effect on firm value results only from tax benefits, which, for reasons discussed earlier, are likely to be modest. In short, the financial markets are likely to give credit for the use of debt only after the returns are all in.[9]

Financing Costs

Another motive for using debt has to do with financing costs. For many firms, and nearly all small firms, debt raised via financial intermediaries is very much cheaper than debt or equity raised via the public financial markets. The main types of financial intermediaries are commercial banks, insurance companies, savings and loan associations, savings banks, and pension funds.

Intermediaries reduce financing costs by reducing the costs of matching up borrowers and lenders. The intermediary acts as "agent" for both borrower and lenders in the tasks of gathering funds, credit analysis, record-keeping, and so on. Savers with small amount can lend much more cheaply and safely by going through a commercial bank than by lending directly to firms. A firm that wants to borrow a million dollars can do so much more cheaply by making one stop at a bank than by gathering small amount from hundreds or even thousands of individual savers. The net effect is that the entire process of borrowing and lending is much less expensive than it would be if intermediaries did not exist. In technical jargon, financial intermediaries reduce "friction" due to costs of search, acquisition, and information-processing. [10]

Commercial banks are the primary suppliers of funds to small firms. By law, commercial banks deal only in debt contracts. The net result is that debt represents a very economical source of outside funds for many small firms, much more economical than equity capital raised by the public financial markets. For small or little-known firms, raising equity capital via the public financial market is prohibitively expensive because it requires a substantial amount of information-processing and credit analysis by hundreds or even thousands of different individuals. The commercial bank performs this credit analysis and information-processing function on behalf of all of those individuals. Since the commercial bank offers only debt, debt becomes the cheapest source of funds.

Large firms also often find debt obtained via financial intermediaries an attractive source of funds. Firms with many profitable investment opportunities may find internally generated funds insufficient to satisfy all requirements. Raising the necessary funds by a sale of stock may be considered undesirable because of control considerations or because of the costs and fanfare of a public offering. The alternative of obtaining debt via a loan from a commercial bank or a "private placement" of long-term debt with an insurance company may be quite attractive. [11] By dealing with a financial intermediary, the firm raises the required funds cheaply and conveniently in a single transaction.

We can conclude that there are three main motives for borrowing by firms. One motive is to capture the tax benefits of deductibility of interest. Just how large these benefits are to shareholders after personal taxes is open to some question. Another motive is to exploit the effects of favorable financial leverage. A final motive is to use debt when the sale of stock may dilute existing control of the firm or involve large issuance costs. [12]

Even if there were no tax benefit at all, many firms would borrow for one of the other two reasons. Firms with access to either debt or equity via the public markets might choose to borrow in order to exploit the effects of financial leverage. Firms that cannot raise equity economically choose debt because it is the only economical source of external funds.

Key Terms and Concepts

tax subsidy   the convention of allowing interest payments for debt as a business expense, reducing tax obligations. This is seen as a "tax subsidy."

deductibility of interest   refers to the exemption of taxation on interest of
debt.

financial leverage   financial methods to help the growth of a business.

equity   Free enterprise system recognizes the private ownership of property.
Roughly speaking, equity means "ownership." An owner's equity represents all of the claims of the owner that are recognized under the law, such
as investment in buildings, machinery, and tools.

The piper must be paid   Those who seek benefits must assume responsibility
and costs.

EBIT   earnings before interest and taxes, also known as operating profit
which measures the firm's performance without regard to financing or
taxes. Therefore, interest of EBIT refers to the interest of debt.

securities   Security is a general term for stock exchange investment, while securities refer to bonds, share certificates, and other titles to property.

financial intermediary   go-between between a lender and a borrower, institutes of financial intermediary include saving and loan associations, life insurance companies, mutual savings banks, etc.

saving and loan association   a financial institute which is very much similar to a
bank, mainly focusing on leasing and property investment.

equity capital   a phrase to describe capital structure of a firm. Equity capital is
from stock issues, while debt capital is from bond issues.

financing cost   the cost of seeking, obtaining and borrowing money.

private placement   an individual or a small group rather than a company to
borrow money from an insurance company.

NOTES

1. The "tax subsidy" due to deductibility of interest is often cited as a major
   advantage to the use of debt.   通过(债务)利息免税而产生的"税收补贴",

经常被看作是利用债务的一大好处。

2. ...from the use of debt is probably modest. ……（股票持有者）利用债务得到的（税收方面的）好处是有限的。

3. If operating return is greater than interest cost, then increasing financial leverage by replacing equity with debt will have a favorable effect on earnings. 如果经营收益比支付利息所花费的成本高，利用金融杠杆，用债务来增加投资，对增加收益还是有效的。

4. worse off with debt 由于债务而变得更糟

5. ...advantage of financial leverage that accrues if things turn out well. ……如果事情发展好的话，金融杠杆自然会带来好处。

6. better off because of the debt 由于债务而使情况变好

7. The increase in risk offsets the increase in expected return in the eyes of suppliers of capital, and current value of the firm is affected only to the extent of tax benefits. 在提供资金的人的眼里，增加的风险会抵消期望收益，而企业的即时价值只在税收这一范围内受到影响。

8. ...the financial markets are unlikely to place a higher current value on the firm's securities simply because the gamble is being taken. ……金融市场似乎不会过高估价企业的债券，因为情况并不明朗。

9. ...the financial markets are likely to give credit for the use of debt only after the returns are all in. ……只有当已经有了收益时，金融市场才会信任利用债务这种举动。

10. ...due to costs of search, acquisition, and information processing. ……由于查询、得到和处理信息的费用。

11. ...a "private placement" of long-term debt with an insurance company may be quite attractive. ……私人向保险公司借长期债务可能会很有吸引力。

12. ... when the sale of stock may dilute existing control of the firm or involve large issuance costs. ……当销售股票会削弱公司现有的控制能力，或是发行费用过大时，……

Trade Credit

Earlier, we defined trade credit as credit extended in connection with goods purchased for resale[1]. It is this qualification—goods purchased for resale—that distinguishes trade credit from other related forms. Machinery and equipment, for example, may be purchased on credit by means of an installment purchase contract of some sort. But if the equipment is used by the firm in its production process rather than resold to others, then the financing usually is not called "trade credit". Credit extended in connection with goods purchased for resale by a retailer or wholesaler, or raw materials used by a manufacturer in producing its products, is called "trade credit". Thus, we exclude also consumer credit, which is credit extended to individuals for purchase of goods for ultimate use rather than for resale.

Trade credit arises from the firm's normal operations, specifically from the time lag between receipt of goods and payment for them[2]. The sum total of a firm's obligations to its trade creditors at any point in time normally is called "accounts payable"on the balance sheet. An increase in accounts payable represents a source of funds to the firm;a decrease in accounts payable is a use of funds.

The extent to which trade credit is used as a source of funds varies widely among firms. In general, manufacturers, retailers, and wholesalers make extensive use of trade credit[3]. Service firms purchase less and therefore rely less on trade credit. There is considerable variation also with respect to firm size; small firms generally use trade credit more extensively than large firms. When monetary policy is tight and credit is difficult to obtain, small firms tend to increase their reliance on trade credit. Large firms often have better access to financial markets and more bargaining power relative to commercial banks and other intermediaries than do small firms. During periods of tight money, small firms that are unable to obtain sufficient funds through normal channels may obtain financing indirectly from large suppliers by "stretching"their payment periods[4] and expanding accounts payable. Large firms often are willing to finance their smaller customers in this manner in order to preserve their markets.

Within certain limits, a firm has discretion with respect to the extent to which it uses trade credit as a source of funds. By altering its payment period, a firm can expand or contract its accounts payable. In theory, a firm could reduce accounts payable to zero and not use trade credit simply by paying each invoice on the day received. However, since trade credit is not interest-bearing, it represents a desirable source of financing;but if used beyond certain limits, it can entail significant costs. Let us now consider some of the factors pertinent to the decision regarding trade credit as a source of funds. Our concern here is with the use of trade credit extended by suppliers.

Forms of Trade Credit

Most trade is extended via the open account. Under this arrangement, goods are shipped and an invoice is sent to the purchaser, but the purchaser normally does not acknowledge the debt in writing. Payment is made later according to the terms of the agreement (discussed below). The major advantage of the open account is its simplicity and low administrative cost. Before granting credit via an open account, most suppliers perform a credit check.

A less common form of trade credit is the promissory note, usually called "note(s) payable, trade"on the balance sheet. The note is a written promise to pay that must be signed by the purchaser. Such notes usually bear interest and have specific maturity dates. They are used most often in situations in which the purchaser has failed to meet the terms of an open credit agreement and the supplier wishes a formal acknowledgment of the debt and a specific agreement regarding payment date.

Terms of Payment

Since the open account is by far the most common, we will restrict our discussion of payment terms to this form. A common arrangement is to specify a net period within which the invoice is to be paid. Terms of net 30 indicate that the payment is due within 30 days of the date of the invoice.

Suppliers often give cash discounts for payment within a specified period. Terms of 2/10, net 30 indicate that a discount of 2 percent may be taken if the invoice is paid within 10 days of the invoice date; otherwise the net (full) amount is due within 30 days. Such prompt-payment discounts[5] are to be distinguished from quantity discounts given for purchase in large quantities, and also from trade discounts given at different points in the distribution chain (wholesale versus retail, etc.). Prompt-payment discounts are very common.

Cost of Trade Credit as a Source of Funds

In the final analysis, the principal consideration in the use of trade credit is cost. Trade credit on open account normally bears no interest, but its use does involve costs. If prompt-payment discounts are allowed by the supplier, a cost is incurred if the discount is not taken. For example, suppose a firm purchases goods on terms of 2/10, net 30. If the invoice is for $1000, the firm can take a discount of $20 and pay only $980 if payment is made within 10 days. If the firm foregoes the discount, it pays $1000 by day 30, assuming it maintains its accounts on a current basis, as it should. By foregoing the discount, the firm has the use of $980 for 20 days, for which it pays interest of $20. This is an interest rate of $20/$980=2.05% for a 20 day period. Annualized, the effective interest cost is

$$\frac{\$20}{\$980} \times \frac{365 \text{ days}}{20 \text{ days}} = 0.372 = 37.2 \text{ percent}$$

We find that in this case, not taking the discount is equivalent to borrowing at 37.2 percent per year, a rather expensive financing arrangement.

We can use the following expression to calculate the approximate cost of foregoing cash discounts:

$$\text{Cost} = \frac{\text{Discount } \%}{100 - \text{Discount } \%} \times \frac{365}{\text{Net period} - \text{Discount period}}$$

Applying this expression to the example above we get

$$\text{Cost} = \frac{2}{100 - 2} \times \frac{365}{30 - 10} = 0.372 = 37.2 \text{ percent}$$

Other Considerations in Using Trade Credit

If there is no discount offered and the firm pays during the net period, trade credit still is not free. The supplier must operate a credit department to conduct credit analyses, maintain records, and proceed against overdue accounts. The accounts receivable on the supplier's books must be financed. These administrative and financing costs, like all costs of doing business, in the long run are borne by the buyers of the supplier's output. We should note, however, that the purchaser is bearing these costs whether credit granted by the supplier is used or not.

Another element of cost is incurred if the firm delays payment beyond the net period. When a firm becomes overdue in its payments, its relations with suppliers are bound to suffer. Some suppliers can be "stretched" farther than others. Just how far a firm can push its suppliers depends on circumstances. A policy of late payment, however, is bad business practice, and in the long run is likely to be costly. At the least, late payment damages a firm's credit reputation, which is a valuable asset and, once lost, is difficult to regain. At worst, late payment can cost a firm its sources of supply. During times of severe financial difficulty, a firm may be unable to avoid late payment. As a matter of long-run policy, however, obligations to suppliers[6] should be discharged on schedule.

While late payment is dangerous and costly in the long run, early payment is uneconomic. Where prompt-payment discounts are offered, they should be taken if attractive, as they nearly always are. Otherwise, payment should be made within the net period. In either case, the full extent of the credit period should be utilized.[7]

John J. Pringle and Robert S. Harris, *Essentials of Managerial Finance* © 1984, pp. 655-658. Reprinted by permission of Scott, Foresman and Company, Glenview, Illinois.

Key Terms and Concepts

trade credit   credit between resellers. Usually a seller trusts a buyer and allows the buyer to pay later but within certain period.

consumer credit   credit between a seller and a customer, usually a seller trusts a customer and allows the customer to pay later but under certain specified arrangements.

tight money   refers to tight monetary policy with high interest rate and tight money supply.

open account   credit arrangement which allows a buyer to make a payment at a later date specified in the agreement.

credit check   checking on the financial background of a buyer.

quantity discounts   price reductions for large quantity order.

trade discounts   price reductions granted to wholesalers or retailers by manufacturer.

NOTES

1. ... we defined trade credit as credit extended in connection with goods purchased for resale.   ……我们把以转卖为目的的购买的信用定义为贸易信用。

2. the time lag between receipt of goods and payment for them   收到货物与支

68

付货款之间的时差

3. In general, manufacturers, retailers, and wholesalers make extensive use of trade credit.　一般说来,制造商、零售商和批发商经常利用贸易信用。

4. by "stretching" their payment periods　用延长付款期限的手段

5. prompt-payment discounts　即时付款折扣

6. obligations to suppliers　对供货者所负的责任

7. ...the full extent of the credit period should be utilized.　……(在这两种情况下)信用期限的全部内容都应当利用起来。

Suggestions for Further Study

To learn specialized English, the main consideration is on English, not on the theories of economics or management. To practically and accurately evaluate a student's English, the critical focus should be on his writing. Why? Two reasons. First, society assesses writers on the basis of their published works. Secondly, spoken English is a skill that even an illiterate can master.

To learn writing, what should be done in the early stages? If a student traces the early stages of learning Chinese, he would find that he learned first those phrases or words that connect words or sentences. In the early stage of learning English, people should do the same. Thus, those typical English expressions using gerunds, present or past participles, conjunctions, passive forms, and infinitives are very important. Hereafter, when reading a text, pay close attention to those words, phrases, and typical expressions. The words and phrases below, extracted from this textbook and printed in bold font, are some examples. For more examples, see Appendix B of this textbook. But, remember, no one can systematically present all the concerned words and phrases. One has to explore these elements himself through continuous reading until he knows what is important and what is not in terms of learning writing.

Economists first began to analyze consumer behavior over a century ago when it was fashionable in psychological circles, to assert that much of human behavior could be explained by people's desire **to realize** as much "pleasure" and **to avoid** as much "pain" as possible. (From The Concept of Utility in Part One Microeconomics)

Economists first began to analyze consumer behavior **over a century ago** when it was fashionable in psychological circles, to assert that much of human behavior could be explained by people's desire to realize **as much** "pleasure" and to avoid **as much** "pain" **as possible.** (From The Concept of Utility in Part One Microeconomics)

Key Words   Word   Phrase   Typical expression

PART EIGHT
ORGANIZATIONAL BEHAVIOR

What Is OBM?

An appropriate starting place for understanding OBM is to look at how it has been defined. A recent survey of OBM practitioners (Frederiksen and Lovett, 1980) asked individuals to give their own definition of the field. Based on their responses, a consensus definition began to emerge:

OBM is the application of principles of behavioral psychology and the methodologies of behavior modification/applied behavior analysis[1] to the study and control of individual or group behavior within organizational settings. (Frederiksen and Lovett, 1980, p. 196)

A less formal but perhaps more descriptive definition of the field was offered by Hall (1980). Writing in an editorial for the Journal of Organizational Behavior Management, he explains:

The field of OBM consists of the development and evaluation of performance improvement procedures which are based on the principles of behavior discovered through the science of behavior analysis. These procedures are considered to be within the scope of OBM when they focus on improving individual or group performance within an organizational setting, whether that organization be a business, industrial setting, or human service setting, and whether that organization was established for profit or not.[2]

The goal of the field of OBM is to establish a technology of broad-scale performance improvement and organizational change so that employees will be more productive and happy, and so that our organizations and institutions will be more effective and efficient in achieving their goals.

These two definitions share a number of common characteristics. First, there is clear agreement on the subject matter of the approach.[3] The focus is on the behavior of both individuals and groups in organizational settings. These settings can include businesses, industries, schools, government, community organizations, hospitals, or human services. Likewise the behavior can be quite diverse. Absenteeism, the completion of assigned tasks, unit production per hour, quality, safety, and customer service are just a few examples. In short, the focus is on almost any behavior that affects productivity or satisfaction in the work environment.

There is also agreement on the purpose of OBM. The purpose is not simply the description or academic understanding of behavior.[4] While such an understanding may be a necessary prerequisite for change, the primary focus is on the improvement of performance and satisfaction. It is not enough simply to describe, classify, or label behavior.[5] Rather the goal is to make organizations more effective at achieving their goals through improving the performance of both workers and managers. In this respect OBM is very much a practical, action-oriented endeavor.

A third important feature of OBM is its theoretical or conceptual basis. While a variety of different terms, such as behaviorism, behavioral psychology, operant psychology, or behavior analysis have been used, the thrust is the same. The primary emphasis is on the behavior of individuals rather than their personality, attitudes, perceptions, needs, deep-seated motives, or other things, that supposedly go on beneath the surface. Rather than inferring these internal states from behavior, the focus is on the behavior itself.

There is a parallel focus on the role that the environment plays in shaping that behavior.[6] Attention is paid to the role of events in the setting that set the occasion for certain types of behavior. There is an equally strong emphasis on the consequences of behavior, or put another way, the context in which behavior occurs.[7] A host of theoreticians and researchers have contributed to this perspective, as will be discussed later.

A final important characteristic of OBM is the methodology employed. Methodology refers to the techniques used for assessing and analyzing behavior. The methodology used in OBM differs from that traditionally used to study individuals or groups in organizations in two important respects. First, there is the ongoing and direct observation of behavior as it occurs in the organization. Rather than focusing on what people tell you about how they act or feel, OBM actually looks at what they do. This doesn't mean that an individual is never asked about feelings or perceptions, but rather that actual accomplishments are more important than internal feelings. This focus is ongoing: rather than basing assessments on one-time surveys, collecting repeated observations over time becomes important. In other words, there are repeated measurements of what people are actually doing over time rather than a one-time assessment of how they feel about what they are doing. A second important characteristic of the methodology is the use of within-group comparisons of performance. What this means is that a single individual or groups of individuals are observed over time as the conditions are changed. Employees' current performance is compared to the baseline of their past performances[8] as programs are introduced or other conditions changed. This contrasts with the traditional approach of comparing different groups of individuals. It forces one to look for practical significance rather than statistical significance as the criteria for improvement. This is an important consideration, since sometimes a statistically significant change in behavior may be of little or no practical significance to the organization. There are many variations on this within-group methodology that will be covered later in this volume.

In summary, OBM concerns itself with the behavior of individuals and groups in organizational settings. It is very much concerned with improving performance in a way that makes organizations more efficient in achieving their objectives. These two characteristics are not particularly new. What is new is the theoretical perspective and methodology that OBM brings to these tasks. It takes a perspective of behavioral psychology and uses the related methodology in its attempt to understand and improve performance. What further distinguishes this approach is that it works. [9]

Lee W. Frederiksen, *Handbook of Organizational Behavior Management*, © 1982, pp. 4-6. Reprinted by permission of John Wiley and Sons, Inc., New York.

Key Terms and Concepts

OBM Organizational Behavior Management, one of the foundation fields of business administration.

organization settings　organizational units.

human service setting　human service units.

broad-scale performance improvement　performance improvement in many aspects and fields.

absenteeism　frequency of individual not showing up for work.

action-oriented endeavor　efforts to accomplish a goal with actual action.

internal states　states of people's mind.

statistical significance　percentage of confidence in terms of the statistical result.

NOTES

1. behavioral psychology and the methodologies of behavior modification/applied behavior analysis　行为心理学和行为变动分析或应用行为分析的方法

2. ... whether that organization was established for profit or not.
……无论这个组织是否为盈利而建立。（注：企业组织与事业组织一般以是否盈利来区分。）

3. the subject matter of the approach　探讨的主题

4. academic understanding of behavior　对行为的学术上的理解

5. ... to describe, classify, or label behavior.　……描述、划分或定义行为。

6. There is a parallel focus on the role that the environment plays in shaping that behavior.　同样也注重影响行为形成的环境方面的作用。

7. the context in which behavior occurs　行为形成的来龙去脉

8. the baseline of their past performances　过去工作的基本情况

9. What further distinguishes this approach is that it works.　因为这种探讨方式能行得通，因而更能显出它的正确性。

Areas of Application

OBM has been applied in a wide range of organizational settings, including businesses, industries, health care organizations, governmental units, social service agencies, schools, mental health institutions, and volunteer organizations. Within these settings it has also been applied to a wide range of problem areas. The purpose of the current section is to enumerate some of these. This effort should be viewed as illustrating the range of topics in which

OBM has been applied rather than an exhaustive list of all possible applications.

Production-Task Completion

Probably the single largest area of application for OBM has been increasing worker performance or task completion. This is evident in both practitioners' surveys (Andrasik, McNamara, and Edlund, in press; Frederiksen and Lovett, 1980) and systematic literature reviews (Andrasik, 1979; Andrasik, Heimberg, and McNamara, 1981; Frederiksen and Johnson, 1981). The target of somehow improving either the quantity, timeliness, or quality of employee output cuts across virtually all organizational settings and virtually all intervention techniques. [1] Examples include performance feedback and supervisory praise to improve factory worker output (Chandler, 1977; Emmert, 1978), financial incentives to increase seedling planting in the forest product industry (Yukl and Latham, 1975; Yukl et al., 1976), and monetary rewards to increase output in manufacturing facilities (Orpen, 1974). Social praise and monetary reinforcement have also been successfully employed to improve task completion in human service settings (Montegar, Reid, Madsen, and Ewell, 1977; Hollander and Plutchik, 1972; Pommer and Streedbeck, 1974). Given the consistency of improvement found across organizational settings, it does not seem unreasonable to conclude that OBM has wide applicability for performance improvement (Frederiksen and Johnson, 1981).

Training and Development

Principles of OBM have also had a heavy influence on how training is conducted. One of the most important trends has been the development of programmed instruction as an approach to training. Babb and Kopp (1978) argue that programmed instruction probably represents the single largest application of behavior modification principles to business settings. [2] It has been used in a variety of America's largest corporations to teach a range of skills such as blueprint reading, basic electronics, office procedures, industrial safety, keypunch operation, computer programming, communications, statistics, management decision making, increased product knowledge, and sales. Programmed instruction involves breaking the material into small, discrete units of ascending difficulty. This allows for self-paced individualized instruction with frequent feedback and mastery of the material.

Another area where OBM has had an impact is in the social skills training. Examples of this training include providing feedback to a subordinate, handling interpersonal conflict,[3] delegating authority, and interviewing (Eisler and Frederiksen, 1980; Goldstein and Sorcher, 1974). Here again, an OBM approach takes a basic skill and breaks it into its component parts. These component parts are then taught using a combination of background rationale and specific instructions, demonstrations or modeling of appropriate behavior, actual practice of the targeted behavior, and praise and feedback (sometimes employing videotape or audiotape replays). Although meager, the available research seems to support the efficacy of this approach (Frederiksen and Eiser, 1980; Kraut, 1976). Its acceptance also seems to be growing. Moses (1978) reports that over 10 thousand managers have been trained using this basic approach at the Bell Systems and General Electric alone.

Absenteeism and Tardiness

Reduction of absenteeism and tardiness represents another area where OBM has been used extensively. The procedures often involve some combination of rewards for attendance and disapproval or punishers for nonattenders. Some examples of these programs include the use of small monetary bonuses (Hermann, deMontes, Dominguez, Montes and Hopkins, 1973) or lottery incentive systems, (Pedalino and Gamboa, 1974) to increase attendance in industrial work forces. One of the largest controlled studies was reported by Kempen and Hall (1977). This study involved 7500 production workers at two factories. Intervention included a two-pronged approach that both specified disciplinary action for excessive absences as well as installing a reinforcement program for good attendance. As attendance improved, workers could earn privileges such as freedom from punching the time clock, time off with pay,[4] and the like. The results of this study indicated both improvement in attendance as well as acceptance by management and union employees.

Sales Management

The area of improving sales presents an interesting challenge. On one hand, some aspects of sales are not under control of the individual employee (e. g. , economic conditions, nature of the product, pricing considerations).

On the other hand, the behavior of the individual sales person is amenable to change. However, "sales behavior" can be difficult to accurately measure. These problems notwithstanding, OBM has made some important progress in the modification of sales-related behavior.[5] Gupton and LeBow(1971) reported an early study designed to change the selling patterns of two part-time telephone solicitors.[6] These solicitors had to sell both new and renewal service contracts. The intervention consisted of setting up a schedule in which the opportunity to sell renewal contracts was made contingent upon placing five new service calls. This contingency resulted in an increase of both type of sales.

Another approach has been to look at customer service behavior. In a recent study (Komaki, Blood and Holder, 1980), feedback and management recognition were used in a systematic way to increase friendliness in a fast food franchise. The authors specified what constituted friendliness (e. g. , smiles at the appropriate time), and measurements were taken. The introduction of the techniques resulted in a marked increase in friendliness in one area and a partial increase in another. A similar approach was used to improve several aspects of customer service behavior in a large department store setting (Brown, Malott, Dillon, and Keeps, 1980). Again the targeted behavior was defined and baseline measurements taken. A training program was first provided and found to result in only minimal increases in targeted behavior. However, when a behaviorally based feedback system was introduced, behavior showed marked improvement. These few examples certainly don't represent the last word in modifying sales behavior.[7] However, they do stand in marked contrast to prevailing approaches that emphasize internal motivation, the selection of individuals who have "natural talent, "and sales training.

Safety

Safety, or the reduction of accidents, also presents a difficult challenge. Accidents tend to occur at a relatively low frequency. However, when they do occur they can be associated with injury, death, or disability. Rather than focusing on accidents per se,[8] OBM has generally focused on improving compliance with safe practices. There are number of examples in the literature. Most have employed programs in which safe performances were specifically targeted, measured, and some sort of feedback or incentive provided for safe performance. The settings in which these programs have been used are diverse. They include a commercial bakery (Komaki, Barwick, and Scott, 1978); research laboratories (Sulzer-Azaroff, 1978); coal mines (Rhoton, 1980). In each of these diverse settings and OBM approach has been associated with either reduction in identifiable hazards[9] or an increase in safe performance.

Conservation

In the ear of rapidly accelerating energy cost, conservation takes on increasing importance. While there is clearly a role for technological innovations and capital expenditures in this area (e. g. , improving insulation, streamlining manufacturing processes, developing more efficient power sources), there is also an important role for behavior change. It seems that the single most cost-effective way to reduce expenditures on energy-related cost is to promote changes in certain types of behavior patterns (Stobaugh and Yergin, 1979). It is in this area, the promotion of behavior change, that OBM has made its major contributions to conservation. Examples include feedback and incentives to modify driving in a way that produced increased fuel mileage in a trucking fleet[10] (Runnion, Watson, and McWhorter, 1978) as well as the development of strategies that help people comfortably adapt to working in warmer or cooler environments (Winett, Hatcher, Leckliter, Ford, Fishback, and Riley, in press).

Key Terms and Concepts

blueprint reading   reading and understanding a draft of design.

basic electronics   principles of electronics.

keypunch operation   typing or inputting data, in other words, punching on computer or typewriter keyboard or on ten-key bar.

lottery incentive systems   systems in which ways of drawing lots are used to stimulate employees to work harder.

telephone solicitors   people who make phone-call to make buyer and seller in

78

touch so as to complete transaction and sell contracts.

fast food franchise   right to serve fast food.

NOTES

1. ... the quantity, timeliness, or quality of employee output cuts across virtually all organizational settings and virtually all intervention techniques.

    ……（改进）雇员工作成果的数量、完成时间或质量（的任务）实际上贯穿在所有部门和所有处理方法中。

2. ... programmed instruction probably represents the single largest application of behavior modification principles to business settings.   ……经过计划的教学，大约代表着企业对改变行为的原理的最重要的应用。

3. ... handling interpersonal conflict, ...   ……处理人与人之间的冲突，……

4. ... such as freedom from punching the time clock, time off with pay, ...
    ……比如免除上工打卡报到或是带工资休假，……

5. These problems notwithstanding, OBM has made some important progress in the modification of sales-related behavior.   尽管有这些问题，组织行为学还是在改变与销售相关的行为方面有了一些重要的进展。

6. ... change the selling patterns of two part-time telephone solicitors.
    ……改变两个兼职电话推销人员的销售内容。

7. ... the last word in modifying sales behavior.   ……（肯定不能代表）全部改变销售行为的方法。

8. ... rather than focusing on accidents per se, ...   ……而不是只看事故本身，……

9. reduction in identifiable hazards   减少能估计到的问题的发生

10. ... to modify driving in a way that produced increased fuel mileage in a trucking fleet...   ……用减少油耗的方法来改变一个卡车运输队的（过去的）行车方式……

Suggestions for Further Study

Same as learning Chinese, when learning English, identifying and enjoying good sentences helps a student to improve his sense of language. Through the improvement of the sense of language, a student improves his fluency in writing.

With the sense of English, a student can feel a sentence or taste its rhythm, tone, and appeal. Examples of good sentences extracted from the Part Twelve International Economics are presented below. For more examples, please see Appendix C of this textbook.

The American entertainer, Walt Disney, summarized the challenge clearly. **"Change is inevitable. Growth is not. "** The lesson applies not alone to the United States, but also to the rest of the world. (From Free Markets and Growth in Part Twelve International Economics)

All of this is driven by a new respect for satisfying consumer wants, instead of being burdened by the lead jacket of tradition or historic convention. Nations, as individuals, are not to be seen as ants riding on the back of a turtle. **Both individuals and nations can create an improved future, if they have the wit, the will, and the courage to change.** (From New-World Realities and Competitiveness in Part Twelve International Economics)

Key Words Sense of language

PART NINE
FINANCIAL ACCOUNTING

Elements of the Accounting Model

The traditional accounting model, or the basis for the accounting process, relies on three major assumptions about business and commerce. The first is that business activity is conducted by distinct entities or identifiable business units. Second, it is assumed that business activity is conducted through economic transactions that may be observed and measured. Finally, the assumption is made that a transaction can be described meaningfully in terms of standard units of information, or accounts. A better understanding of these assumptions may be gained by considering a specific business venture.

A Business Venture

Two long-time friends, Harry Hawke and William Wizzard, decided to start a business upon graduation from college. Each has a limited amount of cash to invest, but they have received assurances of a sizable loan from a local bank. After a brief period of negotiation, they receive authorization to act as a local distributor for a manufacturer of electronic calculators. The terms of the distributorship agreement call for Wizzard and Hawke to form a company that will buy calculators at a wholesale price from the manufacturer and, then, resell them to college students at a higher price. The agreement specifies that they can add 75 percent to the wholesale price to arrive at a retail selling price.

During the month of June, the business was organized. The owners of the business, Hawke and Wizzard, each invested $5,000 in the venture and named their company Basic Calculators. Recognizing that the business needed a supply of calculators for inventory, the owners, acting through Basic Calculators, borrowed $10,000 from the local bank. The terms of the loan called for the business to pay 12 percent annual interest, or $100 each month that the loan was outstanding[1] ($10,000×0.12×1/12).

During the month of August, Basic Calculators opened for business, and several things happened quickly. First, the company rented a store for $500 a month and promptly paid the first month's rent. Store furnishings of $5,000 and calculators worth $7,000(the wholesale price)were purchased for cash. A salesman was hired at a salary of $700 per month. At the end of the month, the first $100 interest payment was made to the bank and the salesman was paid. During the month, the salesman sold $3,000 worth of the calculators for a retail price of $5,250($3,000 cost plus 75 percent of $3,000), which was promptly collected from the customers.

Accounting Entity

An accountant seeking to compile information about this particular business would first clearly identify the business organization for which to account. The specific organization under consideration is referred to as the accounting entity.[2] Therefore, Harry Hawke, as an individual, may be an accounting entity; financial data pertaining to Harry may be collected, measured, and reported. Similarly, Basic Calculators, the company owned by Hawke and Wizzard, may be an entity. Basic Calculators is the entity of interest in this example.

All accounting entities are treated independently of one another. Thus, data relating to the entity Harry Hawke (the individual)are not confused with, or included in, data concerning Basic Calculators (the company).[3] This assumption—which restricts the accountant's attention to a specific individual or organization—is known as the separate entity assumption. Under the separate entity assumption, a business is treated as being separate and distinct from its owners. The accounting records of Basic Calculators should reflect economic events relating solely to that entity.

Transactions

After an entity has been identified, the accounting model measures the economic effect of transactions on the business. A transaction is a simultaneous exchange between the accounting entity and other parties such as customers, suppliers, employees, or owners. The exchange is characterized by each party giving and receiving something of value. Thus, an exchange of economic value must take place for a transaction to occur.

Examples of transactions would include the following:

* Sale of goods for cash—an exchange of property for cash took place.

* Purchase of store furnishings for cash—the firm received store furnishings and exchanged (gave) cash for it.

* Paying a salesperson's salary—the business received the salesperson's services and gave cash in return.

The transactions concept relies on the assumption of a rational, economic individual; people and organizations are always assumed to exchange things of equal value. For example, if a college student buys a best-selling novel for $15, it is assumed that the book was worth exactly $15 to the student, or she wouldn't have exchanged her money for it. The same logic prevails with respect to the seller of the book and with all business transactions included in the accounting system.

Such an assumption of economic rationality aids in valuing accounting transactions; once one element of a transaction is valued, the value of the other element is also known. Thus, if $3,000 is paid for store furnishings, the furnishings will be valued at $3,000 by their new owner. The transaction concept also adds to the definition of an entity. An accounting entity must be an economic unit capable of entering into transactions.

A list of transactions for Basic Calculators during its first month of operations is given in Table 9-1. Observe that the dollar impact of objectives given and received is the same. Each transaction between a business and another party can be characterized in a similar fashion.

Table 9-1   A List of Transactions for Basic Calculators

Objects or Services Received	Objects or Services Given	Dollar Impact
Money	Promise to repay bank (note)	$10,000
Use of store (Rent)	Money	500
Furnishings	Money	5,000
Salesman's labor	Money	700
Use of bank's money (Interest)	Money	100
Money	Calculators	5,250

Furthermore, most business transactions are evidenced by source documents that describe the event. For example, a promissory note is a legal instrument that provides evidence of borrowing money. A purchase order, sales slip, shipping invoice, and canceled check all evidence the acquisition of furnishings. Business forms, documents, and memos reflect each transaction. Creating source documents coincident to a business transaction lies at the heart of most accounting systems, since these documents usually activate the accounting process.

Accounts

Accounting systems classify transactions into broad groups such as sales transactions, purchase transactions, and borrowing transactions. Data relating to each type of transaction is accounted for, or recorded and processed, in the same manner as all other transactions of the same class. They are recorded consistently. For example, identical accounting procedures are applied to all sales for cash even though one sale is of calculators and another of typewriters; similarly, it makes no difference that Mrs. Jones is the first customer and that Mr. Johnson is the second. Preprinted source documents or business forms ensure that corresponding data are collected for similar transactions. [4]

Information in the accounting system is recorded in accounts that reflect the characteristics of various types of transactions. Accounts are used to accumulate information about both elements of each transaction—that is, what an entity receives and what it gives in a transaction. [5] An account identifies the name under which information about a specific element of data is recorded. Accounts represent the names of objects or activities that are accepted as part of the same account. Thus, all information relating to cash will be reflected in the Cash account. (Following standard practice, names of specific accounts are capitalized. [6]) The ability to record, classify, and summarize information in accounts is fundamental to the operation of all accounting systems.

By Ronald M. Copeland

Key Terms and Concepts

accounting entity   unit as a basis to proceed with accounting.
cash account   an account which describes the cash flow.

84

purchase order   a form with all the details of buying, such as name and code of item, mode of payment and so on. This kind of form is usually sent to a seller by a buyer.

sales slip   a piece of paper marked with the details of transaction, such as the title of item, the amount of payment, and the date of purchase.

canceled check   a check returned to an endorser by a bank after completion of the transaction.

NOTES

1. ... the loan was outstanding...   ……贷款尚未偿付……
2. ... is referred to as the accounting entity.   ……是指会计主体。
3. Thus, data relating to the entity Harry Hawke (the individual) are not confused with, or included in, data concerning Basic Calculators (the company).   因此，哈里·霍克个人会计单位里的数据不能混于或包括在比塞克计算机公司的数据资料中。
4. Preprinted source documents or business forms ensure that corresponding data are collected for similar transactions.   印好的单据或业务表格，保证了对相应的交易中有关数据的收集。
5. Accounts are used to accumulate information about both elements of each transaction—that is, what an entity receives and what it gives in a transaction.   账目用于积累会计事项的收支情况——也就是，一个计账单位的收入是什么与支出是什么。
6. ... names of specific accounts are capitalized.   ……每项会计事项的名称是大写的。

Accounting Reports

Although schematic presentations can reveal information about a business venture,[1] they are limited. A thorough understanding of most business organizations and their activities demands other means of reporting. Accounting reports attempt to present relevant information about a specific entity. These reports culminate several activities, including:

   * Measurement—Economic information about business transactions is measured and quantified.

* Collection—Pertinent economic information is collected and entered into the accounting system.

* Summarization—Data in the accounting system are summarized to facilitate reporting.

* Classification—Summarized data are classified and combined to prepare accounting reports.

Three kinds of accounting reports are prepared regularly to address different aspects of a business.

The Balance Sheet

On August 31, the owners of Basic Calculators, Harry Hawke and William Wizzard, wanted to know the status of their investment in the venture. Accordingly, their accountant prepared a balance sheet or statement of financial position (shown in Table 9-2).

Table 9-2　Balance Sheet

BASIC CALCULATORS

Balance Sheet

August 31,19×6

Assets		Claims(Equities)	
Cash	$11,950	Liabilities	
Calculators	4,000	Bank Loan	$10,000
Store Furnishings	5,000	Owners' Equity	
		Hawke Investment	5,000
		Wizzard Investment	5,000
		Owners' Profit	950
Total	$20,950	Total Claims	$20,950

The balance sheet shows the specific assets, or resources of the venture and the specific claims against these assets at one particular point in time. [2] The report is called a balance sheet because it discloses the "balances, " or summaries, of the various assets and claims. Also, the statements is "in balance, "since conventional accounting procedures automatically equate assets and claims.

The balance sheet identifies the balances of specific asset liability and equity accounts as of a specific date. Since account balances change in response to additional transactions, balance sheets at different dates present different balances. Therefore, the balance sheet usually is prepared on a regular schedule, such as annually, quarterly, or monthly, and it reflects the final position as of one period in time. [3]

Consider the example of Hawke and Wizzard. The August 31 balance sheet reflects the items of economic value controlled by Basic Calculators: three assets, cash, calculators, and store furnishings. Also, the balance sheet discloses the nature and extent of claims against these assets: a bank claim of $10,000 and the owners' claims of $10,950. [4] Although this information is important, it does not relate directly to questions about the efficiency of the business venture. For example, the cash balance decreased from an initial balance of $20,000 to its current level of $11,950. Although the balance sheet reports a $950 profit, the owners could question how this profit was determined. An income statement relates information about a venture's profitability.

The Income Statement

As its name implies, the income statement presents information about the profitability, or income, earned by a business venture. An income statement for Basic Calculators is presented in Table 9-3. This statement shows the results for the first month of operations—August. Basically, it is a summary of sales activity (distributing goods and services to customers) and expense activity (utilizing goods and services to generate sales).

The income statement first identifies the sales made during the period, which is measured by the total amount of cash that was or that will be received from customers. This portion of the statement shows the amount customers paid or promised to pay the business for the product or service that they received. In accounting terminology, this is called revenue, or sales revenue, or sales. [5]

The next section of the income statement focuses on the cost of providing the product or service to customers of the business. These costs are referred to as expenses. The expenses of Basic Calculators included the cost to the company of the calculators sold during the month, the rental fee for the store, the salesman's salary, and the interest on the bank loan. These expenses represent the cost of doing business for the month of August.

The last section of the income statement shows the difference between revenues and expenses, or the profit. Common synonyms for profit are earnings and income. In this case the specific profit figure indicates that Basic Calculators earned $950 more than the expenses incurred to distribute the product to its customers. Profit can be considered as the return to owners for initiating the business.[6] The $950 profit of Basic Calculators compensates the owners for investing $10,000 in the business, lending their managerial skills and time to the venture, and performing an entrepreneurial function[7]—that is, starting a business and assuming any risks that may be involved.

Table 9-3 Income Statement

BASIC CALCULATORS

Income Statement

For the Month of August 19×6

Sales to Customers(as measured by cash paid or promised to be paid)—Revenue		$5,250
Cost of Operation(as measured by cash paid out or promised to be paid out to make sales to customers)—Expense:		
Cost of calculators sold	$3,000	
Rental of store	500	
Salesman's salary	700	
Interest paid on loan	100	
Total Cost of Operation		4,300
Profit on Month's Operations		$950

The income statement provides management with an insight into strategies or price policy. It gives answers to questions such as: "Are prices high enough to recover costs?" The income statement also provides the user with the information needed to review expenses and evaluate their magnitude and relationships. The summarization and classification included in the statement makes this task feasible.

Owners of a business may also want to know how resources were used during a particular period of time. For example, Hawke and Wizzard might be concerned about the decrease in the cash balance from $20,000 to $11,950 during the month of August. The funds flow statement, or cash flow statement, describes the changes that affect specific resources, such as cash, during a time period.

The Cash Flow Statement

A cash flow statement for Basic Calculators is shown in Table 9-4. This statement isolates activities that affected the asset Cash during the month of

August. Sources and uses of cash are identified, and the change from the beginning balance to the ending balance is explained.

After establishing the beginning balance, all sources and uses of cash are presented in the statement. The difference between the sources and uses represents the change in the Cash balance (cash decreased by $8,050, from $20,000 to $11,950). The cash flow statement for Basic Calculators for the month of August was very similar to its income statement, but this merely reflects (a) the low number of transactions initiated during August, (b) that most of these transactions dealt with revenue or expense activities, and (c) that

Table 9-4   Cash Flow Statement

BASIC CALCULATORS
Cash-Flow Statement
For the Month of August 19×6

Cash Balance, August 1, 19×6		$20,000
Sources of Cash during the Month:		
Received from customers		5,250
Total Cash Available to Be Used during the Month		$25,250
Uses of Cash during the Month:		
Purchased calculators	$7,000	
Store furnishings	5,000	
Store rental	500	
Salesman's salary	700	
Interest payment	100	
Total Uses of Cash during the Month		13,300
Cash Balance, August 31, 19×6		$11,950

none of the transactions involved the use of credit. In a more typical example, the cashflow statement reflects activities different from those shown on the Income Statement.

By Ronald M. Copeland

Key Terms and Concepts

assets   Assets are resources, or things of value, owned and controlled by the business. Cash, land, or buildings are several types of assets in an accountant's accounts.

claims   rights to demand.

equities   Free enterprise system recognizes the private ownership of property. An owner's equity represents all of the claims of the owner that are recognized under the system of private enterprise.

liabilities   Liabilities are claims by creditors of a business and commit the firm to convey assets or perform services at some future time.

use of credit   refers to later payment granted by a seller.

NOTES

1. Although schematic presentations can reveal information about a business venture,...　虽然图解可以揭示一个企业的情况，……

2. The balance sheet shows the specific assets, or resources of the venture and the specific claims against these assets at one particular point in time.　资产负债表展示企业某一个时刻具体的资产或资源以及与资产相对的权益情况。

3. ... it reflects the final position as of one period in time.　……它反映某个时刻的最后的情况。

4. ... the balance sheet discloses the nature and extent of claims against these assets:a bank claim of \$10,000 and owners' claims of \$10,950.　……资产负债表展现了与资产相对的债务的性质与范围:银行的债权 \$10,000 和企业主的财产 \$10,950。

5. ... this is called revenue, or sales revenue, or sales.　……这被称做收入、销售收入，或销售额。

6. Profit can be considered as the return to owners for initiating the business. 利润可以看做企业主开业的收益。

7. ... lending their managerial skills and time to the venture, and performing an entrepreneurial function...　……把管理技能和时间花在经营上，从而执行企业家的职能……

Suggestions for Further Study

In the previous sections of "Suggestions for Further Study", we have discussed all the fundamental ideas concerning the study of English. In the rest of sections of Suggestions for Further Study , let's shift to the areas of application. English can be used in many fields. One of the most important fields is communication. People write letters to pass information to others or share feelings with others. In daily business, many arrangements are made through business letters.

There is an old saying in China asserting that "Handwriting shows all of a man." In international communication, a business letter does the same. People present themselves to others through a business letter. The skill of communication is very complex and is beyond our present discussion. But, the format of a letter, as if it were the face of a man, can be learned by following the samples in Appendix D of this textbook.

There are many types of business letters in daily business. A customer may write a letter to request information or to complain about a billing problem or a bad product. A businessman may write a letter to inquire about a product he is interested in purchasing, or to provide a thorough explanation about the reason for a late delivery. Letters of application, of course, are written by people looking for prospective positions as an employee, a student, or a member.

In the secretarial handbooks published in the past, people can find as many as eight types of formats. Some put the address of sender on the right upper corner, and the signature of sender on the right bottom corner. Some put the date of letter on the right upper corner, and the signature of sender on the left bottom corner. Some leave five spaces before the first letter of a paragraph typed, some keep eight spaces for the beginning of each paragraph. However, after the arrival of the worldwide computer era, most people have changed their letter format and think of efficiency first. The letter format presented in Appendix D is a format widely adopted, taking efficiency as the first consideration and wiping off all the spaces at the beginning of each paragraph. To make the context clear, space lines are set to separate different parts of letter as well as different paragraphs. For details, see Appendix D.

Key Words Business letter

PART TEN
MONEY AND BANKING

Sources and Uses of Bank Funds

Because the activities of commercial bankers have such fundamental and widespread implications for the behavior of the economy, at times one might be tempted to forget that they are business men and women and think of them as a kind of public servant. Unlike most temptations, this one should be resisted. Bankers are interested in earning a living[1] by making a profit for their stockholders. And like other people in business, the activities of bankers can be usefully classified into two categories: the getting and spending of money. In high-class financial circles, it is customary to dress up this somewhat grubby phrase by calling it the sources and uses of funds.[2]

A full explanation of what is meant by the sources and uses of funds in a formal accounting sense[3] would take us too far afield for our limited purposes here. But the general idea can be readily understood by performing the following imaginary experiment: Think of a bank as a business with a certain amount of cash in its vaults. Now mentally list all of the bank's other balance-sheet items, and in each case ask yourself if an increase in the item would increase or decrease the bank's vault case. If an increase in the item would increase the bank's cash, then the item is a source of funds to the bank; if an increase in the item would decrease the bank's cash, then it is a use of bank funds. For example, an increase in the bank's deposits is a source since a deposit of funds increases the bank's cash, and an increase in the bank's loans is a use since lending draws down the bank's cash.

If you now take a sheet of paper and list all the sources of bank funds in one column and all the uses of funds in another, you will notice an interesting thing: Under "Sources of Funds" you will have listed all the bank's liability and capital items, and under "Uses of Funds" you will have listed all its asset items. In short, you will have duplicated the balance sheet you began with, except that changes in assets are now called uses and changes in liabilities and capital are now called sources.

The purpose of the experiment, of course, is to make precisely this point.[4] But the game is not a trivial one, designed only to test the reader's patience. For in performing the experiment you will have gained two insights: First you now have an alternative and meaningful interpretation of the nature of a balance sheet; and second, you should now have a more intuitive understanding of the nature of banking. In the long run a bank gets money (source) from its capital and liabilities accounts and spends this money (use) on its asset accounts. It is the interest earned on these assets that constitutes the main source of a bank's earnings, or profits. The major categories of the balance-sheet items of the United States commercial banking system are shown in Table 10-1.

Table 10-1   Principal Assets, Liabilities, and Capital Accounts
of United States Commercial Banks, March 20,1978(Billions of Dollars)

Assets	
Cash assets	131.4
Investments	
United States Treasury securities	97.9
Other securities	159.2
Loans	677.2
Other	68.9
Total assets	1134.6
Liabilities and capital accounts	
Demand deposits	
Interbank	37.6
United States government	4.8
Other	279.4
Time deposits	
Interbank	9.1
Other	561.5
Borrowings	107.3
Capital accounts	83.2
Other	51.7
Total liabilities and capital accounts	1134.6

Source: Federal Reserve Bulletin, April 1978, p. A16. Figures partly estimated.

Because the balance sheet is both a meaningful and familiar system of classification, the discussion of banking in the remainder of this chapter will be organized along similar lines. [5] Before beginning this discussion, however, a few warnings to the reader seem in order. First, the reader should be clear about exactly what it means to say that a change in a liability is a source of funds and a change in an asset a use of funds. It means that if a liability item goes down, the bank's resources go down. In other words, liabilities and resources vary in the same direction, and assets and bank resource vary in opposite directions. In the long run, over a period of years, the liabilities of the banking system will grow as the economy grows, and hence on the average liabilities will be a source of funds, and assets a use of funds. But in the short run, on a day-to-day basis, liabilities and assets may move in either direction, and hence each may be both a source and a use of funds. Thus a fall in the demand deposits of the bank (deposit withdrawals) will use bank resources, and a decrease in bank loans (loan repayments) will be a source of funds to the bank. In short, a negative use is a source, and a negative source is a use.

Table 10-2　Controllable and Uncontrollable Factors in Short-Run Bank Adjustments

---

Controllable balance sheet items
Excess cash reserves (asset)
Open market investments (assets)
Negotiable certificates of deposit (liability)
Borrowing from the Federal Reserve (liability)
Federal funds (liability)

Partially controllable balance sheet items
Loans (assets)
Correspondent balances (asset)

Uncontrollable balance sheet items
Cash items in the process of collection (Asset)
Demand deposits (liability)
Time and savings deposits, except negotiable CDs (liabilities)
Capital accounts (capital)

On a day-to-day operating level, it is the banker's job to constantly juggle all these daily asset and liability changes so that the bank's goals of liquidity, solvency, and profitability are achieved. This brings us to the second warning to the reader: In the short run, all balance-sheet items are not equally under the banker's control. Changes in demand deposits, for example, are something that, from the workaday viewpoint of the individual banker, "just happen."[6] Although the bank may be able to predict deposit fluctuations, it cannot control them. Changes in the bank's holdings of Treasury bills, on the contrary, are wholly under the control of the bank; within the limits set by its size, it can buy and sell exactly as many of these as it wants. In addition to the "sources and uses" classification of balance-sheet items, therefore, it is equally revealing to classify these items according to the degree of short-run bank control over them. This is done in Table 10-2. Note that the classification of Table 10-2 is not unambiguous. That is there are some items over which the bank has some control, but not complete control. The most conspicuous of these is bank loans. It may seem strange to suggest that the bank lacks complete control over the size of its loan portfolio, but it is nevertheless true— although not in a legal sense, of course. Legally, the bank may refuse a loan to anyone at any time. But as a practical matter, the bank is obliged to take care of the loan needs of many of its customers.

Viewed together, Table 10-1 and Table 10-2 explain a great deal about both the long-run and short-run behavior of the typical commercial bank. In the long run (Table 10-1), the bank earns a profit for its owners by expanding its liabilities (sources) and using the funds thus acquired to buy assets (uses). In the short run (Table 10-2), the bank manages those items over which it has control to adjust to fluctuations in those items over which it does not have control. It is this latter activity in particular that requires most of the skill needed to manage a commercial bank.

Dudley G. Luckett, *Money and Banking* 2nd ed. © 1980, pp. 153-156. Reprinted by permission of McGraw-Hill Book Company, New York.

Key Terms and Concepts

balance sheet a statement showing the assets and liabilities of a business at a certain date.

demand deposits a term used in the United States for deposits on current account, that is, withdrawable on demand by check.

time and saving deposits Time and saving deposits are offered in a variety of different forms. Their common characteristics are that they pay a rate of interest and that the bank may require a waiting period before the deposits can be withdrawn. There are three basic forms of the time and savings deposits: passbook savings deposits; time certificates of deposit; and time deposits, open account.

borrowings　notably refers to federal funds and Eurodollars.

interbank　among banks.

capital accounts　The capital accounts are subdivided into four categories: capital stock, surplus, undivided profits, and others. Therefore, a bank's capital accounts represent the equity, or ownership, of this bank's stock holders.

deposit withdrawals　money taken away from bank.

federal funds　Federal funds are balances held in the Federal Reserve System. Member banks of the Federal Reserve System are required by law to hold a certain percentage of their deposits as cash-reserve assets. These reserves, except for vault cash, are held in the form of deposit balances at the district Federal Reserve Bank.

Eurodollars　Eurodollars are dollar-denominated deposits in foreign commercial banks and in foreign branches of United States banks. By dollar denominated is meant that the amounts on deposit are stated in terms of dollars rather than in the monetary unit of the country in which they are held, such as pounds in England or marks in Germany. Eurodollars are lent and borrowed freely at market-determined rates of interest.

correspondent balances　In the United States, correspondent balances are due to the existence of branch, holding-company, and chain banking. Separate banks are connected with one another. Some banks hold demand deposits in other banks just as individuals and other businesses do. These demand deposits are called correspondent balances.

negotiable certificates of deposits　A negotiable CD is a receipt given by a commercial bank for a deposit of funds, which stipulates that the holder of the receipt at maturity will be paid interest plus principal. The CD may not be redeemed by the bank before it matures, but because it is negotiable, it may be sold by the initial buyer on a secondary market.

NOTES

1. in earning a living　使业务发展下去
2. In high-class financial circles, it is customary to dress up this somewhat grubby phrase by calling it the sources and uses of funds.　在较高层的金

融界，习惯地把这有点不怎么样的说法披上外衣而称作资金的来源与用途。

3. in a formal accounting sense　就正式的会计概念来讲

4. The purpose of the experiment, of course, is to make precisely this point.
这种试验的目的当然是为了很实际地展示一下这个问题。

5. along similar lines　依相似的思路(来组织)

6. ... from the workaday viewpoint of the individual banker, "just happen."
……以每个银行家日常工作的眼光看总是会发生的。

Instruments of the Capital Market

The main capital market instruments include stocks, corporate bonds, bonds issued by state and local government units, U.S. government notes and bonds, and mortgages.

Stocks

Common stocks are ownership claims on real capital assets of a firm. Unlike debt-instruments issued in the United States, stocks have no maturity date. They are perpetuals, outstanding as long as the corporation is in business. For this reason, the existence of viable secondary markets in stocks is imperative. [1] These secondary markets provide liquidity and enhance the marketability of new issues of stock, thus reducing the real costs to business firms by expanding the scope for obtaining funds[2]. Stocks are traded by brokers in organized stock exchanges and over-the-counter markets. Any corporation having more than 300 stockholders may have its stock traded over-the-counter. [3] Large corporations meeting certain standards of size and stability may apply to the Securities and Exchange Commission for listing on the organized stock exchanges.

The preponderant portion of stock transactions is carried out in the secondary markets. The annual magnitude of new issues of stock ($10 billion to $20 billion) is quite small relative to the existing supply of stock (more than $1,500 billion). The annual volume of new issues varies considerably with economic and financial conditions. When stock prices are depressed, firms shy away from issuing new stock[4] and may in fact buy up some of the existing shares. When the value of equities is rising, it is easier to raise new funds through stock issues. And the increasing valuation of real capital assets, as reflected by the rising share prices, may induce firms to expand real investment expenditures. For this reason, a healthy stock market is an important ingredient in the capital-formation and economic-growth processes.

Corporation Bonds

This instrument is a debt claim against the assets of a corporation. [5] This claim may or may not be secured by mortgages and other assets of the corporation. Unsecured corporate bonds are known as debentures and are generally issued only by firms of high credit rating. New corporate bond issues substantially exceed new stock issues each year in spite of the fact that valuation of the total holdings outstanding of corporate bonds is perhaps only one-fourth of that of stocks. This is explained by the rollover factor in bonds and the fact that many bonds may be called in by the firm prior to maturity. [6] As previously stated, corporate stocks are perpetual issues.

A corporation contemplating a capital investment in new plant and equipment may consider several alternatives: issuing equities, issuing bonds, borrowing from banks, or deferring the project until a later date. The bond yield is a factor entering into the firm's planning. Corporate bond issues exhibit a procyclical pattern, rising in the later stages of cyclical expansion as capacity utilization rates rise and declining in recessions as utilization rates and profits fall off. The instruments generally have maturities of 10-30 years and are traded over-the-counter in a market which is "thin"[7] compared to the major stock exchange markets and the government securities market. Many of the corporate bonds have call features,[8] inserted for the benefit of the issuing corporation. Some are convertible into common stock, a feature which "sweetens" the bond for potential buyers and therefore allows the corporation to borrow at lower interest expense. Primary buyers of corporate bonds are institutions not requiring highly liquid financial assets. [9] These buyers include life insurance companies, private pension funds, state and local government retirement funds, and nonporfit organizations.

Municipal Bonds

State and local governments and other political subdivisions must finance capital investment projects such as schools, bridges, sewage plants, airports, subways, etc. Roughly two-thirds of these capital expenditures are financed by issuing municipal bonds. In 1985, some $500 billion of municipal bonds were outstanding. New issues of municipal bonds are generally purchased by investment bankers and are then sold to commercial banks, property and casualty insurance firms, and high-income individuals. The market in municipal bonds is thin because of the limited number of participants in the market. Also, the number of dealers handling a given issue is quite limited, and many of these dealers hold small inventories.

Many years ago, Congress decreed that interest on municipal bonds would be nontaxable by the Internal Revenue Service, ostensibly to subsidize capital investments of municipalities by helping them to borrow at lower interest costs. As a result of the tax-free interest status, municipal bond yields tend to be slightly lower than U. S. government bond yields and considerably lower than yields on high-grade corporate bonds. The result is that only high-tax-bracket investors find it advantageous to purchase municipal bonds. Commercial banks, typically in the 46 percent corporate income tax bracket, are the biggest buyer of municipal bonds. Owing to its tax-free feature, a bank investment officer might consider a municipal bond yielding 10 percent to be equally as attractive as a U. S. government bond or business loan at 18 percent interest. Between 1946 and 1984, banks upgraded the portion of their total loans and investments devoted to municipal bonds from 5 percent to 10 percent.

U.S. Government Notes and Bonds

The nature of U. S. government notes and bonds was discussed in some detail earlier in this chapter. Here, we shall merely point out that U. S. government bonds and notes are very popular instruments because of the absence of default risk and because of the extremely well-organized and efficient market in which they are traded. Major purchasers include commercial banks, and other financial institutions, nonfinancial corporations, and individuals.

Mortgages

A mortgage is a long-term loan secured by a lien on the real property being financed. [10] Interest rates traditionally have been fixed over the life of the mortgage and, since the 1930s, the mortgage payments have been amortized. This means that part of each regular payment goes to interest and part contributes to the repayment of the principal. At maturity of the mortgage, the debt has been extinguished and the property is owned free and clear.

The mortgage market is the largest debt market in the U. S. capital market. As of 1985, some $2,000 billion in mortgages were outstanding. Some 60 percent of these financed one-to-four family homes. The remainder financed business property, apartment buildings, and farms. Many years ago, individuals were the main mortgage lenders. Today, saving and loan associations, mutual savings banks, commercial banks, and life insurance companies hold the mortgages. Another institution—the mortgage company— makes mortgage loans and then arranges for a life insurance company or other corporation to buy a block of these mortgages. [11]

Largely because of the belief that home ownership should be accorded a high social priority,[12] the federal government has become heavily involved in the mortgage market. Three agencies have been created which help to improved the secondary market in mortgages with a special view toward assisting the market in periods when credit is tight and interest rates are high. The Federal National Mortgage Association(FNMA or "Fannie Mae")issues short-term and intermediate-term securities to the public and uses the proceeds to purchased mortgages. The Government National Mortgage Association ("Ginnie Mae"or GNMA)acts in a similar vein[13], helping to absorb the flow of mortgages especially when the regular channels do not have sufficient funds. This tends to happen in periods of high money market yields, when institutions such as savings and loan associations and mutual savings banks suffer withdrawals of deposits and therefore are forced to restrict new mortgage lending. In the rare periods of low interest rates "Fannie Mae"and "Ginnie Mae"might sell off mortgages and retire some of the debt outstanding.[14] In 1970, Congress created a new agency, the Federal Home Loan Mortgage Company (FHLMC or"Freddie Mac"). This agency issues securities to the public and buys mortgages, primarily from savings and loan institutions. Part of the rationale for forming this new agency was that "Fannie Mae"had become somewhat specialized in buying blocks of mortgages from mortgage companies.

Lloyd B. Thomas, Jr. *Money, Banking, and Economic Activity* 3rd ed. © 1986, pp. 50-53. Reprinted by permission of Prentice-Hall, Inc., Englewood Cliffs, New Jersey.

Key Terms and Concepts

secondary markets stock market, next to the main market—capital market.

liquidity nearness to money or ease with which an asset can be converted to money. The lower the cost in terms of time, transactions cost and risk of depreciation of principal, the greater the liquidity is.

brokers agents who stand to facilitate transactions in some financial instrument by bringing together buyers and sellers.

over-the-counter markets Security transactions take place in over-the-counter security markets as well as in organized security exchanges. In over-the-counter transactions, prices are determined by negotiations between buyers and sellers instead of by centralized bids.

Securities and Exchange Commission The Wall Street Crash (1929) brought heavy losses to investors in stocks and shares throughout the United States. Therefore, in 1933, the U. S. government established this Commission to supervise American stock markets. The goal is to stop unfair trading and the dissemination of false information, especially prior to a new issue of shares.

debentures vouchers or certificates that acknowledge a debt owed by the issuer. In finance a debenture bond is an unsecured bond backed only by the general credit standing of the agency that issued it.

Internal Revenue Service a government administration under Department of Treasury, in charge of tax issues, headquartered in Philadelphia, Pennsylvania.

high-tax-bracket investors investors subjected to pay high tax under certain law.

U.S. government notes treasury notes, one of the three types of U. S. government securities. Others are Treasury bills and Treasury bonds. Treasury notes generally are of one to ten years maturity when issued, while bonds are longer-term instruments.

Federal National Mortgage Association It operates in the secondary market for mortgages, authorized to "intermediate" by selling its own short-term notes and buying government-guaranteed mortgages. By doing so, it redirects funds toward home mortgages.

NOTES

1. ... the existence of viable secondary markets in stocks is imperative ......
有生命力的第二市场的存在是很要紧的。

2. by expanding the scope for obtaining funds 用扩大获得资金的范围的方法

3. its stock traded over-the-counter 它的股票直接参与交易

4. ... firms shy away from issuing new stock... ……企业不宜发行新股票……

5. This instrument is a debt claim against the assets of a corporation 公司债券是企业资产中的债务项目。

6. ... many bonds may be called in by the firm prior to maturity ……许多债券可能未到期便被企业兑付了。

7. ... which is "thin"... ……小一些……

8. Many of the corporate bonds have call features, ... 许多公司的债券具有应召兑付的性质，……

9. ... institutions not requiring highly liquid financial assets 一般购买公司债券的机构为那些不需大量资金流动的单位。

10. A mortgage is a long-term loan secured by a lien on the real property being financed. 抵押是对被资助的实体财产保留留置权的一种长期贷款。（注：留置权是在债务人清偿债务之前，法律授予债权人对抵押财产的拥有权。）

11. a block of these mortgages 一批这样的抵押

12. ... home ownership should be accorded a high social priority, ... ……拥有家庭住宅应受到社会的优先考虑，……

13. in a similar vein 以类似的方式

14. ... retire some of the debt outstanding ……偿还一些未偿还的债务。

Suggestions for Further Study

When a student works on his paper, a lot of information is presented along with his creative ideas. Moreover, inevitably, he will also borrow some ideas or theories from other people's works, or even cite some words directly. In such cases, he needs to mark and declare in his paper the ideas and passages that he has borrowed from others. So, primarily, the purpose of footnotes is to acknowledge sources of information and quotations used in a paper. In rare cases, a footnote is also used to present additional explanation that an author wants to tell readers. Students writing papers must acknowledge the source of direct quotations as well as the source of tables and figures that are borrowed from other people. The sources of ideas or facts that a student paraphrases or summarizes from books, periodicals, magazines, and newspapers should also be acknowledged in footnotes. Remember, in a footnote, distinct from the bibliography, the rule for the author's name is "first name first and last name last".

Samples of a few detailed footnotes are presented in Appendix E of this textbook.

Key Words   Footnote

PART ELEVEN
STRATEGIC MANAGEMENT

Company Goals: Survival, Growth, Profitability

Three economic goals guide the strategic direction of almost every viable business organization. Whether or not they are explicitly stated, a company mission statement reflects the firm's intention to secure its survival through sustained growth and profitability.

Unless a firm is able to survive, it will be incapable of satisfying any of its stockholders' aims. Unfortunately, like growth and profitability, survival is such an assumed goal that it is often neglected as a principal criterion in strategic decision making. When this happens, the firm often focuses on short-term aims at the expense of the long run. Concerns for expediency, a quick fix, or a bargain displace the need for assessing long-term impact.[1] Too often the result is near-term economic failure owing to a lack of resource synergy and sound business practice.[2] For example, Consolidated Foods, makers of Shasta soft drinks and L'Eggs hosiery, sought growth in the 1960s through the acquisition of bargain businesses. However, the erratic sales patterns of their diverse holdings[3] forced the firm to divest itself of more than four dozen of the companies in the late 1970s. The resulting stabilization cost Consolidated Foods millions of dollars and hampered its growth.

Profitability is the mainstay goal of a business organization. No matter how it is measured or defined, profit over the long term is the clearest indication of a firm's ability to satisfy the principal claims and desires of employees and stock holders. The key phrase in the sentence is "over the long term." Obviously, basing decisions on a short-term concern for profitability would lead to a strategic myopia. A firm might overlook the enduring concerns of customers, suppliers, creditors, ecologists, and regulatory agents. In the short term the results may produce profit, but over time the financial consequences are likely to be detrimental.

The following excerpt from the Hewlett-Packard Company's statement of corporate objectives (i.e., mission) ably expresses the importance of an orientation toward long-term profit:

104

Objective：To achieve sufficient profit to finance our company growth and to provide the resources we need to achieve our other corporate objective.

In our economic system, the profit we generate from our operations is the ultimate source of the funds we need to prosper and grow. It is the one absolutely essential measure of our corporate performance over the long term. Only if we continue to meet our profit objective can we achieve our other corporate objectives.

A firm's growth is inextricably tied to its survival and profitability. In this context, the meaning of growth must be broadly defined. While growth in market share has been shown by the profit impact market studies (PIMS) to be correlated with firm profitability, other important forms of growth do exist. For example, growth in the number of markets served, in the variety of products offered, and in the technologies used to provide goods or services frequently leads to improvements in the company's competitive ability. Growth means Change, and proactive change is a necessity in a dynamic business environment. Hewlett-Packard's mission statement provides an excellent example of corporate regard for growth：

Objective：To let our growth be limited only by our profits and our ability to develop and produce technical products that satisfy real customer needs.

We do not believe that large size is important for its own sake; however, for at least two basic reasons continuous growth is essential for us to achieve our other objectives.

In the first place, we serve a rapidly growing and expanding segment of our technological society. To remain static would be to lose ground. [4] We cannot maintain a position of strength and leadership in our field without growth.

In the second place, growth is important in order to attract and hold high-caliber people[5]. These individuals will align their future only with a company that offers them considerable opportunity for personal progress. Opportunities are greater and more challenging in a growing company.

The issue of growth raises a concern about the definition of a company mission. How can a business specify product, market, and technology sufficiently to provide direction without delimiting unanticipated strategic options? How can a company define its mission so opportunistic diversification can be considered while at the same time maintaining parameters that guide growth decisions? Perhaps such questions are best addressed when a firm outlines its mission conditions under which it might depart from ongoing operations. The growth philosophy of Dayton-Hudson shows this approach:

> The stability and quality of the corporation's financial performance will be developed through the profitable execution of our existing businesses, as well as through the acquisition or development of new businesses. Our growth priorities, in order, are as follows:
>
> 1. Development of the profitable market preeminence of existing companies in existing markets through new store development or new strategies within existing stores;
>
> 2. Expansion of our companies to feasible new markets;
>
> 3. Acquisition of other retailing companies that are strategically and financially compatible with Dayton-Huston;
>
> 4. Internal development of new retailing strategies.
>
> Capital allocations to fund the expansion of existing operating companies will be based on each company's return on investment, in relationship to its return-on-investment (ROI) objective and its consistency in earnings growth, and on its management capability to perform up to forecasts contained in capital requests. [6]
>
> Expansion via acquisition or new venture will occur when the opportunity promises an acceptable rate of long-term growth and profitability, acceptable degree of risk, and compatibility with the corporation's long-term strategy.

John A. Pearce II and Richard B. Robinson, Jr. , *Strategic Management* 3rd ed. © 1988, pp. 78-80. Reprinted by permission of Richard D. Irwin, Inc. , Homewood, Illinois.

Key Terms and Concepts

quick fix   swift solution to the temporary situation.

Consolidated Foods   name of a company.

Shasta　brand name of beverage.

bargain businesses　businesses using price cuts to gain market share.

the principal claims　major equities in a balance sheet, including items such as liabilities and owner's investments.

strategic myopia　person's views that lack strategic considerations for the future.

Hewlett-Packard Company　one of the biggest computer companies in the world.

profit impact market studies（**PIMS**）　a study designed to measure the profit impact of market studies and posed by Schoeffler, Buzzell, and Heany in 1974. This PIMS project involved the effects of strategic planning on a firm's return on investment（ROI）.

Dayton-Hudson　name of a company.

return-on-investment　the ratio of net profit to total investments.

NOTES

1. Concerns for expediency, a quick fix, or a bargain displace the need for assessing long-term impact　权宜，短期补偿，以及讨价还价方面的考虑，将把长期影响的考虑搁置一边。

2. a lack of resource synergy and sound business practice　缺乏资源的配合及充分的经营实践。

3. the erratic sales patterns of their diverse holdings　多样化产品的反复无常的销售方式

4. To remain static would be to lose ground.　保持现状会失去竞争的基础。

5. high-caliber people　能力强的人

6. ... to perform up to forecasts contained in capital requests.　……来与资金需求的预测相吻合。

Strategic Considerations for Multinational Firms

　　Special complications confront a firm involved in international operations. Multinational corporations （MNCs） headquartered in one country with subsidiaries in others experience difficulties understandably associated with operating in two or more distinctly different competitive arenas.

Awareness of the strategic opportunities and threats posed and faced by MNCs is important to planners in almost every domestic U. S. industry. [1] Among U. S. -headquartered corporations that receive more than 50 percent of their annual profits from foreign operations are Citicorp, the Coca-Cola Company, Exxon Corporation, the Gillette Company, IBM, Otis Elevator, and Texas Instruments. In fact, according to 1983 statistics, the 100 largest U. S. multinationals earned an average of 37 percent of their operating profits abroad. Equally impressive is the impact of foreign-based multinationals that operate in the United States. Their direct "foreign investment" in America now exceeds $70 billion, with Japanese, West German, and French firms leading the way[2].

Understanding the myriad and sometimes subtle nuances of competing in international markets or against multinational firms[3] is rapidly becoming a focus on the nature, outlook, and operations of MNCs.

Development of an MNC

The evolution of a multinational company often entails progressively involved strategies. The first strategy entails export-import activity but minimal effect on existing management orientation or product lines. The second level involves foreign licensing and technology transfer but still little change in management or operation. The third level of strategy is characterized by direct investment in overseas operations, including manufacturing plants. This level requires large capital outlays as well as management effort in the development of international skills. At this point, domestic operations continue to dominate company policy, but the firm is commonly categorized as a true MNC. The most involved strategy is indicated by a substantial increase in foreign investment, with foreign assets comprising a significant portion of total assets. The company begins to emerge as a global enterprise with world approaches to production, sales, finance, and control.

While some firms downplay their multinational nature — so as never to appear distracted from their domestic operations — others highlight their international intentions. For example, General Electric's formal statement of mission and business philosophy includes the following commitment:

> To carry on a diversified, growing, and profitable worldwide
> manufacturing business in electrical apparatus, appliances, and

supplies, and in related materials, products, systems, and services for industry, commerce, agriculture, government, the community, and the home.

A similar worldwide orientation is evident at IBM, which operates in 125 countries, conducts business in 30 languages and more than 100 currencies, and has 23 major manufacturing facilities in 14 different countries.

Why Companies Internationalize

The past 30 years has seen a dramatic decline in the technological advantage once enjoyed by the United States. In the late 1950s, over 80 percent of the world's major innovations were first introduced in the United States. By 1965 this figure had declined to 55 percent, and the decline continues today. On the other hand, France has made impressive advances in electric traction, nuclear power, and aviation. West Germany is a proclaimed leader in chemicals and pharmaceuticals, precision and heavy machinery[4], heavy electrical goods, metallurgy, and surface transport equipment. Japan leads in optics, solid-state physics, engineering, chemistry and process metallurgy. Easter Europe and the Soviet Union, the so-called COMECON (Council for Mutual Economic Assistance) countries, generate 30 percent of annual worldwide patent applications. However, the United States can regain some of its lost competitive advantages. Through internationalization U. S. firms can often reap benefits from emerging industries and evolutionary technologies developed abroad.

Multinational development makes sense as a competitive weapon in many situations.[5] Direct penetration of foreign markets can drain vital cash flows from a foreign competitor's domestic operations.[6] The resulting lost opportunities, reduced income, and limited production can impair the competitor's ability to invade U. S. markets. A case in point[7] is the strategic action of IBM, which moved to establish a position of strength in the Japanese mainframe computer industry before two key competitors, Fiyitsue and Hitachi, could gain dominance. Once it had achieved an influential market share, IBM worked to deny its Japanese competitors the vital cash and production experience they needed to invade the U. S. market.

Considerations Prior to Internationalization

To begin their internationalizing activities, businesses are advised to take four steps.

Scan the International Situation. Scanning includes reading journals and patent reports and checking other printed sources — as well as meeting people at scientific — technical conferences and / or in-house seminars.

Make Connections with Academia and Research Organizations. Enterprises active in overseas R&D often pursue work-related projects with foreign academics and sometimes form consulting agreements with faculty members.

Increase the Company's International Visibility. Common methods of attracting attention include participation in technological trade fairs, circulation of brochures illustrating company products and inventions, and hiring technology-acquisition consultants.

Undertake Cooperative Research Projects. Some multinational enterprises engage in joint research projects to broaden their contacts, reduce expenses, diminish the risk for each partner, or forestall entry of a competitor into the market.

In a similar vein, external and internal assessments may be conducted before a firm enters international markets. External assessment involves careful examination of critical international environmental features with particular attention to the status of the host nation in such areas as economic progress, political control, and nationalism. Expansion of industrial facilities, balance of payments, and improvements in technological capabilities over the past decade should provide some idea of the host nation's economic progress. Political status can be gauged by the host nation's power in and impact on international affairs. [8]

Internal assessment involves identification of the basic strong points of a company's present operations. These strengths are particularly important in international operations because they are often the elements valued most by the host nation and thus offer significant bargaining leverage. Both resource strengths and global capabilities must be analyzed. The resources to be examined in particular include technical and managerial skills, capital, labor, and raw materials. The global capability components include assessing the effectiveness of proposed product delivery and financial management

110

systems.[9]

A firm that gives serious consideration to internal and external assessment is Business International Corporation, which recommends that seven broad categories of factors be considered. These categories include economic, political, geographic, labor, tax, capital source, and business factors.

John A. Pearce II and Richard B. Robinson, Jr., *Strategic Management* 3rd ed. © 1988, pp. 144-49. Reprinted by permission of Richard D. Irwin, Inc., Homewood, Illinois.

Key Terms and Concepts

Citicorp   name of a company.

Exxon Company   one of the largest petroleum companies in the United States as well as in the world.

Gillette Company   a company noted worldwide in decades with its good quality razors.

Otis Elevator   name of a company.

Texas Instruments   one of the largest computer companies in the United States.

existing management orientation   existing management behavior or outlook.

foreign licensing   A foreign owner offers the right to a trademark, patent, trade secret, or other valued item in return for a royalty or fee.

technology transfer   the process of introducing advanced technology from its innovative source to other firms.

General Electric   one of the largest producers of electronic appliances and instruments.

Fiyitsue   name of a company.

overseas R&D   overseas research and development.

bargaining leverage   the strength of one's position in negotiation, such as market share, access, financial assets, etc.

NOTES

1. Awareness of the strategic opportunities and threats posed and faced by MNCs is important to planners in almost every domestic U. S. industry.
   了解多国企业面临的机会与威胁,这对几乎每一种美国工业的计划都十分重

111

要。

2. leading the way 一路领先

3. Understanding the myriad and sometimes subtle nuance of competing in international markets or against multinational firms... 对国际市场上，或是多国企业面对的无数的、有时仅有细微差异的竞争的理解……

4. precision and heavy machinery 高精度和重型机械

5. Multinational development makes sense as a competitive weapon in many situations. 把多国发展作为竞争武器，在很多情况下是有意义的。

6. ... drain vital cash flows from a foreign competitor's domestic operations. ……从外国竞争者的国内经营中吸引大量资金。

7. A case in point 一个合适的例子

8. Political status can be gauged by the host nations's power in and impact on international affairs 可以从国际事务中的力量与影响来判断被投资国的政治状态。

9. The global capability components include assessing the effectiveness of proposed product delivery and financial management systems 总的能力考察包括评价交付订货的情况及财务管理系统的工作情况。

Suggestions for Further Study

A bibliography is always required as a part of a paper, essay, thesis, or dissertation. A bibliography tells readers all the sources of information an author has used when he worked on his paper. The author may quote, paraphrase, or summarize information from all kinds of sources, such as books, magazines, newspapers, periodicals, websites, or even government documents. With the sources provided by a bibliography, readers can search further information concerning the research that the author presents to the public. Remember, in a bibliography, unlike a footnote, the rule for the author's name is "last name first and first name last".

For more knowledge of bibliography, see the sample bibliographies in Appendix F.

Key Words Bibliography

PART TWELVE
INTERNATIONAL ECONOMICS

Free Markets and Growth

Adam Smith, in his Wealth of Nations (1776) is often given credit for starting the industrial revolution. [1] Adam Smith believed that selfishness, in an ethical sense, is not highly rated. [2] However, in an economic sense, if we encourage individuals to believe that their own hard work would provide direct economic rewards to them, this new "release" of human energy would set in motion economic growth. [3] First, self-interest, freely expressed, would jump-start the economy. Secondly, the gain falling to the hard-working individual could not be fully captured by this economic man. [4] This is because in the quest to build personal wealth, one needs others. Inevitably and automatically, he reasoned, an "invisible hand" assured that the reach of the individual would produce benefits, even if unintended — for all others. [5] Two concepts: the economic man (interested largely in himself) and the invisible hand became the twin pillars of capitalist or free market ideology.

Behind these central forces, the conservative "free market" economists of the 19th century said that economies could only grow if those were generating wealth were also generating capital. Thus, the wealthy economic man should not "consume" his own prosperity, but save and invest that high income flow. [6] In this way, the volume and value of capital made available to workers in society would increase. With more capital per worker, each worker would be more productive. And high productivity would cause wages, employment and prosperity to be enjoyed by all. And the only certain way that economic men could add to their wealth was to produce goods that consumers wanted to buy. In this ideal world of a "free market" economy, there was a tight knit circle of interdependence: Self-interest created high personal energy which created high profits which allowed for high investments which allowed for high productivity which allowed for higher levels of consumption which allowed for — and encouraged — ever higher levels of investment to satisfy that consumption. The circle was complete. In retrospect, conservatives concluded that capitalism required capital. Capital creation was possible if those who had the cake... or the economic surplus... did not eat much of the cake, but invested it. [7]

Faith in this mechanism expanded rapidly in much of the 19th century, and the first half of the 20th century. But the "Great Depression" of 1930s demonstrated that growth was no longer automatic. For many economists, the depression was created because consumption growth was not sufficient to encourage capital growth. With sagging investment — and consumption — capitalist economies spiraled down to a deep depression. In 1933, some 25% of all US workers were unemployed.

The British economist, John Maynard Keynes, proposed a solution. If private investment was not forthcoming, why not undertake, with budget deficits, public investment projects. [8] This pump priming would encourage[9] private investment, and soon the economy would be on its way to expansions of both consumption and investment. But the depression was so severe that it shattered the confidence of free market economists.

Today, as the United States views the global economy, the U. S. is obligated to try to figure out ways to expand economic growth and foreign export markets. Clearly, the United States needs much more capital formation if it is to regain its position as a leading economic power. One U. S. government agency, the General Accounting Office (GAO) observed that in 1990, Japan invested 33% of its Gross Domestic Product, double the level of the U. S. France, Germany and Canada were investing over 21%. Indeed, the U. S. rated last not only for the largest industrialized nations, but also last for the 24 OECD (Organization for Economic Cooperation and Development) nations. U. S. investment levels were reaching new lows in a three decade experience. (GAO, Transition Series, "Investment" Dec 1992, p. 7)

An equally respected element in conservative free market economics is the theme that individual consumers are "sovereign." This simply means that they must be free to spend money they have earned in any way they want. But as we noted above, the classical writers explained that while such freedom must be respected, surely any rational consumer would recognize the importance of capital formation to its own growth, or to its own economic future. Thus, while technically "free" to consume, he would be sensible enough not to consume in excess. [10] The nation state must not consume its own seed corn. If it wants to grow, it must add, each year, to that stock of seed corn.

114

Today, Americans have opted too often for consumption instead of saving. Americans spend, each year, $5.6 billion on cookies, $8 billion on pornography, $62 billion on toiletries, $19 billion on lottery tickets, $15 billion on toys, $19 billion for alcoholic beverages, and $47 billion for cigarettes. To offset the damage that this does to our human bodies, we spend $2 billion for home exercise equipment and $5 billion for health club memberships. But 70% of Americans who own running shoes don't run.

The implications of this explosion in consumption are reflected, too, in a reluctance to pay taxes for the services that we expect from government. The growth of the government deficit reflects the disarray of an economy where gross national appetites have exceeded gross national product.

The free market classical economists offered important advice to any culture hoping to enjoy rapid economic growth or an improved future. The sacrifices of one generation set the stage for the potential for growth — but only if those who receive the funds (including governments) — make prudent use of those resources by investing in growth. Americans have neglected this axiom. They have neglected the needs of the future, and already the future is neglecting America. The high consumption low investment pattern has reduced productivity growth, and with that the rate of GNP growth. America's future will be prosperous — as is the case for all economies — only if we invest in that improved future. Free market mechanisms taken alone do not provide automatic prosperity. For the market is not a disembodied force that assures effortless or automatic prosperity. Growth is something that each generation must earn. Growth generates a stock that each generation must leave as a legacy for the next generation.

The American entertainer, Walt Disney, summarized the challenge clearly. "Change is inevitable. Growth is not." The lesson applies not alone to the United States, but also to the rest of the world.

By Paul E. Sultan

Key Terms and Concepts

economic man　For most individuals, the drive for self-interest is greater than all other motivation. This is not the highest motive, Adam Smith believed, but the strongest single motive.

invisible hand　Adam Smith explained that as the economic man worked for himself, he would automatically benefit others. This benefit was realized by the invisible hand.

market economy   This is one driven by consumer needs, where needs are defined by those who have money to spend. Production is free to respond to capture consumer income by offering goods that are attractive to consumers.

savings   This is the decision not to consume; it is often assumed that savings will lower the cost of borrowing funds, and thus encourage investment activity.

investments   These are expenditures made to build physical capital, plant capacity. In more recent times, they are used to describe investments in education or building human capital. National income accounts not to call stock purchases as investments as these simply involve changes in the ownership of "titles" and not building new capital.

inequality and growth   Conservative economists believe that inequality can encourage economic growth, simply because those with high incomes have the unusual opportunity to save and invest, thus improving the living standards (through the invisible hand) for everyone.

high consumption economy   This is one where people have a strong preference to consume rather than not consume (or save). High consumption levels may choke off chances for capital formation and technology gains.

John Maynard Keynes   a famous British economist who wrote the "General Theory of Employment, Interest and Money" in 1936. Keynes charged that capitalist economies could not always transfer savings into investment. That failure would trigger the reduction of demand, and hence a depression. He believed that government investment could fill the void, until private sector confidence — and investment — was revived.

NOTES

1. ... is often given credit for starting the industrial revolution.   ……经常被赞誉为兴起了工业革命。

2. ... selfishness, in an ethical sense, is not highly rated.   ……从道德观念讲，自私并不好。

3. ... this new "release" of human energy would set in motion economic growth.   ……这种关于人的动力的新说法会启动经济的增长。

4. ... the gain falling to the hard-working individual could not be fully captured by this economic man.   ……一个努力工作的人（即经济人）所创造

116

的，并不全部为他自己所得。

5. ... an "invisible hand" assured that the reach of the individual would produce benefits, even if unintended — for all others.   ……一只"看不见的手"保证了获得个人利益的同时，也为所有其他人带来好处，即使这并非个人本意。

6. ... but save and invest that high income flow.   ……把高收入储蓄起来和用于投资。

7. ... if those who had the cake ... or the economic surplus ... did not eat much of the cake, but invested it.   如果这些有"蛋糕"或经济上有富余的人，不"吃"那么多而用于投资，……

8. If private investment was not forthcoming, why not undertake, with budget deficits, public investment projects.   如果缺乏个人投资，为什么不通过预算赤字来搞公共投资项目？

9. This pump priming would encourage ...   这种启动方法会推动（个人投资）……

10. ... while technically "free" to consume, he would be sensible enough not to consume in excess.   ……虽然道理上讲消费是自由的，一个人还是能够理解不要过度消费的道理。

New-World Realities and Competitiveness

The Old Doctrine

The doctrine of comparative advantage explains that each nation should focus in producing goods where they have a cost advantage over other nations. With each nation doing this and swapping their low-cost output for the mix of goods they need, the economic status of all trading nations is improved. It's a win-win situation. But if one nation continues to export more than it is willing to import, that nation will end up with the excess of foreign funds accumulated by those exports. That excess will cause the value of currency for the nation with a trade deficit to fall. Or stated in other terms, the value of the currency of the nation with the favorable trade balance will rise. This exchange rate adjustment will increase the costs of exports to those nations who have been importing excessively, having the effect of restoring trade balances between nations. Freely floating exchange rates would have the effect, then, of making certain that one nation could not sustain an excess of exports. This simple apparatus has justified the rapid growth of world trade since the end of World War II. Dramatically expanding export activity throughout the world has been a force elevating living standards for many nations.

The New Doctrine

But as in many aspects of life, what appears to be an ideal and simple model doesn't always work out that way. The United States, as a case in point[1], has been suffering from serious trade deficits for almost two decades. It is estimated that for each $1 billion of trade deficit, the country suffers 30,000 in job loss. And each job loss is estimated to cost the United States $30,000. Indeed, the persistence of the trade deficit has had a devastating impact on the nation's manufacturing base. Manufacturing for many years has provided high value-added jobs.

One of many reasons for this serious erosion of trade status reflects new trade strategies undertaken by America's trading partners. A new strategy for managed trade has emerged in the Pacific that has worked with remarkable force. Indeed, if the United States is counted as part of the European trading bloc, and Japan, China, the four tigers, and the four tiger pups counted as part of the Pacific trading bloc, the Asian trading bloc is now running a $1 trillion surplus, set against the $1 trillion deficit of the US-European trading bloc. The Asian success can be explained by the emergence of a new blueprint, a new roadmap, or what is sometimes called a new "paradigm." What are the elements in this new roadmap?

First: primary attention is given to national growth. This means that production activity — and the means to assure its efficiency and effectiveness — gets top national priority. The surplus generated by profitable enterprise must be re-invested in capital, technology, R&D, and the development of an infrastructure to support that production activity. Enterprise must invest today to assure an improved future tomorrow.

Second: the government emerges as a guiding instrument in directing the stream of private sector energy into channels that are most promising for future markets. The government sees the advantage of job growth realized by generating exports, capturing the windfall of 30,000 jobs for each billion of

118

trade surplus. The government offers guidance, and multiple incentives to the private sector to encourage investment in high growth and high value-added sectors. Government and industry are not adversaries. They are partners.

Third: consumers are expected to understand that the improvement in their own living standard must wait or be deferred, as resources are poured into national-growth priorities identified in (1) and (2) above. Benefits denied today are necessary so that plentiful production can be made available tomorrow.

Fourth: nation states aspiring to growth must learn — quickly — to replicate the technologies of Western nations, learning not only how to use the technologies, but the art for their own manufacture at home.

Fifth: primary attention must be given to education. **Future growth is not commodity based but based on cultivated intelligence. Education is critical for two reasons: First, the highly educated corp can identify high technologies that are important to competitiveness and growth. And secondly, a highly educated workforce can learn — quickly — how to make use or how to operate such technology.**

These are the elements of what can be called a neomercantile policy. The blueprint emphasizes the need for sacrifice today, the need for high savings to make possible capital growth, the need for R&D (research and development) to improve the performance capabilities of capital, the need for a highly intelligence and disciplined workforce willing to work for modest pay, the need for a supporting infrastructure including the network of highways, communication linkages, housing, and schooling. And the need to export — at least during this growth phase — more than you import to access "hard" currencies, and with that the selective purchase or licensing of foreign technologies.[2]

In this context, global competition and trade success is not seen as an automatic consequence of impersonal market forces. Trade advantage and global competitiveness is largely "managed." It is generated by a carefully planned strategy of national technology advance, drawing from around the world advances that can serve domestic needs effectively. To be successful, it requires nation state support of the national growth strategy, the willingness to absorb short-term sacrifice, the commitment to expansion of capital and technology, the harmonization of government and industry policy, the harmonization of labor and management efforts. And behind all of this, the clear understanding that global rivalries for competitive advantage involve a **BRAIN RACE!**

The successful recipe can be reduced to two fundamental "S's" **STUDY and SAVE.**

If these are the elements that provide a good environment for growth and competitiveness, what are some of the strategies for individual firms to follow in supporting this growth process? There are five fundamental elements emerging in advanced manufacturing systems in the United States and Japan, elements being copied throughout the world for companies hoping to survive, or improve their position, in this intensely competitive contest. [3]

One: Giving priority to **QUALITY!** Throughout the world, consumers are insisting on quality products. Quality means that the product must be elegant in its design, simple to manufacture (with few parts), easy to repair, be very durable, flexible, and easy to use. And sold at a low or modest price. Consumer demand in the future will involve a blend of cost and quality considerations, with the quality issue edging the price issue. [4] Such distinguished American firms as Motorola have what they call "six sigma" quality targets. This involves 4 to 5 failed parts per million produced. They are planning to elevate that quality standard to 4 to 5 failed parts per billion produced. They are, in essence, moving to **zero defects! Quality products can be produced only by a quality workforce that is committed to perfection in every thought, every action, in every second of each working day.**

Two: Giving priority to **SPEED!**

Competitive pressures are increasing within the global village. In the past, much attention has been given to the life-cycle of a new product. Often an unusual product might enjoy a favored market position for as much as 35 years. But now, the life-cycle has telescoped dramatically. Firms can no longer expect to enjoy a long-term income flow without constantly improving the product or introducing new innovations. Because competitors are quick to develop their own versions of a new product, firms must always recognize that their own chance to secure profits requires that they race to the market with a new product; and even as that product is enjoying an expanded market share, anticipate a short life-cycle, and prepare for its improved design, or new products to take the place of the old.

120

Three: Making use of **Just-in-Time** Manufacturing. This innovation developed by the Japanese requires that the flow of inputs to the firm be carefully synchronized with production needs, and that the manufacture of goods within the plant assume the features of a continuous stream of flow. The trick is to avoid down time,[5] or any period when value added is not been generated to the production flow. Just-in-time systems expose inefficiencies; they reduce the high costs of accumulated inventory; and they obligate a clean, swift, orderly, and harmonized production flow of zero defect products.

Four: Making use of **Lean Management Systems:** Here again, the Japanese — and particularly the Toyota Company, have shown the world that it is possible to produce world class goods with a much reduced workforce. Attention is given to reducing the large number of indirect functions. Indirect functions are those that do not involve direct service to the production flow. There are, in many operations, a pyramid of staff, often outnumbering those on the production line. These pyramids must be flattened. Instead of having 90 separate job duties, each carefully specialized, it is important to have a smaller number of workers, each with broad-based skills. "Lean Management" systems are now sweeping the world in automobile production, as practice demonstrates that it is technically possible to produce much more of high quality goods with a reduced workforce.

Five: **Production teams.** It is now understood that the know-it-all manager simply does not know it all. Frequently, improvements in how work is to be done can be left to the judgment of the individual worker,[6] or more importantly, newly-organized employee teams. This in the United States, is called **employee empowerment.** Most employees have hidden reserves of talent that can increase the capacity of the firm to produce quality products with speed and efficiency. An extension of this reform involves **concurrent engineering.** This process requires that with the improvement of production, it is important to involve consumers, suppliers (or vendors), design engineers, production staff, employees, sales and marketing staff. When all these groups are pulled together into a joint effort to define what is best, often products can be designed that are more easily manufactured with fewer parts, and with durable or reliable service to the consumer.

To summarize, a revolution in **thinking** is now underway throughout the global village, with changes most evident in Pacific Rim nations. Added to this is a revolution in **working.** The way goods are produced must involve smaller teams, concurrent engineering, an empowered workforce, primary focus being given to consumer needs (rather than producer convenience or custom).

Again, those operations which understand the runaway dynamics of the "new world"[7] will improve their market position, increase quality jobs, and be assured of high growth and prosperity. A workforce now becomes a **thinkforce.**[8] Working hard is much less important than **working smart.** All of this is driven by a new respect for satisfying **consumer wants**, instead of being burdened by the lead jacket of tradition[9] or historic convention. Nations, as individuals, are not to be seen as ants riding on the back of a turtle. Both individuals and nations can create an improved future, if they have the wit, the will, and the courage to change.

By Paul E. Sultan

Key Terms and Concepts

doctrine   a belief system; a way of thinking; a blueprint for how the economy should be run.

win-win trade relationship   This is where both nations benefit from trade or where two parties in a competitive relationship negotiate outcomes that benefit both parties.

trade deficit   exists when one nation's exports do not match its imports.

high value added jobs or functions   These involve activities or work that makes a major difference in the value of the product or service to consumers.

exchange rates   the ratio of one nation's currency value compared to another nation's.

infrastructure   represents the support systems for effective production. It includes transportation, communication, sanitation networks, as well as producing a highly intelligent and motivated workforce.

technology   This is distinguished from capital because technology represents new forms — usually more efficient forms — of capital instruments. Technology represents changes in the performance capacities of capital.

brain race   This is the new metaphor for international trade competitiveness. Nations who want to be competitive are in a race to develop attitudes and abilities in the workforce that "invent" new technologies, as well as have the ability to transfer their uses to workplace settings.

empowered workers　These are employees who have been trusted to help figure out how to produce goods more efficiently; it involves a transfer of authority and responsibility to the individual. It is usually developed around workforce teams.

just-in-time production　Vendors supply the inputs to manufacturing as these inputs are needed. This eliminates the cost of inventory, and also reveals where inefficiencies in production interrupt the production stream.

lean management　This involves the thinning out of the labor force, particularly the heavy layers of management that are not directly involved in production, moving from pyramids to pancakes.

concurrent management　This involves the deep consultation in joint decision making that involves every one from beginning to end on how changes in product design and production technique can be made. Changes are driven by consumer needs.

NOTES

1. as a case in point　作为一个恰当的例子来说

2. And the need to export — at least during this growth phase — more than you import to access "hard" currencies, and with that the selective purchase or licensing of foreign technologies.　出口辅以选购外国的技术或技术许可证来获得硬通货——至少在成长期内——比进口必要得多。

3. ... elements being copied throughout the world for companies hoping to survive, or improve their position, in this intensely competitive contest.　……世界上所有希望在激烈竞争中生存和发展的公司都要与这些因素打交道。

4. ... with the quality issue edging the price issue.　……而质量问题比价格问题更重要。

5. The trick is to avoid down time,...　诀窍是避免停工期,……

6. ... improvements in how work is to be done can be left to the judgment of the individual worker,...　……怎样做好工作留给工人自己去决定,……

7. ... which understand the runaway dynamics of the "new world"...　……理解"新世界"的决定性动力的……

8. A workforce now becomes a thinkforce.　体能大军现在变成了智能大军。

9. the lead jacket of tradition　固有的传统的禁锢

Suggestions for Further Study

A résumé, or vita, is a tool for a person to introduce himself to a unit, such as company, agency, government administration, university, or institute.

Usually a résumé is sent with a formal letter addressed to the unit to which the applicant aspires. Internationally, résumés are similar in format, telling first the name, address, telephone number, fax number, email address and the position the applicant is interested in, then his education, experience, publication, special interests, and references. Some personnel departments have special requirements for the contents of résumé, such as asking the applicant to put a photo in the upper corner of the résumé, either on the left or on the right. In this case, an applicant should not casually pick a photo and stick it on. The photo, as well as the paper of résumé, say, color and quality, or the design of the format and the words written, are all clues for the staffs of personnel departments to judge the essence and quality of an applicant. Remember, always carefully design the format of a résumé, seriously write every word, and have each piece of information well clarified. For a sample of a detailed résumé, see Appendix G of this textbook.

Key Words　Résumé

PART THIRTEEN
INTERNATIONAL MARKETING

Advertising Abroad — Creative Challenges

The growing intensity of international competition coupled with the complexity of marketing multinationality demand[1] that the international advertiser function at the highest level of his creativity. Advertisers from all around the world have developed their skills and abilities to the point that advertisements from different countries reveals a basic similarity, and a growing level of sophication. To complicate matters even further, boundaries are placed on[2] creativity by company policy, legal, language, cultural, media, production, and cost limitations.

The advertising man must overcome all of these limitations, but he also may have to do a major selling job to convince his company or client that he is going in the right direction. When Qantas, the Australian airline, wanted to sell some used Boeing 707 jets in the United States, the agency suggested using a theme that they were "flown only on Sundays by little old pilots from Pasadena," but reportedly had great difficulty selling the ad to people in Australia who couldn't get the connection. Ultimately the ad ran and was extremely successful.

Company Policy Limitations

A multinational advertiser helps establish the environment for creativity through its basic advertising policies. Every area of advertising activity needs basic policies covering centralized or decentralized authority, use of single or multiple foreign or domestic agencies, appropriation and allocation procedures[3], copy, media, and research. All other areas covered by policy statements in domestic advertising should also be governed by policy statements in foreign operations. One of the most widely debated areas of policy pertains to the degree of advertising variation[4] from country to country. One view is that advertising has to be customized for each individual country or region, because every country is a special problem. Executives in such companies argue that the only way to achieve adequate and relevant advertising is to develop separate campaigns for every country. Such individual treatment seems to be passing out of popularity,[5] largely because of the extreme cost involved in such a program. Although almost no companies argue for completely standardized ads from country to country, most seem to be taking the position that a basic theme should be developed.

Most companies with long experience in international advertising have found that the question of standardization or modification[6] depends more on the motivation patterns than on geography. Advertising must be related to motivation; if people in different markets buy similar products for significantly different reasons, then obviously the advertising campaigns should be reoriented to these reasons. When the various markets react best to similar stimuli, then it would be unwise to vary the stimulus just for the sake of variation. In most instances, since the purchase motivations are similar for a given product, the majority of companies follow a compromise course. They attempt to maintain the basic elements or basic message[7] and provide only language translation and other minor advertising changes. Even cultural barriers may be transcended if basic purchase motivations are similar. Pepsi-Cola advertises in dozens of countries, yet its policy allows variation in specific detail to suit local market conditions. Certain elements of Pepsi advertising remain constant, whether in Africa, Europe, or South America: the Pepsi-Cola logotype[8], the basic color combination, the Pepsi crown[9], and fundamental point-of-purchase units such as illuminated plastic signs[10], metal tackers, brand signs, etc.

In summary, contemporary thinking on the subject seems to be that international advertising campaigns should be modified from country to country only when absolutely necessary.

Legal and Tax Considerations

In some countries advertising is more closely regulated than in others, requiring modification of the creative approach from country to country. Laws pertaining to advertising[11] may restrict the amount spent on advertising, the media used, the type of product which may be advertised, the manner in which price may be advertised, the type of copy approach and illustration material which may be used, and other aspects of the advertising program. In

Germany, for example, it is against the law to use comparative terminology; an advertiser cannot say that his soap gets clothes cleaner than another, because the statement implies that other products do not get clothes clean. Advertisers live under the threat of immediate lawsuit from competitors[12] if they claim that their brand is best. Similar restrictions exist in most European countries. In Italy even common words like deodorant and perspiration are banned from television.

Some countries have special taxes which apply to advertising and which might restrict creative freedom in media selection[13]. The tax structure in Austria probably best shows how advertising taxation can distort media choice by changing the cost ratios of various media. In federal states, with the exception of Bergenland and Tyrol, there is a 10 percent ad tax on ad insertions. For posters there is a 10-30 percent tax, according to state and municipality. On radio advertising there is a 10 percent tax; however, in Tyrol it is 20 percent.

The Monopolies Commission in England has accused Procter & Gamble and Unilever of creating a monopoly (duopoly?) situation[14] by spending nearly one fourth of their revenues on advertising; incidentally, the companies were also criticized for earning too much. Legislation for new taxes and restrictions on advertising is introduced, and some passed, nearly every year in countries which have traditionally imposed minimal restrictions on advertising and free competition.

Language Limitations

Language is one of the chief barriers to effective communication through advertising. The problem involves not only the different languages in different countries or even different languages within one country, but also the subtler problems of linguistic nuance and vernacular. [15]

Incautious handling of language has caused problems for all kinds of companies in nearly every country. Some automotive examples suffice. Chrysler Corp. was nearly laughed out of Spain[16] when it copied the U. S. theme advertising, "Dart is Power." To the Spanish the phrase implied that buyers lack but are seeking sexual vigor. Ford foundered on the linguistic problems of number; in many languages the word company is plural rather than singular, as in English. "Ford Have Something for It" trumpeted one headline in English. Ford goofed again when it named its low-cost "third world" truck "Fiera," which means "ugly old woman" in Spanish.

Low literacy in many countries seriously impedes communications and calls for greater creativity and use of verbal media[17]. Turkey, for example, has a literacy rate of approximately 25 percent; an advertiser attempting to reach a large segment of the population is forced to utilize radio advertising. Multiple languages within a country or advertising area provide another problem for the advertiser. Even a tiny country like Switzerland has three separate languages.

Language translation encounters innumerable barriers which impede effective, idiomatic translation and thereby hamper communication[18]. Especially is this situation apparent in advertising materials. Abstractions, terse writing, and word economy[19] all pose problems for translators. Some firms, including the Philips Company of Holland and Volkswagen, are using Esperanto in an attempt to overcome language barriers in international markets. Esperanto is a simplified international language used fairly widely in countries with large numbers of foreign visitors or troops and with obscure or varied local dialects and languages. It is doubtful that such a basic language of which no one is really a master can be expected to render forceful, effective advertising in any but the most elementary applications, but its use shows the desperate need for a simple communication vehicle[20].

Cultural Diversity

Overcoming the problems of communicating to people in diverse cultures is one of the great creative challenges in advertising. It is axiomatic that in messages moving from one culture to another, communication is more difficult; this is so partly because cultural factors largely determine the ways various phenomena will be perceived. If the perceptual framework is different, perception of the message itself will differ.

International marketers are becoming accustomed to the problems of adapting from culture to culture. Knowledge of differing symbolism of colors is a basic part of the international marketer's encyclopedia. He knows that white in Europe means pure, but that in Asia it is more associated with death.

Existing perceptions based on tradition and heritage are often hard to overcome. Marketing researchers in Hong Kong found, for example, that cheese is associated with Yeung-Yen (foreigners) and rejected by the Chinese.

128

The concept of cooling and heating of the body are important in Chinese; malted milk is considered heating, while fresh milk is cooling. Brandy is sustaining, whiskey harmful.

As though it were not enough for advertisers to be concerned with differences among nations, they find that subcultures within a country require attention as well. In Hong Kong, for example, 10 different kinds of breakfast eating patterns exist. The youth of a country almost always constitutes a different consuming culture from the older people, and urban dwellers differ significantly from rural dwellers.

As shown by the examples in this section, cultural diversity requires the advertising man to be constantly alert to cultural variation because it constitutes one of the greatest creative challenges in international business.

Media Limitation

Media limitation may diminish the role of advertising in the promotional program and may force marketers to emphasize other elements of the marketing mix. A marketer's creativity is certainly challenged when he is limited to showing a television commercial 10 times a year with no two exposures closer than 10 days, as is the case in Italy. Creative advertising men in some countries have even developed their own media for overcoming media limitations. In some African countries, advertisers run boats up and down the rivers playing popular music and broadcasting commercials into the bush as they travel[21].

Production and Cost Limitations

Creativity is especially important when the budget is small or where there are severe production limitations. Such limitations exist in nearly every advertising medium. Poor quality printing and unavailability of high-grade papers[22] are simple examples. The necessity for low cost reproduction in small markets poses another problem. In many countries, for example, hand-painted billboards must be used instead of printed sheets because the small number of billboards does not warrant the production of such printed sheets.

The cost of reaching different market segments can become nearly prohibitive in some instances. In Hong Kong, for example, it is imperative that ads be run in both English and Chinese. Even if the market being sought is

Chinese, English must be used so Orientals will know the product is not inferior and being advertised only to Asians. To continue the Far Eastern example, advertisers in Bangkok must use English, Chinese, and Thai languages. In Singapore, besides English and Chinese, Malay and Tamil are necessary if the market is to be reached. All of these factors, even translations alone, impose significant cost and production burdens for the advertiser.

Philip R. Cateora and John M. Hess, *International Marketing* © 1975, pp. 400-406. Reprinted by permission of Richard D. Irwin, Inc., Homewood, Illinois.

Key Terms and Concepts

compromise course   refers to the implement of one of the many advertising strategies. Through the course, the core idea and content in an advertisement is kept but with language translation or other minor advertising changes.

Bergenland   name of a state in Austria.

Tyrol   name of a state in Austria.

ad insertion   advertisements together with mails delivered by Post Offices.

poster   advertisement on the wall.

segment   Market segmentation divides up a market into distinct groups. These groups are called segments. People in the same segment have common needs and will respond similarly to a marketing action.

Esperanto   a simplified international language used in countries with many foreign visitors, troops, as well as many languages and dialects.

billboard   outdoor advertisement. The visibility of billboard is most effective in reminding people of well-known products.

inferior   refers to the inferior goods in the concept of microeconomics. Inferior goods are purchased in smaller amounts — or not at all — when people's income rises.

Malay   major language used in Malaysia.

Tamil   a language used in many countries of Southeast Asia.

NOTES

1. marketing multinationality   多国营销

2. boundaries are placed on ...　范围延至……

3. appropriation and allocation procedures　拨款及款项分配的步骤

4. degree of advertising variation　广告变化的程度

5. Such individual treatment seems to be passing out of popularity，...　这种个别对待的方法似乎变得不普遍了，……

6. question of standardization or modification　稳定还是变动的问题

7. ... to maintain the basic elements or basic message...　……保持基本要素或基本内容……

8. the Pepsi-Cola logotype　百事可乐的作为标志的语句（注：指广告的核心语句）

9. the Pepsi crown　百事可乐的标志

10. illuminated plastic signs　有灯光照明的塑料标志

11. Laws pertaining to advertising ...　与广告有关的法律……

12. Advertisers live under the threat of immediate lawsuit from competitors...　广告人生活在竞争者会很快起诉的威胁之中……

13. in media selection　广告媒介的选择

14. The Monopolies Commission in England has accused Procter & Gamble and Unilever of creating a monopoly (duopoly?) situation...　英国的反垄断委员会指责 P&G 公司和 Unilever 公司制造垄断（或两家垄断）的局势。

15. ... but also the subtler problems of linguistic nuance and vernacular.　……而且也有语言中土语与地方话造成的微妙的问题。

16. laughed out of Spain　从西班牙被人笑跑了

17. use of verbal media　使用言语媒介

18. thereby hamper communication　因此妨碍交流

19. Abstractions, terse writing, and word economy...　语言的概括、写作的精练和用词的经济性……

20. a simple communication vehicle　简单的交流手段

21. In some African countries, advertisers run broadcasting commercials into the bush as they travel.　在一些非洲国家，做广告的边走边向丛林播送广告。（注：实际是向丛林中的村落播送广告。）

22. unavailability of high-grade papers　得不到高质量的纸张

Evaluating Alternatives for International Operations

Once a company has evaluated the international market and decided it makes sense to enter it in light of the company's financial goals[1] and willingness to take risks, a means of entry must be selected. The option chosen is that most closely matching its willingness and ability to commit financial, physical, and managerial resources. As Table 13-1 demonstrates, the relative difficulty of entry increases as the firm moves from exporting to direct investments.

Table 13-1 Models of Entry into International Market

Least ←————————————————————————————→ Most

Amount of commitment, control, risk, and profit potential

Indirect exporting (through intermediaries)	Direct exporting (directly to buyers)	Licensing	Joint ventures	Direct investments

Indirect Exporting (Through Intermediaries)

Having another firm sell products in a foreign country is exporting. This entry option allows a company to make the least number of changes in terms of its product, its organization, and even its corporate goals. Exporting may be undertaken occasionally to get rid of surplus products, or a company may begin exporting as a means of familiarizing itself with international marketing[2] and a specific foreign market.

Indirect exporting, or marketing through an intermediary, involves the least amount of commitment and risk but will probably return the least profit.[3] This kind of exporting is ideal for the company that has no overseas contacts but wants to market abroad.[4] The intermediary has the international marketing know-how and the resources necessary for the effort to succeed.

A company has a choice of three primary intermediaries when exporting indirectly:

* A domestic-based export merchant actually buys the products and sells them in foreign markets.

* A domestic-based export agent simply agrees to find a buyer for the products and acts as a go-between.

* A cooperative organization represents several producers and is controlled by them to a degree.[5] This relationship is most common among producers of primary products like fruit.

Direct Exporting (Directly to Buyers)

When a company handles its own exports directly, without intermediaries, this is direct exporting. Most companies become involved in direct exporting when they are approached by buyers or when their exporting becomes sufficiently large to merit more explicit attention within the company.[6] This increases the risk that the company is taking but also opens the door to increased profits.

Several alternative means of direct exporting can be undertaken:

* A domestic-based export department or division is one made up of the company's staff.

* An overseas branch or subsidiary[7] is a separate entity set up in the desired market and handling exporting from there. The branch serves as a warehouse, promotion and sales center, display outlet, and customer service locale.[8] This method offers more control to the exporter. A sales subsidiary may also sell merchandise that is produced within the foreign country.

* A traveling export sales representative is sent to various locations throughout the target markets to generate business.

* Foreign-based distributors or agents do not work for the company directly. The product is sold to them and in turn is sold to the foreign buyers. Exclusive or general rights are often sold along with the product.[9]

Licensing

Under licensing a company offers the right to a trademark, patent, trade secret, or other valued item in return for a royalty or a fee. The advantages to the company granting the license are low-risk and a capital-free entry into the international market. The licensee gains some piece of information that allows it to start at a point beyond the beginning. Yoplait Yogurt is licensed from Sodima, a French cooperative, by General Mills for sales in the United States.

There are some serious drawbacks to this mode of entry, however. The licensor foregoes control of its product and any profits gained from it. In addition, while the relationship lasts, the licensor may be creating its own competition. Many licensees adapt the product somehow and enter the market with product and marketing knowledge gained at the expense of the company that got them started. To offset this disadvantage, many companies strive to stay innovative so that the licensee remains dependent on them[10] for improvements and successful operation. Finally, should the licensee prove to be a poor choice, the name or reputation of the company may be harmed.

Two variations on licensing, contract manufacturing and foreign assembly, represent an alternative way to produce a product within the foreign country. Contract manufacturing is considered the next step up from licensing. U. S. companies may contract with a foreign firm to manufacture products according to certain specifications. The product is then sold in the foreign country or exported to the United States. Foreign assembly, the next step from contract manufacturing, involves using foreign labor to assemble (not manufacture) parts and components that have been shipped to that country. The advantage to the foreign country is the employment of its people, and the U. S. firm benefits because import tariffs are lower on parts than they are on finished products. U. S. firms also take advantage of cheaper labor forces when products are assembled overseas.

Joint Ventures

When a foreign company and a local concern invest together to create a local business, it is called a joint venture. These two companies share ownership, control, and profits of the new company. Investment may be made by having either of the companies buy shares in the other or by creating a third and separate entity.

The advantages of this option are twofold. First, one company may not have the necessary financial, physical, or managerial resources to enter a foreign market alone. The alliance between Renault and AMC is an excellent example: without Renault's cash, it is unlikely that AMC would still be in existence today. Second, a foreign government may require a joint venture before it allows a company to enter its market. Japanese car manufacturers are forming joint ventures to produce subcompacts of U. S. consumers — to such a degree that by 1990 all U. S. subcompacts will bear a foreign stamp. For example, General Motors and Toyota are producing Chevrolets in Fremont, California; Ford and Toyo Kogyo (Mazda) are producing subcompacts in Hermosillo, Mexico; and Chrysler and Mitsubishi are producing Omni and Horizon models.

The disadvantages arise when the two companies disagree about policies or courses of action. For example, U. S. firms place a high priority on marketing a product, whereas foreign companies rely more heavily on selling. It is also common for U.S. companies to reinvest earnings gained, whereas some foreign companies may want to spend those earnings.

Direct Investments

The biggest commitment a company can make when entering the international market is by direct investment, which entails actually investing in an assembly or manufacturing plant located in a foreign country. For example, Honda's Marysville, Ohio, plant produces Civics and Accords, and Nissan's Smyrna, Tennessee, plant produces pickup trucks.

Many U. S. multinational corporations are also switching to this mode of entry[11] because the strength of the dollar has decreased their competitiveness in many markets. To bring costs and quality in line,[12] direct investing is a solution for those who depend on sales revenues from international marketing. McDonald's chose this alternative in Great Britain and built a plant to produce 2 million rolls a week when no local bakers would make them to McDonald's specifications.

The advantages to direct investment are many:

* Cost economies. Labor, materials, and freight costs are all reduced; many countries also offer investment incentives.

* Improved image. Creating jobs of locals definitely improves relations.

* Better marketing insight. Through closer involvement with government, customers, local suppliers, and distributors, a company gains greater insight into marketing needs and can adapt products to the market more accurately.

    * Greater control. Policies of the subsidiary will reflect the long-term goals of the company.

    * Fewer restrictions. A great deal of red tape can be eliminated, including many trade barriers.

However, because the commitment is so great in direct investing, the risks that accompany this alternative are also great. These include risks other than financial. When a company enters a new market, there is a responsibility to the host country. The responsibility can be the honest sale of a safe product or, as Union Carbide can attest, the responsibility can become much more than that. The chemical disaster at Union Carbide's plant in Bhopal, India, in which thousands of people were killed is a horrifying example of how one firm's attempt at international marketing became a nightmare for the host country.

Eric N. Berkowitz, Roger A. Kerin, and William Rudelius, *Marketing* © 1986, pp. 592-596. Reprinted by permission of Richard D. Irwin, Inc., Homewood, Illinois.

Key Terms and Concepts

joint venture   business owned by at least two firms or organizations. Joint venture with owners from different countries is called international joint venture.

go-between   intermediaries to connect sellers and buyers.

display outlet   stores or supermarkets to display and sell goods.

royalty   payments of money made by companies to a person, a group, or a company with the ownership or patent of the production.

Yoplait Yogurt   brand name of fermented milk.

General Mills   name of a food company.

contract manufacturing   agreeing to have another firm manufacture products according to certain specifications. If the manufacturing firm is foreign, the products may then be sold in the foreign country or exported back to the home country.

foreign assembly   using foreign labor to assemble parts and components that have been shipped to that country.

136

Renault   a brand name of French car.

AMC   American Motors Corporation. It merged with Chrysler Corporation in late 1980's and no longer existed.

Chevrolet   a brand name of car made by General Motors.

Omni   a brand name of economic car.

Horizon   a brand name of economic car which is quite similar to Omni.

Honda   a Japanese automobile company.

Civic   a brand name of car made by Honda.

Accord   a brand name of car made by Honda.

Smyrna   name of a place in Tennessee.

pickup truck   a kind of small truck used to pull troublesome vehicle.

red tape   various documents with details of regulations or restrictions issued by local or central government.

Union Carbide   name of an American company which was responsible for the chemical disaster in Bhopal, India in late 1980's.

NOTES

1. in light of the company's financial goals   按照公司的财务目标

2. a means of familiarizing itself with international marketing   一种使自己熟悉国际市场营销的手段

3. ... probably return the least profit.   ······大约得到的利润最少。

4. ... wants to market abroad.   ······打算到国外营销。

5. ... controlled by them to a degree.   ······由他们控制到一定的程度。

6. ... when their exporting becomes sufficiently large to merit more explicit attention within the company.   ······当他们的出口量变得相当大,从而引起公司内部的特别注意。(注:意思是值得注意考虑直接出口。)

7. An overseas branch or subsidiary   一个海外分支或子公司

8. customer service locale   顾客服务点

9. Exclusive or general rights are often sold along with the product.   随着产品的售出,特许权及一般的其他权利也随之售出。

10. ... many companies strive to stay innovative so that the licensee remains dependent on them...   ······许多公司坚持有新的发明,这样进行许可证生产的厂家则不断地要依赖他们······

11. ... switching to this mode of entry...   ······转为以这种方式来进入(注:指直接投资的方式)······

Suggestions for Further Study

A memorandum is absolutely not important for school life, but very useful for students when they graduate and have found a job in a foreign company or an international joint venture. A memorandum is frequently used in company daily business, passing information either within a company or between different departments.

A memorandum consists of five major parts: Sender, receiver, subject, date, and initials of the sender. For detailed sample, read Appendix H.

Key Words Memorandum

PART FOURTEEN
INTERNATIONAL BUSINESS

The International Rules of Commercial Policy

As mentioned in Chapter 8, nontariff barriers (NTBs) have increasingly replaced tariffs as a means of protecting domestic industries. Table 14-1 illustrates the consistent, and rather dramatic, decline in average U. S. tariff rates since the Great Depression. The most recent round of international trade negotiations (the Tokyo Round, 1973-1979) will result in a further reduction of average tariff rates among the major industrial nations (the United States, Japan, and the members of the European Economic Community) to 4.7% by 1987.

Table 14-1 U. S. Average Tariff Rates,* 1830-1980

PERIOD	RATE	PERIOD	RATE
1831-40	38%	1926-30	40%
1841-50	30	1931-35	50
1851-60	24	1936-40	38
1861-70	43	1941-45	32
1871-80	42	1950	13
1881-90	45	1955	12
1891-1900	47	1960	12
1901-10	45	1965	12
1911-15	39	1970	10
1916-20	22	1975	6
1921-25	36	1980	6

* Tariff rates calculated as total import duties divided by value of imports subject to duty (tariffs). [1] Source: U. S. Department of Commerce, Statistical Abstract of the United States, 1960 and 1984 (Washington, D. C.: U. S. Government Printing Office, 1960, 1984).

This trend toward freer trade has been interrupted during periods of substantial unemployment. Tariff rates rose during the 1930s, a period of massive worldwide unemployment, and the recessions of the late 1970s and early 1980s brought renewed pressure for protectionism. This "neoprotectionism" is not manifested in higher tariffs, but rather in terms of nontariff barriers,[2] including quotas, "voluntary" export restraints, "orderly marketing agreements," and antidumping codes. The net effect of these NTBs, while hard to quantify, is to directly limit imports or to increase the cost (through various licensing requirements) of importing goods.

We can gain a better understanding of why, and when governments resort to protectionism if we briefly consider the major provisions of the General Agreement on Tariffs and Trade (the GATT)[3]. This agreement, first signed by 23 countries in 1947, established principles for trade negotiations and conduct among the signatory nations[4]. Among its more important provisions are (1) prohibitions on (a) export subsidies (Article VI) and (b) quotas (Article XI), as well as (2) the most favored nation (MFN)[5] clause (Article I), which stipulates that bilateral tariff reductions between contracting nations shall apply to all signatory parties. The agreement also established procedures by which nations could seek retribution from other nations that violate the terms of the agreement by raising tariffs or imposing nontariff barriers (Article XXIII). These principles certainly represent a general endorsement of the principles of free trade.[6]

However, if we wish to deduce why countries restrict trade, it is even more important to understand the "exceptions" to the foregoing principles. The "Escape Clause" (Article XIX) allows nations to withdraw previous tariff concessions, or to protect domestic industries, if trade has caused, or threatens to cause, "substantial damage" to domestic producers. Moreover, the prohibitions on quotas or export subsidies have numerous exceptions, including (1) primary (or agricultural) products, reflecting the propensity of industrialized nations to subsidize domestic agricultural production; (2) the national security clause (Article XI), which permits trade restrictions for military (security) reasons; (3) the rebate of indirect (but not direct) taxes on export goods, which allows nations that use these indirect taxes (such as the value-added tax, commonly used in Europe) to subsidize exports; and (4) the use of trade restrictions to correct "balance-of-payments" deficits. These (and other) exceptions provide sufficient loopholes to allow nations to use protective policies whenever they so desire.

Furthermore, little can be done to punish nations that violate the terms of the GATT. Often, a nation will negotiate a voluntary export restraint (VER) with some foreign government. Under the terms of these agreements, the domestic nation pressures foreign exporters to reduce exports "voluntarily"; in a sense, foreigners agree to impose an export quota on goods bound for the domestic market. [7] Pressure is frequently exerted by the threat of heavy import tariffs or quotas. While these restraints, which protect domestic industries, may seem consistent with the GATT's "escape clause," they are not because (1) they can be imposed without proof that substantial damage has been done to the domestic industry as a result of prior trade concessions and (2) the restraints do not apply equally to all foreign suppliers, a violation of the MFN clause.

While the use of voluntary export restraints has increased, they are not a recent innovation; the United States negotiated a "voluntary" limit on Japanese textile exports to the United States in the 1930s. In the early 1960s the United States threatened to invoke the national security clause as a rationale for protecting domestic textile firms and thereby induced foreign exporters to accept (country-specific) export restraints. This so-called Long-Term Agreement, principally covering cotton products, was replaced in 1973 by the Multi-Fibre Agreement (MFA), which extended protection to textile goods produced with synthetic, as well as natural, fibers.

Recent U. S. trade restrictions include quotas on sugar and petroleum imports, restrictions ("orderly marketing agreements") on color TV imports, "voluntary limits" on Japanese car exports to the United States and similar limits on U. S. steel imports (as well as a "Trigger price mechanism," [8] which imposes an automatic tariff if the price of imported steel is "too" low). Nor is the United States the only villain in utilizing nontariff barriers; the U. S. "voluntary restraints" of the early 1980s limited Japanese car exports to the United States to 1. 68 million (then, about 20% of the U. S. market), while similar restraints in France limited Japanese imports to 3% of the market, and in Italy to 3,000 cars.

Rest assured that the foregoing does not represent all the trade restrictions used by countries. Other types of NTBs include government procurement policies (such as the "Buy American" policies followed by the federal and many state and local governments), export subsidies (such as low interest loans for exports to foreign buyers), and border tax adjustment policies (adding domestic taxes to the cost of imports). Despite the GATT agreements, the ability of governments to restrict trade is essentially unlimited.

Walter Enders and Harvey E. Lapan, *International Economics* © 1987, pp. 158-161. Reprinted by permission of Prentice-Hall, Inc., Englewood Cliffs, New Jersey.

Key Terms and Concepts

nontariff barriers   barriers besides tariff barriers (tax or duty), such as quotas or quantitative restrictions as well as other regulations concerning import of goods.

Great Depression   Economies have proven themselves subject to regularly recurring periods of slump and recovery, which culminated in 1930's and were called "the Great Depression". Depression is one of a sequence in the business cycle. The sequential three include recovery, prosperity, and recession.

orderly marketing agreement   agreement with clauses of certain kind of limitation so that importing country can well restrict exporting country.

antidumping codes   regulations against selling goods at lower prices in a foreign country than in the home country.

Escape Clause   refers to the Article XIX in General Agreement on Tariffs and Trade. It conditionally allows a country to protect domestic industries and withdraw previous regulations on tariffs.

value-added tax   Value of goods beyond certain amount will be taxed.

balance-of-payment   a summary for a country. It records all economic transactions between this country and the rest of the world for a given period of time.

buy American   a slogan to call on American people to buy goods made in U.S.A. so as to promote domestic employment.

NOTES

1. Tariff rates calculated as total import duties divided by value of imports subject to duty (tariffs). 关税比率的计算方法是用进口关税总额除以应付税的进口产品的总价值。

2. This "neoprotectionism" is not manifested in higher tariffs, but rather in

142

terms of nontariff barriers,... 这种"新保护主义"不表现在高的关税，而是用无关税壁垒,……

3. General Agreement on Tariffs and Trade（the GATT） 关税及贸易总协定

4. signatory nations 签约国

5. the most favored nation（MFN） 贸易最惠国

6. a general endorsement of the principles of free trade 对自由贸易原则的普遍赞同

7. ...in a sense, foreigners agree to impose an export quota on goods bound for the domestic market. ……这意味着出口国同意接受对输入到进口国的货物实行的（出口）定额。

8. "Trigger price mechanism." "价格机制的启动键"

Foreign Direct Investment

Foreign direct investment data are the most widely used indicators of multinational enterprise activity. In concept, direct investment relates to financial flows accompanied by managerial involvement and effective control. [1] Since "effective" control is sometimes difficult to determine, the various countries have adopted quantitative criteria from which control is inferred. The United States, for example, defined direct investment as an ownership interest in foreign enterprises of at least 10 percent. Individual country practices diverge, however, using minimum percentages of ownership ranging from 5 percent to 50 percent.

On a global basis, the estimated book value of foreign direct investment was a minimum of U.S. $412 billion at the end of 1978. Book value estimates, however, substantially underestimate current values. They are cumulative totals of historical cost at the time the investment was made. They have not been adjusted for the effects of appreciation in values and inflation since the investment was made.

Also, the global estimate does not include a number of countries for which data are not available. The missing countries include the USSR and other East European nations. In 1976, according to one source, these socialist countries had an estimated 700 manufacturing and trading firms in foreign countries. The oil-exporting developing countries have recently begun to make major direct investments in foreign countries but the governments have not made investment data available. In 1980 the government of Kuwait acquired a 10 percent interest in Volkswagen do Brazil. Kuwait also purchased a 14 percent interest in Daimler-Benz, the West German maker of Mercedes automobiles, and more than 25 percent of Korf-Stahl, a German steelmaker.

A number of developing countries have been spawning their own multinationals and exporting investment capital, mainly to other developing countries. Firms in Brazil, Hong Kong, India, Mexico, the Philippines, and Korea are among those that have gone multinational.[2] Again, data are not available for including these direct investments in our global estimate.

The leading home-base country[3] for the multinationals in 1978 was still the United States, with 41 percent of total foreign direct investment. The United Kingdom was next with about 12 percent. Other important home countries are West Germany, Japan, Switzerland, the Netherlands, Canada, the Benelux countries, and Sweden. Switzerland is a special case because many firms from other countries use Switzerland for tax and secrecy reasons as a conduit through which investment outflows are channeled.[4] Thus the data reflect much more activity than that of truly Swiss firms.

How fast is multinational foreign investment increasing? The quality of the data do not permit a precise answer. The U. S. data are probably the most reliable, making adjustments for divestments overseas as well as expansions. In the case of the United States, the direct investment position abroad[5] has expanded at an annual average growth rate of 10 percent over the 30-year period from 1950 to 1980. Over the last decade, with greatly accelerated rates of direct investment by non-U. S. firms — particularly Japanese and German — the overall growth rate has probably approximated 15 percent annually.

Stefan H. Robock and Kenneth Simmonds, *International Business and Multinational Enterprises* 3rd ed. © 1983, pp. 23-25. Reprinted by permission of Richard D. Irwin, Inc. , Homewood, Illinois.

Key Terms and Concepts

multinational enterprise conglomerate with business in many countries.
book value tangible net worth.
oil-exporting developing countries   wealthy countries of Organization of

Petroleum Exporting Countries, in terms of income per capita. Kuwait is one of them.

Volkswagen   name of an automobile company in Germany. This company is the partner of two joint ventures in China. One is making "Santana" in Shanghai, and the other, "Golf" and "Jetta" in Changchun.

Daimler-Benz   German automobile manufacturer producing Mercedes Benz automobiles. It was the product of a merger between two German automobile manufacturers, Benz et Cie and Daimler Motoren Gesellschaft, in 1926.

Mercedes automobiles   Mercedes Benz automobiles. Mercedes Benz is a brand name of car. It is more popular in China to call it "Benz".

Korf-Stahl   name of a steel company.

divestment   withdrawal of investment.

NOTES

1. In concept, direct investment relates to financial flows accompanied by managerial involvement and effective control.　从概念上讲,直接投资与财务管理和有效的财务方面的控制密切相关。

2. ...among those that have gone multinational.　……也在这些进行多国经营的企业之中。

3. The leading home-base country...　处于领导地位的以自己国家为基地的国家……

4. ...as a conduit through which investment outflows are channeled.　……作为投资向外流动的渠道。

5. the direct investment position abroad　对外直接投资的情况

Suggestions for Further Study

Students in China spend a lot of time learning English. The period of time could be as long as sixteen to twenty years. When students graduate and leave campus, what will they do with English? Of all the possibilities, translation could be a realistic task in future business.

Till now, few people have recognized that translation is a task that requires creativity. The debates about whether translation is science or art have lasted for decades. Some say translation is science, others say translation is art. Putting people's endless debates aside, translation itself is at least some thing that needs artistic creativity, or it will not be accurate and vivid.

There are quite a few rules a translator has to follow, otherwise his translation would not be lucid. Nineteen cases of translation are presented in the Appendix I of this textbook. They can help students to solve most of the common problems in translation. Please read them carefully.

Key Words Translation

APPENDIX A
READINGS IN ECONOMICS AND
MANAGEMENT

Reading is always a very important tool for students learning English. It helps them to improve their listening, writing, and speaking, though not directly. Through reading, students build their vocabulary, nourish their knowledge, and at the same time, little by little, recognize and catch the sense and soul of English language.

The Objectives of Firms in Economics

Economists assume that the principle objective of business firms is to maximize profits. This profit maximizing assumption is useful in analyzing behavior in business enterprises. Economists can easily analyze price and output decisions in firms when profit maximizing behavior is assumed.

The profit maximizing assumption is appealing to economists because it adequately explains the motivation of entrepreneurs and business managers. The entrepreneur's drive for profits will ensure that economic resources are continuously earmarked for activities where such employment is rewarded. Profits reward the entrepreneur for organizing production, making appropriate business decisions, introducing innovations, and assuming risks.

The precedence for using the maximization principle was set forth by Jeremy Bentham during the late 18th and early 19th centuries. Bentham was concerned with maxima and minima of pleasure and pain resulting from alternative actions. Indeed, Bentham employed the words "maximize" and "minimize" in his writings. This utilization of the maxima is the forerunner to the maximization principle used in economics. In economics, the maximization principle is used to analyze the behavior of business firms, consumers, and entire societies.

Augustine Cournot is the first economist to systematically set forth the maximization principle as it applies to the theory of the firm. Cournot's

Researches into the Mathematical Principle of the Theory of Wealth written in 1838 developed an almost completed theory of the firm operating in various types of markets. Cournot identified conditions where price declined and output increased, as the number of sellers increased.

Cournot's mathematical and diagrammatical presentation of his theory of the firm drove away many readers. His theory was not touched until the work of Alfred Marshall. Marshall's *Principles of Economics* written in 1890 went through eight editions during his lifetime. Marshall's book contained understandable discussions of many of the basics presented by Cournot. Marshall also added discussions of the representative firm, fixed costs and variable costs, and increasing, decreasing, and constant cost industries to his analysis.

Edward H. Chamberlin's *The Theory of Monopolistic Competition* in 1933 and Joan Robinson's *Economics of Imperfect Competition* in the same year analyzed market types between competition and monopoly. Indeed, Chamberlin's depiction of market situations was adopted in economics textbooks. The presentation of marginal revenue and marginal cost permeated Robinson's work. Other economists have also contributed to the analysis of profit maximizing behavior in firms.

Profit Maximizing Behavior

The objective of firms operating under purely competitive conditions is to maximize profits. The profit maximizing price and output levels are easily determined in this market structure. In pure competition, there are a very large number of firms in the industry. These firms produce a homogeneous or standardized product with no qualitative differences in output produced.

In the purely competitive model, firms can freely enter or exit the industry. There are no artificial barriers to prohibit firms from entering the industry and producing output. There are few industries that approach the competitive model. Notwithstanding, agriculture in the United States closely approximates the purely competitive situation.

Profit maximizing price and output level in the competitive model are used as a benchmark to compare both real world results and outcomes in other market structures. The profit maximizing price in the competitive model is always lower than in other market situations. The profit maximizing level of

148

output is always greater than in alternative market structures.

The purely competitive situation is the most widely analyzed model because it is considered an ideal market structure. Only in this market can people see a situation with both allocation efficiency and productive efficiency. Allocation efficiency notes that only those goods desired by consumers in the market are produced. This desirability is measured in terms of consumers' willingness to spend money for the output produced. Productive efficiency notes that output is produced in the least costly way. The cheapest means of producing output is utilized which economizes on the use of scarce economic resources.

The profit maximizing objective is also applicable for firms operating in other types of market structures: monopolistic competition, oligopoly, and pure monopoly. In monopolistic competition, there are many firms that are producing a differentiated product. Differentiated products are goods that have real or imaginary differences.

Real product differences are those based on the physical attributes of goods. Imaginary differences are created in the minds of consumers via advertising or sales promotions. Differentiation can also be based on conditions of sales such as a favorable location of the firm. Entry into monopolistic competitive industries by entrepreneurs is relatively easy.

In oligopoly, there are a small number of relatively large firms in the industry. These firms produce either a standardized or differentiated product. Entry into the industry is difficult. This is the case because entering firms must produce a large output to realize the lowest per unit cost. In the case of a differentiated oligopoly, financial resources are needed both to develop and promote a differentiated product.

There is only one firm in pure monopoly and entry into the industry is blocked. Monopolies exist because government grants to a single firm the exclusive right to produce the output. The output produced by the monopolist is unique because there are generally no closely substitutable products available. Monopoly is the polar extreme to pure competition.

An Illustration

Profit maximizing price and output levels can be determined using a total revenue and total cost approach. Total revenue is a price times quantity relationship.

It is the number of goods sold multiplied by the selling price. Total cost is also a price times quantity relationship. It is determined by multiplying the number of goods produced by the cost of producing the units. Firms will maximize profits when the difference between total revenue and total cost is the greatest. Hence, firms will attempt to make total revenue as large as possible while keeping total cost at a minimum.

Profit maximizing behavior of firms can also be determined using the marginal revenue equals marginal cost approach. Marginal cost is the change in total cost associated with producing one more or one less unit of output. Marginal revenue is the change in total revenue which results when output is increased or reduced by one unit. Marginal revenue equals marginal cost is the most useful approach for firms to determine the profit maximizing level of output. This is the case because firms have direct control over changes in output produced.

The equality of marginal revenue and marginal cost for profit maximization is applicable under each market structure. In all market situations, firms will find it profitable to produce successive units of a product as long as the output produced adds more to revenue than to cost. At the profit maximizing level, the output produced adds the same amount to both the firm's revenue and cost.

For the purpose of illustration, assume a firm can produce 10 bicycles at a total cost of US $2000. The firm is capable of expanding production to 11 bicycles at a cost of US $2500. If production is further expanded to 12 bicycles, the total cost increases to US $2800. Thus, to increase production an additional unit — from 10 to 11 bicycles — the increase in total cost is US $500. The marginal cost for the 11th bicycles is the US $500 additional cost. The marginal cost of increasing output from 11 to 12 bicycles is US $300.

If the selling price for bicycles is US $300 each, the total revenue for selling 10 units is US $3000. Eleven bicycles will generate a total revenue of US $3300 and twelve bicycles US $3600 in revenue. The marginal revenue from increasing the number of bicycles sold from 10 to 11 units is US $300. The marginal revenue is also US $300 when the number of bicycles sold increases from 11 to 12 units.

The profit maximizing level of output is 12 bicycles where marginal cost = marginal revenue = US $300. Thus, producing the 12th bicycle adds US $300 to the firm's cost and the same amount to its revenue.

150

Other Firm Objectives

The assumption that firms will seek to maximize profits is a useful first approximation. However, business managers may pursue objectives other than profit maximization. Managers may attempt to maximize their own utility which includes the amount of leisure they are able to consume. Managers may be more interested in being good corporate citizens in the community than with maximizing profits.

Managers, instead of maximizing profits, may be more interested in maintaining employment at existing levels. The concern for employment may be the result of managers attempting to create positive images for both the company and its products. Moreover, managers may also be reluctant to layoff people which may be necessary to maximize profits. The reluctance to layoff workers may be to avoid any strong negative reactions from the public and government.

Managers may be more interested in maximizing the growth of the firm or increasing market share which may conflict with profit maximization. Business managers may focus more attention on increasing their salaries or the size of their staff. These and other interests may lead managers to pursue activities that do not maximize profits.

In the United States, corporate managers may not diligently pursue profit maximizing behavior because there is a separation of ownership and control. Stockholders own the corporations but managers exercise control over the operation of the firms. In following behaviors that do not maximize profits, managers are pursuing objectives that are not in the best interest of the stockholders. Stockholders are interested in maximizing the return on their investment in the corporation.

Managers are constrained in the extent to which they pursue strategies that do not maximize profits. These behavioral constraints include board of directors which monitor performance outcomes of firms. There are also capital markets that may impede the borrowing ability of firms that are not profitable. Stockholders may voice dissatisfaction when the return on their investments is not maximized. Also, competitive pressures from rival firms in the industry may force managers to pursue profit maximizing behavior. It may become necessary for firms to pursue cost cutting strategies to remain competitive.

The Role of Government

The most efficient way for firms to pursue profit maximizing behavior is to respond to market forces. Notwithstanding, government may assist firms in developing profit maximizing behavior. Government can attempt to set the myriad of prices that competitive markets establish automatically. Plant managers are then told to maximize profits subject to the prices established by the public authorities. Managers would then equate marginal cost of producing some specified output to the price which is established by government.

The advantage of government setting prices is that it is not involved in establishing production goals for managers. However, a significant disadvantage is that government must become involved in the complicated process of determining appropriate prices. Competitive conditions will establish correct market prices quite easily without any involvement on the part of government.

Government may intervene in the economy because of a concern for fairness or a more egalitarian distribution of goods and services in the society. Hence, the government is concerned with maximizing social welfare not profit maximization. Social welfare is concerned with promoting the well-being of individuals in society.

Social welfare can be determined in a variety of ways. It can consists of the sum of the utility or satisfaction level of all individuals in society. Utility depends on the quantity of commodities each individual has to consume. The social welfare may consist of the satisfaction level of a small number of powerful individual in the society. Moreover, the utility level of members of the dominated political party may be the most important consideration in social welfare. However the amount is determined, the attempt by firms to maximize social welfare may conflict with profit maximization.

The assumption that firms will maximize profits is a very useful one in economics. This assumption leads to explainable and predictable behavior on the part of business managers. Also, the profit maximizing assumption leads to predictable price and output results in all types of market structures.

By Christopher Jeffries

Key Terms and Concepts

maximization principle   the attempt by firms to increase total revenue while keeping total cost at its lowest level.

marginal revenue   the change in total revenue resulting from a change in units of output produced.

marginal cost   the change in total cost resulting from a unit change in output produced.

market structure   the organization of an industry that is based on the number of firms in the industry, type of product produced, and entry conditions.

differentiated products   goods that differ from one another based on conditions of sale and real or imaginary differences.

sales promotion   one of the four ways of promotion, the rest three are advertising, personal selling, and publicity.

total cost   an amount that is calculated by multiplying the number of goods sold by the cost of producing the unit.

total revenue   an amount that is determined by multiplying the number of units sold by the selling price.

social welfare   the relative deservedness of individuals and groups in society.

The Maximizing Principle in Economics

The maximizing assumption is a useful first approximation in analyzing economic behavior. This assumption is appealing to economists because it adequately explains the motivation of consumers, firms, and society. Economists assume that consumers are interested in maximizing their utility or satisfaction. In addition, economists assume that business firms are interested in maximizing profits, and society is concerned with maximizing the utility of its members.

Jeremy Bentham's work laid the foundation for the use of the maximizing principle in economics. Bentham established himself as a leading scholar during the late 18th and early 19th centuries. He was principally concerned with maxima and minima of pleasure and pain resulting from alternative actions. Indeed, Bentham employed the words "maximize" and "minimize" in his

153

writings. Bentham's followers used his work as the basis for analyzing maxima positions in the economy.

Maximizing Behavior of Consumers

Hermann H. Gossen, in 1854, was the first to develop a theory of consumption based on the marginal principle. Later, William S. Jevons introduced a new subjective theory of value in 1871. Jevons' book, The Theory of Political Economy, was instrumental in starting the marginal revolution. The marginal revolution is the beginning of modern economic analysis. Carl Menger, also in 1871, wrote a book that presented the marginal principle and subjective value. (Henry William Spiegel, *The Growth of Economic Thought*, 1991, p. 512, 530).

Economists assume that the objective of consumers is to maximize their utility. The consumption of goods and services yields utility or satisfaction to consumers. If it is assumed that utility can be quantified, a consumer will maximize total utility when the ratio of price to marginal utility is the same for all goods consumed. That is, consumers will maximize utility when $MU_a/P_a = MU_b/P_b = \ldots MU_n/P_n$. This is referred to as the "utility maximizing rule".

In the utility maximizing rule, MU represents marginal utility and P is price. Marginal utility is the change in total utility that results from a change in the quantity of the good consumed. That is, marginal utility is the extra or additional satisfaction the consumer receives from a small change in the quantity consumed. The marginal utility is assumed to decline as the individual consumes more units of each good or service.

To illustrate the utility maximizing rule, assume that two goods, Good A and Good B, sell for $2 and $5, respectively. Assume the consumer determines that his marginal utility from consuming 5 units of A is 20 units of satisfaction or "utils," 6 units of A yield 15 utils, and 7 units of A result in 10 units of additional satisfaction. For Good B, consuming 3 units result in 30 utils, 4 units yield 25 utils, and 5 units add 20 units of satisfaction.

In applying the utility maximizing rule, the consumer will consume 7 units of Good A and 4 units of Good B. That is, $MU_a/P_a = 10/2 = 5$ and $MU_b/P_b = 25/5 = 5$. Thus, the extra or marginal utility the consumer gets from spending his last dollar on each of the goods is the same.

The flaw with using the utility maximizing rule is that consumers must know the extra satisfaction they receive from consuming various quantities of different goods. Of course, individuals do not know, or even want to know, the marginal utility of the goods they consume. To circumvent this flaw, the indifference curve and budget line analysis is utilized.

Francis Y. Edgeworth, in 1881, presented the indifference curve in his book, *Mathematical Psychics*. Vilfredo Pareto transformed Edgeworth's indifference curve into one that represents a combination of goods acceptable to the consumer. Today, economists note that the indifference curve shows the various combinations of two goods that leave the consumer with the same amount of utility.

The slope of the indifference curve is the "Marginal Rate of Substitution (MRS)." The Marginal Rate of Substitution is the willingness of the consumer to substitute additional quantities of one good for another. In using the indifference curve analysis, the consumer does not have to know the amount of marginal utility received from consuming various goods. This is a distinct advantage over using the utility maximizing rule.

Enrico Barone, in 1908, devised the budget line or price-ratio line (Henry William Spiegel, *The Growth of Economic Thought*, 1991, p. 525, 526, 557). The budget line shows the various combinations of two goods a consumer can purchase with a specified amount of money income. When considering two goods, Good A and Good B, the slope of the budget line is the ratio of the prices. That is, the ratio of prices is P_a/P_b.

With the budget line and indifference curve, it is possible to determine the equilibrium for the consumer. The consumer will maximize utility by consuming the combination of two goods corresponding to where the budget line is tangent to the indifference curve. Thus, when considering two goods, Good A and Good B, the consumer will maximize utility when the $MRS_{ab} = P_a/P_b$.

Maximizing Behavior of Firms

Augustine Cournot is the first economist to systematically apply the maximizing principle to the theory of the firm. Cournot's book, *Researches into the Mathematical Principle of the Theory of Wealth*, written in 1838, presented a full-fledged theory of the firm operating in various types of market structures. Cournot identified situations that caused price to decline and output to rise, as the number of sellers increased. (Henry William Spiegel, *The Growth of Economic Thought*, 1991, p. 510-511).

Edward H. Chamberlin's *The Theory of Monopolistic Competition* and Joan Robinson's *Economics of Imperfect Competition*, both written in 1933, analyzed market structures between competition and monopoly. Chamberlin's depiction of market structures along a continuum is adopted in economics textbooks. The presentation of marginal revenue and marginal cost permeates Robinson's work. (Henry William Spiegel, *The Growth of Economic Thought*, 1991, p. 579-581).

Economists assume that the objective of entrepreneurs and business firms is to maximize profits. The profit-maximizing assumption is applicable for firms operating in all market structures—perfect competition, monopolistic competition, oligopoly, and monopoly. In all market structures, the profit-maximizing level of output can be determined using the total revenue and total cost approach. Total revenue (TR) is a price times quantity relationship. Total revenue is equal to the number of goods sold multiplied by the selling price.

Total cost (TC) is a unit cost times quantity relationship. Total cost is determined by multiplying the number of goods produced by the cost of producing the units. Firms will maximize profits when the difference between total revenue and total cost is the greatest. Hence, firms will attempt to increase total revenue as much as possible while keeping total cost at a minimum.

The profit-maximizing level of output, in all market structures, can also be determined using the marginal revenue equal marginal cost approach. Marginal cost (MC) is the change in total cost associated with producing one more or one less unit of output. Marginal revenue (MR) is the change in total revenue which results when output is increased or reduced by one unit.

Equating marginal revenue and marginal cost is the most useful approach for determining the firm's profit-maximizing level of output. This approach is desirable because firms have direct control over changes in output produced. Any change in output produced that impacts the revenue and cost equally will be acceptable to the firm.

Marginal Revenue = Marginal Cost Approach

To show the MR = MC approach, assume a bicycle firm can produce 10 units at a total cost of US $2,000. Moreover, the firm is capable of producing 11 bicycles at a total cost of US $2,500 and 12 bicycles at a total cost of US$ 2,800. Thus, for the firm to increase production from 10 to 11 bicycles, the marginal cost is US $500 (US $2,500—US $2,000). The marginal cost of increasing output from 11 to 12 bicycles is US $300 (US $2,800—US $2,500).

If the selling price for bicycles is US $300 each, the total revenue for selling 10 units is US $3,000 (US $300 × 10 units). Eleven bicycles will generate a total revenue of US $3,300 (US $300 × 11 units) and 12 bicycles will result in a revenue of US $3,600 (US $300 × 12 units). The marginal revenue from increasing the number of bicycles sold from 10 to 11 units is US $300 (US $3,300—US $3,000). The marginal revenue is also US $300 when the number of bicycles sold increases from 11 to 12 units (US $3,600— US $3,300).

The profit-maximizing level of output is 12 bicycles. The firm will produce the last unit of output where marginal cost = marginal revenue = US $300. Producing the 12th bicycle adds US $300 to the firm's revenue and an equal amount to its cost.

Maximization in Society

The work of Pareto is influential in welfare economics. Building on the work of F. Y. Edgeworth, Pareto identified a situation where it is impossible to make one individual better off without making another individual worse off. Indeed, Pareto identified an infinite number of these "maximum" positions. In economics, these maximum positions are referred to as Pareto efficient points. Each Pareto efficient point is associated with a different distribution of income.

The locus of Pareto efficient points forms the Contract Curve. From the Contract Curve, a Utility Possibilities Curve (UPC) can be constructed. The Utility Possibilities Curve shows the maximum amount of utility that one individual (group) can attain, given the utility level of another.

A Social Welfare Function (SWF) is assumed to exist in economics. The conventional Social Welfare Function depends on the utility of each member of society. However, the Social Welfare Function can also be constructed based on the preferences of a small group of individuals or, indeed, one person. There is controversy among economists over whether, indeed, a Social Welfare Function really exists. There is also contention over how the Social Welfare Function is actually determined.

From the Social Welfare Function, a set of social indifference curves can be derived. A social indifference curve shows the various combinations of utility for two individuals (groups) that leave the entire society with the same level of total utility. If the utility of any member of society increases, the entire society is assumed to be better off. Social welfare is maximized when the social indifference curve is tangent to the Utility Possibilities Curve. This maximizing position corresponds to a particular distribution of money income in the society.

By Christopher Jeffries

Key Terms and Concepts

utility   the ability of goods and services to yield satisfaction to the consumer.

Jeremy Bentham   the individual whose early work laid the foundation for the use of the maximizing principle in economics.

marginal utility   the change in total utility or satisfaction that results from a change in the quantity of a good consumed.

utils   a terminology in economics used to designate the amount of consumer satisfaction.

budget line   this line shows the various combinations of two goods that can be purchased with a given money income.

indifference curve   the indifference curve shows the various combinations of two goods that yield the same amount of utility to the consumer.

market structure   the organization of an industry based on the number of firms, type of product produced, and entry conditions.

marginal revenue   the change in total revenue resulting from a change in the units sold.

marginal cost   the change in total cost that results from a unit change in output produced.

total revenue   the total revenue is the number of units sold multiplied by the

158

selling price.

total cost this cost is equal to the number of units produced multiplied by the cost of production.

social welfare function how society views the relative deservedness of individuals and groups. The social welfare depends on the utility levels of individuals in the society.

An Introduction to the Theory of Economic Growth

As people throughout the world awake each morning to face a new day, they are under different circumstances. Some live in comfortable homes with many rooms and have more than enough to eat. They are well clothed and healthy, with a reasonable degree of financial security. By contrast, others, and these constitute more than seventy-five percent of the world population, are less fortunate. They may have little or no shelter and an inadequate food supply. Their health is poor. They can not read or write. They are unemployed, and their prospects for a better life are bleak or uncertain. The majority of these people live in countries and regions that modern economists now refer to as developing countries or the Third World. The challenge is to find ways to eradicate these conditions and improve the quality of life of these individuals. One way to meet this challenge is through the promotion and achievement of economic growth and development, particularly in the poor nations of the world.

The pursuit of economic growth and prosperity remains an important goal of almost every nation, rich or poor, developed or underdeveloped. There are two common measures of economic growth. The first is the rate of growth of a nation's gross domestic product (GDP), which tells people how rapidly the economy's total real output of goods and services is increasing. The second is the rate of growth of per-capita real gross domestic product, which, according to many economists, is a better measure of the rate of increase of a nation's standard of living.

Availability and Use of Economic Resources

The achievement of economic growth for any nation depends on the availability of economic resources and efficient use of these resources in the production process. Economists classify economic resources under four basic categories: Land, capital, labor, and entrepreneurial ability. Land refers to all natural resources, all gifts of nature, which are usable in the production process. These include arable land, forests, mineral and oil deposits, and water resources. Capital, or investment goods, refers to all manufactured aids to production, that is, all tools, machinery, equipment, and factory, storage, transportation, and distribution facilities used in producing goods and services and getting them to the ultimate consumer. The process of producing and accumulating capital goods is known as investment. Labor refers to all physical and mental talents of men and women which are usable in producing goods and services. The services of a logger, retail clerk, machinist, teacher, medical doctor, and nuclear physicist, all fall under the general heading of labor. Entrepreneurial ability refers to the ability of the individual to take the special initiative of combining the resources of land, capital and labor in the production of a good or a service. This individual, known as the entrepreneur, becomes the catalyst or the driving force in the production process. He or she assumes the risk of involving time, effort and personal financial assets, and makes the critical decisions to ensure the efficient use of the other resources and the eventual success of the business enterprise.

Different countries have different endowments of these economic resources. Some have more, and others have less. But all nations are compelled to do the best with what they have and to reach out toward other countries to acquire those resources in which they are lacking. By using all their resources efficiently to produce the maximum level of goods and services that their people and others may want, national economies reach what economists refer to as their production possibilities frontiers or their potential aggregate output level. Generally, countries with larger endowments of resources face an easier path toward meeting the challenge of economic growth and development for their people. By contrast, countries with an inadequate endowment of resources have to rely on others to provide an adequate level of goods and services to their population. Countries are encouraged to identify resources in which they may have a comparative advantage relative to other countries. Then, they are to use those resources efficiently to produce goods and services which may be used domestically and by other nations. They then will engage in trade with each other for finished products and for available resources, as well.

Thus, a nation's potential output is directly related to the amount of resources it possesses and the extent to which they are used. At any given point in time, an increase in a nation's output depends on an increase in one or more of its resources or inputs, or in an improvement in the level of technology used along with the inputs in the production process. That means, in other words, for output to increase, either the quantity of land, or labor, or capital must increase, or some improvement in the technology pertaining to the use of each or all the resources is necessary. This is consistent with the traditional neoclassical model of economic growth which assumes a direct relationship between the level of output and the number and quantity of input used in production. How is this increase in the level of resources supposed to take place? Can a nation increase its aggregate output without necessarily increasing its resources? Or, can a nation increase its aggregate output in the face of a decline in one or more inputs?

Resource Productivity

Each resource, through the production process, contributes to the level of aggregate output. The quantity of output that is generated by each unit of an input (or a resource) is called the average product of that input, sometimes referred to as the productivity of that input. By dividing the level of output by number of units of a given variable input used in the production of that output, and, at the same time, assuming that the other inputs are fixed in quantity, people can estimate the average product of an input. Hence, economists estimate the average product of land, the average product of capital, or the average product of labor. As a kind of resource, entrepreneurial ability is with special nature. The productivity of this resource is completely tied with the productivity of the other resources. For this reason, people seldom estimate the average product or productivity of entrepreneurial ability. Another measure of productivity often used by economists is the marginal product of an input. It is defined as the increase in the level of output attributed to the use of an additional unit of an input in the production process. It is estimated by dividing

161

the increase in the quantity of output produced by the increase in the number of a given variable input, assuming that the other inputs are used in fixed quantities.

Expansion of Resources

How is the increase in the level of resources supposed to take place? Let's first consider the case of land. Land is nature's gift to mankind. For the most part, the amount of this resource is fixed. If it is currently fully exploited, it is not likely to be increased under normal circumstances. An increase will require the annexation of new territories as a result of a war, for example, or the discovery of new sources of raw materials.

Now, consider the case of capital. This resource is man-made. Its production, acquisition and expansion may require the use of land and labor resources, and additional financial assets or funds which may not be available to the nation. The prospect of increasing the capital base of a nation has been a primary concern of economists since the days of Adam Smith, David Ricardo and their followers in the classical school of the eighteenth and nineteenth centuries and, later, the neoclassical school of the twentieth century. Edwin Mansfield mentioned Ricardo's idea in his *Economics: Principles, Problems and Decisions*. He wrote that Ricardo warned that while capital formation was important for economic growth, the increase in the capital level must be watched carefully because of the law of diminishing returns in production. According to the law of diminishing returns, the average and marginal product of an input tends to increase at first, then reaches a peak, and eventually starts to fall. Hence, Ricardo further stated that investment in new plant and equipment would increase output up to a point. Beyond that point, further investment in plant and equipment would not increase output at all, because increases in the total amount of capital tended to be accompanied by decreases in the marginal product of capital. After Ricardo, his followers at the neoclassical school, Sir Roy Harrod, Evesey Domar, and Robert Solow, to name a few, explored the role of savings, and capital formation on economic growth. The simple Harrod-Domar model of economic growth states that the rate of growth of a nation's aggregate output is equal to the savings-output ratio divided by the capital-output ratio. That suggests a direct relationship between a nation's savings-output ratio and its rate of economic growth and an inverse relationship between its capital-output ratio and its rate of economic growth. The neoclassical school emphasizes the importance of savings for investment financing and for the promotion of economic growth. This conclusion poses a dilemma for poor nations with very little to save. Underdeveloped nations with inadequate savings are forced to rely on external sources of funds to finance their investment initiatives. The external sources of finance may take the form of direct foreign investment in the private sector, loans from foreign commercial banks, loans from international multilateral or bilateral institutions, or foreign aid from donor nations or agencies.

Finally, consider the case of labor. Increases in the amount of labor available to a nation are a by-product of an increase in that nation's population rate. As population increases, eventually the size of the labor force increases as well, which implies a potential increase in the use of labor as an input in the production process. However, just as in the case of capital, the effect of population on economic growth has been the concern of economists since the beginning of economic literature. The classical work of Thomas Malthus provided a warning, implying the law of diminishing returns pertaining to the use of labor as a variable input in the production process. Given a fixed level of technology and the fact that land is fixed, increases in labor due to population growth, will eventually cause the marginal product of labor to get smaller and smaller, and the growth in the labor force will eventually bring about economic decline.

Among some of the developing countries of the world, Malthus's analysis seems to be relevant today. According to Edwin Mansfield, during the past forty years, the population of the less developed nations has grown very rapidly in part because of the decrease in death rates attributable to the recent advancement in medicine. "Between 1940 and 1970, the population of Asia, Africa, and Oceania almost doubled. There has been a tendency for growing population to push hard against supplies in some of the countries of Africa, Latin America, and Asia (Edwin Mansfield, 1992)." In response to population pressures, many countries throughout the world have implemented a series of population control measures, including incentives to families to reduce birth rates and family size.

Can a nation increase its output without increasing one or more of its inputs? Or can a nation increase its output while experiencing a decline in one or more input? An affirmative answer to the above questions depends on one important factor in the production process: the level of technology or the degree to which the current level of technology can be improved. By definition, technology refers to the body of knowledge that can be used to produce goods and services from economic resources. At a given point in time, an improvement in technology will allow a nation to adopt the optimal combination of resources to produce a desired level of output, or to achieve a growth in its level of output. An improvement in labor technology will lead to an increase in the productivity of labor, allowing each worker to contribute more to total output. The same is true for an improvement in capital technology. An improvement in capital technology will allow for more output to be derived from each piece of machinery used in the production process.

Currently, the majority of the nations in the world, developed or underdeveloped, are investing considerable amount of their national budgets in the promotion or development of appropriate technologies to enhance their level of economic growth and to enable them to compete with other nations in the production and distribution of a variety of capital and consumer goods, ranging from computers and electronics, automobiles, air transport equipment, military weapons, agricultural equipment and machinery, etc... The wealthiest nations of the world also spend billions of dollars annually in research aimed at the development of new, faster, and more efficient technology which will reduce the cost of production in the industrial, agricultural, and other sectors, and improve productivity at all levels.

By Jean-Claude Assad

Key Terms and Concepts

economic growth   a percentage change in a nation's annual aggregate output which is measured by the nation's gross domestic product (GDP).

economic resource   any resource, human or material used in the production of goods and services. Economic resources are classified as land, capital, labor, and entreprepreneurial ability.

input   an economic resources, something used to produce an output.

resource productivity   the amount of output generated from the use of one unit of a resource or input. It may refer to the average product of the marginal

164

product of the resource. The average product is estimated by the ratio of the quantity of output produced divided by the quantity of inputs used in production. The marginal product is estimated by the ratio of the change in total output produced over the change in the input used in the production process.

capital-output ratio   the monetary value of a nation's capital resources divided by the monetary value of its aggregate output or gross domestic product (GDP).

less developed nations   nations characterized by a lack of capital goods, intensive-labor technology, high unemployment, low literacy rates, etc... They are also referred to as developing or underdeveloped nations.

Taxation in Western Economics

To compete in the global economy, business professionals must understand not only the private market forces that shape economic activity, but also the business climate of different countries. National and provincial governments strongly influence the business climate of countries through the regulatory practices and systems of taxation that they impose. The discussion below provides a conceptual framework for understanding and comparing the tax systems of different countries.

To meet their public responsibilities, governments must own or acquire the services of economic resources—land, labor, and capital. Although in rare circumstances governments may take control of resources directly through mandate or expropriation, a critical aspect of economic policy in western societies is the choice of how to fund public-sector activity. While governments may charge user fees for some activities or borrow to fund others, the most important source of funds for governments is taxation.

To enhance our understanding of taxation in western economies, we ask the following questions. What philosophies or principles direct tax policy in western economies? What economic measures are subject to tax? How are these bases taxed? How are tax policies evaluated? How do tax systems differ among western economies?

Principles of Taxation

What philosophies or principles direct tax policy in western economies? Two complementary perspectives underpin the design of tax policy: the benefit principle and the ability-to-pay principle.

The benefit principle of taxation emulates the invisible hand of the free market. It states that those who benefit from the provision of a good or service should pay to support it. Under the benefit principle, therefore, those citizens who use a government service should pay taxes to support its provision. For example, rather than charging tolls on many public highways, the government may tax gasoline and use the tax revenues to fund the building and maintenance of roads.

The ability-to-pay principle suggests that those citizens who have the greater ability to pay taxes should pay higher taxes. Because income and wealth may be considered appropriate measures of ability to pay, personal income taxes and estate (inheritance) taxes are consistent with this principle. Consumption is also a measure of ability to pay. Those who consume more goods and services produced by the economy have a greater capacity to pay taxes as well.

Tax Bases and Tax Instruments

What economic measures are subject to tax? How are these bases taxed? In designing a tax policy, the "tax base" is the item or economic activity that is subject to tax. The "tax instrument" is the type of tax that is used to extract revenue from the tax base. In the benefit tax example above, the number of gallons of gasoline purchased by a driver is the tax base. The instrument is the gasoline excise tax. The tax rate is the amount of tax levied per gallon purchased.

Economists often categorize tax bases as follows: income, consumption, and wealth. Examples of instruments that tax various types of income include the following: personal income taxes, wage or payroll taxes, and profit (or corporate income) taxes. Sales taxes, value-added taxes, expenditure taxes and selective excise taxes tax different measures of consumption. Net worth taxes, property taxes, and estate (inheritance) taxes tax forms of wealth.

166

Criteria for Evaluating Tax Systems

How are tax policies evaluated? What constitutes a "good" tax system? How can we tell whether a tax system is good or bad, and, if bad, how to fix it?

Whether a tax system is desirable or not depends upon what we want the tax system to do or not to do in our society. Western economists often evaluate tax systems using some or all of the following criteria: efficiency, equity, revenue yield, administrative ease, and compliance cost.

EFFICIENCY. History has demonstrated that market economies are among the most efficient economic systems in the world. Market prices signal simultaneously both consumer demands and resource scarcity. In balancing the two, markets allocate resources efficiently to those activities that consumers value most. All participants in markets have an incentive to respond to the signals. Consumers have an incentive to allocate their budgets prudently based on the market prices and to conserve where prices are high. Households have an incentive to offer more labor services if wage rates are high. Producers have a profit incentive to supply more goods and services in markets where prices are high and to conserve resources where input prices are high. Taxes, however, often hurt economic efficiency because taxes often reduce incentives and distort price signals. Income taxes, for example, can reduce incentives to work and to save. Excise taxes can substantially increase the gross price of a good or service and reduce its consumption. Both harm economic efficiency.

Taxes can have wide-ranging effects on an economy's efficiency. Taxes that are least harmful to economic efficiency typically minimize adverse effects on incentives and distortions to price signals, or are imposed on commodities that are inelastic in demand or supply. For example, broad-based taxes can raise substantial revenue with very low tax rates, minimizing distortions to price signals and adverse effects on incentives. Also, taxes on goods that are inelastic in demand or supply do not alter market resource allocation and, therefore, have minimal effects on economic efficiency. Similarly, by mimicking the signals and incentives of the market economy, taxes carefully designed to implement the benefit principle are often efficient taxes. A few taxes actually can increase economic efficiency. Such corrective taxes are imposed intentionally to discourage undesirable behavior. Taxes on pollution, for example, enhance economic efficiency by intentionally raising the cost of polluting and thereby providing a disincentive to emit pollutants.

EQUITY. Society's values govern whether or not a tax is viewed as "equitable" (fair). Basic considerations include horizontal and vertical equity. A tax is horizontally equitable if citizens in equal circumstances are treated equally for tax purposes. Following the principle of ability to pay, a tax is vertically equitable if those with greater ability to pay taxes do, indeed, pay higher taxes.

Often the question of vertical equity is explored by asking whether a tax is progressive, proportional, or regressive in its effects on different income groups. A progressive tax takes a greater share of income from higher income groups. A proportional tax takes the same percentage of income from all income classes. A regressive tax takes a greater share of income from lower income groups. In assessing vertical equity, researchers are careful to discern whether the market shifts the tax and, if so, to whom. For example, in the United States, both federal and state governments levy substantial excise taxes against cigarettes, in part for revenue and in part to deter smoking and its associated medical risks. Cigarette manufacturers must pay the taxes, which increase their effective marginal cost of selling each pack. Because the demand for cigarettes is highly price inelastic, the tax is passed forward to consumers in the form of higher gross market prices. Because the demand for cigarettes is income inelastic, lower income households bear a disproportionate share of the increase, resulting in a regressive tax.

REVENUE YIELD. If the purpose of the tax is to provide revenue, then the amount of revenue provided by the tax is an important consideration. Broad-based taxes, such as the personal income tax, value-added tax, and general sales tax, provide substantial revenue and can be designed to minimize loss of efficiency and collection costs. For these reasons, many western economies make substantial use of these tax instruments.

ADMINISTRATIVE EASE. To provide substantial net revenue for the government, the tax must be relatively inexpensive to administer and to enforce. Tax laws should avoid substantial collection costs, opportunities for tax evasion, and potential for judicial challenges.

COMPLIANCE COST. The true costs of the tax system include not only the revenue collected and loss of economic efficiency, but also the costs to society of complying with the tax laws. Public support for government is higher if people understand the tax laws and can comply with them simply. For example, businesses in the United States administer general retail sales taxes by collecting from consumers a flat percentage of tax per dollar of retail sales and sending the proceeds to the government. Such taxes are relatively easy for citizens and businesses to understand and meet. In contrast, the income tax system in the United States has come under severe criticism by citizens and politicians because of its complexity and high costs of compliance. Many citizens and businesses hire tax experts to determine the amounts of income tax due and to complete the voluminous tax forms.

TRADE-OFFS. In designing a tax system, policy makers must often trade off one criterion against another. For example, excise taxes levied against goods with inelastic demand distort economic efficiency the least, yet are often highly regressive. Government could tax medicine or food, both of which are inelastic in demand, but the tax would fall heavily on the poorest members of society. Many would judge such taxes as unfair and unacceptable despite the efficiency of the tax policy. Alternatively, progressive taxes on personal income may be viewed by some as highly equitable, but economic research has raised serious questions about efficiency losses due to adverse effects on incentives. For these reasons, the design of tax systems will always be a political question because of different opinions about the importance of alternative characteristics or criteria of tax instruments.

Tax System of Western Economies

How do tax systems differ among western economies? The Organization for Economic Co-operation and Development (OECD) publishes Revenue Statistics, which provides historical and comparative data for Western tax systems. The perspectives below are based on data from the 1998 edition.

How large are the tax burdens in different economies? In 1996 (OECD, Table 3, p. 79), total tax revenue as a percentage of GDP ranges from 52% in Denmark and Sweden to 16% in Mexico. For the largest economies, the percentages are 28.5% for the United States, 28.4% for Japan, 38.1% for Germany, 45.7% for France, and 36% for the United Kingdom. In general, taxes as a percentage of GDP tend to be lower in OECD America (Canada, Mexico, and U.S.) and OECD Pacific than in OECD Europe.

Which tax bases are taxed most heavily in different economies? In 1996 (OECD, Table 7, p. 81), income and profits taxes were the dominant form of taxation in the United States, Japan, Canada, UK, Scandinavian countries, New Zealand and Australia. In Greece, Hungary, Korea, Mexico, and Portugal, taxes on goods and services (sales and value-added taxes) were dominant. Social security and payroll taxes were important in countries such as Austria, France, Germany, Italy, Japan, and Spain. Taxes on property were less than 14% of revenue in all OECD countries.

Summary

While all governments levy taxes, their tax systems serve different social objectives and have different effects on the economies they serve. Some taxes are levied on those who benefit from a specific government activity, and the revenues from such taxes support the activity. Other taxes are levied against ability to pay in the form of income and profits, wages or payroll, consumption of goods and services, or wealth. Criteria such as revenue yield, equity, economic efficiency, and administrative and compliance costs govern decisions about the mix of tax instruments used in tax systems. Because different societies and political organizations value these objectives differently, the nature of the tax system is political. Most OECD economies, like most developed economies, rely heavily on broad-based taxes such as income taxes, value-added taxes, and sales taxes for revenue. Extensive social insurance funds in some countries increase reliance on social security and payroll taxes. Property and wealth taxes are generally small in relation to other taxes. Overall tax burdens range from 15% to 50% of GDP in OECD countries. In OECD Europe, tax burdens typically range from 35% to 50% of GDP. Tax burdens are typically less than 35% of GDP in OECD Pacific and OECD America.

Taxes are an important aspect of a nation's business climate. Foreign investors and international firms find it important to understand the tax systems of prospective countries. By understanding the underlying philosophies and structures of taxation, business professionals can evaluate the business climates of prospective markets or production sites and, thereby, develop sound business strategies for their firms.

By Donald Elliott

Key Terms and Concepts

ability-to-pay principle of taxation   those citizens who have the greatest ability to pay taxes should pay higher taxes.

benefit principle of taxation   those who benefit from the provision of a good or service should pay to support it.

tax base   an item or economic activity that is subject to tax. Examples of tax bases include measures of consumption, income, or wealth.

tax instrument   the type of tax used to extract revenue from the tax base. Examples include the personal income tax, corporate income tax, excise tax, value-added tax (VAT), general sales tax, property tax, wage tax, and inheritance tax.

tax rate   a ratio expressing the relationship between the tax obligation and the tax base.

efficiency   refers to Pareto's theory of the optimal state of the economy in which no one can be made better off without making someone else worse off.

equity   fairness.

Organization for Economic Co-operation and Development (OECD)
according to the convention originally signed in Paris in 1960, the OECD promotes policies designed to achieve economic growth, employment, and financial stability and to expand world trade. Original signatories include Austria, Belgium, Canada, Denmark, France, Germany, Greece, Iceland, Ireland, Italy, Luxembourg, the Netherlands, Norway, Portugal, Spain, Sweden, Switzerland, Turkey, the United Kingdom, and the United States. Subsequent additional members include Japan, Finland, Australia, New Zealand, Mexico, the Czech Republic, Hungary, Poland, and Korea.

social insurance   government-provided pensions, disability payments, unemployment compensation, and health benefits to buffer citizens against economic loss.

Application of Probability Concepts
in Decision Making

The word probability is quite often used in daily conversations by academicians who hold terminal degrees in statistics and those who have little or no formal training in the subject. No matter who uses the word, it invariably amounts to people referring to the chance or likelihood that a future event will occur. In most cases, a mental estimation is made, and decisions are made based on such estimates. In business decision making, one needs to be more formal, and numerical estimates of probability are required. Since all business decisions impact future events, a working knowledge of probability concepts is essential for effective decision making.

Two Basic Properties of Probability

(1) The probability that a future event A occurs is always between zero and one.

$$0 \leqslant P(A) \leqslant 1$$

An event that is certain to occur has a probability of one (1) while an event that cannot occur is assigned a probability of zero (0).

(2) The sum of the probabilities of all final outcomes for an experiment must equal one (1).

Three Approaches to Probability

The three conceptual approaches to the study of probability include Classical Probability, Empirical Probability, and Subjective Probability.

(1) Classical Probability

In classical probability we assume that the outcomes of an experiment are equally likely. Therefore, the probability of an event A, is given by

$$P(A) = \text{Number of outcomes favorable to } A/\text{Total}$$
$$\text{number of possible outcomes}$$

Example 1 If we need to know the probability of picking a black card from a deck of 52 cards, we have:

$$P_{(\text{Black Card})} = 26/52 = 0.5$$

172

Example 2   If we need to know the probability of picking a defective item from a shipment of 1000 items containing 4 defects, we have:

$$P_{(Defective)} = 4/1000 = 0.004$$

(2) Empirical Probability

Empirical probability is based on relative frequencies. Probability calculation is based on past data. Where such are unavailable, new data are generated by performing necessary experiments.

$$P(A) = \frac{\text{Number of times event A occurred in the past}}{\text{Total number of observations}}$$

Example 3   The products coming out of an assembly line were examined by quality control staff. Out of 1000 products examined, 2 were defective. What is the probability that an item randomly picked from this assembly line will be defective?

$$P_{(Defective)} = 2/1000 = 0.002$$

(3) Subjective Probability

In subjective probability, we do not make any mathematical calculations. Rather, we assign probability based on opinions, experience, and belief. Opinions of experts such as stock market analysts, economists, and scientists play a major role.

Example 4   If we would like to know the probability that the German soccer team will win the next World Cup, they rely on the opinions of soccer experts, say, coaches, players, and commentators.

Probability Concepts in Everyday Business Decision Making

In this section, we shall limit our discussion to discrete probability distributions. A discrete probability distribution refers to the probability distribution of discrete random variables (variables that can take on only whole numbers, e. g. cars, people, cattle, etc.).

Example 5   Craftman Christopher Jenkins sells bicycles to supplement his meager income at Springfield. Examination of past sales data reveals that Craftman Jenkins sells the largest number of bicycles on Sunday. From this data, he established a probability distribution for the number of bicycles that he expects to sell on any Sunday.

Number of bicycles (x)	Probability $P(x)$
0	0.10
1	0.15
2	0.25
3	0.25
4	0.15
5	0.10
	1.00

We have noticed from this probability distribution that two basic conditions are met:

—the probability of making a sale lies between 0 and 1.

—the sum of probabilities add up to one.

Further, from this probability distribution of Craftman Jenkins' sales performance, insights into two very important questions/decisions can be delineated.

Question 1: On a typical Sunday, how many bicycles can Craftman Jenkins sell?

Question 2: What is the variance in the number of bicycles sold.

To address question one, we need to find the mean number of bicycles sold. The formula for the mean of a discrete probability distribution is:

$$\mu = E(x) = \sum xP(x) \qquad (1)$$

where μ is the mean of the probability distribution which is also referred to as expected value of the random variable, $P(x)$ represents the probability associated with each value of the variable.

Keep in mind that the mean of this random variable represents a value that would, on average, occur if this distribution is generated many times.

Applying formula (1):

x	$P(x)$	$xP(x)$
0	0.10	0.00
1	0.15	0.15
2	0.25	0.50
3	0.25	0.75
4	0.15	0.60
5	0.10	0.50
		2.50 approx. 3

$\mu = E(x) = 3$ (Note that we approximate to 3, since fractional values are

174

not possible in a discrete probability distribution). A value of 3 indicates that, on average, over many Sundays, Craftman Jenkins expects to sell a mean of 3 bicycles.

To address Question 2, we need to find the variance of the distribution in Example 1. The formula for the variance of a probability distribution is given as:

$$\sigma^2 = \sum[(x-\mu)^2 \, P(x)] \qquad (2)$$

This variation in performance is popularly stated in terms of standard deviation which is the square root of the variance.

$$\sigma = \sqrt{\sigma^2}$$

Applying formula (2):

x	$P(x)$	$(x-\mu)2$	$(x-\mu)^2 \, P(x)$
0	.10	$(0-3) = 9$	$9 * .10 = 0.90$
1	.15	$(1-3) = 4$	$4 * .15 = 0.60$
2	.25	$(2-3) = 1$	$1 * .25 = 0.25$
3	.25	$(3-3) = 0$	$0 * .25 = 0.00$
4	.15	$(4-3) = 1$	$1 * .15 = 0.15$
5	.10	$(5-3) = 4$	$4 * .10 = 0.40$
			2.30

$\sigma^2 = 2.30$

Therefore, $\sigma = \sqrt{2.3} \approx 1.5$ approx. 2

How do we interpret a standard deviation of 2 bicycles? This standard deviation implies that, while on average, Craftman Jenkins could sell 3 bicycles per Sunday, his weekly sales performance may vary from as high as 5 bicycles to as low as 1 bicycle on any given Sunday. This is given by:

$$\mu + \sigma = 3 \pm 2 = (5,1)$$

Craftman Jenkins can now review his past performance and make a decision whether to continue this business or not. Secondly, any other Craftman contemplating whether or not to emulate Craftman Jenkins now has some preliminary figures to work with.

By Dal Didia

Key Terms and Concepts

event   a collection of one or more outcomes of an experiment.

discrete probability distribution   probability distribution of a discrete random variable.

discrete random variable   a random variable that can assume only countable values or whole numbers.

experiment   refers to the process of making an observation or taking a measurement.

outcome   a particular result of an experiment.

probability distribution   a listing of the outcomes of an experiment along with the probabilities associated with each outcome.

random variable   a variable that can assume different values in an experiment.

standard deviation   an average measure of the variation or dispersion in a distribution. This is obtained by taking the square root of the variance.

variance   a measure of the variation or dispersion in a distribution that takes the arithmetic mean of the squared deviation of each observation from the mean.

The Learning Organization

Several trends have existed in the field of management. The beginning of the Industrial Revolution brought the implementation of financial incentives (purported by Frederick Taylor) where workers were paid according to their productivity. A business process improvement methodology which incorporates learning organization concepts. In the United States, the Industrial Revolution provided an opportunity for the manufacturing sector to become dominant and more people sought employment in plants. With the involvement of the United States in World War I and World War II, the country was able to build world dominance as a leading manufacturer. However, most companies did not share a high concern for quality in their products. Subsequently, other countries were able to find a niche and developed products that had more durability and reduced failure rates. One such country was Japan.

Total Quality Management

In the late 1970's and 1980's, U. S. companies, in the automobile and electronics industries, started to see dramatic declines in sales because of their inability to compete with products made in other countries. Many American organizations faced extinction unless they incorporated a process that would emphasize quality instead of quantity. The theory of total quality management (TQM) served as a method by which U. S. companies could achieve this goal.

Total quality management, a method supported by Edward Deming, is a process by which a company works toward a level of excellence with regard to its goods and services. As result, these companies began a process by which they changed their structure, goods and services, and production methods in order to reflect an environment whereby organizations achieve a high level of quality. Customers were viewed by TQM companies as driving forces of change. With total quality management, there are internal as well as traditionally external customers. Production processes were developed to subscribe to the needs and wants of the customer. Thus, TQM incorporated a drive to improve quality as well as attend to the customer's product requirements. However, total quality management soon became a buzz word and organizations moved away from this set of techniques to the next phase of quality.

Re-engineering

The next trend in production processes was re-engineering. Re-engineering entails the drive for quality products by an organization's willingness to completely change all of its organizational structure, production processes, and culture. In order to implement re-engineering, an organization must determine its core businesses and build its framework around that core vision. As a result of building the organization around the core business, the organization is able to analyze each part of the business to ensure that quality is maintained in all parts of the company. One problem associated with the implementation of both re-engineering and TQM is that companies view the techniques as fads.

The Learning Organization

Managers have realized that trends alone cannot sustain the organization's survival. One of the present issues for management is how to respond to the variety of complexities within the organization. In order to sustain or improve performance, organizations must create an environment where changing influences such as globalization, workforce diversity, and technology advances will not disturb its progress. The learning organization is a view of the company that can produce this environment. The learning organization was developed by Peter Senge, author of the book, *The Fifth Discipline: The Art and Practice of the Learning Organization*. Senge stated that organizations have to learn how to learn. This is an abstract concept. However, the argument is that if an organization wants to be able to handle the rapid changes that come with doing business, it becomes necessary that the organizational culture be designed to fit environmental complexity. In his widely acclaimed text, Senge discusses five disciplines essential for the learning organization. Those disciplines are as follows:

1. Building a shared vision: the practice of unearthing shared "pictures of the future" that foster genuine commitment.

2. Personal mastery: the skill of continually clarifying and deepening each individual's personal vision.

3. Mental models: the ability to unearth our internal pictures of the world, to analyze them, and to make them open to the influence of others.

4. Team learning: the capacity to "think together" which is gained by mastering the practice of dialogue and discussion.

5. Systems thinking: the discipline that integrates the other disciplines and putting the complete framework into action.

As evident from the above definitions, the learning organization must become skilled at creating, acquiring, and transferring knowledge. The knowledge is then placed into action by employees at all levels of the organization. The primary reason why an organization would go through this process is that it may attain a competitive advantage that will ultimately yield higher levels of performance.

Organizational learning can take place in many forms and it is viewed as a company specific. Senge notes that there are some tools used by employees that will assist in the facilitation of learning. One tool is known as left-hand, right-hand columns. This technique is to be used in meetings. During the meeting, each employee is expected to take notes as he or she normally would. However, the employee would also write notes depicting his or her feelings about the meeting. After he or she leaves the meeting, the employee is asked to review both the meeting notes and the respective feelings. Next, an analysis is made of how those feelings may provide biases that inevitably interfere with the attainment of group or overall company goals.

Another tool used by individuals is the concept of the ladder of inference. This process allows the employee to find causes for his or her behavior. Similar to a behaviorist perspective, it is important in organizational learning that individuals be able to determine how their behaviors affect the ability of the organization to prosper. Although there are some assumptions involved in determining the cause of behavior, this exercise allows the employee to take control over his or her behavior. Consequently, the power of change resides within the individual employee.

A third tool of organizational learning is called the "container". It is used in meetings. In traditional companies, meetings can become complicated because employees include their personal feelings as part of the meeting agenda. Therefore, the meeting takes longer and some goals are not accomplished because of a focus on impertinent issues. The container idea attempts to reduce some of this problem. Using the container, each employee has an imaginary place in which he or she can place his or her negative feelings. These feelings, in other settings, might be vented and disturb the meeting's progress. The container also gives the employee additional time to consider the impact on his or her angry comments on the feelings of others. Senge's perspective is that if given more time, employees might not make angry or fearful comments. Thus, the container reduces the probability that employees will act out of anger or fear.

Another technique used in organizational learning is the causal loop. Harder to implement, the causal loop is the integrative step for employees because it requires that the organization view itself from a systems perspective. Systems thinking requires that an organization consider the effect of one influence on other organizational factors. In a system, an organization's managers, employees, and other resources affect each other. It is essential that an organization give consideration to a systems effect because it indicates the importance of employees across functions working together.

The Implementation of Organizational Learning

As the aforementioned discussion indicates, the implementation of organizational learning is difficult to accomplish. Some scholars have suggested that it is impossible to develop a pure learning organization. As a result, some experts have proposed that organizations should implement those elements of the learning organization that would be most applicable to that entity. To the extent that a company chooses to implement organizational learning, the Institute for Strategic Learning in Illinois denotes some of steps inherent in the strategy.

The first step to becoming a learning organization is to conduct an assessment of the company's current situation. The company must assess what organizational learning properties it currently possesses. This step acknowledges the fact that there are some things that an organization has done correctly. The next step for the organization is to develop an intervention plan whereby the organization searches for areas to which it can ascribe. Once the intervention has been refined, an action plan is put into motion.

Assessment is an analysis of the company's current situation. It is used to provide direction for future planning. However, a side benefit to this assessment is the perception on the part of employees. Typically, assessment involves heavy interaction with all employees in the organization, using interviews and surveys. The message of a traditional assessment is that the organization must change. Therefore, assessment has a positive indirect effect because it symbolizes that the organization is preparing for a change. The next challenge in an organizational learning strategy is to select the manner by which the company is going to use in order to execute the change. There are several areas of focus including overall strategy, organizational culture, organizational structure, and performance management. By determining the areas of focus, companies can assess the level of learning that will be conducted—individual, team, and/or organizational.

The next step in building an organizational learning strategy is to determine initiatives that will address individual or departmental responsibilities. Different groups and individuals are given assignments that will promote learning. One source for building initiatives is through the use of cases. Cases provide a resource for organizations that do not know the steps needed to ensure effective implementation. Using cases enables companies to explore best practices and successful plans of action. Thus, companies can develop intervention plans with fewer errors because of the stories of other companies.

The implementation of an organizational learning initiative is accomplished in several ways. One recommended method is through small pilot initiatives. Caution should be taken when replicating past successes of other companies. Often, the language between two organizational cultures differs. In addition, companies should reflect on instances of triumph within their own boundaries and consider how to build upon the good aspects of the company. More importantly, in addition to implementation, organizations must measure performance.

Any effective strategy implementation should include a basis for assessment to determine an intervention's success. There may be characteristics within an intervention plan that are more conducive to higher levels of productivity. For instance, a company may decide to offer incentives to employees or departments in order to increase the probability that employees or departments will engage in learning. One performance measure would be the amount of financial reward disbursed to employees after a defined time period. The important element to this discussion is that measurement is a key factor to define effectiveness. Often, new organizational development initiatives are created, but no measurement follows. Therefore, each organization must develop and account for its own growth, with respect to its intervention.

The inclusion and participation of all employees is essential for a company to be considered a learning organization. Each organizational member must give commitment and effort to the idea of learning. Each employee must believe that learning is necessary, continuous, and a part of organizational change. The responsibility of management is to develop an environment where learning is possible and encouraged. The premise is that the learning organization implies some experimentation and there may be instances when new processes are attempted and fail. If management reacts badly to the "failures", employees will know that the organization's commitment is not present and consequently, the effort to engage in learning will not survive. Senge notes that organizational learning is an idea or a vision and it is the organization that defines the action taken. Therefore, each company engaged in organizational learning must go through a process of defining and enacting a vision of the learning organization appropriate for their objectives.

By Alisa Mosley

Key Terms and Concepts

Industrial Revolution   it refers to a period of history in the United States that symbolizes a transition from agriculture to manufacturing.

organization   a group of people brought together in a structured manner to accomplish a purpose.

re-engineering   refers to a radical redesign of all or part of a company's work processes to improve productivity and financial performance.

learning organization   refers to an entity that focuses on its ability to adapt to change and to involve its members in individual and collective learning.

total quality management   refers to a process by which organizations review and modify their businesses in order to achieve a zero-defect environment.

The Goal of Financial Management

In America, shareholders represent owners of a corporation and the managers are hired employees. The shareholders invested their money in the company for a financial return. Therefore, managers are hired to maximize the shareholders wealth. In order to accomplish this goal, the managers play important roles in the areas of capital budgeting, working capital management, financial structure, and dividend policy. This section discusses the following issues involving the maximization of shareholder wealth: (1) measure and rationale of shareholder wealth maximization, (2) deficiencies of profit maximization as a goal, (3) agency problems, and (4) corporate wealth maximization as an alternative goal.

Measure and Rationale of Shareholder Wealth Maximization

In principle, the shareholder wealth is measured by the value of stock that represents the fundamental economic value of a company's common stock. There are several ways to measure the value of stock. Dividend valuation models are most frequently used. The dividend valuation models calculate the present value of an expected stream of future dividends as the proxy value of stock. It is based on the belief that the distribution of earnings in the form of cash dividend payments is the ultimate value to the shareholders.

Earnings valuation models assume that earnings are the main income streams for valuation. A variation of earnings valuation model would combine earnings per share data with a P/E (price-earnings) ratio. This variation would calculate the value of stock by aggregating the present values of a dividend stream for a fixed number of periods and the market value of stock at the end of the periods calculated by the earnings per share multiplied by the P/E ratio.

Shareholders in a firm have a residual claim on the assets of the firm. Other stakeholders such as creditors, employees, suppliers, consumers, and governments have claims on the assets of the firm prior to shareholders. If the shareholder wealth is increasing, then it means that the value of other claimants has also been increasing already. Therefore, the goal of shareholder wealth maximization is an umbrella measure that covers the interests of all other claimants.

182

Deficiencies of Profit Maximization as a Goal of Financial Management

Maximizing profits for a firm is a necessary condition for wealth maximization, but it is not a sufficient condition for wealth maximization. Here are some of detailed discussions on the deficiencies of profit maximization as the sufficient condition.

First, profit maximization is inferior to earnings per share measure. For example, let's assume: you own 100 shares of company X; company X has 1,000 shares outstanding with $2,000 profits this year; company X's dividend payout percentage is 100%. Then, the earnings per share and the dividends per share are $2. As a shareholder, your dividend income is $200 this year. Now, let's assume that the company sells 1,000 additional shares with $3,000 profits during the following year. The earnings per share and the dividends per share become $1.5. And your dividend income reduces to $150. At the same time, the per share price of stock would have been drastically decreased due to the dilution of share value. As a shareholder, would you be happy about your stock performance? Absolutely, not. This example demonstrates that the increase in profits does not mean the corresponding increase in the shareholder's wealth. Thus, maximization of the earnings per share would be better than maximization of profit as the goal of financial management.

Second, profit maximization ignores time value concept. To explain this problem, let's assume that you are considering two mutually exclusive projects A and B: project A will generate a single cash profit of $100,000 at the end of the tenth year; project B will generate a series of cash profits of $6,500 at the end of each of next ten years. Which project would you choose? Would you choose the project A because its total cash profit of $100,000 is greater than $65,000, the total sum of cash profits generated by project B? If you choose project A because of this reason, then you are ignoring the timing of cash flows. Obviously, $1 today is worth more than $1 in a future time, since $1 today can earn the simple and compound interests through passage of time.

To make a correct decision on the above mutually exclusive projects, people should have applied the present value concept. For example, let's assume that the appropriate discount rate for analyzing these projects is 10%. The present value of project A's cash profit is $38,600. The present value of project B's annuity cash profits is $39,942.50. Therefore, project B would be a better choice. Wealth maximization embraces this concept, but profit maximization ignores it.

Third, profit maximization ignores the riskiness of profit streams. To discuss this deficiency, let's assume that you are comparing two mutually exclusive projects C and D. Project C will have a sure profit of one million dollars regardless of different conditions of economy. Project D will have no profit in a recessionary economy, one million dollars in a normal economy, and two million dollars in a booming economy. The probabilities of a recessionary economy, a normal economy, or a booming economy are, respectively, 0.25, 0.5, 0.25. The expected profits of both projects are one million dollars. Which projects would you choose? According to profit maximization, two projects would be indifferent. However, project C would be better since it has a certain profit while project D has a risky profit. Wealth maximization would choose project C, incorporating the degree of riskiness.

Fourth, profit maximization ignores the impact of financing structure. Let's assume that you are examining two mutually exclusive projects E and F. Project E will be financed by a half million dollars of debt and will have a profit of one million dollars in a year. Project F will be financed by a half million dollars of equity and will have a profit of one million dollars in a year. As far as profit maximization is concerned, two projects are indifferent. That is, profit maximization does not reflect the degree of financial risks involved in different projects. However, project F would be better since it is less riskier than project E. Wealth maximization would choose project F, reflecting the degree of financial risks involved in two projects.

Fifth, profit maximization ignores the impact of dividend policy. Profit maximization would not consider any measure beyond profit. For example, whether the company retains the full profit or pays out the full profit as cash dividends, it would be indifferent with profit maximization. However, wealth maximization takes the dividend policy into account, since stockholders' welfare is affected by the dividend policy as well as profits' growth rates.

Because of all these reasons, wealth maximization is superior to profit maximization. Profit maximization has a limited value. Other things being equal, profit maximization leads to wealth maximization. The goal of financial management ought to be wealth maximization.

Agency Problems

Agency problems are problems resulting from agency relationships. An agency relationship exists whenever a "principal" engages an "agent" and

184

grants the agent some decision-making power. In a firm, stockholders are principals and managers are agents of the stockholders. Agency costs are the costs associated with monitoring management's actions to insure that these actions are consistent with the shareholders' wealth maximization, or shareholders' interests.

Agency costs are all costs to encourage managers to maximize shareholders' wealth rather than to act in their own self-interests. There are three major agency costs: (1) expenditures to monitor managerial actions, such as audit costs; (2) expenditures to limit undesirable managerial actions, such as performance-based incentive plans, e. g. , stock options and stock grants diluting the company's stock value; (3) opportunity costs resulting from shareholders' restrictions, such as requirements for shareholder votes on certain managerial actions, limiting the ability of managers to take timely actions that could increase shareholder wealth.

Corporate Wealth Maximization as an Alternative Goal

The philosophy that the goal of financial management should be to maximize shareholders' wealth is dominant in the Anglo-American areas. However, in Europe, Japan, and some of their neighboring countries, people believe that the goal of financial management should be to maximize corporate wealth. Corporate wealth maximization is based on the rationale that the corporation should deal with shareholders on a par with other corporate stakeholders, such as creditors, governments, consumers, suppliers, management, labor, communities, and so on.

Gordon Donalson and Jay Lorsch in their book *Decision Making at the Top: The Shaping of Strategic Direction* explain the corporate wealth as follows: The definition of corporate wealth is much broader than just financial wealth, such as cash, marketable securities, and unused credit lines; consequently, it goes beyond the wealth measured by conventional financial reports to include the firm's market position as well as the knowledge and skill of its employees in technology, manufacturing processes, marketing and administration of the enterprise.

The corporate wealth maximization is a long run perspective in that what is best for the firm's all interest groups would make the firm continue to grow and remain viable. However, as John M. Keynes said, "Long run is a misleading guide to current affairs. In the long run, we are all dead." In contrast, the belief of shareholders' wealth maximization is a short run perspective in that what is best for the shareholders should be also best for the interests of all other claimants.

By Geungu Yu

Key Terms and Concepts

P/E   price earnings ratio. Price per share divided by earnings per share. It measures how much investors are paying per dollar of earnings.

mutually exclusive projects   projects that are perfectly negatively dependent on each other, so that taking one project prevents the taking of other project.

compound interest   interest earned on interest.

stock option   right to buy or sell a stock at a predetermined price within a given period.

stock grant   a stock given by a company as a reward or an incentive.

Anglo-American   the United States, United Kingdom, Canada, Australia, and New Zealand.

credit line   also called bank line. It is bank's commitment to make loans to a particular borrower up to a specified amount for a short period of time, usually up to one year.

Global Advertising Regulations

Conflicting national advertising regulations pose grave problems for marketers and advertising agencies promoting multinational corporations products and services. Advertising has become global as multinational corporations continue to target, reach and penetrate target market consumers in foreign markets to sell goods and services. Government restraints on international advertisers are more stringent than those imposed in the United States and Canada. Specific products advertised, media selection regulations, commercial scheduling and timing, usage of comparative advertising., advertising to children and sexism in advertising are prime areas where international advertisers face guideline limitations in the international marketplace. William F. Arens wrote in his book *Contemporary Advertising*, "Companies advertising abroad typically face markets with different value systems, environments, and language. There customers have different purchasing abilities, habits and motivations. Media customary to U. S. and Canadian advertisers may be unavailable or ineffective. The companies will therefore likely need different advertising strategies. But they face a more basic problem: How to manage and produce the advertising? Should their U. S. agency or in-house advertising department do it? Should they use a foreign agency or set up a local advertising department?" Interesting though, similar advertising campaigns and ads used in the United States have been successfully launched in host country markets. Some examples are Coca-Cola, Federal Express, British Petroleum and Max Factor using global advertising marketing strategies with their commercials and ads. Ultimately, it is quite apparent that external legal, economic, political, social and cultural factors have a vast impact on the type of goods and services advertised in foreign markets.

Advertising Laws and Regulations Governing Comparative Advertising

Advertising laws and regulations governing comparative advertising advertising vary in European countries. In their book *International Marketing*, Williams F. Arens, Philip R. Cateora and John L. Graham mentioned that Germany, Belgium, Luxemburg and Spain ban comparative advertising if used to degrade the competitor's image or products and services marketed to the consuming public. Austria, Denmark, Italy, Netherlands and United Kingdom welcome comparative advertising so long as the information is accurate, relevant and fair and the ad does not degrade or belittle the competitor's company image, or products and services advertised. Comparative advertising is also heavily regulated in other countries. In Asia, an advertisement showing chimps choosing Pepsi over Coke was banned from most satellite television; the term "the leading cola" was accepted only in the Philippines. An Indian court ordered Lever to cease claiming that its New Pepsodent Toothpaste was "102% better" than the leading brand. Colgate, the leading brand, was never mentioned in the advertisement although a model was shown mouthing the word "Colgate" and the image was accompanied by a "ting" sound recognized in all Colgate ads as the ring of confidence. Banning explicit comparisons will rule out an effective advertising approach heavily used by U. S. companies at home and in other countries where it is permitted.

Regulations on the Commercials Advertising Specific Products

Regulations on the use of commercials advertising tobacco, alcoholic beverages and pharmaceuticals are mixed in the global marketplace. The advertising of tobacco is banned in all media in Italy, banned on TV and radio in Austria and the United Kingdom and restricted on TV in Spain. Austria, Belgium, Denmark, France, Germany, Italy and Netherlands follow the European Union guidelines on the limitation of commercials. That is, commercials cannot exceed 15 percent of daily broadcast time. Michael R. Czinkota and Ilkka A. Ronkainen. alleged in their book *International Marketing* that after several years of debate within Europe to prohibit tobacco advertising everywhere (except point-of-purchase ads in tobacco specialty shops), the EU decided that the final ratification of the Maastricht Treaty completed the single European market, and the mandate to come up with community wide directives ended. The issue will be handled by each member country separately. The Maastricht Treaty calls for a commitment to economic and monetary union (EMU) with the cue to become a common European currency by 1999. Cateora and Graham specifically noted that the government controlled TV network in Kuwait only allows 32 minutes of advertising per day in the evening. Commercials are controlled to exclude superlative descriptions, indecent words, fearful or shocking shots, indecent clothing or dancing, contests, hatred or revenge shots, and attacks on competition. The authors also noted that it was illegal to advertise cigarettes, lighters, pharmaceuticals, alcohol, airlines and chocolates or other candy.

Advertising Regulations Regarding Children

Advertising regulations regarding children are quite diverse in Western Europe. The European Union prohibits the showing of children in danger; exploiting their ignorance or credulity; or encouraging them to persuade adults to buy. While Belgium, Denmark and France follow the EU guidelines, Austria and Germany ban direct appeals in radio and TV ads. Spain restricts exploitation of children while Switzerland has no general regulations regarding advertising to children.

According to the book *International Marketing* written by Philip R. Cateora and John L. Graham, there are more than 50 different laws restricting the advertising of products and services to children in Europe. (a) In the Netherlands, confectionery ads must not be aimed at children, and can't be aired before 8 p. m. or feature children under 14. Further, a toothbrush must appear on the screen, either at the bottom during the entire spot or filling the whole screen for the last $1\frac{1}{2}$ seconds. (b) There is a ban on toy advertising in Greece on television between 7 a. m. and 10 p. m. (c) War toys cannot be advertised in Spain or Germany. (d) French law prohibits children from being presenters of a product or to appear without adults. A Kellogg Company spot that runs in the U. K. featuring a child assigning a different day to each box could not be used in France. (e) Sweden prohibits TV spots aimed at children under 12 and no commercials of any kind can air before, during, or after children's programs. It's interesting to note that Sweden passed the law at least a year before commercial television was permitted. Although some advertising laws have been harmonized, there still exist some major differences in advertising laws among the EC countries. The European Commission continues to review these bans, case by case, and it is striving for some agreement on a set of standards directives. As yet this goal has not been achieved.

Regulation Governing the Use of Sexism in Advertising

The use of sexism in advertising has increasingly gained public attention in the international marketplace. It would be ideal for countries to self-regulate and police the use of sexism in advertising predicated on their ethical and moral cultural standards of acceptable behavior cutting short of international advertising associations imposing restrictions and regulations. Cateora and Graham discussed this problem in their book *International Marketing* and said, "One of the problems in controlling decency and sex in ads is the cultural variations around the world. An ad perfectly acceptable to a Westerner may be very offensive to someone from the Middle East, or for that matter, another Westerner. Standards for appropriate behavior as depicted in advertisements vary from culture to culture. Regardless of these variations, there is growing concern about decency, sex, and ads that demean women and men. International advertising associations are striving to forestall laws imposing self-regulation, but it may be too late; some countries are passing laws that will define acceptable standards."

In summary, multinational corporations advertising in foreign markets must have a thorough understanding of the do's and don'ts of overseas countries because of language, cultural, literacy, governmental, political, economic and media availability differences that exist. Acquiring legal services of law firms familiar with local host countries' advertising rules and regulations should be considered a priority marketing strategy for multinational corporations.

By James R. Smith

global advertising   refers to advertisements placed in different media that are consistent in the world marketplace.

multinational corporation   refers to a corporation doing business in foreign markets beyond its home boundaries.

target market   refers to the specific segment of potential consumers toward which an organization directs its marketing program.

comparative advertising   refers to a company advertising of its products as superior to it's competitors' products.

international marketplace   refers to the global or world marketplace where home corporations operate business across borders and in host countries.

Financial Intermediation: Assets and Liabilities Management in a Profit-Seeking Environment

The study of Banking and Financial Markets has become one of the most fascinating areas in the field of economics. In recent years, the development of emerging financial markets in Asia and Latin America has accentuated the traditional interdependence among countries and regions. On a daily basis, developments or activities in one country's financial markets undoubtedly have broad repercussions for other countries. Changes or fluctuations in the value of a country's currency have consequences not only for that country but for numerous other countries as well, and over the years, as financial markets become more prominent, the role of commercial banks and even central banks has evolved as well. These days, commercial banks diversify their portfolio of activities in areas historically reserved for investment banks, thus continuing to lead the financial industry.

However, despite the growing expansion of the nature and types of their activities, banks have not abandoned their traditional role as premier financial intermediaries. Their ability to develop new technologies and strategies aimed at attracting deposits from savers and extend loans to borrowers continues to expand. It is that traditional role that fundamentally defines the function of commercial banks. The primary purpose of this section is to offer a comprehensive look at commercial banks and their ability to continue to maintain efficiency and profitability in an emerging financial world, while promoting the economic development of their communities.

Role and Function of Banks—The Intermediation Process

Banks are financial institutions that accept money deposits and make loans. Although the term "banks" has become more associated with the traditional commercial banks, to many individuals it includes other depository institutions such as savings and loan associations, mutual savings banks and credit unions. The other group of financial institutions is referred to as non-depository financial institutions. These institutions include finance companies, investment banks, pension and retirement funds, insurance companies, and mutual funds.

Banks and other financial institutions perform the role of intermediaries in the economy. A financial intermediary helps transfer funds from the lenders/savers to the borrowers/spenders. For example, a bank might acquire funds by issuing a liability to the public in the form of savings deposits. It might then use the funds to acquire an asset by making a loan to an individual or a corporation or by buying a bond in the financial market. This intermediation process is known also as indirect finance. According to Frederic S. Mishkin, although the media focus much of their attention on securities markets, particularly the stock market, financial intermediaries are a far more important source of financing for corporations than securities markets are. Without the existence of financial intermediaries, funds transfers would be limited, difficult, or almost impossible in most economies. For transfers to be carried out, lenders would experience high transaction costs and assume relatively high risks. Imagine having to assume the risk of lending your hard-earned money to individuals or businesses without the necessary information about the borrower's history of debt repayment or the borrower's ability to pay.

Mishkin pointed in 1997 that financial intermediaries can reduce transactions costs because they have developed expertise in lowering them. For example, a bank knows how to find a good lawyer to produce an airtight loan contract, and this contract can be used over and over again in its loan transactions, thus lowering the legal cost per transaction. Instead of a loan contract costing $500, a bank can hire a good lawyer for $5000 to draw up a loan contract that can be used for 2,000 loans at a cost of $2.50 per loan.

Assets and Liabilities Management

The depository activities of a bank are referred to as its liabilities. Once a bank collects funds from the savers/depositors, it becomes liable to them and must pay them for the use of their funds. The deposits constitute sources of funds used by the bank to make loans to borrowers. Loans are referred to as income-earning assets. All banks maintain a balance sheet where:

$$\text{Total Assets} = \text{Total Liabilities} + \text{Capital}$$

Primary assets of a commercial bank include the following categories:

—**reserves at the central bank:** all banks in the system are required to maintain a certain fraction of their deposits at the Central Bank. In the United States, the Central Bank is designated as The Federal Reserve Bank, usually referred to as The Fed. The Fed determines what percentage of their deposits banks must maintain in reserves. Bank reserves are a critical element in the money creation or expansion process. The lower the percentage of the reserves that banks are required to maintain at the Central Bank, the greater the bank's ability to issue loans and accumulate assets. For example, if the reserve requirement ratio on deposits is 10 percent, upon collecting 10 million dollars of deposits, the bank will be required by law to maintain one million dollars at The Fed and issue new loans in the amount of 9 million dollars.

—**vault cash:** currency that commercial banks hold on location (in their vault) to meet the needs of their depositors for cash withdrawals from their accounts.

—**cash items in the process of collection:** any item other than currency that is deposited at a teller's window, such as a personal check or a payroll check, is a cash item until the check clears, that is, until the check is honored by a payment through the issuer's financial institution.

—**deposits at other banks:** deposits that are held at other private banks. They are also referred to as correspondent balances.

—**government securities:** a wide category of financial instruments which include U. S. government securities, as well as state and municipal securities.

—**commercial and industrial loans:** a very important asset category which includes all loans to businesses. These loans may have varying degrees of default risk and maturity.

—**real estate loans:** loans made primarily to businesses to finance construction or purchase of new buildings.

—**consumer loans:** loans extended to individuals for the purchase of a variety of consumer goods.

—**interbank loans:** loans issued to other private banks. They are usually short-term in nature.

—**other assets**: bank buildings, computers and other equipment.

Commercial bank liabilities include:

—**checkable deposits**: these accounts consist of demand deposits on which the bank generally pays no interest, and other transactions deposits such as NOW accounts, on which the bank pays interest to the depositor.

—**small-denomination time deposits**: deposits with fixed maturities and denominations below $100,000.

—**savings deposits**: these deposits have no maturity. They include passbook savings accounts, statement savings accounts and money market deposit accounts.

—**large-denomination time deposits**: these accounts have denominations of $100,000 or more. They typically have maturities of less than six months.

—**loans from the Central Bank**: also referred to as Federal Reserve discount window borrowing. These loans may be obtained for a variety of reasons such as fluctuations in liabilities due to seasonal variations, or a temporary liquidity shortfall.

—**loans from other banks and financial institutions**: banks borrow from other banks and financial institutions in the federal funds market. These loans are overnight loans through which the banks raised funds to deposit at the Fed in order to meet the amount required by the Fed.

Bank capital is the difference between total assets and total liabilities. These funds are raised by selling new equities or from retained earnings.

Although the level of sophistication may differ from country to country and even from bank to bank, it is fair to assume that the liabilities and assets categories listed above are typical for banks throughout the world. Through the efficient management of its assets and liabilities, the bank is able to generate a profit to finance its operations and pay dividends to its shareholders.

In practice, the bank generally pays a relatively low interest to its depositors while charging a relatively higher interest on the loans that it issues to borrowers. Typically, interests on demand deposits are non-existent, or very low. Special checkable deposits which require high daily balances, such as NOW accounts, offer attractive rates of interests. Passbook savings deposits pay relatively low interest rates generally 2 to 3 percent per year while large denomination time deposits may pay interest at the rate of 5 to 6 percent annually. The interest paid on deposits represents costs to the banks.

The interest rate charged on a loan depends on a variety of factors: first, the type of loan, whether it is a business loan, a consumer loan, a secured loan, an unsecured loan, etc; second, the maturity of the loan, i. e. , how long it will take the borrower to repay the loan; third, the credit worthiness of the borrower.

The interest payments earned from the loans constitute the revenue of the bank. The bank's profit is estimated by computing the difference between its revenue from assets and its costs on liabilities. The objective of a bank is to manage its assets and liabilities in order to earn the highest possible profit.

According to Mishkin, the bank manager has four primary concerns. First, he must make sure there is enough ready cash to pay depositors. To keep enough cash on hand, the bank must engage in the liquidity management, i. e. , acquisition of sufficiently liquid assets to meet the banks obligations to depositors. Second, the bank manager must pursue an acceptably low level of risk by acquiring assets that have a low rate of default and by diversifying asset holdings (asset management). Third, the bank must acquire funds at low cost (liability management). Finally, the manager must decide the amount of capital the bank should maintain and then acquire the needed capital (capital adequacy management).

The bank manager who is successful in satisfying those four concerns will likely earn a considerable profit for the bank, and through the process of intermediation benefit the savers, the borrowers and the community as a whole. The role of financial intermediaries in promoting economic growth has received significant attention in economic literature. Financial institutions affect economic growth through their ability to efficiently attract and allocate savings, thus playing a vital role in the savings investment process. According to Rita Maldonado, "financial intermediaries, by providing indirect finance, hence a better and more efficient means of eliciting and allocating savings, do effect the economy as a whole. They raise the levels of savings and investment and therefore promote growth in employment and real national income. "

Numerous well-respected economists including J. A. Schumpeter, R. Goldsmith, R. McKinnon, E. Shaw, etc. endorsed the significance of an efficient financial sector in the process of economic development. Most agree that an efficient financial system must be innovative and assertive in promoting entrepreneurship and assist businesses in effective and productive businesses practices. This practice is referred to in the literature, as supply-leading finance. Prominent historical examples often cited for the supply-leading phenomenon include the financial development experiences of Germany since 1830 and Japan since 1870.

Supply-leading finance offers a model for banks to follow, particularly in communities in need of financial flows and professional expertise. As the bank manages its assets and liabilities in search of an economic profit, it can simultaneously assume a leadership role in ensuring the overall economic development of the community. A growing economy will provide a broader population of income earners in search for both the depository services of the banks and its supply of loanable funds to satisfy their ever-increasing desire to consume varying goods and services.

By Jean-Claude Assad

Key Terms and Concepts

financial intermediation   the process by which financial institutions transfer funds from the lenders/savers to the borrowers/spenders.

liability management   the ability to acquire funds at low cost. Examples of such funds are deposits collected from savers.

demand deposits   another term for checking accounts that pay no interest.

NOW accounts   negotiable order of withdrawals, interest paying checking accounts where the account holder may be limited to a specific checking accounts where the account holder may be limited to a specific number of withdrawals (or check writing) over a specific period of time.

statement savings accounts   typical small savings accounts on which the bank provides a statement to the account holder on a periodic basis, generally every three months.

money market deposit accounts   deposits with limited checking privileges that generally pay an interest rate comparable to the U. S. treasury bills or other money market instruments, such as certificates of deposits (CDs).

liquidity management   the ability to keep enough cash on hand to respond to the demands of depositors.

asset management   the ability of the bank to acquire and maintain assets with a low rate of default.

capital adequacy management   the ability of the bank to acquire and maintain the adequate level of capital to ensure growth and profitability.

Qualitative Characteristics of Accounting Information

The FASB develops two types of guidelines, standards and concepts which establish basic fundamentals to be observed by accountants. The Concepts are designed to aid the FASB in developing standards that accountants use in preparing financial reports and statements. Standards developed by the FASB are mandatory and must be observed by members of the AICPA. However, Concepts are not mandatory and serve only as a reference or guide to the accounting profession.

To date, the FASB has issued six Statements of Financial Accounting Concepts. The objective of the FASB in issuing these concepts is to establish a framework that developers, users and preparers of accounting information can use as a reference in making a business decision.

This article will explain the second concept, FASB Concept No. 2, Qualitative Characteristics of Accounting Information. It will list each quality of information defined in the concept and give a short uncomplicated explanation for that quality.

Accounting information is the data used to prepare any of four financial statements required under Generally Accepted Accounting Principles (GAAP). Thus, accounting information in this context is the actual numbers used in preparing the required accounting statements. The required statements are the Statement of Income, Balance Sheet, Statement of Cash Flows and the Statement of Stockholders Equity.

Concept No. 2 is organized in the form of a hierarchy of qualities which should be possessed by accounting information. At the top level are benefits and costs, the "pervasive" or universal constrains. On the second and third levels, the decision-specific qualities are understandability and decision usefulness.

The fourth level contains two separate and equally valuable qualities, relevance and reliability. Relevance and reliability are primary decision specific qualities that influence each decision and make accounting information more desirable. Although, relevance and reliability are equally important in the hierarchy, users often sacrifice a loss of one quality for a gain in the other. Since decision makers require useful accounting information when selecting among different alternatives, it is important that these data possess both of these qualities.

Relevant and reliable accounting information is a key portion of any rational accounting decision. If either is missing, the accounting information will be useless.

Both relevant and reliable information are composed of secondary qualities in much the same manner as a favorite dish is made from a recipe of ingredients. The ingredients in relevant information are timeliness, predictive value and feedback value. The secondary qualities of reliable information are verifiability, representational faithfulness and neutrality. In addition to the above, relevant and reliable information interacts with two additional secondary ingredients, comparability and consistency.

Benefits and Cost

All accounting information, including that required by the FASB, has costs. However, due to the scope and nature of accounting reports, the information will not benefit each user equally. Thus, each user will benefit from accounting information only to the extent that it is needed and used. For example, some decision makers prefer that information is more relevant than reliable; while for others, the reverse is true. This requires the FASB, as standard setters, to seek a balance between the two. Because decision makers have different needs, the FASB cannot sacrifice either relevance or reliability for the other. In fact, the FASB must weigh the expected cost of gathering accounting information by preparers against the benefits gained by users. As a result of this balancing, if the FASB determines that the costs associated with implementing a proposed standard are greater than the benefits to be realized, the standard will not be implemented. This is true even if the proposed information is both relevant and reliable.

Understandability

If accounting information is to benefit users of financial statements, the information must be presented in a form that is comprehensible or understandable by users. This assumes that users will have a "reasonable understanding of business and economic activities". By directing information to users with a moderate understanding of business, the FASB seeks to allow those users who are willing to study the information opportunities to enjoy maximum benefit from the information.

Decision Usefulness

Decision usefulness is the second user specific quality of accounting information. Decision usefulness is important since each decision maker must individually determine what information is useful. Often individual judgment will not be based solely on the numbers in the financial statements. Thus, judgments are unique to the individual decision maker. In fact, each judgment will probably be based largely on individual experience and other information already possessed. However, the judgment will be made in conjunction with useful data from the financial statements.

Relevance

If accounting information is to be useful to decision makers, then it must be relevant to the decision. Relevant information is information which influences or makes a difference in the decision. Relevant information can affect decisions in several ways. First, it can assist the decision maker with a past or present prediction. Second, it can cause the decision maker to rethink past expectations or change current expectations.

Feedback, Predictive Value and Timeliness

Predictive value and timeliness are the ingredients that make up relevant information. Feedback and predictive values are evident when decision makers use accounting information to confirm or correct prior assumptions. Decision makers use accounting data as a basis to improve their decision-making abilities. Confirmation and correction of prior assumptions are the direct result of influential information or relevant information. Timeliness is a critical ingredient, for if relevant information is not received in time to make the decision, the information is useless.

Reliability

Reliability is defined as the quality of information that assures the user that the information is reasonably free from error or bias and that is neutral and represents what it purports to represent. It is evident from the definition that the FASB understands and recognizes that once financial statements are released to the public, users will base a number of decisions on them. Therefore, by presenting Concept No. 2, decision makers are expected to gain more certainty that the information provided in the financial statements

198

represents what it claims to represent.

Neutrality

Neutrality applies to both standard setters and users of accounting information. Neutrality is more important to those that issue regulations than to the typical users that are applying standards. However, Concept 2 tells us that the primary concern, whether implementing standards or applying standards, is to present information that is both relevant and reliable. In effect, the goal of standard setters is to issue rules that have no effect on any user, that is, to be neutral.

Bias

Under Concept 2, biased information is described as data that has the tendency to be "too low" or "too high". If, for example, in the preparation of an entity balance sheet, the preparer shows depreciation of an asset consistently low, then these balance sheets will be unreliable. When users cannot depend on statements to represent what preparers claim they represent, the statements are unreliable. This is true since the balance sheets are designed to show the economic resources, obligations, and events that change those resources in the business.

Conservatism

Often, as in the case of depreciating assets, accountants are required to use estimates in preparing financial statements. Estimates, by definition, are uncertain and can mislead the readers of accounting statements. Through the years, when presenting data which purports to measure the operations or results of operations of a business, accountants have developed preferences for understated rather than overstated data. This practice of understating of data is called conservatism and was considered, by some, to be a virtue. The FASB, in Concept No. 2 indicates that the consistent and deliberate understatement of data in financial statements introduces bias into those statements. Additionally, it indicates that the deliberate understatement of data impacts the representational faithfulness, neutrality, and comparability of statements. Moreover, in Concept 2, FASB points out that an understatement in one year causes distortions for subsequent years.

Representational Faithfulness

Under Concept No. 2, representational faithfulness is an ingredient of reliable information. Simply, it is the agreement between the accounting information presented in the financial statements and the economic resources and obligations that actually exist in the business.

Comparability

Concept No. 2 describes comparability as a characteristic that makes accounting information more useful. Comparability is defined as the quality of information that enables users to identify similarities in and differences between two sets of economic phenomena. Additionally, Concept No. 2 distinguishes "comparable" data from relevant and reliable information and describes it as the relationship between more than one piece of information. Decision makers can compare financial statements based on these relationships and note any similarities or differences. However, the concept cautions that if data from businesses are to be compared, then the input procedures for applying data and the system used for classification of accounting information must be the same. If decision makers compare accounting information with data gathered from other businesses or from the same business in different years, then that information becomes more beneficial.

Consistency

Concept No. 2 describes consistency as an important quality that makes accounting numbers more useful. It defines consistency as conformity from period-to-period with unchanging policies and procedures. This conformity can be of enormous value to decision makers as it aids analysis and facilitates an understanding of the numbers presented in the statements. In effect, when presenting accounting data over time, there is a strong preference for preparers not to vary their policies and procedures. However, this preference is not intended to prevent changes that will allow the profession to develop and move forward. If there is a need for change, the Concept No. 2 admonishes decision makers to weigh the decision in terms of tradeoffs versus advantages.

Materiality

Finally, Concept No. 2 discusses materiality as a threshold that must be achieved when presenting accounting numbers. Materiality considers the quantitative aspect of accounting information. The determination, as to whether an accounting number is material or immaterial, is generally made by auditors reviewing accounting reports. Auditors decide whether or not to recognize errors and omissions in accounting numbers based on individual judgment. That judgment is generally affected by the size and nature of the number. If the accounting numbers arise from normal circumstances and are too small to influence the accounting report, then they are immaterial and the auditor will ignore them. However, if these numbers arise from circumstances that are abnormal, they may be considered material and are included in the auditors' reports.

By Richard L. Russell

Key Terms and Concepts

FASB (Financial Accounting Standards Board) a seven-member board whose mission is to establish and improve or set standards of financial accounting.

AICPA (American Institute of Certified Public Accountants) a national organization for professional Certified Public Accountants.

GAAP (Generally Accepted Accounting Principles) accounting principles which have substantial authoritative support. GAAP consists of FASB Standards and Interpretations, APB Opinions and Interpretations, and CAP Accounting Research Bulletins.

statement of income a statement that measures net income or profit by listing revenues and subtracting expenses for a fiscal period.

balance sheet a accounting report that shows the business assets, liabilities and owners equity as of a specific date.

statement of cash flows a statement that shows the items that caused cash to flow into or out of a business for a fiscal period.

statement of stockholders equity an accounting report that explains the owners' equity for a fiscal period.

depreciation the process of allocating the cost of tangible assets over their useful lives.

economic resources the assets obtained or controlled by a particular entity as a result of past transactions.

obligations liabilities that will cause probable future economic sacrifices or transfer assets or services to others in the future.

The Rise of China's Joint Ventures
in an Interdependent Global Economy

China intends to modernize its industry, its agriculture, its science and technology, and its defense by the year 2000. On the way to these "four modernizations", China has started to implement economic reforms and to introduce an "opening-up" policy for the presence of foreign industry. China and multinational enterprises (MNEs) each have different objectives. Each must find a way to identify mutual rewards through cooperation and accommodation. The number of cooperative ventures between China and MNEs is increasing, and so is the number of joint ventures.

A Brief Background on the Rise of China's Joint Ventures

China's first joint venture appeared in 1951. The rapid growth of multinational enterprise in China started during the 1960's. Throughout the world, in the past decades, we saw an expansion of foreign direct investment and joint ventures, particularly in less developed countries (LDCs). In this period, joint ventures grew up in planned economies as well. The growth of joint ventures in previous Yugoslavia was a case in point. China's joint ventures were continuing to accelerate in the 1980's.

At the present time, this exposure to the outside world is seen as a long-term and basic state policy. China has acknowledged that while ensuring its sovereignty and independence, it must open its doors to the outside world. It must increase its strength through ever-growing economic exchanges with other countries. This is also viewed as an unavoidable way as well as a necessary expedient to speed up the development of its economy.

What is a joint venture? The definition of joint venture can be found in most contemporary research on this emerging business form. Historically, a joint venture was "any association between two or more juristic persons for a business purpose." Another brief definition says that "joint ventures are separate entities with two or more active firms as partners." In China, the concept of joint venture remains somewhat vague. Some accept a broad concept viewing all the activities involving joint partnerships as joint ventures. These could include cooperative production and management, compensatory trade, processing and assembling supplied parts and components, leasing, license

202

trade and cash purchases. However, this kind of view ignores the fact that a joint venture should be an entity owned by two or more partners doing business together.

Two conditions are most important for the concept of joint venture. One condition is that it has to be an entity owned by two or more partners. The other condition is that both parties are active in the management of the joint enterprise. In the United States, direct investment is defined as an investment that is greater than 10 percent, presuming some influence in management because of that level of capital. Investments less than 10 percent are categorized as portfolio investments. In China, the law requires a minimum participation of 25 percent for foreign partners. A joint venture is an entity which is owned by two or more partners who act together in the business of the entity.

The presence and growth of joint ventures in China have raised many questions: Why do China and MNEs opt for these cooperative arrangements? What is the investment environment in China? What is the future prospect for joint ventures in China?

Different Objectives of China and MNEs

The significant impact of the multinational enterprises is in the internationalization of production and in the development of a world economy. In a global economy, enterprise investment decisions and operations are increasingly combined with allocations of world resources and maximization of world welfare. In order to understand the nature of the multinational enterprises which will increasingly affect our economy at the present and in the future, we should be familiar with the characteristics of those multinational enterprises. For the very large multinational, there is a capacity to draw resources from throughout the world. It communicates with its branches throughout the world in order to identify the advantages of drawing selectively from alternative areas. It takes a global view and many have substantial technical knowledge or expertise to integrate resources drawn worldwide into a profitable joint venture.

It is clear that for China and off-shore multinational enterprises to enter into a joint venture, there must be the promise of benefits for both sides. China is seeking technology imports, the development of its infrastructure, access to techniques for high-value-added production, and the means to accelerate the development of its basic resource base. The presence of foreign firms in such joint ventures builds on their hope of profits, and perhaps, a sustained or durable market position to serve not only foreign markets, but the substantial potential of the massive Chinese market as well.

Multinational enterprises have their own objectives worldwide. These objectives can be summarized as follows:

(a) Advancing profitability: The gain of short-term and long-term profits.

(b) Market access: The opportunity to secure local market penetration.

(c) The resource dividend: Having access to low-cost labor and other material resources.

(d) The "risk minimization" motive: This involves risk-sharing.

There are several ways to realize these objectives. Five options are found to be most effective. They are direct exports, sales agency, contract manufacturing, undertaking a wholly-owned subsidiary, and having a partner to a joint venture. Of these five types of entry, direct export is less risky. But it has little long-term potential for growth, particularly as local production expands. Having a sales agency in a host country is similar to direct export. But the physical presence of sales agency in a host country offers some advantage over the direct export, for it can provide valuable feedback to the parent company. Contract manufacturing does not involve a legal liaison between a local manufacturer and parent company. The local manufacturer produces goods and exports them all. The arrangements concerning production can be various. The responsibility to provide equipment, raw materials, semi-finished parts, technology, design, quality requirement are all specified in the contract. A wholly-owned entity as a subsidiary for an MNE may have problems. Unlike a joint venture, a wholly-owned subsidiary assumes all the risks itself.

In an interdependent global economy, China has its own objectives. It is encouraged with the development of its economy. China's objectives are:

(a) Financial interests: China needs investments and foreign exchange.

(b) Industrialization needs: China wants technology to improve domestic productivity.

(c) Employment needs: China must sustain creative employment for its large workforce.

As noted at the outset, to realize these objectives, China has started implementing the "opening-up" policy. It is to expedite rapid economic development through international cooperation. To make that possible, it is undertaking compensatory trade agreements, provision for processing and

204

assembling needed parts and components. It is willing to enter into leasing and licensing agreements, and to participate in joint ventures as well.

A Common Strategy for China and MNEs

There are so many strategies available to both multinational enterprises and China to reach their objectives. Joint venture obviously is one of the best choices for both China and MNEs in the development of an interdependent global economy. What factors make a joint venture to be so attractive for the multinational enterprises and China?

In the development of Chinese economy, joint ventures are playing a main role at least in five aspects. Hence, a joint venture is by no means a way of hiding weaknesses, instead, a successful joint venture creates strength.

First, similar to other LDCs, the resources of financing are always considered the most important factors in the development of economy. In the establishment of the joint ventures, foreign enterprise will introduce its own investments and China will need foreign exchange and accept technology transfer. Apparently, joint ventures can serve as a highly effective mechanism to secure foreign exchange.

Secondly, joint ventures offer an opportunity for China to acquire updated technology on a continuing basis in both production and management and to raise its productivity. In addition to the capital expenditure and the improvement of labor skills, productivity growth is attributed to the progress of technology. The partner's continuing interest in the venture brings in new technology. As the technological time span continuously shortens, the necessity for continuity will become an increasingly important consideration.

Thirdly, joint ventures benefit China in marketing. Joint ventures often generate shared brands and joint distribution channels. Therefore, joint ventures lead to ever expanding marketing opportunities. In the primary period, most of China's joint ventures rely on their foreign partners' international distribution channels to sell joint ventures' products.

Fourthly, joint ventures can weaken potential crisis of employment and provide more job opportunities. In the next ten years, there will be millions and millions of new job seekers entering China's labor market. They need jobs.

Fifthly, a joint venture is a way to share risks. People frequently view joint ventures as a risk-allocating mechanism for partners to pursue their objectives. In resource-based ventures, economic risk sharing is particularly important. The scale of resource projects forms the scenario that no single firm is willing to risk its future on a single project. In the exploration of oil and coal, a large amount of investment is required. Considering that the price of energy is more likely to go up in the long-run, China is making its effort to have more partners in resource exploration and other capital intensive projects.

The multinational enterprises will search the benefits from a different angle. In general, China has abundant resources and cheap labor, but needs investment and technology transfer. Multinational enterprises need resources, labor, and access to local markets. All of these elements provide a mosaic for mutual benefits through joint ventures.

Joint venture is not a simple story. One cynic describes these as a situation where "the joint venture process starts out with one partner having the money and the other the expertise, and ends up reversing these positions — the latter having the money and the former the expertise." There are many reasons for multinational enterprises to establish joint ventures worldwide. The follows are five major considerations.

First, trade barriers are growing. Tariffs, import quotas, and currency controls severely limit foreign markets. For example, China in 1980s imposed 40% to 200% tariffs on more than a dozen of imports. Consequently, direct exports become difficult for MNEs. Therefore, a joint venture provides an effective means for assured market access.

Secondly, excess capacity in most of the durable goods industries leads many firms to look for more attractive investment opportunities in foreign countries. However, China has its long-term objectives focusing on both technology transfer and independent production capacity. Gradually, manufacturing that involves only assembly and processing draws less and less attention in China.

Thirdly, anticipation of lower corporation income taxes and higher profits is promising since certain countries do offer lower income tax rate. China, as a host country, may offer a better investment environment.

Fourthly, patent laws in some countries require firms to manufacture locally in order to obtain patent protection and to achieve the legal status necessary to assert infringement claims.

Fifthly, in some large or risky projects as off-shore petroleum exploration, the MNEs do need to share risks with China.

Prospect of Joint Ventures in China

China has also established many joint ventures abroad. As China's joint ventures expand worldwide, a significant transition is taking place in China's position in the growth of interdependent global economy. The basic change arises from China's objectives and strategies. The objectives which are usually set by the multinational enterprises now can be China's. At the same time, the strategies which are usually used by the multinational enterprises now can be helpful to China. Compared with developed countries, China apparently lags behind. However, in terms of the ability of investment and technology, China is in the lead of most LDCs. For this reason working as both host country and parent country to establish joint ventures at home and abroad is a logical outlet for China in an interdependent global economy.

By Xianyuan Dai

Key Terms and Concepts

multinational enterprise　very large company with business worldwide.

less developed countries　also called developing countries, most of them are making great efforts in speeding up their own economies.

direct investment　investment in a host country by a foreign country.

portfolio investment　investment in the form of securities. A good portfolio investment will show a wide spread of investments in order to reduce the risk of loss.

joint venture　a joint venture is an entity which is owned by two or more partners who act together in the business of the entity.

world welfare　benefits to make the whole world better off.

wholly-owned subsidiary　a company completely owned by a parent company.

shared brand　two companies share a brand which is jointly created by them. The brand usually is composed of two separated brands which were used respectively by two companies in the past.

distribution channels　the network to distribute and sell products. Channel members may involve manufacturers, wholesalers, retailers, brokers, and agencies.

History of the International Monetary System

Many international agreements have shaped the international monetary system. A brief history of the international monetary system will provide opportunities to evaluate strengths and weaknesses of various system. It also provides a better understanding of the current system. This section will discuss the following systems: (1) the gold standard, (2) the freely fluctuating, (3) the Bretton Woods, (4) the eclectic monetary system, and (5) the European Monetary System (EMS). The section will draw several financial implications for business and economic policy makers.

The Gold Standard (1876-1913)

The value of each national currency under the gold standard is fixed in terms of gold. That is, each currency is defined as the amount of gold of standard purity. For example, the dollar of the United States could be converted into gold at a rate of US $20.67 per ounce of gold. This was called mint parity. Whether the currency itself is gold, or whether it is fully or partially backed by gold is not important. What is important is that each government is willing to buy and sell gold freely for the national currency in unlimited quantities, so that gold can be freely transported internationally.

The gold standard system was consistent with the doctrine of laissez-faire. An automatic self-correcting mechanism was built in the system. A country with a surplus in its balance of trade would experience a gold inflow. This would lead to an increase in domestic money supply and a corresponding increase in domestic price level. In turn, this would result in an increase in imports and a decrease in exports. This process would continue until the country's balance of trade equilibrium is reached. On the other hand, a country with a deficit in its balance of trade would experience a gold outflow. Following the logic opposite to the country with a surplus in its balance of trade, the deficit country would accomplish its balance of trade equilibrium as well. Thus, the system had the effect of implicitly maintaining the balance of trade equilibrium. Through this mechanism, each country would sustain the long run stability of money supply and price level. The gold standard operated reasonably well until the outbreak of World War I disrupted trade flows and the free movement of gold among countries. Consequently, the trading countries suspended the operation of the gold standard.

The Freely Fluctuating (1914-1944)

After the collapse of the gold standard system, the value of each international monetary unit was allowed to fluctuate freely in terms of gold. The exchange rate, the price of one currency in terms of the currency of other country, became determined by the free market forces of supply and demand. During this period, the exchange rates became seriously unstable. This instability upsets international patterns of trade and capital flows. For some countries, as the exchange rates rose, the domestic prices of imported goods rose, and so did wages. A conspicuous result was that the volume of international trade did not grow in proportion to world outputs. The decline was one of the direct causes of the Great Depression in the 1930s. The main trading nations made efforts to return to the gold standard during the interwar period. The United States returned to gold in 1919, the United Kingdom in 1925, and France in 1928. However, the Austrian banking system's collapse caused most trading nations to abandon the gold standard again. In 1934, the U. S. dollar was devalued to US $35 per ounce of gold and it was to be traded only with foreign central banks.

The Bretton Woods (1944-1973)

As World War II neared toward a close, forty-four nations adopted a so-called gold exchange standard at an international conference at Bretton Woods, New Hampshire in 1944. They adopted a fixed exchange rate system that evolved from the gold standard but differed from it in that, under its operation, international reserves consisted of both gold and convertible national currencies. Each country fixed the value of its currency in terms of gold but was not required to exchange its currency for gold. Only the U. S. dollar remained convertible into gold at US $35 per ounce. This form of international monetary organization evolved after World War II, not with deliberate planning but as a natural outcome of the economic, military, and political world dominance by the U. S. at that time.

The conference created the International Monetary Fund (IMF), a mechanism for member countries to prevent large devaluation and defend their currencies against adverse economic consequences such as balance of payments and exchange rate problems. It also established the International Bank for Reconstruction and Development (IBRD), also known as the World Bank.

The IMF was the key institution in the international monetary system (and remained so to the present). To carry out its task, the IMF was originally funded by each member's quota. The quota assigned to each member determined not only the size of its contribution to the Fund, but also the amount of the Fund's resources that it could borrow. The quotas originally consisted of two components: 25% in gold and 75% in the member's own currency. The quotas have been expanded and the distribution modified to accommodate growth in world trade, new membership, and the relative importance of member countries. Under this mechanism, each member was obligated to establish a par value of its currency in terms of gold, and to peg the exchange rates within a range of one percent above and below that par value. When a member country experienced difficulty maintaining its parity value because of balance-of-payments disequilibrium, it could borrow from the IMF. Such loans would be subject to IMF conditions regarding domestic economic policy to restore balance-of-payments equilibrium. To correct a fundamental disequilibrium in the country's balance of payments, the par value could be changed permanently.

As mentioned above, the Bretton Woods system allowed for changes in exchange rates when the fundamental disequilibrium forced such changes. Thus, the system could be better described as an adjustable fixed exchange rate system. Nonetheless, it was a gold exchange standard because its key currency, the dollar, was convertible into gold for official holders of dollar such as central banks and treasuries.

The Bretton Woods system served reasonably well through the 1950s. However, in the 1960s, fundamental international economic problems such as incompatible national monetary and fiscal policies, differential inflation rates, and unexpected external shocks eventually led to the system's crises. One solution to the problems was to create Special Drawing Rights (SDRs) in 1970. It was a genuine net addition to international reserves, which was credited to the account of each IMF member country according to the established quota. Nevertheless, the failure to readjust currency values to accommodate the fundamental economic changes led to the eventual breakdown. The system collapsed in August 1971, when President Nixon declared to stop the convertibility of the dollar into gold. This declaration was prompted by the dollar glut resulting from the situation that the foreign dollar liabilities of the U. S. were much larger than its gold stock. A key cause of the system collapse was the U. S. dollar problem. The sources of the dollar problem were multiple. The U. S. ran persistent and growing deficits on its balance of payments. Because of financing the Great Society program and Vietnam war, the inflation was inevitable. There was a rampant speculation that other currencies would revalue against the dollar. There was an essential need to devalue the dollar, but it was the standard currency so that it was difficult to do so. This dollar problem led to a lack of confidence in the ability of the United States to convert dollars into gold. Consequently, the U. S. suffered outflows of about one-third of its official gold reserves in the first seven months of the year 1971.

In December 1971, a group of ten leading trading nations reached a compromise agreement at a Washington, D. C. meeting. This was later called the Smithsonian Agreement. The U. S. agreed to devalue the dollar to US$38 per ounce of gold. As the dollar was being devalued, the other countries agreed to revalue their own currencies. Furthermore, the trading band was expanded from one percent to 2. 25% of the stated parity.

Even though the dollar was devalued, the dollar remained inconvertible into gold. The speculative flows of currencies led to a further devaluation of the dollar in February 1973, to US$42. 22 per ounce. Finally, in March 1973, the major currencies were allowed to float to levels determined by market forces.

The Eclectic Monetary System (1973-Present)

Since March 1973, the system would be described as a managed float system. Under the managed float system, most central banks would intervene to obtain a politically favorable exchange rate that would be different from the rate determined by the free market forces. However, exchange rates became much more volatile than they were during the Bretton Woods period (when changes occurred less frequently). The foreign exchange markets became dominated by three major currencies, the U. S. dollar, the German mark, and the Japanese Yen. There were several major events in the 1970s and the 1980s that shaped the current system.

The Jamaica Agreement was adopted at the meeting in Jamaica in 1976, which was attended by all IMF members. The agreement declared that floating rates were acceptable. It also declared to abandon gold as reserve asset, and to readjust IMF quotas upward. The Plaza Agreement was accepted by Group of Five (G-5) at the Plaza Hotel in New York in 1985. The U. S. and others acknowledged the need to control the volatility of international currency markets and to establish currency target ranges in the agreement. The G-5 involved the United States, Japan, United Kingdom, West Germany and France. The Plaza Agreement emphasized that the intervention would require close cooperation among major trading nations. The Louvre Accord, reaffirming the Plaza Agreement, was adopted by Group of Six, the G-5 plus Canada, in Paris in 1987. The Accord intensified economic policy coordination to promote global growth and reduce external imbalances. The Accord agreed to realign exchange rates to be consistent with underlying economic fundamentals. The international monetary system that emerged from the Louvre Accord can be described as a floating exchange system with somewhat wide ranges that are periodically revisable. However, the implied intervention levels remain flexible.

The European Monetary System (1979–Present)

The European Monetary System (EMS) is a system in which the member countries maintain fixed exchange rates among themselves, yet the exchange rates float against the rest of the world. The 12 member countries are Germany, Denmark, Belgium, Luxembourg, Ireland, Italy, the Netherlands, France, Great Britain, Greece, Spain, and Portugal. The EMS is a monetary arrangement of the European Economic Community formed in 1979 to provide greater exchange rate stability, economic cooperation, and promotion of trade and development of the European community. The key mechanism is called the Exchange Rate Mechanism (ERM), which is the process by which the member countries maintain the managed exchange rates. A highlight of the mechanism involves the creation of a common unit of account called the European Currency Unit (ECU). The ECU is an index currency based on a weighted average of the currencies of the 12 members of the European Union. The ECU's value varies as the members' currencies float jointly with respect to the U.S. dollar and other nonmember currencies.

The 12 members met at Maastricht, the Netherlands and had a treaty in December 1991. The Treaty specified a timetable and a plan to replace all the individual currencies with a single currency. In September 1992, high German interest rates induced massive capital flows into Germany, eventually causing the withdrawal of Britain and Italy from the ERM. The mechanism of fixed exchange rates among the ERM collapsed in 1993. Most ERM members allowed a 15% deviation band on either side of EMS-agreed par values in 1993. As of January 1994, Britain, Italy, and Greece were not committed to ERM parities. They are still hoping to accomplish a single currency mandated by the Maastricht Treaty. A common currency would mean truly fixed rates among members.

Main benefits of the common currency would include the following: The common currency serves as a more favorable framework for economic growth and employment. The single currency will reduce the foreign exchange risk that hinders the development of investment and international trade. It will give Europe genuine cohesion, and monetary sovereignty will be shared and exercised in the common interest. It will allow Europe to negotiate trade and monetary issues on an equal ground with its major competitors such as United States and Japan on the international stage. However, the single currency might bring some negative impact on the individual member countries before long. In some countries the single currency could probably create instant recession and increased unemployment.

Financial Implications

First, there exist so many different currency arrangements today. It is important for any participant in the international monetary system to understand the currency regimes specifically in which it operates. Second, the foreign exchange risk adds an additional burden on international affairs. However, it could also provide speculative opportunities. Third, developing effective hedging strategies against the foreign exchange risk would be essential in international affairs. Fourth, understanding of the international monetary system is crucial for international financing.

By Geungu Yu

Key Terms and Concepts

laissez-faire   a French term meaning "allow to do" that connotes nonintervention by government in economic affairs.

balance of trade   an entry in the balance of payments measuring the difference between the monetary value of merchandise exports and merchandise imports.

equilibrium   a condition of perfect balance, in which opposing forces are of equal weight, countering any tendency to change in any direction.

exchange rate   the price of a unit of one country's currency expressed in terms of the currency of some other country.

devaluation a drop in the spot foreign exchange value of a currency that is pegged to other currencies or to gold.

speculation an attempt to make a profit by trading on expectations about future prices, i. e., taking an informed risk.

hedging an attempt to reduce risk by protecting an owner from loss.

International Banking

International banking involves activities such as import and export financing, foreign exchange transactions, deposits and loans in the Eurocurrency markets, international loan syndication, and information service to multinational clients. This section discusses the following topics: a brief history of international banking; major requirements for international financial centers; comparative advantages of international banking; organizational types and expansion strategies; Eurocurrency markets and advantages of offshore banking; risks in international lending.

A Brief History of International Banking

C. P. Kindleberger in his paper "The Formulation of Financial Centers: A Survey in Comparative Economic History" finds that British foreign lending can be traced back to 1571 when usury laws were imposed that limited the interest charged on domestic loans to a stipulated rate, thereby diverting financial resources from domestic lending to foreign lending. The history of international banking has been linked to the historical development of international financial centers. In the early nineteenth century, the London financial market became the international financial center. European cities such as Amsterdam, Hamburg, and Paris gained some international financial eminence in the late nineteenth century primarily due to their physical locations and central roles in international commerce. In the early twentieth century, New York emerged as a financial center directly competing against London. After the World War II, the international financial leadership shifted to New York.

Taeho Kim in his book *International Money & Banking* explains that there are four waves of the recent internationalization of banking which began a significant pace in the 1960s. At first, relatively large-sized U. S. banks began rapid expansion of their overseas operations around the early 1960s as a natural extension of their domestic banking in response to the rising demand for international financial intermediation combined with their relative advantages. As the second wave, a similar pattern of expansion was started by banks of other industrial countries, notably Canada, Japan, and Germany. Although banks from the United Kingdom and France experienced a substantial reduction in overseas presence in their former colonies in the 1950s and 1960s, they began expanding their presence in other industrial countries, notably the United States, in the 1970s. The third wave of internationalization came from banks of developing countries in the late 1970s. The fourth wave which may be regarded as the globalization of banking started after the Single European Act of 1986 within the European Community upon removal of barriers to international capital flows.

Major Requirements for International Financial Centers

New York, London, and Tokyo are the world's most important international financial centers today. The major requirements for success as new international financial centers can be classified as follows. First, the location should be known as a center for commerce and business. Second, it should have a competitive time zone. Third, it should have an existing trade and financial expertise. Fourth, it should have dependable telecommunications available. Fifth, it should have economic and political stability. Sixth, it should have a regulatory climate that protects domestic and foreign depositors and borrowers but it should not be improperly restrictive to financial institutions.

Based on the above criteria for international financial centers, Australia's Sydney emerges as a new international financial center. This is because Sydney is well known as a center for international commerce and trade. It has a competitive time zone, since it is between the U. S. West coast and Japan. Its trade and financial expertise is adequate and growing. It has dependable telecommunication systems. It also plays a role of financial center of major Pacific Rim countries.

Let's examine the qualifications of Shanghai, China. First, Shanghai is well known as a center for commerce and business. Second, it has a competitive time zone, since it is between Tokyo and Hong Kong. Its trade and financial expertise is growing fast. Fourth, its telecommunication system develops rapidly. Fifth, the economic and political environment is reasonably stable. Sixth, its regulatory climate will improve in the near future. If this assessment is correct, Shanghai could become a major international financial center in the Asia.

Comparative Advantages of International Banking

Why are banks involved in the activities of international banking? We can summarize three distinctive advantages associated with international banking activities. First, there are advantages stemming from the factors related to the host countries. The factors include: an absence or reduction of bank regulations that lowers operational costs; clustering of a banking community that reduces communication cost; in some cases, unique profit opportunities resulting from monopolistic market characteristics. Second, there exist advantages resulting from the factors involved with home countries. Main sources of the advantages include: the home currency being used as international currency; the home country's skilled workers to be deployed in the host country. Third, there are advantages specifically related to the individual bank such as improved bank-customer relationship. Consequently, any international location which can promote all three types of advantages could emerge as a new international financial center.

Organizational Types and Expansion Strategies

A multinational bank can offer global needs of its client firms by distinctive organizational types and strategies. Host banking offices in a global financial network include correspondent banks, representative offices, shell branches, subsidiaries, and affiliates. Additionally, the United States (U. S.) allows International Banking Facilities (IBFs) and Edge Act and Agreement corporations in the U. S. Let's discuss the essential functions and the main benefits and costs of each form.

Correspondent banks provide services such as accepting drafts, honoring letters of credit, and furnishing credit information on import and export transactions. The major advantage would be that the cost of market entry is minimal and can be adjusted to the local scale of service. The major problem is that the correspondents might assign low priority to the needs of the home country's customers.

Representative offices help parent bank clients when they are doing business in the host country. They also obtain economic and political intelligence on the host country and the local market. The main advantage is to obtain the relevant information on the local market at a low cost. The disadvantage is that the benefit might be outweighed by an ineffective market penetration.

A shell branch is a legal part of the parent bank. Its principal service is to extend credit as well as to take deposits. The advantages include: to provide a full range of banking services under the name and legal obligation of the parent; as for U. S. banks, to take deposits that are not subject to reserve requirements or FDIC insurance unless the deposits are reloaned to the U. S. parent bank. One other important advantage of a shell branch is that the deposits can be loaned to U. S. residents. The main disadvantage is that the parent bank is liable for any claims against the branch.

A subsidiary is an incorporated bank, acquired entirely or in major part by a home bank. The subsidiary must comply with the regulations of the host country. The advantages include: the parent is not liable for liabilities of the subsidiary; acquiring an existing local bank will make it possible to access to the local deposit market; the subsidiary may appear to be a local rather than foreign bank. A disadvantage is that it might give the impression to the local customers that the prestige or financial backing of the parent bank is not behind the subsidiary.

An affiliate is a locally incorporated bank owned in part, without controlling interest, by a home bank. Several home or host banks can join together as owner of the affiliate. The main advantage is that the host bank acquires the expertise of two or more owners. Another advantage is that the host bank maintains its status as a local institution while keeping continuous relations with its home bank. The main disadvantage is that several owners may not agree on particular policies important to the viability of the host bank.

IBFs are established in 1981 to help U. S. banks capture a larger proportion of the Eurocurrency business. They are in-house shell branches to maintain a separate set of asset and liability accounts. IBFs are account entities authorized by the Federal Reserve Board of the United States to facilitate U. S. bank competition. They are not subject to the reserve requirements or Federal Deposit Insurance Corporation (FDIC) insurance premiums on deposits. Their deposits and loans are limited to customers of host countries.

Edge Act and Agreement corporations are the subsidiaries of U. S. banks financing international commerce, chartered by the Federal Reserve Board under a 1919 amendment to the Federal Reserve Act. They are allowed to operate interstate branches, physically located in the United States. They represent precursors of eventual U. S. nationwide branch banking.

Eurocurrency Markets and Advantages of Offshore Banking

A Eurocurrency market is the international financial market fulfilling a need for international deposits and loans in different currencies. The banks that fulfill this need are called Eurobanks. They mostly involve offshore banking. Using the prefix Euro is somewhat deceiving since the activities are not limited to Europe. For example, as discussed under the above section of IBFs, Eurodollar banking may occur in the United States through the IBFs and other organizational forms. A Euroyen market deals with yen-denominated bank deposits and loans outside Japan. There are also Euromarks, Eurosterling, and Eurofrancs.

There are many advantages of offshore banking for customers. Properly established and managed, the offshore accounts can help the customers reduce tax burdens or other regulations. The customers can maintain confidentiality in trades and transactions. Offshore accounts also enable them to invest in foreign financial assets that are not registered with their home country's regulatory agencies. So the transaction costs made through offshore accounts might be lower than those of investment vehicles in the home country. They can use the accounts to manage the foreign exchange risk and invest in foreign financial assets to earn the higher interest rates available in foreign countries. Because of all these advantages, offshore banking activities have grown rapidly since the late 1950s. However, since the authorization of IBFs in 1981, the offshore activities have experienced little or no growth.

Risks in International Lending

International lending involves more complex risk than those in domestic lending. The risks of international lending include commercial risk and country risk. Commercial risk is the risk for a foreign customer's inability to meet their obligations due to business reasons. Assessing credit quality of a foreign customer is more difficult than that in domestic lending. This is due to the fact that international lending has to deal with differences in culture, economy, politics, and other dimensions.

Country risk is the risk of a foreign customer's inability to pay due to host country's unexpected political or foreign exchange events. Country risk can be classified as sovereign risk and currency risk. The risk associated with political events is called sovereign risk. The risk involved in foreign exchanged events is called currency risk.

Sovereign risk occurs when a host government exercises its sovereign power to deny foreign obligations or disallow local firms to honor their obligations. These actions can result from deliberate actions or indirect consequences of ineffectiveness of a host government.

Currency risk is the possibility that an unexpected change in foreign exchange rates will alter the home currency value of repayment of loans by foreign customers. If the loan is denominated in the home currency, the risk is shifted to the borrower. For example, let's assume that a Japanese borrower has $1,000 (or ¥100,000) loan denominated in dollars from a U. S. lending bank and the exchange rate changes from ¥100/$ to ¥200/$. With the new rate, the Japanese borrower has to pay ¥200,000 as a result of depreciation of yen. Even though the direct risk shifts to the borrower in this case, the lending bank will still be subject to indirect risk that the borrower might give up the willingness to pay due to the loss.

However, if the loan is denominated in the host country's currency, then the risk is directly on the lending bank. Let's take the same example except that the loan is denominated in yen. With the new rate (¥200/$), the Japanese borrower will own the same ¥100,000, but the lending bank's claim will be only $500 (100,000/200). That is, the depreciation of host currency results in a direct loss to the lending bank.

By Geungu Yu

Key Terms and Concepts

foreign exchange the system whereby one country's currency is exchanged for another country's currency.

syndication selling securities or making loans by a group of banks that jointly negotiate a contract to do so. This practice is common, since too much capital is required for a single bank to handle the issue alone.

monopolistic market a market in which sellers can influence prices owing to product differentiation. Although there may be many sellers, their products differ from one another at least in some way.

reserve requirements the portion of their deposits that United States banks must, by law, set aside as bank reserves. The purpose of reserve requirements is to protect depositors and to give the monetary authority a means of controlling the money supply.

FDIC insurance Federal Deposit Insurance Corporation insurance. Insurance to maintain public confidence in banks and the financial system. The FDIC currently insures customer deposits up to $100,000 per account.

Federal Reserve   the central monetary authority of the United States, established by the Federal Reserve Act of 1913. Unlike most other advanced countries, the United States has no single central bank. Instead, it operates under a system of 12 Federal Reserve banks owned by the member banks in their respective districts.

Trade Policy in Developing Countries

Generally, every country, whether developed or developing, has a trade policy. In certain countries, the trade policy may be a combination of different trade orientations that may also be in conflict with one another. Countries that have different trade orientations are sometimes referred to as trade neutral. Trade orientation refers to the type or method of trade strategy that a country is pursuing to achieve economic growth and industrialization. Trade policy represents the set of policy instruments that directly affect a country's balance of payments position. Colin Kirkpatrick in a book edited by Norman Gemmell states that the instruments that are used in trade policy include "quotas, tariffs, taxes and subsidies on exports and imports, as well as exchange rate policy and regulation of international capital movements."

Trade policy is not an end in itself, rather a means through which a country can achieve its goals of economic growth and industrialization. Let us briefly take a look at how some developing countries have utilized trade policy to achieve economic growth and industrialization. The two major competing trade strategies are import-substitution trade policy and export orientation trade policy. Import-substitution trade policy emphasizes the use of imports of intermediate and capital goods to achieve economic growth and industrialization as well as achieving a favorable balance of payments position. On the other hand, export orientation trade policy stresses the use of exports to achieve economic growth and industrialization. Several of the developing countries and regions, such as South Korea, Singapore, Taiwan and Hong Kong, and quite a few industrializing countries, say, Brazil, Mexico, China, Indonesia, Nigeria, India and Pakistan have used some form of the trade policy to pursue the goal of economic growth and industrialization.

Among the countries that pursued import-substitution trade policy are Brazil, India, Pakistan, Nigeria, Mexico and Indonesia in the 1960s and

1970s, and in some cases to early or late 1980s. The countries or regions of South Korea, Singapore, Taiwan and Hong Kong all pursued export-orientation trade policy for economic growth and industrialization. Lately, almost everyone of the above countries that pursued import-substitution trade policy has liberalized its markets or moved into some variant of export-oriented trade policy. In certain cases, the export-oriented trade policy was selective as was the case of South Korea while in others it was outright export-growth strategy like the case of Singapore. For some countries like Mexico, Nigeria, Indonesia, import-substitution was moderately practiced or pursued as export-oriented strategy of some kind was simultaneously being practiced. Having summarized and named the various developing countries that have used the two broad trade methods for economic growth and industrialization, let us briefly define and explain the various instruments of the two trade policies which we started to discuss at the very beginning.

Tariffs

Tariffs are taxes imposed on products when they cross national boundaries. There are different kinds of tariffs. A specific tariff represents a fixed tax or amount of money charged per unit of the imported item or product.

An ad valorem tariff, is a sales tax charged as a percentage of the value of the imported item or product. A compound tariff is a combination of specific and ad valorem tariff. Tariffs could be levied on imports or exports. When tariffs are levied on imports we call them import tariffs, and when they are levied on exports we call them export tariffs. A tariff whose sole purpose is to increase revenue or generate revenue for the government is called a revenue tariff. A revenue tariff could be levied on both exports and imports of a country.

In formulating trade policy, developing countries make use of tariffs to achieve both economic growth and industrialization and as well as addressing the problems of balance of payments. Some developing countries use a protective tariff to insulate some of their import-competing industries from foreign competition. Generally, what a protective tariff does is to put the products of the domestic industries in a more competitive advantage over the products from foreign producers, thus making the locally produced products more attractive in terms of price. The reason why a protective tariff is used by many developing countries is that it enables the country to be selective in terms of the products and industries where it applies. Generally, a tariff increases the price of a product. For example, a developing country may elect to use a protective tariff to encourage the development of economies of scale in an industry and at the same time reduce its import bills and thus help its balance of payments position.

Quota

We have both import quotas and export quotas. Quotas represent some level of physical restrictions on the amount or quantities of products that can be imported or exported within a specific period of time. Import quotas allow a developing country to limit the quantities of various products that will be imported into the country during a specified period of time. Export quotas allow a country to set the ceiling on the amounts or quantities of certain products that will be exported during a specified period.

Quotas represent what economists call nontariff trade barriers. There are other forms of nontariff trade barriers that developing countries and developed countries choose to apply in their trade policies. Import quota is one of the favorable nontariff trade barriers that is very attractive to developing countries especially when they face adverse balance of payments situation. Import quotas achieve more than one goal. By reducing the quantity of a product that would otherwise have been imported without such restrictions, it gives the domestic industries the opportunity to increase the domestic production of such a product. Such increase in domestic production to fill the gap from imports means some increase in domestic employment. Furthermore, the domestic industry that produces this product, gains some competitive advantage and thus to help in the overall goal of industrialization while significantly reducing import bills which will help the position of the country's balance of payments as stated above.

Other forms of nontariff trade barriers are voluntary export restraints and local content requirements. These instruments are used by developing countries and developed countries in their trade policies. Voluntary export restraint occurs when an exporting country voluntarily restricts the amount or quantity of exports to a particular country during a specific period of time. Local content requirement is used to enable the domestic manufacturers to produce some of the parts of a product, or that some of the materials used in the production of a product come from the local economy.

Subsidies

A subsidy represents a payment of funds by the government to firms or businesses for goods and services that are produced but not given to the government. Subsidies are some form of transfer payments in the sense that the goods and services produced do not go directly to the government. Subsidies could take various forms. Some are in the form of lower interest rates on borrowed funds, or outright tax with days, or cash payments for the production of such goods. Trade subsidies could be either export subsidy or domestic subsidy. Export subsidies represent the grants or payments given to producers that produce goods which are exported to other countries. Domestic subsidy on the other hand is given to producers of import-competing goods. Giving producers of import-competing goods subsidy helps them to compete with the imports from other countries and insures that such industries continue to produce locally. The export subsidy enables the producers to be competitive in the external markets. The method of subsidy that a country selects depends on the overall trade policy of the nation.

Exchange Rate Policy

Today, exchange rate policies of the developing countries are either pegged to one of the major international currencies or are in one form of managed float or are free floating. Few countries have their currencies fixed. Fixed exchange rate policy was in effect for most countries until the 1970s when the central banks of the western nations could no longer back the currencies with gold. Fixed exchange rate represents the exchange of a currency for a specified amount of precious metal, usually gold, or of other currencies. In other words, the market does not play any role in determining the value of the exchange rate. Flexible exchange rate policies could be freely floating exchange rates or sometimes take any form of the managed float that is determined by the forces of demand and supply of the currency for the case of freely floating. The value of exchange rates in managed floating currencies is somewhat a combination of the forces of the market and level of government intervention or administration. However, the purpose of such policies is to contrast trade and balance of payments position.

Some of the developing countries like Chile, Brazil, were able to lower their tariffs and still able to grow their exports. The use of exchange rate policy not only can affect the balance of payments position of a country, it also has the ability to determine the level of capital imports for development. Most of the developing countries now are pursuing the trade strategy of export promotion and trade liberalization. Export promotion requires that the exchange rate of the developing country not be overvalued. Sometimes, the nominal exchange rate is first devalued by the developing country that is pursuing trade liberalization and export promotion policy. However, the important issue is to have the effective real exchange rate to be in equilibrium. The importance of this is that it increases the ability of the developing country to increase the level of its exports and thus economic growth and industrialization. Furthermore, it increases the level of capital imports to the developing country. A caution that may be necessary here, is that it is possible for some of the developing countries in pursuit of export promotion policy to end up subsidizing their exports at prices that are below free trade prices. Although it is easier to over subsidize imports than exports, it is plausible for a developing country that is pursuing export promotion to over subsidize its exports.

Whatever trade policy a developing country decides to follow, it is very important that the policy should be an integral part of the country's overall economic development and industrialization strategy. For any of the trade policy to achieve its objective, both fiscal policy and financial policy reforms must be in place to complement the trade policy. From the experiences of such countries like South Korea, Singapore, Brazil, Chile and China, there is considerable evidence to suggest that trade policies have been successful in countries that reformed their fiscal and financial policies to be in line with the trade policy.

In light of the above discussion, it is evident that how developing countries use the policy instruments that directly affect trade policy and their balance of payments is key to the type of trade strategy it will pursue. Also, the success or failure of the policy will very much depend on how these instruments are used in combination with the fiscal and financial policies to achieve the country's overall development and industrialization goal.

Regulation of International Capital

The regulation of international capital is one of the instruments of trade policy as well as balance of payments correction. Developing countries as well as developed countries use this as an instrument of trade policy. This is used in certain cases to limit the level of foreign control of their economies. Regulation of international capital could take the form of foreign ownership in some key industries or domestic firms participation in joint venture projects. Other forms will be the number of years required before a foreign firm could repatriate profits, the time period necessary for application and approval of foreign exchange forms.

There is clear evidence that most of the developing countries that pursued export-oriented trade policy have more liberal control on the inflows and outflows of international capital. On the other hand, those developing countries that pursued import-substitution trade policy seem to have more control or regulation on the level of international capital. Furthermore, in countries where there are less restrictions on international capital inflows and outflows, the exchange rate policies have also been very flexible or are some type of managed floating exchange rate. However, when developing countries face adverse balance of payments problem, it is more attractive from a policy perspective to institute some control or restriction on the outflows of foreign exchange. This is especially true if the problem is for a short period of time.

Another form of regulation of international capital that a developing country may adopt is the structure of bank assets and ownership in the developing country. If a developing country wants to effectively monitor the inflows and outflows of capital, it must be able to regulate the banks that operate within its shores. This is even more important in today's global financial markets.

By Dennis O. Anyamele

Key Terms and Concepts

balance of payments   a financial statement that compares all reported payments by residents of one country to residents of other countries with payment to domestic residents by foreign residents.

quota   a restriction on the quality or amount of a product that can be imported or exported within a specific period of time.

tariff   a tax levied on products when they cross national boundaries.

subsidy   a payment of funds by the government to producers for goods produced.

exchange rate policy   a policy that uses a country's currency price or ratio to affect prices of goods and services.

capital goods   goods used in the production of other goods.

ad valorem   taxes on commodities are calculated in two ways, either according to quantity or according to value. In the case of ad valorem tax the amount to be paid is proportionate to the value of the commodity.

trade liberalization   trade and economic policies that emphasize market allocation of resources and price determination.

APPENDIX B
WORDS, PHRASES, AND TYPICAL EXPRESSIONS

Economists first began to analyze consumer behavior over a century ago when it was fashionable in psychological circles, to assert that much of human behavior could be explained by people's desire **to realize** as much "pleasure" and **to avoid** as much "pain" as possible. (From The Concept of Utility in Part One Microeconomics)

Hence, utility has both objective and subjective features and, most particularly, utility is **a matter of** individual taste, preference, perception, personality makeup, and state of mind. (From The Concept of Utility in Part One Microeconomics)

Peanuts, **for instance**, are bought **by some people** to serve at cocktail parties, **by others** to make peanut brittle, and **by some** to feed to squirrels, with potentially different utilities to each buyer in each case. Moreover, the utility of a good can vary **from time to time**, or **place to place**. (From The Concept of Utility in Part One Microeconomics)

In ordinal preference patterns, one only has to be able to rank alternatives — **from highest to lowest, best to worst, or most satisfying to least satisfying;** no attempt is made to quantify the amount by which one alternative is better (or worse) than others. (From The Concept of Utility in Part One Microeconomics)

In contrast, we say there are "few" sellers of a product whenever the actions of any one firm will **be noticed and reacted to** by rival sellers. "Few" means few enough **so that** firms find it imperative to follow each other's moves closely. Fewness of sellers also means that each firm is large relative to the size of the market **in which** it operates; often, when firms are few in number each firm is large in absolute size as well. (From How Markets Function in Part One Microeconomics)

The sales clerks in one store may be more courteous, **or** its location more convenient, **or** its checkout system faster, **or** its delivery service more dependable, **or** its credit terms or accommodating. Such factors can cause buyers to prefer **one seller over another**, even though the item purchased is the same. (From How Markets Function in Part One Microeconomics)

The classification of spending as consumption or investment remains to **a significant extent a matter of convention**. From **the economic point of view**, there is little difference between a household **building up** an inventory of peanut butter and a grocery store **doing** the same. (From Outlays and Components of Demand in Part Two Macroeconomics)

Nevertheless, in the national income accounts, the individual's purchase is treated as a personal consumption expenditure, **whereas** the store's purchase is treated as investment in the form of inventory investment. (From Outlays and Components of Demand in Part Two Macroeconomics)

Policy makers have **at their command** two broad classes of policies with which to affect the economy. (From Macroeconomic Policy in Part Two Economics)

Those who regard the costs of unemployment as high, relative to the costs of inflation, will run greater risks of inflation to reduce unemployment than **will those** who regard the costs of inflation as primary and unemployment as a relatively minor misfortune. (From Macroeconomic Policy in Part Two Macroeconomics)

Because desk clerks and receptionists are generally **unskilled and not permanent staff**, reservation equipment is designed to be simple to operate. (From Hotel Computer Applications in Part Four Management Information System)

It can do so **either through** pushing its goods and services to consumers through distribution channels **or through** pulling its goods and services to consumers **by means of** promotional efforts designed to motivate consumers to choose its particular goods and services. (From Pulling and Pushing Marketing Strategies in a Market-Oriented System in Part Six Marketing)

A variation of this kind of promotion is the offer of a membership in a "trying and buying" club. Prospects are invited to apply for membership **in order to be granted** club privileges to buy products **at special introductory low prices.** (From Pulling and Pushing Marketing Strategies in a Market-Oriented System in Part Six Marketing)

Do the financial markets place a higher value on firms that bet on the future **by using debt**? If there existed managers that could predict the future with certainty, the answer would be yes. But even managers **with access to** the best information cannot do so, and suppliers of capital in the financial markets know they cannot. Debt can **make the owners worse off**, perhaps **very much worse off**, if things do not go well. (From Motives for Using Debt in Part Seven Managerial Finance)

Three economic goals guide the strategic direction of almost every viable business organization. **Whether or not** they are explicitly stated, a company mission statement reflects the firm's intention to secure its survival through sustained growth and profitability. (From Company Goals: Survival, Growth, Profitability in Part Eleven Strategic Management)

Profitability is the mainstay goal of a business organization. **No matter how** it is measured or defined, profit **over the long term** is the clearest indication of a firm's ability to satisfy the principal claims and desires of employees and stockholders. (From Company Goals: Survival, Growth, Profitability in Part Eleven Strategic Management)

A firm might overlook the enduring concerns of customers, suppliers, creditors, ecologists, and regulatory agents. **In the short term** the results may produce profit, but **over time** the financial consequences **are likely to** be detrimental. (From Company Goals: Survival, Growth, Profitability in Part Eleven Strategic Management)

The stability and quality of the corporation's financial performance will be developed **through** the profitable execution of our existing businesses, **as well as through** the acquisition or development of new businesses. (From Company Goals: Survival, Growth, Profitability in Part Eleven Strategic Management)

Faith in this mechanism expanded rapidly in much of **the 19th century**, and **the first half of the 20th century**. But the "Great Depression" of 1930s demonstrated that growth was no longer automatic. (From Free Markets and Growth in Part Twelve International Economics)

Indeed, the US rated **last not only for** the largest industrialized nations, **but also last for** the 24 OECD (Organization for Economic Cooperation and Development) nations. US investment levels were reaching new lows in **a three decade experience**. (From Free Markets and Growth in Part Twelve International Economics)

An equally respected element in conservative free market economics is the theme that individual consumers are "sovereign." This simply means that they must be free to spend money they have earned **in any way** they want. But as we noted above, the classical writers explained that **while** such freedom must be respected, surely any rational consumer would recognize the importance of capital formation **to** its own growth, **or to** its own economic future. (From Free Markets and Growth in Part Twelve International Economics)

But if one nation continues to export more than it is willing to import, that nation will **end up with** the excess of foreign funds **accumulated by** those export. That excess will cause the value of currency for the nation with a trade deficit to fall. Or stated **in other terms**, the value of the currency of the nation with the favorable trade balance will rise. (From New-World Realities and Competitiveness in Part Twelve International Economics)

Enterprise must invest today to assure **an improved future** tomorrow. (From New-World Realities and Competitiveness in Part Twelve International Economics)

APPENDIX C
SAMPLES OF GOOD SENTENCES

Adam Smith, in his Wealth of Nations (1776) is often given credit for starting the industrial revolution. **Adam Smith believed that selfishness, in an ethical sense, is not highly rated.** However, in an economic sense, if we encourage individuals to believe that their own hard work would provide direct economic rewards to them, this new "release" of human energy would set in motion economic growth. (From Free Markets and Growth in Part Twelve International Economics)

In this ideal world of a "free market" economy, there was a tight knit circle of interdependence: **Self-interest created high personal energy which created high profits which allowed for high investments which allowed for high productivity which allowed for higher levels of consumption which allowed for — and encouraged — ever higher levels of investment to satisfy that consumption.** (From Free Markets and Growth in Part Twelve International Economics)

The sacrifices of one generation set the stage for the potential for growth — but only if those who receive the funds (including governments) — make prudent use of those resources by investing in growth. Americans have neglected this axiom. **They have neglected the needs of the future, and already the future is neglecting America.** (From Free Markets and Growth in Part Twelve International Economics)

The American entertainer, Walt Disney, summarized the challenge clearly. **"Change is inevitable. Growth is not."** The lesson applies not alone to the United States, but also to the rest of the world. (From Free Markets and Growth in Part Twelve International Economics)

They are planning to elevate that quality standard to 4 to 5 failed parts per billion produced. They are, in essence, moving to zero defects! **Quality prod-**

ucts can be produced only by a quality workforce that is committed to perfection in every thought, every action, in every second of each working day. (From New-World Realities and Competitiveness in Part Twelve International Economics)

All of this is driven by a new respect for satisfying consumer wants, instead of being burdened by the lead jacket of tradition or historic convention. Nations, as individuals, are not to be seen as ants riding on the back of a turtle. **Both individuals and nations can create an improved future, if they have the wit, the will, and the courage to change.** (From New-World Realities and Competitiveness in Part Twelve International Economics)

APPENDIX D
BUSINESS LETTERS

A Business Letter in Daily Business

November 12, 2005

Mr. John Neter
President
Trade and Industry Development Company
1053 Dongfang Avenue
Beijing, P. R. China 100199 (fictitious)

Dear President Neter:

You are welcome to advertise for your products or techniques in the catalogue INTERNATIONAL EXHIBITION OF INVENTIONS OF GENEVA (IEIG), Switzerland. You are also welcome to present and sell your products and techniques in the exhibition with the help of our agency.

In this letter, we have enclosed the copies of instructions and samples concerning the procedure of advertising, as well as an application form. In 2003, we presented in Geneva the products from China Medicines and Health Products Import and Export Corporation. In 2004, we had several advertisements of Chinese companies in the catalog, such as TML, MCT, and so on. In 2006, we would like to offer more opportunities to Chinese firms and companies for the purpose of promotion in international markets. If you are interested in exploring the international markets, please return the enclosed forms as soon as possible to the following address:

Mr. Sherwin Tang
Representative
Exclusive Agency in China
    for Advertisement of IEIG
P. O. Box 8059
Beijing, P. R. China 100088

We are always with your future opportunities in international markets.

Sincerely,
(Signature of sender)
Sherwin Tang
Representative

A Business Letter to Customers

June 19, 2005

Dear Friend:

Thanks for your interest in our catalog! A copy of our latest issue is enclosed.

We have recently begun an export service, but unfortunately we cannot yet export to your country — sorry! Many nations impose restrictions on commercial imports of textiles and apparel, and we are currently investigating these requirements as they apply to your country. If and when we are able to ship our merchandise to you, we will be happy to serve you directly.

In the meantime, if you have a friend, relative or business contact in the United States who would be willing to forward the package to you, we would be happy to ship your order to them. Your order should include either your credit card number (MasterCard, Visa or American Express) and expiration date, or a check for U. S. funds drawn on a U. S. Bank.

Again, thanks for your interest in Sun's.

Sincerely,

Your friends at Sun's

SUN'S, INC.
108 Sunset Avenue, Brightsville, NM 10668
The United States
1-800-123-4567 (fictitious)

A Recommendation Letter

December 6, 2005

Dr. Shiro Yabushita
Dean and Professor
School of Political Science and Economics
Waseda University
1-6-1 Nishi-Waseda, Shinjuku-Ku
Tokyo, Japan 169-8050

Dear Dr. Yabushita:

It is my pleasure to recommend to you a promising student of mine, Ms. Dan Wu, to be a candidate in an international exchange program between Japan and China. Although I am not quite aware of the details of the program, I know there is certainly an opportunity for Beijing Normal University to choose its most promising students and to send them to Waseda University, for the sake of a previous agreement between Japan and China, or between Waseda University and Beijing Normal University.

I taught Ms. Wu when she was a junior. She was a very good student in my class of Marketing. I have two classes of Marketing each year. One is in Chinese, and the other , in English. Both classes use Dr. Philip Kotler's *Principles of Marketing*. The Chinese class uses the Chinese edition translated by two colleagues and myself. The English class uses the English edition. Ms. Wu was in my Chinese class, for her first foreign language is Japanese. Japan is in her feelings and emotion. I was educated in America. I regret that I cannot offer a class in Japanese, though my grandfather studied and worked in Japan in the early years of last century. (Later he became one of the key persons in 1911 revolution. They left Japan and overthrew the Qing Dynasty in China.) In my class, Ms. Wu got a grade of 98. Apparently she had a complete understanding of all the questions I raised in the final examination paper. It seems girls in China always do better in exams than boys. And, year after year, boys lag behind until they graduate.

Ms. Wu is a serious student, spending most of her time in the library. In China, few university students would choose such a way of study and life, but those who would like to do further study abroad would stick to reading. They know they have to spend much time before entering the gate of a foreign university. Now, Waseda University has become the opportunity and expectation of Ms. Wu. I hope that she will be able to enter the academic exchange program hosted by such a wonderful university. I know, in the hearts of ninety-nine percent of Chinese scholars, Waseda University ranks No. 1 in Japan. If Ms. Wu goes to your school to study, she can learn a lot. What she will learn there, probably would change her whole life. If so, it is the strength of a marvelous university.

Ms. Wu was an intelligent student in my class and always had the right answers in problem solving. I usually do not assign too much homework to students, but I think questionnaire design is important. In my record, Ms. Wu did very well in the assignment of questionnaire design. The reason for me to pay very much attention to the assignment of questionnaire design is that I think those students who can have a questionnaire well done are with better understanding of the world as well as the details of people. As I know, she had done well in other tough assignments as well. These assignments required students to complete time-consuming readings.

My school offers a complete undergraduate program in economics. Students enrolled in our program are well trained in those fundamental areas such as microeconomics, macroeconomics, finance, and econometrics. There should not be any problem for Ms. Wu to complete a one-year academic exchange program in Waseda University. Plus, she just got a first-class scholarship in my university. That is the mark of a rank asserting first three among one hundred and twenty students.

Japan is with one of the best education systems in the world. If you can offer Ms. Wu an opportunity to do further study in your school, I will be most grateful to you, and to your university. Scholarship is very important for Ms. Wu as well. In China, a lot of families have got rich and they are able to pay tuition for their kids. Yet Ms. Wu's family is not in the group like that. Here, I am sincerely applying scholarship for her. I am expecting the completion of a smooth international exchange program between Japan and China.

If you need further information, please let me know.

Truly,

Xianyuan Dai

Xianyuan Dai
Professor of Economics
School of Economics and Business Administration
Beijing Normal University
Beijing, P. R. China 100875
Tel: 86-010-58807847 / 13961311452 (fictitious)
Email: xydai @ bnu. edu. cn

APPENDIX E
SAMPLES OF FOOTNOTES

Books

BOOK WITH ONE AUTHOR
Adam Smith, An Inquiry into the Nature and Causes of the Wealth of Nations (London: J. M. Dent & Sons, Ltd. , 1910), p. 15.

BOOK WITH TWO OR THREE AUTHORS
Eric N. Berkowitz, Roger A. Kerin, and William Rudelius, Marketing (St. Louis, MO: Times Mirror/Mosby College Publishing, 1986), p. 455.

A LATER EDITION
X. J. Kennedy, An Introduction to Poetry, 4th ed. (Boston: Little, Brown and Company, 1978), pp. 122-130.

A TRANSLATION
Philip Kotler, Principles of Marketing, trans. Ping Zhao, Xianyuan Dai, and Junxi Cao (Beijing: Tsinghua University Press, 1997), p. 155.

A BOOK WITH AN EDITOR
Xianyuan Dai, eds. , A Textbook of College English of Economics and Management, 2nd ed. (Beijing: Peking University Press, 2000), p. 180.

Magazines, Periodicals, and Newspapers

A SIGNED ARTICLE IN A PERIODICAL
Bruce H. Clark, and David B. Montgomery, "Managerial Identification of Competitors," *Journal of Marketing*, Vol. 63, July 1999, p. 14.

A SIGNED ARTICLE IN A MAGAZINE
Bruce Montgomery, "Who Are Competitors," *Time and Space*, 7 December 2005, p. 13.

A SIGNED ARTICLE FROM A NEWSPAPER

Dana Alden, "Kissing Death or Surviving?" *Home Daily*, 15 November 2004, p. 5.

AN UNSIGNED ARTICLE FROM A MAGAZINE OR NEWSPAPER

"The Fall of Philip's Curve," *World Economy*, 22 March 2005, p. 34.

APPENDIX F
SAMPLES OF BIBLIOGRAPHIES

Books

BOOK WITH ONE AUTHOR
Smith, Adam. An Inquiry into the Nature and Causes of the Wealth of Nations. London: J. M. Dent & Sons, Ltd., 1910.

BOOK WITH TWO OR THREE AUTHORS
Berkowitz, Eric N. , Roger A. Kerin, and William Rudelius. Marketing. St. Louis, MO: Times Mirror/Mosby College Publishing, 1986.

A LATER EDITION
Kennedy, X.J. An Introduction to Poetry. 4th ed. Boston: Little, Brown and Company, 1978.

A TRANSLATION
Kotler, Philip. Principles of Marketing. trans. Ping Zhao, Xianyuan Dai, and Junxi Cao. Beijing: Tsinghua University Press, 1997.

A BOOK WITH AN EDITOR
Dai, Xianyuan, eds. A Textbook of College English of Economics and Management. 2nd ed. Beijing: Peking University Press, 2000.

Magazines, Periodicals, and Newspapers

A SIGNED ARTICLE IN A PERIODICAL
Clark, Bruce H. , and David B. Montgomery. "Managerial Identification of Competitors." *Journal of Marketing*, Vol. 63, July 1999.

A SIGNED ARTICLE IN A MAGAZINE
Montgomery, Bruce. "Who Are Competitors." *Time and Space*, 7 December 2005.

A SIGNED ARTICLE FROM A NEWSPAPER

Alden, Dana. "Kissing Death or Surviving?" *Home Daily*, 15 November 2004.

AN UNSIGNED ARTICLE FROM A MAGAZINE OR NEWSPAPER

"The Fall of Philip's Curve." *World Economy*, 22 March 2005.

APPENDIX G
RÉSUMÉ

Ms. Yingying Tian

Graduate Student of 2003

School of Economics and Business Administration

Beijing Normal University

Beijing, P. R. China 100875

Tel: 010-58807847 / 13682224444 (fictitious)

Email: y. y. tian@bnu. edu. cn

Position desired   Editor

Education

2003 to present   Beijing Normal University.
                  Current standing: graduate student, MS in Economics expected in June 2006.
                  Major: International Economics.

1999-2003   Peking University, graduated with BS in Economics.

Experience

2003 to present   Editor of *Economics Review*, student periodical of School of Economics and Business Administration, Beijing Normal University. Responsibilities include writing *Words from Editor*, editing, and proofreading.

Summer 2002   General Assistant of *Modern Conglomerates*, in charge of taking phone calls and assorting drafts and files.

Publications	Yingying Tian, "Why Sky Is Blue", *Reader*, January 2002, pp. 35-36.
	Yingying Tian, "Utility Falls", *Economics Review*, December 2004, pp. 15-18.
Special interest	Writing essays, reading, photography
References	Graduate academic references available from the Office of Student Affairs at Beijing Normal University, Beijing, P. R. China 100875; undergraduate academic references available from the Office of Student Record at Peking University, Beijing, P. R. China 100083.

Employment Reference	Dr. Weiming Dong
	Chief Editor
	Modern Conglomerates
	Beijing, P. R. China 100003
	Tel: 010-35541166 / 13998886666 (fictitious)

Personal Reference	Dr. Weizhong Dong
	Professor
	Department of Economics
	School of Economics and Business
	Administration
	Beijing Normal University
	Beijing, P. R. China 100875
	Tel: 010-58807777 / 13992223333
	(fictitious)

APPENDIX H
MEMORANDUM

To: Robert Sampull   Date: December 3, 2005
           Michael Collery
           William Heckerman

From: John Weinrich
           President

Subject: Yearly Report to Board of Directors

Several expressions need minor revision. Please give your comments and have the report returned before December 15, 2005.

J.W. (Initials of sender)

APPENDIX I
TRANSLATION

APPENDIX H
MEMORANDUM

Although reading, listening, writing, and speaking are four very important areas of learning English, translation is also frequently involved in people's cross-cultural communication. Sometimes the process of translation arises unnecessarily in a person's thinking and interrupts either his own meditation or his communication with others. Most of the time translation is a bridge to link people with different cultures. When students graduate from universities, translation techniques become a useful tool to enhance the quality of their communication. Good translation transmits accurate information to people and enables them to understand ideas explained within their native language. The translation technique is often neglected by students. Consequently, translated sentences can be awkward, distorted or simply unclear. No one is able to tell all the translation techniques systematically, simply because the art of language and expression is characterized by diversity. To clarify, major translation techniques should draw student's attention for they are basic points in terms of cross-cultural communication.

Normally, there are three fundamental standards to assess a translated sentence or work. They are accuracy, clarity, and fluency.

In this appendix, the techniques of translation from English into Chinese are discussed in a series of cases, while the process of translation from Chinese into English, is skipped. By nature, the problem of translating from Chinese into English for Chinese students is more likely to be expression-oriented, whereas the problem of translating from English into Chinese is more technique-oriented.

The cases here are written in Chinese to give students better understanding. Each case contains an underlined typical sentence selected from a sample paragraph. It is then followed by an example of translation and a discussion of technique. At the end of each, a rule of translation is presented for students to follow in future. For a thorough understanding of these cases, it is suggested that students translate the whole paragraph first before they start to read the discussions and rules. In this manner, they can compare sample sentences with their own translation and have a deeper impression.

CASE ONE

【正文】Indeed, U.S. top companies can no longer ponder over the question of whether to use separate market and advertising strategies and tactics to reach these attractive markets for the reason of tendering the white Anglo majority consumer market.

【译文】真的,对于是否运用其他的市场和广告策略及战术,接近这些有吸引力的市场,补偿英国裔消费者大市场的问题,美国的大公司再也不能犹豫了。

【讨论】英译汉时,英语的长句子一定要切换成汉语的短句子。英语与汉语最大的区别之一,就是英语可以利用从句或介词宾语,把一个句子写得很长,并且在句子中间不使用标点符号。英译汉时,如果单纯使用"更换前后位置"的一般原则,一句翻一句,译文多半会别扭。

CASE TWO

【正文】Also, there is no need to provide goods and services that consumers do not want because their wants and needs for other things are basically unlimited.

【译文】也没有必要提供消费者不需要的商品或服务,因为还有许多他们所需要的其他商品或服务。

【讨论】英语和汉语表达方式略有不同时,应避免"直译",而采取"意译"。本句后半部如果译成"他们对其他东西的欲望和需要基本是无限的",会与句子前半部分脱节。

CASE THREE

【正文】The swaps market is the market for simultaneous purchase and sale of foreign exchange with the purchase being effected at once and the sale back to the same party to be carried out at a price agreed upon today but to be completed at a predetermined future date.

【译文】交易市场是购买和销售同时发生的市场,购买生效的同时,外汇又销售给了卖方,价格是当天定的,但交易在预先定好的一个未来的日子完成。

【讨论】英语与汉语表达方式完全不同时,"意译"也不能奏效,必须根据原文的意思,用汉语进行写作。以语言差别而论,这种情况并不多见,进行翻译工作的人,不可随意使用这个原则,使译文走神。

CASE FOUR

【正文】The marketing orientation period began after the 1950s. Companies sales capacities and competition had grown extensively during this period and companies were turning their attention to new product research, production and distribution efficiency and widening their product categories and lines to continue increasing sales. This period saw the creation of a marketing department and all marketing activities were controlled within the department.

【译文】以市场营销为主体概念的时期从 20 世纪 50 年代开始。

【讨论】涉及专业理论的概念，一定要依照专业理论来翻译。市场营销学的发展过程分为三个阶段(或四个,市场营销学界有不同看法,本例中的思想为"三阶段论"),一是"生产论"阶段,二是"销售论"阶段,三是"市场营销论"阶段。

CASE FIVE

【正文】The segment's market potential should be measurable. Ease of measurement facilitates effective target marketing by helping to identify and quantify group purchasing power and to indicate the differences among market segments.

【译文】测量的简单,也就是能够辨认和定量分析群体购买力,指出各个子市场的差别,保证了有效的目标市场营销。

【讨论】翻译要注意意识的转换。"helping"是"帮助"的意思,但此例中不能译成"帮助"。上文中如果译成"通过帮助辨认和衡量购买力,以及指出子市场的差别,……",则不妥,会与句子的前半部脱节。

CASE SIX

【正文】Import substitution approach allows a country to be able to utilize the imported capital goods to manufacture the finished goods or manufactures that were previously imported.

【译文】进口替代法使一个国家能利用进口设备材料,生产以前需要进口的最终产品或产品。

【讨论】翻译要注意概念转换。本例中的"capital goods"原意是指用于生产的那些物资,但中文很难找到一个对应的词,所以将"capital goods"转换成"设备材料"。

CASE SEVEN

【正文】To begin with, there are third party externalities which arise indirectly from a transaction or chain of transactions. Consider developing and industrial base in a city. <u>Should capital gains, low cost raw materials and skilled labor, and the promise of expanding sales and profits be the objectives for decision making or should environmental spoliation be given weight?</u>

【译文】决策目标考虑的应该是资产收益、低成本原材料、熟练的劳动力、销售与利润增加的前景，还是防止环境被破坏？

【讨论】英译汉有时为了句子的连贯，译文中需要添加一些词。本例中如果只写"决策目标"，会与句子后半部分脱节，所以加字译成"决策目标考虑的……"。

CASE EIGHT

【正文】<u>Factors are third-party firms that buy accounts receivable from a trading firm at a discount and then assume responsibility for collecting the receivables.</u> Most factoring is on a nonrecourse basis. This means that the factor assumes all the credit and political risks.

【译文】代理商是第三方企业，它们从贸易公司打折购买应收账款单据，然后再去收账。

【讨论】英译汉有时不能依字进行翻译。本例中的"accounts receivable"是"应收账款"的意思，但不能译为"购买应收账款"，后面也不能译成"收集应收账款"。

CASE NINE

【正文】Who need foreign exchange? They are international traders in goods and services, capital investors, tourists, and governments. A typical procedure in the market starts with a customer who goes to the foreign exchange department of the bank when he wishes to sell or buy foreign exchange. <u>The bank tries to match this demand and supply among their own customers, but if this is not possible, then they turn to other banks and brokers.</u>

【译文】银行试图满足自己客户的需求和供给，但是如果做不到，客户就会转向其他银行和经纪人。

【讨论】有些代词翻译时必须写明所指的人或物。本文的"they"译成"他们"后含糊不清,必须译为"客户"。同类词还有"it",多数时候译为"它",特殊时候必须指明。

CASE TEN

【正文】To fully appreciate the international trade policy of any nation will require one to understand the major interest groups and industries in that country or nation. Since sovereign nations will always act on perceived benefits that will accrue to the interest groups that control the resources, this implies that it is the conflicts of interests within nations that are dominant as a factor and not the conflicts of interest between nations in shaping the trade policy of a nation.

【译文】由于主权国家总是从国内控制资源的各派的既得利益出发,因此就一个国家贸易政策的形成来讲,国内利益冲突是一个主要因素,而不是国家间的利益冲突。

【讨论】**翻译时需要注意对关键词的理解。**本例中的"within"和"between"两个介词,虽然后面跟的都是"nations",但一个是指"国内",另一个是指"国家之间"。原文如果能够写成"within a nation",则会更清楚。

CASE ELEVEN

【正文】Today, the advances in technology especially in the areas of computers and telecommunications have accelerated the rapid integration of national capital markets. The problems and risks of international capital markets are becoming the central issues in international transactions. There are risks of currency fluctuations and defaults.

【译文】国际资本市场上的问题和风险正在成为国际交易中的主要事务,货币价值波动和拖欠的风险都存在着。

【讨论】**英语画句号的地方,翻译时不一定需要句号。**

CASE TWELVE

【正文】The exporter delivers the merchandise alongside the transportation medium, within reach of the medium's loading facilities. The importer is responsible for all other costs beyond this point.

【译文】出口商在运输工具装卸设备可及之处交付货物。

【讨论】**英语画逗号的地方,翻译时不一定需要逗号。**

CASE THIRTEEN

【正文】Second, a letter of credit (LOC) is a written document issued by a bank if required conditions are satisfied.

【译文】第二,信用证明是由银行开具发出的文件,但必须符合条件。

【讨论】英译汉时,有时需要打破原有的英语句子结构。这里如果将"... a written document issued by a bank"译为"由银行发出的写好了的文件",句子就很不简洁。

CASE FOURTEEN

【正文】Today, exchange rate policies of the developing countries are either pegged to one of the major international currencies or are in one form of managed float or are free floating. Few countries have their currencies fixed.

【译文】今天,发展中国家的汇率政策,或者局限于一种主要国际货币,或者是有序浮动,再不就是自由浮动,很少的国家使用固定汇率。

【讨论】英译汉时,一个词在句子里重复出现时,要注意语言的多样化。本例中的"or"出现两次,如果都译成"或者",文字表达就显得十分平淡。

CASE FIFTEEN

【正文】To begin with, there are third party externalities which arise indirectly from a transaction or chain of transactions.

【译文】首先,存在许多第三方外部因素,他们非直接地由一项交易或一系列交易引起。

【讨论】英语名词为复数形式时,即使原文表示中没有用"许多"一词,译文中也需要加上。

CASE SIXTEEN

【正文】Market segmentation is the process of dividing identifiable heterogeneous larger markets into smaller homogeneous submarkets or market segments.

【译文】市场细分是将可以区别的差异性大市场,划分成同质的子市场或小子市场。

【讨论】英译汉时,特殊专有名词的译法是自然形成的,但以贴切为好。比如"market segmentation"和"market segment"两个词,经过很长时间和多种译法,才变成今天的"市场细分"和"子市场"。

CASE SEVENTEEN

【正文】Procter&Gamble（P&G）makes as many as eleven brands of laundry detergent, including Tide, Ivory Snow, Cheer, Bold, and so on.

【译文】P&G 公司生产多达 11 种洗衣粉,包括汰渍牌（Tide）、Ivory Snow 牌、Cheer 牌和 Bold 牌等。

【讨论】已在中国注册的品牌,按注册中文名称译,并加注原文,未注册的品牌,保留原文。如果随意地按音译,反而造成混乱。

CASE EIGHTEEN

【正文】Jennifer Flores's cultural background will affect her camera buying decision.

【译文】詹妮弗·佛罗瑞的文化背景会影响她的照相机购买决策。

【讨论】字典上有的人名字依照字典上的译法译,字典上没有的名字,进行音译。翻译名字时要考虑人的性别,并且选择符合习惯和妥帖的字。

CASE NINETEEN

【正文】According to a recent *Redbook* ad, "She's a product of the 'me generation,' the thirty-something woman who balances home, family and career — more than any generation before her, she refuses to put her own pleasures aside. She's old enough to know what she wants. And young enough to go after it." According to *Redbook*, this consumer makes an ideal target for marketers of health food and fitness products. She wears out more exercise shoes, swallows more vitamins, drinks more diet soda, and works out more often than do other consumer groups.

【译文】据最近的 Redbook 杂志中的广告说,"她是'自我为中心'这代人的产物。30 岁左右的女人要平衡家、家庭和事业,比她前面任何一代人都要做得多,而且也决不愿放弃享乐。"

【讨论】把英语单词翻译成中文词的时候,不同的英语单词可能被误译成相同的中文词,翻译时要注意选择最贴切的词表达中文的意思。本例中的"home"和"family"两个词在英汉字典中都有"家"的意思,但英语的"home"多数是在说住的那个地方或者那所房子,而"family"一般是指家里的人,也就是家的成员的总称。类似的词还有"vague"和"blur"两个词,在中文的解释里都是"模糊",但前者指看不见的"模糊",比如思想不清;后者指看得见的"模糊",比如泪水把眼前弄模糊了。再有就是"essay"、"thesis"和"dissertation"三个词,在英汉字典上

252

都是"论文"的意思，可是第一个是"本科论文"，第二个是"硕士论文"，第三个是"博士论文"。通常这类词在做汉译英时更容易出问题，因为母语为汉语的人做汉译英时，有时会在字典中找对应的词，找到便用，至于字面之外意思深处的内容，就不可能太清楚了。

CASE TWENTY

【正文】This (small farmers), whether from Pakistan or Indonesia or Kenya or Mexico, appear to represent common needs and behavior patterns. Most of them till the land using bullock carts and have very little cash to buy agricultural inputs. They lack the education ... to appreciate fully the value of using fertilizer and depend on government help for such things as seeds, pesticides, and fertilizer. They acquire farming needs from local suppliers and count on word-of-mouth to learn and accept new things and ideas. Thus, even though these farmers are in different countries continents apart, and even though they speak different languages and have different cultural backgrounds, they may represent a homogeneous market segment.

【译文】这些(小农场主们)，无论是在巴基斯坦还是印度尼西亚，或者肯尼亚、墨西哥什么的，都表现出同样的需要和行为方式。……因此，即使这些农场主在不同的大陆板块的国家里，讲着不同的语言，有着不同的文化背景，他们可能代表着同一子市场。

【讨论】**翻译要注意译文意思的准确。**例如"Indonesia"不能译成"印尼"，一定要写成"印度尼西亚"；"in different countries continents apart"不能只译成"在不同国家"就算了，因为原文中特意提了"continent apart"，尽管原文表达有些过于复杂，翻译还是要以忠实原文为本，所以要译成"在不同大陆板块的国家里"，但也不必依据原文字词表达顺序而译成"在各大陆板块的不同国家里"。